D0360798

Berkley Prime Crime titles by Laura Morrigan

WOOF AT THE DOOR
A TIGER'S TALE

A Tiger's
TALE

Laura Morrigan

BERKLEY PRIME CRIME, NEW YORK

THE BERKLEY PUBLISHING GROUP
Published by the Penguin Group
Penguin Group (USA) LLC
375 Hudson Street, New York, New York 10014

USA • Canada • UK • Ireland • Australia • New Zealand • India • South Africa • China

penguin.com

A Penguin Random House Company

A TIGER'S TALE

A Berkley Prime Crime Book / published by arrangement with the author

Berkley Prime Crime Books are published by The Berkley Publishing Group.
BERKLEY® PRIME CRIME and the PRIME CRIME logo are trademarks of
Penguin Group (USA) LLC.

For information, address: The Berkley Publishing Group,
a division of Penguin Group (USA) LLC,
375 Hudson Street, New York, New York 10014.

ISBN: 978-0-425-25720-3

PUBLISHING HISTORY
Berkley Prime Crime mass-market edition / May 2014

PRINTED IN THE UNITED STATES OF AMERICA

10 9 8 7 6 5 4 3 2 1

Cover illustration by Mary Ann Lasher.
Cover photos: *Paw prints* by Dzmitry Haishun/Shutterstock;
Leopard print by zimmytws/Shutterstock.
Cover design by Diana Kolsky.
Interior text design by Kristin del Rosario.

For my brother, Dan, the bravest guy I know.

ACKNOWLEDGMENTS

Heartfelt gratitude to:

Editor extraordinaire, Faith Black, and all of the great people at Berkley Prime Crime, who make books their business and do it well.

Jingle Davis for teaching me about tabby and all its colonial wonder. Officer Shannon Hartley, thank you for answering random questions about the JSO. I'm going to write a dive story one day!

The ladies of my writers group: Amelia Grey, Dolores Monaco, Frances Hanson-Grow (aka Mom), Geri Buckley Borcz, Hortense Thurman, and Sandra Shanklin. Your support and knowledge are priceless. Nikki Bonanni for reading and being my cruise director.

My aunt, Oma Laura, who is always full of Jacksonville insight, and my cousin, Angie, see—I remembered this time!

My family for being my cheerleaders—especially my niece, Claire, for handing out bookmarks to strangers.

And, of course, my husband, Blake, who puts up with the utter madness that is life with a writer. Thank you.

CHAPTER 1

The weathered sign on the gate read:

Happy Asses Donkey and Big Cat Rescue
Tours: Tues–Fri 1:00–dark.

Affixed below was a newer sign. The reflective white letters glowed in my headlights, and though the effect caused the words to blur, the message came across loud and clear.

ABSOLUTELY NO TRESPASSING!
We are not responsible for death
or injury due to your own stupidity.
There are wild animals inside this gate.
If one of them eats you, it's your own fault.
~Ozeal Mallory, proprietress

I smiled. I'd never met Ozeal, but I liked her already. From what I'd heard, Ozeal Mallory was dedicated, competent, and experienced at handling all manner of big cats.

Judging from the sign, no-nonsense could be added to the list of her attributes. I wondered what had gone wrong.

The minute hand on my dashboard clock ticked to twelve past six. I was supposed to be attending a black-tie gala on Jacksonville Beach at seven o'clock. I was going to be late.

Usually, I'd welcome an excuse to avoid any event that had the words *black-tie* and *gala* in the title, but tonight's fund-raiser was an exception.

A local animal charity had teamed up with the sheriff's office to raise money to provide Kevlar vests for police dogs. As someone who felt the canine officers deserved as much protection as their handlers, I had decided to donate my services as an animal behaviorist to be sold in the silent auction. Unfortunately, this required I be present to smile, answer questions, and talk up what I do.

As much as I appreciated Ozeal's signage, it was time to get the show on the road.

The problem was, there was no one on the road. Nor was there anyone in the parking area on the other side of the gate. I squinted against the dusky gloom of twilight and was able to make out the shape of a small building nestled in a clump of pine trees at the far end of the lot.

I stared for a few moments but detected no movement.

I knew there were animals just beyond the building. I could feel the low hum of their brains. Equine. Probably the rescued donkeys referenced in the sign.

Not long ago, I wouldn't have been able to sense their presence, but my telepathic ability had taken a step forward recently. My range for connecting to an animal's mind used to be limited to about twelve feet. But I'd been faced with a desperate situation and discovered you can accomplish a lot when you're fighting for your life.

Not that my new, long-distance skill would help me get through the gate. Unless there was a Houdini donkey somewhere in the vicinity, I was out of luck.

I thought about honking the horn but not knowing the scope of the situation, I decided to eschew any loud, unexpected noises. I don't have many friends—well, human friends, anyway.

Dr. Hugh Murray was one of the few. When he'd called to ask for help dealing with an angry tiger, he'd been in one piece. I wanted to keep it that way.

The thought made my gaze drift back to the warning sign and I noticed a faded arrow painted on the gate's railing. Following its direction, I spotted what looked like an over-sized doorbell with the words RING FOR DELIVERY written in block letters underneath.

Above it was a security keypad.

I cut my engine, pushed my door open, then stopped myself just as I was swinging my legs over the running board and caught sight of my new shoes.

My new *high-heeled* shoes.

I peered out at the muddy ground then glared at my inadequate footwear. After a moment's consideration, I tugged off the heels and climbed into the backseat of my car, a vintage Skyline Blue Suburban named Bluebell. She's big and loud and her cargo area is roughly the size of Rhode Island, so it took a minute before my fingers brushed over the hard rubber tread of one of my all-weather boots.

I fished out its mate, clambered into the front seat, shoved my bare feet into the boots, and hopped out of my Suburban, landing with a splat on the sodden ground.

The evening was damp and breezy, the temperature hovering in the mid-sixties, not unusual for October in North Florida. The rain we'd had in the past weeks, however, had been excessive, and I slipped and slid my way over the muddy drive.

I'd just pressed my finger to the buzzer when a four-wheeler appeared, skidding to a stop just on the other side of the fence. The driver, a young, willowy blonde, called out over the soft putter of the idling engine.

"Are you Grace Wilde?"

"Yep."

The girl swung her leg over the seat and hurried to a post

half a dozen feet inside the gate. She pressed something I couldn't see, and, with a whirring *click,* the gate popped open.

"Ozeal said to come and get you as quick as I could," the girl said as she opened the gate wide enough for me to walk through.

"What about my truck?"

She glanced up, eyes wide. If it hadn't been for the numerous piercings dotting her pale skin, I would've said she looked like a typical girl next door. Big hazel eyes, a dash of freckles dusting her nose and cheeks.

"Oh—um . . . I guess you should pull in and park up by the office."

I clomped back to Bluebell and hauled myself behind the wheel as the girl swung the gate open.

I drove through, parked, and grabbed the dainty beaded bag that was to serve as my purse for the evening.

A moment later the girl arrived on the four-wheeler. Her brows rose when she got a good look at my outfit.

Maybe she didn't think the rubber boots went with the formfitting cocktail dress.

"Problem?"

"Um . . . I'm not sure you'll be able to ride in that."

I looked at the four-wheeler's long, narrow seat and sighed.

"I'll ride sidesaddle." As we started off, I added, "Just try not to fling too much mud on me, okay?"

My sister would have a fit of apoplexy if she knew what I was doing. Emma had worked hard on putting me together for the evening. She'd chosen everything from my earrings to my underwear, and I was grateful.

It wasn't that I lacked the ability to dress myself. The issue was dressing myself *up.* Every time I diverged from my standby jeans and T-shirt ensemble, I ended up looking like a clown in drag.

Really, I had to think of the children.

And my date.

Kai Duncan was a crime scene investigator for the Jacksonville Sheriff's Office. I'd been surprised to learn he owned a tux, but I was looking forward to seeing him in it.

Aside from quick lunches here and there or meeting at the shooting range where Kai was teaching me how to handle a firearm, we'd had a hard time getting it together in the date department. Inevitably, one of us would have to cancel because of work.

I'd be damned if I was going to do it tonight.

"Pick it up, girl. I got someplace to be," I called over the growling engine.

We zipped around a barn and turned onto a narrow road that most likely ringed the perimeter of the property to provide access to the buildings that housed the animals. We passed several enclosures as we went. Most were empty, their occupants secured in the adjoining houses for the night. Finally, we slowed to a stop when a figure came into view.

Trying not to flash anyone on my dismount from the four-wheeler, I walked to where the woman stood and introduced myself.

"Ozeal Mallory," she said and gave my hand a firm shake. She didn't so much as blink at my odd outfit.

I couldn't attempt to guess her age in the harsh glow of the four-wheeler's headlights, but judging from other physical characteristics I'd say she was a mix of Hispanic and Sasquatch.

Tall and barrel-chested, with skin like mocha cream and rowdy black curls framing her face, she looked like she could play safety for the Steelers.

"I don't want to spook Boris any more than he already is. We'll walk the rest of the way." She motioned for us to continue down the access road.

"What happened?" I asked, struggling to keep up with her long strides. My boots squeaked with every swift step.

"I wish I knew," she muttered, then fell silent as we neared a large concrete-block building, where I assumed Boris was fed and housed at night.

Attached to the building was a large enclosure. We slowly made our way along the side of the tall, chain-link fence,

Ozeal's troubled gaze fixed on the Siberian tiger as it paced in a tight circle around the base of a spindly pine tree.

We stopped and I reached out mentally for a quick evaluation, brushing the tiger's mind with my own. No trace of aggression. Boris had moved past whatever had spurred him to go for Hugh and moved on to neurotic pacing.

I pulled my focus back and scanned the enclosure. I saw neither hide nor hair of Hugh—but there also wasn't any blood, which I took as a good sign.

"Where's Hugh?" I asked.

Ozeal started to answer when a wolf whistle cut through the air. The tiger glanced up and I realized the sound had come from the flimsy pine sapling growing in the center of the enclosure.

I followed the tiger's gaze to see Hugh grinning down at me from the precariously bent treetop. He cocked an eyebrow.

"Nice boots."

"I have a date and didn't want to get my heels muddy."

His grin widened. "Must not be a very hot date if you came all the way out here just for me."

"Careful, Dr. Murray, these boots are made for walkin'. I might just leave you up there."

"Sorry. What I meant to say was, you look amazing and if you get me out of here in one piece I will make sure you have a chance to wear your heels. Even if I have to take you to dinner myself."

I shook my head. "Do you ever give up?"

"Why? One day you might say yes."

Not long ago, his flirtation would have ticked me off but I'd gained some perspective in the last few months. Maybe it was the whole almost-getting-murdered thing, but I didn't take Hugh as seriously as I once did.

I turned to Ozeal, who stood with her hands on her stocky hips, frowning through the chain-link at the tiger.

"Okay, give me the short version," I said.

"Boris has been agitated for the last couple of days so I asked Hugh to come out and take a look at him. He's the most gentle cat we have. Even-tempered. Low-key." She shook her head. "If he was a horse, he'd be giving pony rides to three-year-olds."

"Okay," I said. It was the best I could come up with. We all knew there was a big difference between a horse and a tiger. To my knowledge, horses didn't eat people. Tigers, on the other hand . . .

"It's just so out of character," Ozeal continued, mystified. "There must be something wrong."

"Your concern is touching," Hugh called out.

Ozeal sent him a dismissive wave. "You're not on the endangered species list."

"Actually, at the moment, I'm not so sure about that."

As we'd been talking, I'd noticed the lion in the pen across from Boris was watching us with interest—and hunger. It wasn't that he wanted to eat us. He didn't know what the humans were doing with the tiger and he didn't care. It was past dinnertime and he expected Ozeal to get on with it.

Lions can be pretty bossy when it comes to keeping a schedule.

"Have you fed the other cats?" I asked Ozeal.

"Not everyone. I was in the middle of the evening feeding when—"

The lion chose that moment to voice his impatience with a roar. The reverberating bellow cut off Ozeal's words. I was expecting it, but my heart still leapt at the sound. Even Ozeal flinched.

It didn't matter how many times you heard it, a lion roaring that close made the caveman inside want to haul ass in the opposite direction.

"The natives are getting restless. Why don't you deal with dinner and I'll work on Boris."

Ozeal gave me a long look. "Hugh says you're the best. Can you get him out of there?"

"Yes."

Probably.

"How?"

"I'm going to get Boris inside his house." I motioned to the building.

"I already tried to lure him with food."

"He's beyond taking that bait. I'll have to try something else."

"And by 'something else' you mean . . . ?"

"I have a few ideas."

"She eez the tiger wheesperer," Hugh said.

I cast him a quick, unamused glance.

Ozeal gave me one last appraising look. "All right. Don't let Hugh get killed. I'll lose my accreditation." With that, she turned on her heel and walked away.

I looked up at Hugh. "Dr. Murray—"

"Yes, Dr. Wilde?" I narrowed my eyes at the title. Though I kept my license current, I no longer practiced as a veterinarian and it sounded weird to be addressed as *doctor*.

I pointed my finger at him in warning. "Not a sound."

"You're the boss."

Strictly speaking, Hugh had no idea how I did what I did. He just knew it worked. I have a good reason for hiding my telepathic ability: People would think I was nuts. I couldn't do my job if people thought I was nuts. You have to have a certain amount of street cred to do what I do.

Before I could solidify my plan, or rather, wing it and pretend I had a plan, I needed to understand how the tiger's compound was configured.

I walked back along the fence to the attached building and stepped through the door. Buzzing, fluorescent lights clearly illuminated the space. The layout was pretty standard. A hallway ran the length of the structure along the back wall. A trio of tiger-sized runs lined the corridor. Each had two doors—an access gate that opened into the hall and a guillotine door that led to the exterior enclosure.

I noticed several offerings had been tossed through the chain-link to entice Boris to come into his run so he could easily be secured.

I clasped the lock on the gate that separated the hallway from the run and gave it two swift tugs.

Better safe than dinner.

I checked to make sure my phone was on vibrate—which

was about the only thing I knew how to do with the new iPhone—and noticed it was nearing six thirty.

I was going to be so late.

Pushing the thought away, I stuffed the beaded clutch under my arm and walked out to where I could see Boris, pulled in a slow, calming breath, and began speaking in a low monotone.

"Hey there, Boris. Hey, gorgeous boy."

I continued my litany of praises and slowly, gingerly opened my mind to the tiger's.

The neurotic pulse of his thoughts matched his pacing. But there was an undercurrent of worry or fear that kept flashing to the surface.

Ozeal's instincts had been spot on; something was wrong with the big cat.

Boris. I gave the tiger's mind a little nudge and his head swiveled toward me. Like many animals, Boris had never encountered a human like me. Curiosity short-circuited the pacing for a moment and he slowed.

Gotta love cats.

Now that I have your attention . . .

"Come here, big guy." I urged the cat to come to where I stood, halfway between the outside corner of the fence and the guillotine door leading into his indoor enclosure.

Boris came toward me and I edged sideways toward the door. All the while, mentally urging him to follow. I lost sight of him for a moment as I rounded the corner into the hall but by then he already knew where I wanted him to go and it didn't take much to coax him through the door into the interior pen.

As quickly as I could, I released the latch, slid the guillotine door closed behind him, and let out a relieved sigh.

The tiger pressed his head against the chain-link that separated us.

Pet.

I smiled and obliged by rubbing my fingertips on his forehead. For a moment, I could understand why Hugh would have trusted the cat. Boris seemed docile and calm, but I could sense something very different. The undercurrent of emotion I'd felt earlier remained.

My ability worked better with physical contact so I placed my other hand through the fence and rested it on the smooth fur between the tiger's ears.

I focused and tried to understand the origin of the tiger's unease. The emotions were jumbled. A mix of fear, anger, and a touch of . . . sadness?

It was almost as if he missed someone.

Separation anxiety?

I'd experienced this mix of emotions plenty of times in my work but there seemed to be more to it for Boris.

But what?

I can't look through an animal's mind the way you flip through a magazine. I can only read their thoughts and feelings as they experience them.

"Talk to me, handsome. What's going on?"

I tried to focus on the mysterious feeling, but trying to lock on to an abstract, underlying emotion was like trying to grab an eel. Finally, I managed to catch just a wisp of it, and pull it to the front of both our minds.

Boris let out a low, mournful growl, and I instantly moved to soothe him.

"It's okay."

Gone.

Who's gone?

Taken.

The murky image of a dark-haired girl fluttered through my mind. The girl laughed. She smelled like peppermint. But she was too out of focus to distinguish her features. I tried to latch on to the image and projected back to the tiger with a question.

What happened?

I got a flash—the merest blink of an image.

The girl was standing outside a fence, her face in profile as if she was turning to look at something behind her.

A sharp stab of alarm pulsed from the cat, followed by a surge of anger so strong I felt my lips curl back in an answering snarl.

"Whoa." I blinked and struggled to get a hold on my own emotions.

Boris let out a growl—it seemed to rumble endlessly against the bare, block walls.

"It's all right," I said. Though my heart was still pounding, I tried to smother the burning helplessness radiating from the cat with calming thoughts.

Easy.

The echoing growl subsided.

"I see he's back to being Dr. Jekyll," Hugh said quietly from the doorway. Obviously, he'd made it out of the tree and through the enclosure's exterior gate.

I eased up on the connection with the tiger and turned my attention to Hugh, motioning for him to head outside.

Thanks to the tiger's eruption of emotion, I was feeling jumpy and on edge. Suddenly, I was irritated with Hugh.

"The cat has an issue and you go in the enclosure with it to do an evaluation? What were you thinking?"

He shrugged. "I wasn't."

"You could have been killed."

"I had my tranq gun." He motioned to the pistol holstered at his side.

I arched my brows. A tranquilizer gun would have knocked Boris out about ten minutes too late, and we both knew it.

"Okay," he conceded. "I only wear it to look cool." Hugh offered me a charming half smile that could probably be weaponized to disarm a legion of Amazon warriors.

I wasn't in the mood. "Next time you decide to be dinner for someone, don't call me to clean up the mess."

"All right." His smile faded a notch and he eyed me with curiosity.

I understood why. Usually, I'm as calm as a glacial lake when I deal with animals. I have to be.

Shielding against the onslaught of an animal's thoughts and emotions was the only way I could help them—and keep my sanity. I had rushed it tonight and was paying the price—and so was Hugh.

I took a deep breath. I still wanted to berate him for being careless, but I'd known Hugh a long time. If he'd gone into the enclosure, he'd had his reasons.

"Sorry—let's just focus on what's making Boris suddenly want to eat people he supposedly likes."

"No, you're right, Grace, it was reckless of me to go in there. But to be fair, Boris isn't like any other tiger I've known. He bonds with people quickly. And he's never so much as sneezed at a human. His previous owner rescued him from a breeder as a cub—she was training him to work in movies—so he's been socialized with people and other animals."

"Then what's he doing here?"

"The woman was injured in a car accident and had to give him up."

Ozeal approached, stuck her head through the door to check on Boris, and turned to beam at me.

"Well, I have to say, I am truly impressed."

I acknowledged the compliment with a nod. "We're trying to understand the root of what's upsetting Boris. It's almost as if he has separation anxiety. Has someone he was attached to left recently?"

Ozeal's brow furrowed.

"Brooke."

"Who's Brooke?"

"One of my volunteers."

"When did she leave?" Hugh asked.

"Wednesday. Which is when Boris started acting strange." She shook her head. "I should have made the connection. Boris loves Brooke. He took a shine to her right off."

"Is Brooke coming back?" I asked.

Ozeal pressed her lips together. "I don't know," she said with a sigh. "We had a disagreement and when I went to ask her to help with one of the tours, she was gone."

"She didn't say anything?"

"I didn't even see her leave."

"What about her car?"

"Brooke just turned sixteen. She doesn't have a car."

I felt a knot of apprehension tighten in my stomach. Sixteen.

Taken.

I stepped away from Ozeal and Hugh, who had started talking about the best treatment for Boris's separation anxiety. I opened the little beaded clutch, pulled out my phone, and called Kai.

"Have you made it to the restaurant yet?"

"I'm pulling up to the valet now."

"Do you have your crime scene stuff with you?"

"My field kit? Yes. Why? Your friend didn't get eaten, did he?"

I hesitated a bit too long.

"Grace?" There was an edge to his voice.

"No. Hugh's fine." I explained the situation as quickly as I could.

"So you think this girl, Brooke, is missing?"

"Not just missing. Taken." Boris's description echoed through my mind. "Kai, I think she was kidnapped."

CHAPTER 2

I hesitated before turning back to where Ozeal and Hugh stood. Over the years, I'd gotten pretty good at tiptoeing around the truth when it came to my telepathic ability. Kai, being one of the few people who knew the truth, had kept his questions brief when I'd asked him to come to the rescue facility, before hanging up with, "I'm on my way."

Explaining to Ozeal why I wanted a crime scene investigator to come snoop around her place would be more complicated.

I couldn't tell her the truth—that Boris had told me Brooke had been taken. Maybe it was a cop-out, but I was guessing claims of psychic abilities would come under the category of nonsense in her book.

So, I decided to rely on a tried and true method—when in doubt, make something up.

With the phone still pressed to my ear, I walked back to Ozeal and Hugh.

"Ozeal, does Brooke have dark hair?"

"Yes, why?"

"Can you describe her physically?"

"Average height, I guess. Pretty. She wears her hair long."

Acting as if I was still talking to Kai, I grimly relayed this news into the phone and then said, "Okay, we'll be here." I turned my attention to Ozeal as I slipped my phone into my bag. "That was my date. He works for the sheriff's office. They've been investigating a series of missing persons cases involving girls who match Brooke's description. He wanted to come by and ask a few questions. Is that okay?"

"You think Brooke was kidnapped?"

The idea clearly troubled her and I felt a pang of guilt. I hated being deceitful but sometimes it was the only way to express what would otherwise take a lot of explaining on my part as I tried to prove I really could talk to tigers.

"I think it's possible," I said.

"Weren't there tour groups here that day?" Hugh asked Ozeal.

She nodded. "We had a school field trip and a few other groups."

"That's a lot of people. What are the chances of someone snatching a sixteen-year-old girl in broad daylight with a tour group snapping pictures in every direction?"

"We'll ask Kai when he gets here."

"When will that be?" Ozeal asked.

"Wait, your boyfriend's name is Kai? Isn't that a type of tea?" Hugh said with a lopsided grin.

I ignored him. "He's coming from Jax Beach so, thirty, maybe forty-five minutes."

Ozeal nodded. "We're running behind schedule tonight. Hugh, why don't you make yourself useful and help me get the rest of the big guys put up before the next bout of storms moves in. Grace, could you take another look at Boris? I want your opinion on the best treatment for his anxiety."

And just like that, I was recruited into the ranks—sparkly purse, mud boots, and all.

We'd just finished getting everything secured for the night and made it to the main building when lightning splintered across the sky. Rain swept over the grounds in a rush. The temperature dropped on a gust of wind, causing goose bumps to cascade over my skin, but I lingered on the porch as Ozeal and Hugh filed inside. I liked to watch storms, and smiled when the monotonous roar of the downpour was punctuated with sporadic bursts of thunder and the echoing caterwaul of a bobcat.

Caitlyn, the girl who had fetched me on the four-wheeler when I'd arrived, had gone home, and Hugh had been volunteered for gate duty. He stepped out of the front door and lifted a bright yellow raincoat from a peg on the wall.

"Ozeal's putting on some coffee," he told me as he shrugged into the jacket. "I'll wait here till your boyfriend pulls up and let him in."

I started to correct Hugh's designation of Kai. Technically, he wasn't my boyfriend but I decided to let it go. I nodded my thanks and went inside to find the kitchen. It was easy to spot. Judging by the avocado green stove and matching Frigidaire, in the seventies the building had been a ranch-style family home. Now it functioned as reception, gift shop, and offices.

Ozeal handed me a mug displaying the Happy Asses logo: a rear view of a donkey and a tiger side by side, their tails entwined like friends holding hands.

"Donkeys and big cats? Seems like an unlikely combination."

Ozeal let out a short laugh. "Well, you have the asses to blame for the cats."

She lowered herself into a chair at the kitchen table and I did the same. I took a sip of coffee, breathing in the rich aroma, and waited for her to continue.

"I bought this house after my husband died. Thought I could have a nice, quiet life out in the country. My son and I showed up with our U-Haul and found three donkeys in the pasture. The previous owners had left them to fend for themselves."

She shook her head as if she found the idea of someone abandoning an animal baffling.

I shared the feeling.

"So you decided to keep them?"

"What else could I do? We got them fixed up and fed. One of them, Jack-Jack, is a mini. Only three feet tall at the withers, but he has the biggest personality. Smart as a whip, loves to play, and he's an escape artist. He used to get out of his pen and wander all over the place. One day, he came home with another donkey. A little jenny—she was in poor shape, too."

I raised my eyebrows at that. "Jack-Jack rescued another donkey and brought it home?"

She nodded.

"A few weeks after that, he showed up with a stray dog."

"A dog?" That surprised me even more. "Donkeys usually don't like canines."

"Not as a rule, no. But Jack-Jack is not one to go by rules." Her lips quirked into a smile. "Guess what else he brought me."

"I have no idea—a fawn?"

"A bobcat kitten."

"You've got to be kidding." I was going to have to meet Jack-Jack.

"Believe me, I was as shocked as you are. I called the wildlife rescue, but they had a full house and asked if I could keep the kitten for a few days. I agreed, and they sent a veterinarian out to do an exam. He explained that the wildlife sanctuary was full because they'd gotten a whole litter of bobcat kittens some breeder had abandoned, along with their mother. They planned to reintroduce the kittens to the wild but the mother had never been out of a cage. She needed to be placed in a rescue facility, or she'd be euthanized."

"Terrible." I'd muttered the word to myself, but Ozeal nodded.

"It was. But that young veterinarian was fresh out of school and full of energy and ideas. The more he talked about the need for a place these cats could go, the more I agreed."

"So you took the mother."

"Once the kittens were weaned. You can figure out the rest of the story."

I looked at her and knew I'd been right to judge a woman by her signage. "The world needs more people like you, Ozeal."

She shook her head. "The world needs fewer idiots who think lion cubs make good Christmas presents."

A flash of headlights cut through the kitchen window.

A sudden thought occurred to me. "What happened to the young vet who talked you into all this?"

Hugh tromped into the room as I finished the question.

"Oh, he comes around from time to time to drip on my floor." Ozeal's tone was dry but her eyes shone with affection.

Hugh's raincoat was so slick from his dash to open the gate for Kai, he looked like a melting lemon gummy bear.

"Sorry," Hugh said, glancing at the puddle at his feet. "I'll hang my jacket outside."

He turned to go but stopped as Kai entered the room. Kai was wearing his tuxedo shirt under a dark rain jacket. Hugh paused to give him the once-over, then held out his hand.

"Hugh Murray. You must be the guy who got Grace in a dress."

"Kai Duncan. You must be the guy she had to come rescue."

The men shook hands but seemed to study each other a beat too long. I'd never been terribly astute when it came to men, but even I could tell there was some posturing going on.

Ozeal said, "Hugh, you're still dripping. Mr. Duncan, would you like some coffee?"

The men moved apart. Hugh continued outside and Kai turned to smile at Ozeal. "Coffee would be great, thanks."

He fixed his attention on me and I tried to ignore my body's instant reaction. Kai's Polynesian and Scotch heritage had gifted him with features I found very appealing. Dark hair and complexion. Green, almond-shaped eyes. Lazy surfer-boy smile.

Kai accepted a mug from Ozeal but waited for her to lower herself into a chair before taking a seat himself.

His manner tended to be disarming, his gaze and tenacity intense. The combo had affected more than just my libido. Kai had been the first person in years I'd told about my psychic ability. The admission had not been easy, but he'd promised to keep my secret.

I was banking on that promise now.

"I know I probably shouldn't have," I said, "but I told Ozeal about the other missing persons cases."

Ozeal locked her steady gaze onto Kai. "Grace said the police are looking into disappearances of girls who look like Brooke."

Kai shot me a look.

"Sorry." I was apologizing for dragging him into a lie but Kai went with it.

"It's not really something I can discuss." He quickly moved past the fabled disappearances and began asking questions about Brooke. He covered several questions I'd already asked, then moved on to the ones I hadn't even considered. Which is probably one of the many differences between someone with a degree in criminology and, well, me.

"Have you talked to her parents?" Kai asked.

Before Ozeal could answer, Hugh reappeared in the doorway.

"I've got to head out. One of our rhinos has gone into labor and I'm on the first watch."

"Before you go," Kai said, shifting his attention to Hugh, "do you know Brooke?"

"Not well. I've only met her a few times. She seems like a nice kid. I hope you find her."

"Hugh," I said before he could turn away. "Good luck."

"Thanks. And thanks for coming to my rescue . . . especially in that dress."

Kai watched him go then glanced at me. I wasn't sure how to categorize his expression, but it wasn't happy.

Now was not the time to explain Hugh's teasing so I chose to bring the conversation back to the topic.

"You said you talked to Brooke's parents?"

Ozeal nodded. "I called them when she didn't come in

yesterday. They weren't surprised. Honestly, it sounded like they had been expecting me to call. Brooke has had issues with dealing with her problems."

"Rather than facing them, she runs away?" Kai asked.

"According to her stepfather, yes." There was a long pause. Ozeal seemed to be choosing her next words carefully.

"Brooke is part of the rehabilitation program," she finally said.

"Rehabilitation?"

"For young people. They volunteer and get the chance to work with some of the animals. It teaches them responsibility and it keeps them off the streets and out of trouble."

"You're saying Brooke is a—what?" I asked, truly shocked. "A troubled teen?"

"I don't believe in labels. The kids in the program are promised a clean slate here. They come to me as volunteers. Ready to work and learn—not as junkies or thieves."

"And Brooke had access to Boris?" I didn't bother to hide my disbelief. The idea that a troubled teenager would have access, or possibly even keys, to a rescue facility that housed some of the world's largest predators completely boggled my mind.

Ozeal met my eyes with a steady gaze. "I'm not a fool, Grace. Brooke's contact with the animals was always supervised. I have rules. They apply to everyone. No lying. No stealing."

"You use the honor system?" Kai sounded as stunned as I was.

"I believe in giving these kids a fair shot. But I'm not completely naïve. This ain't my first rodeo." She motioned to the clump of keys clipped to her belt. "Every one of these goes to a lock on this property."

"So you keep certain things locked up."

"We have twelve cats in this rescue facility. A tiger, a lion, two panthers, six bobcats, and two caracals. So yes, I keep a good deal locked up."

"I meant—"

"I know what you meant, Mr. Duncan, but before you jump to conclusions, or make judgments on my policies, maybe you should ask how many times in the last three years I've had an incident of any kind involving one of my volunteers."

"I'm guessing zero."

"Not once since I started the program have I had more than a few minor issues. Kids that drop out, mostly."

It was an impressive claim.

"Do you think Brooke is one of the dropouts?" Kai asked.

Ozeal shook her head. "I'll say this—I have a lot of hope for Brooke. She's smart, and she's got a good heart. Most of our animals come from less-than-ideal situations. Someone buys one of these cats as a cub without any real understanding of the kind of care and environment they need. That ignorance usually leads to severe health and behavioral problems. Brooke had taken it on herself to do some research. She wanted to figure out a way to make things better for them."

"Enrichment projects?" I asked.

Ozeal nodded.

"Brooke thought it was only right. If she was getting a chance to turn things around, they should, too."

"What does your gut tell you is going on with her?"

The big woman was quiet for a long time. She looked down at her empty mug and then raised her gaze to meet my eyes.

"I don't know. People do things for reasons you can't understand. I've been wrong plenty of times, but if you'd asked me two days ago, I wouldn't even have considered the idea that she would up and leave."

We all sat there in silence as the rain thrummed against the roof.

Finally, Kai said, "Thanks for taking the time to talk to me, Ozeal. If I have any more questions, I'll call."

"Don't you want to look around?" I asked.

"It's pitch-dark and pouring," Kai said, as if I was just tuning in to the program.

I met his eyes and held his gaze for a long, uncomfortable moment, then I turned to Ozeal.

"Do you have an extra jacket?"

"Should be one on the peg by the front door."

"Excuse me." I stood more abruptly than I intended, and my chair skidded backward and bumped into the cabinet. I gave Ozeal a quick nod, turned, and walked out the door.

Outside, I shoved my arms into the raincoat and flipped up the hood. Kai caught up to me at my Suburban, where I was pulling a flashlight from the door's side pocket.

"Grace, what are you doing?"

"Going to look around," I said, turning to march toward Boris's enclosure.

"Brooke has been gone since Wednesday," Kai said, walking beside me. "It's been raining almost nonstop since then. If there was any evidence, the chance of finding it in the dark is slim."

"If?"

"Yes, if."

"You don't think she was kidnapped."

"I didn't say that. But you have to look at the facts."

"Okay, let's start with this one: Boris said Brooke was taken. He didn't say she'd run away. Taken."

I tried to stay calm and keep my argument as logical as possible, reminding myself that Kai was a scientist, and even though he accepted my ability, it had been a while since we talked about it, at least as it applied to his world. No matter how much my temper was riding me, I had to remember that as a crime scene investigator, Kai was used to working with facts and evidence.

"Could Boris have misunderstood?"

"He didn't."

"Grace." As we trudged past a small pavilion dotted with picnic tables, he snagged my arm and pulled me out of the rain. "Just stop for a second and listen. Brooke is a teenager with issues. Her own parents think she ran away."

I could barely see his face in the glow of the distant security light. But I could tell he was irritated. Water ran down the lines of his furrowed brow and dripped from the tips of his hair.

I knew it was hard to understand that a tiger's worry trumped Brooke's own parents. But that's what I needed—to be understood. Having Kai question me hurt.

A calming chill swept over me. My self-defense instinct has always been to freeze people out. But in my heart I knew something was different with Kai.

Once you let someone in . . .

The thought brought my hackles up. "Look, if you don't believe me—"

"I never said I didn't believe you. But you've told me that you feel an animal's emotions. It affects you."

"Not really," I lied.

"So that night you came over to watch a movie and fell asleep in the first five minutes wasn't because of Dusty?"

I flushed. It had been one of our first dates. Kai's cat, Dusty, had curled up in my lap—content and comfy—and his mellowness had washed over me like a warm bath. I'd conked out almost instantly.

"That wasn't my fault. I'd had a really long day. You remember the deal with the water buffalo and the lady with the chickens?"

"Not easy to forget that story."

"Well, I was tired and I didn't have my guard up."

"Exactly. You can be influenced, which makes you less objective."

"This is different."

"How?"

"It just is."

I started pacing to release some of the frustration that had started to boil through me. After a few seconds, I realized it was a very tigerlike thing to do and stopped.

"Why can't you just take me at my word?" I asked.

"I'm not doubting your word. I'm questioning the circumstances of the situation."

"Fine. You have questions—ask."

"It's never that easy with you."

"Why not?"

"Because you don't like to answer."

"That's not—"

He held up a hand and cut me off. "I'll rephrase. You don't like to *explain* your answers."

I shook my head, at a loss. Where had all this come from? I felt like I was back at square one with him, trying to substantiate something too nebulous to be proven.

"There's nothing to explain," I told him as rain pounded around us. "Brooke was kidnapped. No explanation needed."

"What do you want me to do, Grace? I can't call in a kidnapping based on what a tiger told you."

I knew that, logically. The trouble was, I wasn't feeling very logical.

"We have to do something, Kai."

"Okay, how's this—wait till tomorrow morning. I'll meet you here first thing and we can look around then."

I started to say no but I knew he was right. Wandering around in the dark would be futile. Thinking like a cat didn't mean I could see like one.

I agreed with a grim nod. Thunder rumbled overhead as we stepped from the pavilion into the downpour. In the distance, I heard the muted, lonely roar of a tiger.

• • •

I dragged myself into my sister's condo just after nine o'clock. Wet, grumpy, and worried, I was so distracted by thoughts of a missing sixteen-year-old and hurt by Kai's obvious lack of faith in my ability, I almost didn't notice my dog, Moss, enter the foyer to greet me.

Being that Moss is a wolf hybrid who outweighs me, he's pretty hard to miss. As tall as his timber wolf relatives, his head comes to my waist. This meant I never had to bend over to pet him and he could peruse the kitchen counters freely—much to my sister's dismay.

I'd been house hunting, but so far hadn't found a place with a moat and twenty-foot wall.

"Hey, big guy."

Sensing my mood, Moss let out a low, questioning grumble.

Okay?

I'm fine.

Before I could place my hand on his head for an appreciative pat, Moss caught the scent of tiger and other exotic wonders wafting in the air around me. He was used to me coming home coated with animal smells, but always got especially excited by the scent of a big cat. I assumed this had something to do with the fact that as a pup, he'd been BFF with a jaguar cub.

Whatever motivated his zeal, I knew his nose would be twitching over me as long as I smelled of *Panthera tigris*.

I was heading toward my bedroom to take a quick shower and change when the front door opened.

My sister, Emma, decked out in all-black vampire chic, strolled in carrying a purse in the shape of a tiny coffin. She took one look at me and shook her head.

"Dare I ask?"

"I didn't make it to the gala."

"That's a relief. I'd hate to think you showed up in those boots."

I glanced down at my feet, then at my sister. "At least I'm not sporting fangs. What's with the outfit?"

"Theme wedding. October tends to inspire the Goth crowd."

Emma was a premier party planner in Jacksonville, and she always attended the events she planned, which meant dressing the part. From Wild West to rockabilly, Emma had a closet full of costumes.

"I had planned to come home and change before meeting up with you at the soirée," she said as she set the mini-coffin on the island separating the kitchen and open living room. "Clearly that's not going to happen."

Moss had continued to sniff me from toe to waist and back again, finally nudging at my fingers where I'd touched

Boris. His brain was in high-excitement mode—which was wearing on me.

Moss, enough!

I bent and yanked off my boots.

"Here—see if I stepped in anything interesting." I tossed the boots aside and stepped away.

"Eew." Emma made a face.

I waved her off. "I'm too tired to block him out and talk to you at the same time."

"Well, it worked," Emma said, watching as Moss zeroed in on a spot on the bottom of one boot. "But I don't want to know."

"Neither do I. Come on."

We fled to her room and shut the door. I let out a sigh of relief. Fatigue always made it harder to shield my mind, especially from Moss.

Emma turned her back to me and motioned to the laces of her boned corset. As I went to work freeing her from what I considered a torture device, we talked about the events of the night.

"Then," I said, pulling the corset over her head, "Kai went all *CSI* on me. He's not convinced Brooke was taken, because he thinks my emotions are too tangled up with Boris's."

"It's a valid point."

"For the record, as my sister, you have to agree with me."

"I didn't say I disagreed with you. Just that it's a good point. And," Emma went on as she shimmied into a red dress that worked perfectly with her dramatic eye makeup and ruby lips, "I think there's something else to consider. Your emotions might have been influenced by the tiger's but what about Kai's? He may not have been as upset if you'd run off to save someone else."

"What do you mean?"

"From what you've said, Dr. Murray is a bit of a flirt. I've seen his picture—he's a hottie. Is he still asking you out all the time?"

"I told you, that's just Hugh being Hugh." I'd recently come to understand that all the flirting and silliness that used to irritate me were simply Hugh's way of letting me know he cared about me. "He likes to tease me. It doesn't mean anything."

"You might know that, but Kai doesn't."

"What does that have to do with him believing me?"

"Maybe nothing. But let's look at the situation in another way. You ditched Kai for Hugh."

"That's ridiculous. I didn't ditch anyone. Hugh was being stalked by a tiger—"

Emma held up a finger and continued. "Then, you call Kai, expecting him to rush to your side and when he does, you're still unhappy because he doesn't want to go charging into a thunderstorm—in a tux, mind you—to search for a girl who might not even be missing."

"She's missing, Emma."

"Understood. I'm just trying to illustrate how a person's perspective can change things."

"You really think Kai would be petty enough to let jealousy cloud his judgment?" I asked, standing behind Emma as she checked her appearance in the full-length mirror in her room.

"It's not petty, it's human nature. Everyone is influenced by their emotions. And you," she said, glancing at my reflection before turning around to face me, "you get the bonus plan. You have to deal with your own emotions in addition to the influence of whatever animal you're doing the Vulcan mind-meld on."

"Em, this isn't about Boris's emotions," I said, frustrated.

"I never said it was. I think there's another reason you're so convinced something happened to Brooke." Emma walked into her closet and emerged a moment later with a black satin clutch. "You identify with her."

"You're right," I said with a dramatic sigh. "Those years I spent on the street were really hard."

Emma cast me a sharp look and clarified. "I mean you're on the same page—mentally."

"I'm on the same mental page as a sixteen-year-old habitual runaway with a criminal record? Really, Em—you keep saying stuff like that and I'll have to revoke your sister card."

"You can't revoke my sister card."

"Yes I can."

She shook her head. "Nope."

"Then I'll suspend your sister card."

"So I'll be on sister probation? You don't have the authority."

"Says who?"

"Mom." Emma's smile widened. "Let's call her and ask."

There was an unspoken rule between us—the first one to threaten to call our mother during a disagreement always won. You only called Mom if you knew you were right.

Of course, from time to time bluffs were made, but for the most part the "Let's call Mom" declaration settled any dispute.

Knowing this, in addition to the fact that our parents were RVing out of cell range somewhere in Yellowstone, Emma pressed on with her point. "Brooke has found friendship with at least one animal at the rescue place. You should consider the idea you might be projecting, because you understand where she's coming from."

"No, I don't. All I know is she's some poor kid whose parents are deadbeats that don't care about their daughter."

"Do you know that for a fact?"

"Come on, Em . . ."

"I'll take that as a no. So, find out," she said as we walked out of her room, down the hall, and into the living room. "Talk to her parole officer or whatever kids her age have. Before you jump back into an argument with Kai, get more facts. Why try to make him see something he can't?"

Dammit, my sister was right.

"You might also want to make a point of telling Kai you have no romantic interest in Hugh—just for clarity's sake."

I rolled my eyes. "I'm not going to do that. Kai's not

stupid, Emma." Even as I said it, I remembered how he and Hugh had sized each other up in Ozeal's kitchen.

"No, but he's human. And for the record," she said, mimicking my earlier comment, "I'm always on your side."

CHAPTER 3

Kai stood me up. Kind of. He'd actually gotten called to a murder scene. I understood. But I was still irritated to be on my own, looking for clues.

My mood didn't improve when an hour of traipsing through the woods surrounding Happy Asses yielded nothing more than a few scratches on my arms. I was pulling another twig from my hair when I remembered something.

I fished my phone out of my back pocket and called Hugh.

"You took your tranquilizer gun in with you, right?"

If my abrupt question bothered him, he didn't comment. "Right. Why?"

"Did Boris see it before or after you entered the enclosure?"

"I don't know. I keep the gun in my holster. Though I did check the CO_2 before I went in. You're thinking he wigged out because of a tranq gun?"

"It's a thought."

"Ask Ozeal if Boris has an issue with being tranquilized— maybe that will solve the mystery."

I made a noncommittal sound. Mostly because I had a

different mystery to solve. Could Brooke have been taken at gunpoint?

That might explain why Boris went after Hugh. Not because whoever grabbed Brooke looked like Hugh—which had been my working theory—but because they'd had a gun. Hugh couldn't have had it out of the holster for more than a minute to check the CO_2.

There was an easy way to find out if Boris had a reaction to someone holding a gun.

I walked to Bluebell, opened the back, and unlocked my metal storage box. The box was bolted down and contained medications that were considered controlled substances. It also contained the Glock Kai was teaching me how to shoot.

I lifted the gun and checked to make sure the clip was empty and there was no round in the chamber. I even went as far as to dry fire the gun twice with it pointed to the ground.

Safety check finished, I locked my strong box, closed Bluebell's rear doors, and, with the gun tucked into the waistband of my jeans, made my way down the access road to see Boris.

The tiger was lounging in his small concrete pool when I walked up. He saw me, surged to his feet, and let out a low whine followed by a series of rumbling, slow, sneeze-like sounds.

It was called *chuffing,* and was the tiger equivalent of "Howdy, friend!"

I pursed my lips and mimicked the sound, placing my hand on the wire between us when he rubbed his face against the fence.

"How you doing today, Boris?"

As I asked, I gently probed his mind to get a feel for his mood. There was still an undercurrent of sadness, but he seemed calm and relaxed.

Pet.

He pressed his forehead squarely against the fence and I scratched between his ears and down his nose.

Contentment filled the big cat and rolled over me in a

soft wave. I hated to upset him, but I needed to know whether or not the sight of a gun might have prompted his reaction to Hugh. There was also a chance that seeing a gun would trigger a flash of memory and I might actually get a clearer glimpse of what happened.

I pulled my hands away with a mental apology and drew the Glock out of my waistband. I didn't point the weapon at the cat—I just let him see it.

Boris blinked his golden eyes, then pressed his head against the fence.

Pet.

"Well, I guess that answers that question."

"Grace? What the hell are you doing?"

I turned to Ozeal, who had probably seen me waving a gun around in front of the tiger and thought I'd gone completely crazy.

"I thought maybe Boris had turned on Hugh because he saw a dart gun and had some negative associations with it."

Ozeal's frown deepened.

"I'm sorry. I should've asked. My tranquilizer gun isn't a pistol so I had to use this. Obviously, the gun isn't loaded."

Ozeal seemed to consider my logic, then slowly nodded.

"I'm not sure I understand your methods, but as long as you're doing what you're doing to help Brooke or Boris, you've got my okay."

I nodded and looked away, both moved and dismayed at her declaration of trust—something that came so unnaturally to me.

"I was wondering," I said, hoping to redirect my thoughts, "how many other people work here?"

"Well, there's my son, Ben, who mostly works in the commissary. Once a week I have a maintenance guy, Paul, who comes in to fix the list of odds and ends that need doing from the week before. In the office, we've got Debbie. She handles all the paperwork, the website, and answers the phone and e-mails."

"Can I talk to them?"

"I already talked to everyone that was here on Wednesday. No one saw anything."

"What about the girl I met last night?"

"Caitlyn. She's a volunteer in the rehabilitation program."

"Are she and Brooke friends?"

"As far as I can tell."

"And she didn't have any insights?"

A ghost of a smile played on Ozeal's lips. "Caitlyn's not the most insightful girl. Bless her heart, she's as thick as rhino hide."

"I know you don't believe in labels, but do you know what Caitlyn had gotten in trouble for?"

Ozeal blew out a slow breath. "A little bit of everything. I haven't asked her about it, but I get the feeling that, more often than not, she's influenced by her friends. Does something stupid by following someone else's lead."

"And Brooke?"

A look clouded her features, but she answered.

"Stealing."

Something about the way she said the word made me wonder. "Is that what you and Brooke argued about?"

She was silent for several moments. "Before we go into that, I want you to know that I trust Brooke. And not just in a hypothetical way. She's been here almost a year and has earned privileges I haven't ever given a volunteer."

"Like?"

"Brooke has the code to the front gate so she can come in early. And after she got her driver's license, I let her go pick up supplies from the feed and seed on her own."

"But?" I prompted.

"Wednesday, I caught her in the clinic."

"You think she was trying to get drugs?"

"She says she wasn't. And when I asked her what she needed, she lied and told me she was looking for some pliers."

"I take it you don't keep pliers in the clinic."

"I don't. And Brooke knows it. We both got upset, and I told her if she stepped out of line again I'd write her up and send the report to her probation officer. I didn't see her after that."

I thought quietly for a minute. "Did she tell you why she wanted the pliers?"

"She said there was a loose spot on the fence behind Boris's enclosure. I had Paul check, but he didn't find anything."

"Paul, the maintenance worker? He was here on the day Brooke went missing?"

She nodded. "Usually he comes on Sundays. We're closed, so if he needs to get into any of the enclosures for repair I can make sure he has access. But he had planned a trip with his family this weekend, so I asked him to come Wednesday."

"Did you talk to him?"

"No. I didn't think about it, because he usually isn't here."

"I'd like to get his contact information."

She nodded. "You may not be able to reach him. Paul's out of town till tomorrow. But he'll be here Monday—I've got an electrical issue he has to see to." She pointed past me to a light pole. I could see an electrical box—the kind that has a cover to keep out the elements—affixed to the side of the pole. The plastic was warped and blackened.

"Lightning?" I asked.

"Last night. Which reminds me—I've got to head to the office and make sure Debbie checks the surge protectors. I'll let her know you're coming. She'll get you whatever you need."

With a parting nod, she strode off.

Past the pole, I noticed two sets of pale, golden eyes peering at me.

Cougars.

They must have already been secured in their overnight housing when I'd ridden to Hugh's rescue the night before. Could they have seen what happened to Brooke? I started toward their enclosure to ask. One of the cougars, a female, crouched lower as I approached.

I hadn't focused my mind to mentally connect with her

but I could still feel aggression and mistrust rolling off her in hot waves.

Stranger.

"Only because we haven't been introduced," I said, opening my mind to hers just as she lunged at the fence with a screeching snarl.

The burst of hostility hadn't caught me completely off guard, but it zinged through me nonetheless. That, along with the eerie noise only a cougar could make, sent a surge of goose bumps rushing over my skin.

"Nice," I spoke softly, snuffing out the lingering ferocity with a blanket of calm. "You're a very scary girl, aren't you?"

The cougar growled, crouching low again.

I sent her gentle thoughts. Calm. Friendly.

Safe.

You're safe. I won't hurt you or your friend.

The cat's mind, which had been a tangle of savage, frightened thoughts slowly calmed. After several minutes, her tense muscles relaxed. She even started to purr when I knelt in front of her.

I smiled. Cougars are the largest cat that can still purr—it's a wonderful sound.

I spent some time talking to the cougars, but realized quickly that they had no insight into what had happened to Brooke.

After bidding them good-bye, I made my way to the office to talk to Debbie.

Ozeal had been right, at least about Debbie witnessing what had happened to Brooke. Her office was in the main building, about as far away from Boris's enclosure as possible.

The woman was small and birdlike, with huge Coke-bottle glasses and a fluff of bleached blond hair that made her look like Tweety.

"Ozeal said you thought Brooke might have been kidnapped," she said. "I hope not. I can't imagine something like that happening out here."

"I hope not, too. I know Brooke was in the program. Do you have a file or anything I can take a look at?"

She nodded and her giant glasses slipped down her nose. She shoved them back into place and opened a file drawer.

"I'm afraid there's not much in it. Just her application to the program. The volunteers sign in when they get here and make a note of the time. There should be a photocopy in the file."

"Thanks. Can I take a quick look and bring it back after I make a few notes?"

"Take your time."

I walked to the picnic tables and flipped through the very light file.

The application listed Brooke's home address and gave the name and phone number of another contact, listed as "Mrs. Johnston, PO."

PO must mean Brooke's probation officer.

I made a few notes on the little notepad app that came with my phone and returned the file to Debbie.

Okay, now what?

I'd noticed on the log-in sheet that Brooke usually arrived in the morning and Caitlyn in the afternoon. I assumed the girl wouldn't be in until later. I thought about going directly to Brooke's house to see for myself why her parents had decided to blow off her disappearance but wanted more info first.

I looked at my notes again and decided to call Mrs. Johnston, hoping to get more information on Brooke and maybe a perspective on her home life. I tried the number but got the Department of Juvenile Justice's voice mail.

I didn't have the faintest idea how to track down a government employee. Kai, the logical go-to for information, was obviously busy, so I tried to outline the steps I'd need to find someone when all I had was a last name and a work phone number. I might be able to locate her office, but what were the chances that Mrs. Johnston would be working on Saturday?

Pretty slim.

I didn't have anything else pressing to do until my first

client appointment, which left me with a couple of hours to kill.

The only other person who might shed some light on detective techniques was my friend Wes.

Wes and I had been friends since grade school. He was an attorney, and though he now lived in Savannah, he maintained his connections in Jacksonville.

I found his number in my contacts and called.

"Well, hello, Gracie–pooh. To what do I owe this honor?"

I rolled my eyes. Wes had a flare for nicknames. "I have a question."

"Oh?"

"How do you find someone if you only have a last name and phone number?"

"Apparently, I'd start by calling the most amazing attorney I knew."

I smiled. "And then?"

"Then, I'd promise to go dancing with him the next time he was in town."

"Uh . . ." Dancing with Wes was hazardous to my health. He was an amazing dancer, but the last time we'd gone out, he'd nearly salsaed me into cardiac arrhythmia.

"That didn't sound like much of a promise."

"If Emma comes to take some of the heat off me, then fine."

"Hummmm . . . bring your hot cop and we have a deal. Unless there's a reason you're asking me and not Kai-candy?"

"Kai-candy?"

"Not my best, I admit. Sergeant Dunc-a-licious?"

I snorted out a laugh. "Where do you come up with this stuff?"

"I have to find an outlet for my creativity."

"*Kai-candy* is working a murder. But I'll invite him dancing—that's a promise."

"Spectacular. Now, give me the name and phone number of the person you're looking for and I will set my minions on the task. They should find something soon."

"Thanks, Wes."

"Anything for you, my sweet."

I hung up and wandered in the direction of the barn. Several donkeys grazed in an adjacent pasture, and I walked toward the split-rail fence that separated us.

Whoever came up with the term *dumbass* probably never knew a donkey. Generally speaking, donkeys are intelligent, calm animals. They like attention, and when the small herd noticed my approach, they moved forward en masse—heads up and ears pricked. The feeling from the group was a mixture of anticipation and interest, along with mild curiosity.

"Hi, guys."

I folded my arms to lean on the rough-hewn wood of the top rail and propped one foot on the bottom.

"Jack-Jack, you in here somewhere?" I scanned the group and finally saw the miniature donkey. To say he was cute was an understatement. Like a lot of donkeys, his coloring was a grayish dun with the characteristic cross of darker hair at his withers. Light tan capped his muzzle and ringed his eyes.

All in all, he didn't look like a genius donkey—but looks could be deceiving.

Curious, I zeroed in on his brain and learned two things.

One—the little guy was off-the-charts smart; and two—he didn't want to talk to me.

The donkey was hiding something.

Okay, you little sneak. Just as I was about to pull out the big guns, hop the fence, and lay my hands on him for a proper Grace mind-meld, my phone chimed.

I glanced at my screen. A text message from Wes with Mrs. Johnston's information.

"That was fast," I said.

According to the text, Clara Johnston was fifty-one and married. It listed both her office and her home address, which, as luck would have it, was only a little out of the way from my first consultation appointment. Before I headed for Bluebell, I turned to Jack-Jack.

"When I get back, we're gonna have a talk."

Jack-Jack pulled his lips back in a donkey snicker, then turned and trotted away.

• • •

My appointment was with Brian Crews and his exceedingly hyper and loving Labrador, Jacoby. I'd worked with them before, so was able to quickly determine the catalyst behind Jacoby's sudden need to turn his owner's new flower beds into WWI-worthy trenches.

Bonemeal. A great fertilizer, but to a dog like Jacoby, it was a buried treat that could never be located.

With some effort, I was able to explain to Jacoby that all the digging in the world would never yield the bone his nose promised, and I suggested Brian use something else to feed his plants.

All in all, the appointment took around half an hour, so it was barely past eleven when I started on my own hunt for Brooke's caseworker.

I spotted Clara Johnston's house as soon as I turned onto her street. It was hard to miss the profusion of giant, inflatable Halloween decor covering her lawn.

There was so much vivid orange and violent purple that it was hard to make out the house.

Halloween has always been one of my favorite holidays. Probably something to do with the magical concept of trick-or-treating and staying out past my bedtime. But as much as I liked the holiday, and as inept as I was at understanding design and decor, even I knew Mrs. Johnston had taken things a little too far.

Like a cobra entranced by the movements of a mongoose, I was so mesmerized by the colors that it took me a minute to notice a woman had pulled into the drive.

Like always, I wrestled with the best approach. I figured in her line of work, the woman had been fed enough BS. I'd probably be better off playing it straight and telling her the truth. Well, except for the bit about a tiger seeing Brooke's kidnapping.

"Mrs. Johnston?" I called out as I passed the VW-sized pumpkin marking the corner of her lawn.

She turned to me and nudged her car door closed with one hip. "Yes?"

"My name is Grace Wilde. I was hoping I could ask you about Brooke Ligner."

"Who?

"She's one of your . . ." I wasn't sure of the term. *Client?* "You're her probation officer."

And just like that a switch was flipped.

"If you want to report a problem or file a complaint, you'll have to call the office Monday." She turned away before she'd even finished the sentence.

"Wait, that's not why I'm here." I faltered at the entrance of the poofy orange tunnel leading to the front porch, then hurried through, nearly bumping into the woman as I walked up the steps and emerged on the other side. "I think something may have happened to Brooke."

"Then I suggest you contact the police."

"Come on. We're talking about a sixteen-year-old girl."

"So are most of my other cases." She spoke without looking at me and unlocked her front door.

"So, what? You only care Monday through Friday?"

"Pretty much."

The door slammed in my face and I stood there for a moment, too stunned to move. I had a hard time equating the cheerful decorations with the cold woman I'd just met.

Maybe she was married to someone with a sunny disposition and a love of hyperbole. Either that, or she was like the witch in "Hansel and Gretel," and the decorations were Mrs. Johnston's version of the gingerbread house. A tool to lure children close so she could snack on them later.

"The witch gets it in the end, you know!" I called out before turning with a sigh to walk back to Bluebell.

Discouraged by my lack of progress with Mrs. Johnston, I was not in the best mood when Kai called.

"Hey. Sorry about earlier. Did you find anything?" he asked as I drove back to Happy Asses.

"Yes. Mud, dirt, leaves, and pine needles."

"No squirrels to interrogate?"

I knew he was only teasing, but after last night, I was feeling sensitive so I didn't reply.

"Grace?"

I choked back the snippy comment I wanted to make and tried to be logical.

"No squirrels. But I'm hoping to talk to the other volunteer. Maybe she can tell me something."

"One of the other teens in the rehab program?"

"Her name is Caitlyn. She and Brooke are friends—or at least I hope they are. I'm batting zero today."

"I don't know about that."

"Trust me, I feel like I'm running on a hamster wheel."

"I mean you might not want the girls to be friends. If Caitlyn and Brooke are buddies, she's probably not going to tell you anything. Loyalty is big with these kids. Snitching is a no-no."

"Snitching? How can talking to me be snitching? I'm not a cop."

"You're an adult."

Crap.

"So what do I do?"

"If you talk to her, don't jump in with a bunch of questions. Talk about something else. Find something you have in common."

"In common?" First Emma, now Kai. My people skills must have been worse than I thought for them both to compare me to juvenile delinquents.

"If you can get her talking first, you'll have better luck. Trust me."

Great, I had to chitchat. I sucked at chitchat.

Over the phone, I could hear a gruff voice speaking with the abruptness and cadence of a Yankee.

"Is that Jake?" I asked.

"Yeah. He wants to talk to you. Hang on."

A moment later, I got Detective Jake Nocera's signature greeting.

"Yo."

"What's up, Jake?"

"When are you bringin' Moss over for a playdate?"

"Soon. How's Jax doing?"

"Getting fat. Mary says I need to take him for more walks, but with this knee I'm lucky to make it off the toilet in the morning."

"Nice. Thanks for that visual."

"No problem. So, I'm thinking if you bring Moss over, he and Jax can play and I'm off the hook."

"For a day."

"I'll take what I can get."

I understood. Keeping up with a young Doberman pinscher who was trained as a personal protection dog wasn't easy. But Jax was such a good dog, it was worth the time and effort.

"Okay, I'll call Mary and set something up."

Jake handed the phone back to Kai with what might have been a *thanks,* but with Jake's Northern accent and general grumpiness, it was hard to tell.

"I was going to ask if you wanted to grab lunch," Kai said, "but I'm going to be stuck here awhile. What are you doing for dinner?"

"What did you have in mind?"

"How about the Pizza Bar?"

"Sounds good."

I heard more voices in the background.

"I've got to go. Maggie is turning things over to us. I'll see you tonight." I knew from past conversations that Maggie was the medical examiner, and the fact that she had only just turned the crime scene over to the police meant Kai would be busy for a while.

After we hung up, I concentrated on divining a way to approach Caitlyn.

I thought about calling my sister for advice. Emma could make small talk with anyone. Infant or octogenarian— people loved my sister. But I knew the glam Goth wedding was later that night and Emma was probably up to her eye-balls in black tulle and brocade velvet.

I was on my own. Hopefully, I would do better with Caitlyn than I had with Ms. Nasty Pants Johnston.

I parked near the Happy Asses office and hopped out of Bluebell. It didn't take long to spot my quarry. Caitlyn was dragging a large trash can toward the donkey pen and carrying a fan rake and an oversized shovel. Though she was taller than me—not hard given that I'm barely five foot three—she was fine boned, a bit scrawny, and was having a tough time maneuvering the can along with the tools.

I sighed and started toward her.

It looked like I was going to be cleaning up donkey poop. The glamour of my life is almost too much to take sometimes.

"Hey, let me help you." I held the gate and took the rake and shovel.

"Thanks."

The donkeys, eager as ever, had surrounded us by the time we took two steps into the enclosure.

Their expectations were clear. Even if I hadn't been inundated with *Treat. Treat? Where treat? Have treat?* the nosing at our pockets and hopeful expression in their large, liquid eyes would have told me what they wanted.

I pulled up my mental shield to cut off the pleas.

"So, how do you plan to scoop if we can't move?" I asked with what I hoped was a casual smile.

"Dang it. I forgot about their treats. Brooke always brought them."

I kept a supply of dog and cat treats in Bluebell but was fresh out of donkey snacks.

Peppermint.

I remembered Boris saying Brooke smelled like peppermint.

"Do they like candy? I have some in my truck."

"Yeah. That would be great."

I went and grabbed a packet of Skittles out of the bag of

Halloween candy I'd picked up in case we had any trick-or-treaters. No peppermint, but they'd have to do.

We fed the donkeys the Skittles and I offered to help Caitlyn rake the pen. As we worked, I tried to chitchat about the only thing we had in common.

"So, you like volunteering here?"

"It's a lot of work, but it's fun, you know? The animals are cool."

"Brooke liked working with the animals, too, didn't she? It seems weird that she'd just take off."

Caitlyn shrugged. Maybe I'd jumped the gun on asking about Brooke. I started to go back to the chitchat stuff and had an idea.

"Hey, I wanted to ask you about last night."

Caitlyn glanced at me before dumping a load into the can. "You mean what happened with Boris?"

"We've been trying to figure out what upset him. Did you see what happened?"

"Yeah!" Caitlyn perked up. Apparently Hugh getting treed like a raccoon warranted her interest. I was happy to use that to my advantage and not only get her talking but also see if she could provide insight into what had triggered Boris's attack.

"It was crazy. Like, I was standing right there with everyone else. One second, Boris was on his back getting his belly rubbed and next thing he's up and after Dr. Murray."

The fact that Boris had been on his back was probably the only reason Hugh had been able to make it up the tree. It was also interesting because by exposing his belly, Boris was expressing trust. Something that had clearly changed in the blink of an eye.

But why?

"So you didn't hear Dr. Murray say something or hear a noise that might have frightened Boris?"

"No. Nothing like that."

"You said you were watching with everyone else. Who else was there?"

"Ozeal, me, and the maintenance guy, Paul. It was crazy.

I was afraid Ozeal was going to have to dart Boris. And that wouldn't have been good."

Even with her limited experience, Caitlyn knew the risks in tranquilizing a large animal, especially in an uncontrolled situation.

"I'm glad we didn't have to," I said.

"Because of you." She looked at me, wide-eyed.

"Yep. I'm like the Ghostbusters."

"Who?"

"Never mind. Ozeal mentioned Brooke had been doing some work trying to get some more toys and stuff for the cats."

"Yeah. Brooke is real smart. You can apply for all this money and stuff. She spent a lot of time filling out forms. She even wrote a paper or something." She made a face as if she found the idea of writing truly horrifying.

"I wonder if that's what's upsetting Boris: Brooke leaving." Grace Wilde, Queen of Subtle.

"That can happen?"

"Sure. Animals are affected by separation anxiety just like people." We dragged the can to the other section of the pen, our shadows stretching out in front of us in the late-afternoon sun. The air was still and warm enough to make sweat bead on my brow as we raked.

"Do you think Brooke is coming back?" I asked.

"I don't know."

"So she didn't tell you she was leaving?"

"I wasn't here."

"I mean before that. She never said she might take off?"

"Me and Brooke have different shifts. We overlap sometimes and grab lunch or whatever, but we don't spend much time together. I mean, like, we talked some, but she wasn't really into sharing."

"I wish I could talk to her. Maybe let her know that Boris was upset. Do you know how I can get in touch with her?"

"Ozeal said she's been trying to call her." Caitlyn hesitated before admitting, "I tried to call Brooke, too, but she hasn't answered."

"Maybe I should go look for her. Do you know any of her hangouts? Someplace she might've gone?"

"She said she liked to hang out at the Regency Mall sometimes. But, you know, they make you stop hanging out with most of your old friends. I used to go out to Jax Beach but my PO says I can't do that anymore. I mean, how is hanging at the beach supposed to be a bad influence? We even have a fu—" She caught herself and cast me a sidelong glance. "Uh. A freaking curfew. It sucks."

"Sounds like it. Was there anyone in particular Brooke wasn't supposed to see?"

"Her boyfriend, Stefan. He got busted for drugs."

"Do you know his last name?"

She shook her head. "Sometimes, Brooke would call him Butter."

"Butter? Is that like calling someone honey?"

Caitlyn giggled. "No. It's his street name. 'Cause he thinks he's smooth as butter." She rolled her eyes.

"I take it you don't think he's so smooth?"

"He's kind of a dick." Her eyes widened. "Sorry."

"Hey, call it like you see it—that's what I do."

She nodded. "I met him a couple of times."

"He came here?"

She shrugged. "Me and Brooke would go to the movies; he'd meet her there."

I thought it was really stupid to risk getting in trouble to see a boy. But it wasn't my place to point that out. "You think he's a jerk, huh?"

"He's a total wangster. Like he's all bad or something because he thinks he looks like that guy on *Pretty Little Liars*—you know, the bad boy, Caleb?" She rolled her eyes again. "Like you can grow your hair out and look like Tyler Blackburn."

I had no idea what she was talking about, but I nodded anyway. "Total wangster. Do you know where Stefan lives?"

"Somewhere off Cesery, I think."

Cesery was a long road with access to everything from

housing projects to mansions, if you crossed over into Oak Park. Not the greatest lead, but it was a start.

We were quiet as we finished our task and finally I asked, "Do you know what's up with Brooke's parents?"

"What do you mean?"

"They haven't reported her missing."

Caitlyn shrugged. "Brooke said her mom told her if she ever ran away again, she shouldn't come back. And her step-dad said she was cut off or something."

"So Brooke and her parents didn't get along?"

"She said her mom was just emotional but her stepdad's a real asshole." She shot me a guilty grimace. "Sorry."

"Apologize to the donkeys, not me."

She blinked at me. "Huh?"

"You know—they're asses and . . . never mind."

I helped Caitlyn maneuver the can through the gate but hung around as she headed off. I had an appointment with a jackass of my own.

CHAPTER 4

I'd kept my eye on Jack-Jack while we cleaned the pen. As soon as Caitlyn was out of sight, I turned to find he'd moved away and turned his back on me.

"You'll have to do better than that, buddy." I slipped back through the gate and crept toward where he stood.

Here, donkey, donkey.

As I edged forward, I nudged Jack-Jack's mind with my own.

Nothing.

He wasn't just ignoring me, he was . . . blocking me?

"No way."

It had taken me years to learn how to block out the intrusive buzz of the animal minds around me. Pulling a mental shield into place was tricky and took practice. I couldn't believe a donkey could do it—not even one as smart as Jack-Jack.

I put my hand out and eased toward him. If I could get my hands on him, my connection would be stronger and I'd know for sure.

The other donkeys watched as I stalked closer to Jack-Jack. I cast out my feelers to them, thankful to find they weren't alarmed. Donkeys could be very protective when they perceived a threat. The last thing I wanted was to be the victim of a misguided donkey stomp.

As I neared, Jack-Jack's ears swiveled backward, listening. I was only a few feet away.

Closer. Closer . . . just before my hand connected with his rump, he trotted away.

I tried again with the same result. Each time, I would get within inches and he would prance off.

A game?

I glanced at my watch and saw I had time before I was supposed to meet Kai for pizza. If the little donkey wanted to play, so be it.

How about hide-and-seek?

I turned in a circle and began scanning the pen. Since Jack-Jack wasn't going to let me come to him, maybe he'd come to me.

The donkeys, being grazers of the highest order, had shorn every blade of grass to oblivion. Their main source of food was a large pile of hay by the barn.

A small lean-to protected the hay container and feed buckets from the elements. I walked to the structure and looked for a good place to lie in wait. A glance over my shoulder told me Jack-Jack still stood with his back to me.

I edged closer to the hay, leapt into the pile, crouched, and covered myself as quickly as I could. I brought up my mental shield so I wouldn't inadvertently broadcast my plan, and settled in with my back against the barn wall.

Now, all I had to do was wait for Jack-Jack to get close and I'd be able to touch him. Simple enough.

After a few minutes, I started to itch. Nothing horrible— just enough to make me want to squirm. I held still so I didn't give myself away.

I could do this. Mind over matter.

The thought inspired a random Dr. Seuss quote to float through my mind.

"Be who you are and say what you feel because those who mind don't matter and those who matter don't mind."

My mother had told me this repeatedly as a child.

It didn't matter that I was different.

Different was beautiful.

But after the age of about five, people no longer thought it was cute when I told them I was talking to the squirrels. They thought it was weird.

Mom had stuck to her guns. "Your true friends will like you the way you are. Forget everyone else."

I'd learned to forget a lot of people. Even people I thought loved me.

In college, I'd been dumped in spectacular fashion by Dane Harrington—of *the* Harringtons, one of the oldest, wealthiest families in the Southeast. He'd broken it off when I'd finally revealed my ability. Not because he thought I was crazy but because he thought I was a freak.

For a long time, I'd used that as an excuse to stay closed off, never letting anyone in.

Then I'd met Kai. A man of science who believed in my psychic ability despite everything he'd been taught. A man who made me feel things that scared me. A man who . . . was probably already on his way to meet me for dinner while I was hiding in a haystack trying to ambush a donkey.

I wasn't crazy and I wasn't a freak, but sometimes, I was really stupid.

I shot to my feet and staggered out of the hay, brushing myself off as I marched past the donkeys, who were clustered in the shade of a tree around a salt lick.

Jack-Jack coughed out a laughing bray—which I ignored—as I walked through the gate. As I climbed into Bluebell, I caught sight of the bag of Halloween candy. I knew one mini-donkey who would not be getting any more Skittles from me.

• • •

I managed to make it to the Pizza Bar only a few minutes late. Like always, I felt a little rush when Kai saw me and smiled.

His smile widened as I slid into the booth across from him.

"Is that a piece of straw in your hair?"

"Probably." Stupid donkey. I reached up and began patting my head as I inwardly vowed to retaliate. After a few seconds, Kai leaned across the table and gently pulled the stalk free.

He held it up, then locked his eyes on me. "You haven't been rolling in the hay with someone else, have you?"

"Uh . . . nope." I met his gaze, ignoring the heat that threatened to flush into my cheeks.

The waitress arrived, saving me from having to come up with anything better. We ordered a couple of beers and a half-veggie, half-pepperoni pizza.

"How did everything go with your call?" The restaurant was packed and noisy enough that I knew we wouldn't be overheard talking about a murder scene.

"Busy. We're shorthanded." He waved the subject away. "What about you? Did you get anywhere with the other girl in the rehab program?"

"Caitlyn. Surprisingly, she opened up to me." At least I thought she had. "She told me where Brooke used to hang out, so I guess I'll look into that. And Brooke has a boyfriend—Stefan someone. He also goes by the name Butter, if you can believe that."

"I've heard some stupid street names."

"Well, according to Caitlyn, Stefan is a total wangster. Whatever that means."

"It means he's a wannabe gangster. Someone who looks the part but isn't a member of any gang," Kai said. "How long has Brooke been on probation?"

"About a year."

He nodded. "Brooke's old hangouts are worth checking on, but they might not lead anywhere. Hot spots tend to move depending on how many times the cops have shown up there. Plus, if you start nosing around, you might spook someone who knows where she is."

I hadn't considered that. "Caitlyn also said Brooke didn't get along well with her parents. No big surprise there. Other than that, I didn't get very far." I explained briefly about my run-in with Brooke's probation officer. "The woman didn't even acknowledge she knew who Brooke was."

"Brooke's a minor. Legally, her probation officer can't tell you anything."

"I know, but she acted like she couldn't have cared less about Brooke. And she was creepy."

He arched an eyebrow at that.

"Trust me. Clara Johnston is like the ice cream man who keeps dead bodies in his truck next to the Dreamsicles."

"You've been watching too many horror films."

"It's almost Halloween, what else is on?"

Our waitress brought the drinks, and I took a sip of cold Abita beer. "I'm not sure where to go next," I said.

"The only thing you can do is hope her parents call the police and report her missing."

I blew out a frustrated breath, shook my head, then angled it as I studied him.

"Are you saying that because you really think there's nothing I can do, or because you still don't think Brooke was kidnapped?"

"I'm trying to help you."

"No, you're trying to discourage me."

"Right. Because that would work."

I narrowed my eyes. "What's that supposed to mean?"

"Grace, you're one of the most hardheaded people I've ever met. It would take a tsunami to discourage you."

"There's nothing wrong with being a little tenacious."

"A little?"

"Okay, a lot. Who cares? If being stubborn means I stick to what I know is right, then so be it. And I *know* Brooke was kidnapped. There's no other reason Boris would tell me she was taken."

"How can he tell the difference between going willingly and being taken by force?"

"Boris may not have a human understanding of some things, but he's a predator, Kai. Whatever happened to Brooke, it wasn't friendly."

The pizza arrived, but I'd suddenly lost my appetite. I stared at my plate, frustrated that I hadn't found any evidence to bolster my argument, and hurt that I needed it.

"Grace," Kai said softly when the waitress left.

I met his gaze, knowing my face reflected the chill I suddenly felt toward him.

He leaned forward, keeping his eyes on mine. "You shouldn't do that if you want my help."

"What?" I asked as he scooped a slice of pizza onto my plate then served himself.

"I want to learn more about your ability, Grace. I can't do that if you freeze me out every time I start asking questions."

I blinked at him. "Wait, you mean all the questions about Boris are because you want to understand?"

"That's how this works. You asked for my help. I can't do that if I don't understand all the facts."

"Oh."

"Why do you think I'm asking?"

"I didn't think you believed me."

"I told you last night I believed you."

"I know, it's just—" I stopped, not knowing how to explain without feeling like more of an idiot.

Flustered, I did the only thing I could think of—I took a big bite of pizza. Though I was going to need more than a moment to work through my thoughts.

I wasn't about to admit that a disastrous college romance had left me hesitant to open up to others—that was pathetic. Even though I'd come to learn that people could accept my ability, I still assumed the other shoe was always poised to drop.

I washed down the pizza with a swig of beer and sighed. "I can confess my deepest fears to a cockatoo but can't figure out how to talk to another person. How crazy is that?"

"A little." His tone was teasing. "I have another question."

"Of course you do."

"Do you have a problem talking to everyone or just me?"

I thought about it. "I don't socialize well. But besides that, you fall into a special category."

He raised his brows with a grin. "Which is . . . ?"

"Outside my family, I can count on one hand the number of people who know about my ability."

"Even your friend, Tiger Bait?"

"Hugh?" I frowned. "He doesn't know."

"Really?" Kai studied my face, though I wasn't sure what he was looking for.

"Yes, really. He'd think I was nuts—like you did."

"So I *am* special. Good." The playful gleam in his eyes heated, as if lit by an inner fire.

Suddenly, it seemed to have grown hot in the small restaurant. "Anyway, you're the only person who's interrogated me."

"Once."

"More than once. And you're doing it again."

"You're telling me no one ever asks you about your ability? What about your clients?"

"They don't know the truth. As long as I get results, people don't care about the how."

"And your family? Your parents never questioned you? Even when you were little?"

"Not the way you do."

He leaned back and studied me. "I like the idea of being special to you, Grace. But not if it means you don't like talking to me."

"I don't like talking to anyone—" Kai's phone rang, cutting me off, which was good because I had no idea what I was going to say.

"I've got to head back in," Kai said and signaled the waitress.

She dropped off the check, then brought us a box for the two remaining pieces of pizza. Kai laid a few bills on the table and asked if I wanted to take home the leftovers.

I shook my head. "Share them with Jake. He always says he doesn't eat when he's working."

"You're going to meet me at the range tomorrow?" he asked as he walked me out.

"Wouldn't miss it."

He smirked. "You miss a lot, which is why you need to be on time."

"I'm getting better."

We reached Bluebell, and I was starting to feel awkward about how we'd ended the conversation earlier.

I hesitated before opening the car door then turned to Kai and blurted, "I want to do it."

His brows shot up.

"Talk to you!" I clarified, embarrassment making my voice an octave higher. "I want to talk to you."

"Okay." Kai moved toward me, a slight smile curving his lips.

"I mean—not now." I swallowed hard and said more calmly, "That's what makes you special—that I want to."

Kai placed his hands lightly on my hips and leaned closer. The heat of his body seemed to wash over me.

"One day, we're going to have a real date—and I'll get to kiss you good night."

"We have to have a real date?"

His smile widened. His gaze heated as his eyes locked on my mouth.

My phone wailed the opening notes of "Crazy Train" by Ozzy Osbourne. I nearly jumped out of my skin and Kai eased back.

Damn Emma and her obnoxious ring tones. I fumbled with my phone, finally hitting the button to silence it.

"Sorry—my sister." A few moments later the phone chimed to announce I had a text message. I glanced at the screen.

Meet me at the condo. Need your assistance.

"I've got to run."

He flashed that killer smile. "See you tomorrow. Maybe we'll call it a date," he said with a wink before turning to walk away.

When I got my heart rate under control, I climbed into Bluebell and headed home. Emma was going to flip when I told her she'd interrupted what might have been our first kiss.

• • •

The sight of my sister stopped me in my tracks.

Emma wore a black and garnet bustier with a ragged, asymmetrical skirt. Her hair was covered by a wild, black wig. Gold bones fanned out to form a crown on her head. More bones dangled from a scarf at her waist.

"What the hell are you supposed to be?"

"A voodoo queen." She gestured in a regal way, and I spotted a voodoo doll dangling from one wrist. Her other hand, which was cupped to her chest, held something black and fluffy. I stepped forward for a better look.

"What is—is that a kitten?"

"Some idiot thought it would make a great costume accessory. Of course, the poor thing flipped out as soon as they carried it into the venue. I found it cowering under a table." She held out the tiny ball of black fur. "I figured you'd know how to deal with it."

I stared at my sister, stunned.

"What?" she asked.

"Nothing, it's just . . . I never expected you to bring an animal into your sanctum sanctorum."

"What was I supposed to do? Toss it in the trash?"

Sadly, that was exactly what some people would've done.

"I'm just surprised, that's all."

She lifted a shoulder, her bone earrings swinging with the movement. "We're starting your house hunt next week. I can put up with that little thing for a little while."

"I'm not sure you'll feel that way when it decides to sharpen its claws on your designer couch."

She dismissed my comment with a wave. "You'll just train it."

"Emma, it's a *cat*."

Of course, we'd grown up with pets. Dogs, cats, squirrels,

birds, snakes, lizards, you name it—if it was stray or injured I brought it home.

My mom was softhearted when it came to animals and welcomed each creature. My father, a master mechanic and certified tough guy, didn't. At least not out loud. He would grumble and complain as he built little houses and cages for every new arrival. Emma reminded me so much of him sometimes, I couldn't help but smile.

"Anyway," she said airily, "if I can deal with Moss, I can deal with that little—" Her eyes widened. "He won't hurt it, will he?"

"He'll be fine. Moss!" I called out for my dog. He ignored me.

I could feel his mild interest, but he was comfortably stretched out on the couch and wasn't inclined to move.

"Come here, Moss."

Nothing.

I have a kitty cat.

Kitty?

I heard the jingle of his tags, and a moment later Moss trotted into the room. His eyes instantly fixed onto the black fuzz ball in my hand.

Kitty!

I held out the kitten and Moss busily began his examination, sniffing every inch of the cat with tail-wagging exuberance.

Moss's kitty.

"Yes, this is your kitty. Be gentle."

I placed the kitten on the floor. It opened its eyes slowly, fatigue and confusion making it wobble as it sat up.

"It's okay, little one." I reassured it with thoughts as well as words.

You're safe.

The kitten mewed. Moss took this as his cue. Unable to pick it up by the scruff of its tiny neck, Moss gently clamped his jaws over the kitten's entire head.

"Um—Grace?"

"It's okay. Moss likes cats."

"Because they taste just like chicken?"

I laughed. "They remind him of his old buddy, Charm."

"That little thing reminds him of a jaguar?"

"Domestic cats and jaguars don't smell the same, but they're close enough."

Moss lifted his kitten and took it back to his spot on the couch. He plopped the kitty down between his forepaws and began giving it a bath. I could hear the purring from where we stood.

I went to the pantry and rummaged through my stockpile of emergency animal supplies. I had a few cans of kitten food and even a small bag of cat litter, but no litter pan.

"Emma, do we have any of those disposable roasting pans?"

My sister opened the cabinet and pulled out an aluminum dish. "Will this work?"

"It will have to."

As I set up a temporary kitty station in my bathroom, I told Emma about meeting Kai for dinner and that his questions seemed to be geared toward helping me rather than doubting my ability.

I held up my hand. "I know—don't say it."

"You do tend to assume the worst in people. I'm just glad Kai continues to prove you wrong."

"So far. The jury is still out."

She shot me an arch look. "Is it?"

"I haven't known him that long. People aren't always who they seem to be."

"I won't argue that. But even so, you never know until you take him for a test drive or two." She bit her bottom lip and grinned. "Or ten."

I pressed my lips together to stifle a giggle.

My sister's eyes narrowed. "Are you blushing?"

"No."

"What happened?"

"Nothing."

"Lie."

"Well, something might have happened if my sister hadn't called and interrupted."

Emma's eyes widened. "Were you going home with him?"

"What? No! Lord, Em, it wasn't like that. I thought he was going to kiss me."

Her mouth dropped open in astonishment. "You haven't kissed him yet? Grace, it's been over two months."

"No it hasn't. And half the time one of us was either working or out of town." I used the small desk chair for balance as I toed off my dusty tennis shoes.

"Okay, fine, one month. That is glacial, even for you. Kai is a fox. He's hot for you. What's your problem?"

"You assume I have a problem?"

"Um, yeah."

"The problem is time. Look at me, Emma." I turned in a circle so she could admire the grime and bits of hay that were no doubt clinging to my clothes. "And this is mild. I can't leave work and go out on a real date. I smell like a barnyard."

"You could make time."

"I've been trying to. But I had to go up to Savannah to help Wes with that cat burglar thing. Kai was gone for two weeks for his cousin's wedding."

"Which you could have gone to."

"In Hawaii?" I gave her an incredulous look.

She shrugged, conceding the point.

"Including tonight, Kai and I have only been out four times. If you don't count meeting at the firing range—which I don't."

"You guys need to get it together and by together, I mean—"

I grabbed her hands before she could elaborate with a gesture. "I get it. Thanks."

"Are you sure time is the only factor?" she asked as I went into the bathroom to turn on the shower. "You're not coming up with excuses to ditch him because of trust issues?"

"I don't have trust issues," I said, walking back into the bedroom. "People are generally not trustworthy. That's not an issue . . . it's a fact."

She stared at me for a long moment then said, "Wow. Just . . . wow."

I waved her off and decided to change the subject. Even with all she'd been through, Emma would forever believe in the power of love. I had my doubts.

"Do you have to go back to the event?"

"Yep. And it will be a late one. Can you train with me in the morning? Sensei will be here at seven."

My sister had converted her garage into a mini-dojo, complete with training equipment and a dressing area for when she had guests. Sometimes, I joined her in her private classes.

"How can you stay up half the night and then go to the dojo so early?"

"This body"—she swept her hand in an arc from head to waist—"is a finely tuned machine."

I snorted out a laugh. "Fueled by martinis and malarkey."

"And vitamins and green tea. So, are you in?"

I used to make excuses to get out of class, but the little aikido I'd learned had helped save my life recently, so I meant it when I said, "I wish I could, but I've got a busy day. I'll have to get the kitten squared away and I want to find Brooke's boyfriend—which could take a while." I pulled off my dirty shirt and tossed it in the hamper. "Have you heard of something called *Pretty Little Liars*?"

"The books or the TV show?"

"The show, I guess. Caitlyn said Brooke's boyfriend looked like the bad boy. Someone named Caleb."

"Tyler Blackburn." Emma turned to my small desk and opened my laptop. A few keystrokes later, the screen showed a teenager with shoulder-length dark hair and a smile too perfect to fit a bad boy. He was cute, though. Wangster or not, if Stefan looked like the actor, I could see why Brooke would be interested.

"How do you know who this kid is?"

"I did a *PLL*-themed sweet-sixteen bash a few months ago."

"*PLL*?"

"*Pretty Little Liars*. And, yes, before you say it—I know

way too much about teenage stuff. It comes with the job. Don't even get me started on Bieber fever."

"Don't worry, I won't." But I'd just realized something. "Since you know so much about it, where would you go hang out if you were a wangster who thought you looked like a teen heartthrob?"

"I'd start at the Regency Square Mall."

Then that was exactly what I'd do.

CHAPTER 5

I had a dream I was on a powerboat. The engine rumbled as we sped over the water. Contentment washed through me as I turned my face to the bright sun, until suddenly I had the feeling I was being strangled. A beach towel had somehow gotten wrapped around my neck. I tried to untangle the towel but couldn't.

I woke with a start and lifted my hands to my neck. My fingers connected with soft fur and I let out a sigh. Apparently, my new kitty had decided my larynx would be a great place to sleep.

Scooping the kitten onto the bed, I sat up and glanced at the alarm clock. Six fifteen. I started to lie back down but noticed Moss was nowhere in sight. My dog was not an early riser. After a quick mental scan, I felt him near the front door. There was a sense of urgency radiating from him.

If he had needed to pee he would have gotten me up. Had someone been knocking? Why hadn't I heard him bark?

Tossing back the covers, I hauled myself out of bed, jabbed my legs into a pair of sweatpants, and shuffled toward the door.

Moss wasn't in the hall or the foyer.

"Moss?"

The door burst open and my sister and my dog came barreling toward me.

"Hang on, you lunatic!" Emma dropped the leash and Moss charged past me. He lost his footing on the marble floor as he tried to turn toward the bedrooms. Skidding and slipping, legs splayed, with a grunt, he crashed into a potted palm.

Oops.

"Moss!" *What are you doing?* I put some force into the question.

He ignored me, scrambled to his feet, and disappeared down the hall.

"Your dog has lost his mind." Emma panted from behind me. "I was going to take him out for a walk, but he didn't want to go past the sidewalk. He stopped and lifted his leg on the first patch of grass and then almost yanked my arm off trying to get back inside."

I stared at her, bewildered, before I realized what was going on. I focused on Moss's thoughts and smiled.

"What's funny about this?" Emma demanded.

"Moss was in a hurry to get back to his kitten."

"Seriously?"

I motioned for her to follow me down the hall. We stopped in the doorway of my bedroom. Moss was on the bed, his body so tightly curled around the kitten that all you could see sticking up out of the wall of off-white fur were the points of two black ears.

"Did he really think something would happen to it?"

I shrugged. "The novelty will wear off soon enough. Once the kitten gets some energy back, Moss will be glad to get a break from his mothering duties."

We headed into the kitchen, where I made coffee and Emma brewed her green tea.

"So, what are you going to name the kitten? It's a girl kitty, right?"

"Right," I said as I poured a cup of coffee. "I haven't thought about names yet."

"How about Voodoo?"

I smiled. "After her queenly benefactor?"

"Why not? It's better than Fluffball or Blackie."

"I like it—Voodoo it is."

Emma finished her tea and headed downstairs to the dojo to warm up before class. I showered and started the manhunt for Brooke's boyfriend, Stefan.

I was so hopped up on caffeine that I'd made it halfway to Cesery Road before I made an astute observation.

My chances of finding a low-life druggie like Stefan out and about before eight on Sunday morning were pretty much zip.

The coffee would not be defeated so easily. I needed a way to channel my energy. I thought about what Kai had said about the police being unable to start the search for Brooke until she was reported missing. What if I could convince Brooke's parents she hadn't just run away?

I called Ozeal, who'd probably been up since dawn, and asked her for Brooke's home address. "I'll have to call you back, Grace. I'm still making the breakfast rounds." Before she hung up, I heard the lion, Larry, belch out a hungry roar.

My stomach grumbled, echoing the sentiment. I spotted a Krispy Kreme up ahead. The HOT DOUGHNUTS NOW sign flashed like a neon beacon guiding the wayward and lost to the goodness of fried dough and sugar glaze.

Five minutes later, I was hopped up on coffee *and* sugar.

My fingers danced on Bluebell's steering wheel and my leg bounced up and down as I sat next to the empty box of doughnuts and stared at the clock.

What seemed like an hour later, Ozeal called me back and read off an address not far from the Krispy Kreme.

"You're going to talk to the Ligners?"

"I'm hoping to persuade them to file a missing person report on Brooke."

"You going to tell them about the other missing girls?"

I winced at the reference to my lie.

"I'll do whatever I can to convince them," I assured her before hanging up, feeling terrible that I had been dishonest.

My conscience chanted *Liar, liar, pants on fire!* as I pulled out of the Krispy Kreme.

The Ligners' neighborhood surprised me. I was expecting an area of Arlington with a harder edge, but the houses were spacious and neat. Solidly upper-middle class. Lawns were manicured and trash cans and skeletons kept well hidden from view.

I parked in the drive behind a newer Lexus SUV and climbed out of Bluebell. A few doughnut crumbs and flakes of glaze clung to the front of my shirt and I brushed them off as I walked down the path toward the front door.

I rang the bell and stood admiring the cheerful Halloween wreath while I waited.

The woman who opened the door looked to be in her forties. A blonde with blue eyes. I wondered if I had the wrong house. Aside from her coloring, she didn't look like the mother of a missing teenager. No trace of worry lining her face or dark circles under her eyes.

"Mrs. Ligner?"

"Yes."

"My name is Grace Wilde. I work with Ozeal Mallory at the rescue facility."

She blinked at me for a moment before seeming to connect the dots. I wondered if this woman, with her perfect hair and spotless shirt, had distanced herself from the unpleasant reality that her daughter was in a program for troubled teenagers.

"I'd like to talk to you about Brooke, if you have a minute."

"Brooke?" A little frown creased her brow.

"May I come in?"

She glanced over her shoulder and back at me. "I don't know . . . we were just on our way to church."

"It won't take long. Do you know that Brooke is missing?"

Again she blinked at me as if she didn't quite understand. I was beginning to think I would get more response from a goldfish. I tried again. "Brooke hasn't been to work in three days."

"Oh, yes, well, Brooke does that. You know how teenagers can be."

"I think you should file a missing person report."

"A what?" Her eyes went wide.

"Anne? Who was at—" A man appeared behind her, stopping when he saw me.

"Hi, Mr. Ligner? I'm Grace Wilde. I work with Brooke," I lied as I offered my hand. He gave me a perplexed smile before taking it.

"She's looking for Brooke."

"Have either of you spoken to her in the last few days?"

Mrs. Ligner shook her head, then looked to her husband as if he held all the answers.

He laid a hand on her shoulder. "Honey, why don't you go finish getting ready." He gave her shoulder a squeeze and she turned and walked away without another word. Her husband watched her go with a small shake of his head.

"Come in, please. I'm sorry about Anne. Everything with Brooke . . . it's just gotten to be too much," he said, pulling the door wide.

I followed him into a foyer that opened onto a spacious living room. The decor was modern—angular, sleek, and white. The wall leading to the backyard was made of solid glass. Sunlight streamed into the room, reflecting off an abundance of stainless steel. I had to squint in the glare.

"I didn't mean to upset anyone," I said when Ligner turned to me. "But I'm concerned about Brooke."

He blew out a hard sigh. "If I had a dollar for every time I've heard those words."

"You're aware that she hasn't come to work since Wednesday?"

He nodded. "I talked to Mrs. Mallory. She's being patient with Brooke, and I appreciate that. I haven't had the heart to tell Anne that Brooke has missed work."

"Why not?"

"Last week, Brooke and her mother had a fight. I don't know what it was about. Brooke left. We assumed she'd run off again and was staying with a friend. I'd hoped she'd keep up with the job. It's really her last chance."

"What do you mean?"

"She has to stick with her job as part of her probation."

"When was the fight?"

"Tuesday night, I think."

The day before Brooke was taken. "I told your wife—I think you should file a missing person report."

"Missing person?" He shook his head "No. Brooke's not missing. She'll call eventually. When she runs out of money or, heaven forbid, needs to be bailed out of jail again."

His jaded attitude wasn't surprising, but it was sad. "You're not worried at all?"

"Of course, we're worried, but I'll be honest with you, Miss Wilde, there's just so much worrying you can do before you drive yourself crazy. Eventually, you have to say enough is enough."

"I understand." I also knew my chance of talking him into reporting Brooke missing was dwindling with every defeated answer he gave me. "It's just that I have a feeling there's more going on with Brooke."

"What makes you think that?"

"It's hard to explain." And I wasn't about to try. I was pretty sure Mr. Ligner wasn't the type of guy who would buy the truth—that I'd gotten the info from a Siberian tiger. "It's just a feeling, really. Brooke was doing so well with the cats, it's hard to believe she just ran off."

Ligner let out a long breath. "I know what you're thinking—Brooke is smart and funny and charming. You meet her and think maybe she's learning responsibility. Maybe she's cleaned up her act. Well, she hasn't. Just when you think she's on the right track, she'll let you down. I look at Brooke and still see a sweet little girl. But that's not who she is anymore."

This guy was killing my sugar buzz. It was hard to tell if he was sincere or just a good actor. I just never knew with people.

The thought prompted my gaze to wander around the room in search of dog toys or other signs of animal habitation. Where was a good, faithful mutt when you needed one to interrogate?

I cast my mental feelers out as far as I could and felt a low buzz to my right. Too far to tell what it was or if it was even inside the house.

"Miss Wilde?" Ligner had picked up on my not-so-covert perusal of the area.

"Um . . . do you mind if I use your bathroom?" I offered him a sheepish smile. "Too much coffee."

He showed me to a door down the hall. The immaculate powder room was so clean it looked as if it had never been used. After I used the facilities, I poked around for all of two seconds, which was all it took to discover there was nothing to discover beyond the brand of toilet paper.

I exited the bathroom and saw Mr. Ligner had donned a sports coat and was holding his keys. I surmised this was a subtle hint that I should go. I thanked him for his time, but just as I reached the front door I paused. The animal presence I sensed earlier had come closer. I heard the distinct flop of a pet door swinging closed.

No jingle of tags and no click-clack of toenails on the tile floor. A cat?

I reached out with my mind to confirm my hunch.

Felis catus.

Not the ideal informant, but beggars and choosers and all that jazz.

I caught sight of the gray tabby just as Mr. Ligner bid me farewell with a solemn nod and closed the door.

I strolled to Bluebell, took my time getting in, and waited until I saw the front door open and the Ligners emerge before backing out of the driveway. I slowly circled the block and pulled back into the drive.

Acting as if I hadn't just been there two minutes before, I moseyed up the walkway and pretended to ring the bell. I located the cat within a few seconds and mentally urged it to come outside and around to the front yard so we could have a chat.

Here, kitty kitty.

No response. I knew the Ligners had gone to church, so

I had time on my side. But just because I could afford to wait didn't mean I wanted to.

Come on, kitty . . .

Nothing.

Here's the thing with cats—they have a fine-tuned ability to ignore anything that's beneath their notice. Cats are like the kung fu masters of the kiss-off.

The only other animal I've ever known who could come remotely close to a feline's capacity to tune out humans was our old basset hound, Bumble. Bumble was so good at playing deaf, my parents believed he had a hearing problem. They took him to the vet and found out his hearing was fine and, after a few tests, suggested that Bumble might be a bit slow. I knew better, but didn't have the heart to tell my parents the truth. Bumble just couldn't have cared less.

This cat was giving my old dog a run for his money.

If I wanted to connect with Brooke's cat, I was going to have to get closer.

Recently, I'd learned the key to avoid getting caught doing something you shouldn't was to act natural. Keeping this in mind, I unhurriedly, but purposefully, walked around to the side of the house. The gate in the privacy fence was unlocked, so I let myself into the backyard, closed the gate, and went in search of Mr. Snobby Cat.

I reached the wall of windows and, through the glass, spotted the tabby crouched at his food bowl, single-mindedly munching away.

"Hey!" I tapped the glass with my finger.

Nothing.

I tapped harder.

A slight ear twitch.

Hey! Cat! I thrust the words at him with my mind.

The tabby paused, swallowed, flicked his tail, and resumed his love affair with his food.

"Oh, you're good," I said, narrowing my eyes.

At that point I was determined to get the cat to at least acknowledge my existence. I glanced around, thinking there was something I could tap harder on the glass with, and remembered the cat door.

I walked to it, knelt, and pushed the flap open.

"Here, kitty kitty!"

Nothing.

I knew the tabby could hear me. His slight annoyance every time I made a noise proved as much. I stuck my head through the cat door and made kissing noises while calling, "Kitty kitty! Come here, kitty."

The cat remained crouched, his back to me.

I'm trying to find Brooke.

There was a slight flutter of interest when I mentioned her name. I gazed at the rear end of the tabby and tried again. Though I had a feeling it was a lost cause, I gave it one last shot anyway.

Tenacity is my middle name.

"Kitty kitty. You like Brooke, right? Come on, buddy, just talk to me for two minutes."

"Are you okay?"

I jumped at the sound of the voice, banging my head as I yanked it out of the cat door. Wincing, I blinked up at the man standing next to me on the patio. He wore cargo shorts and a T-shirt that bore the name of a landscaping company.

"I'm fine," I said as casually as I could before standing up.

The first thing I noticed when I straightened to face him was that he was probably a foot taller than my five feet three inches. The second thing I noticed was his eyes—they were a light golden amber. Not friendly or warm. In fact, they were so similar in color to a wolf's I found myself leaning forward and squinting to see if the yard guy was wearing colored contacts.

His brows knit at my overt scrutiny.

"You have eyes like my dog," I told him, as if that explained everything.

One brow arched at that but he didn't ask for clarification. Instead he asked, "What are you doing back here?"

"I was . . ." I trailed off when he glanced at the cat door.

"Talking to the cat?" he asked.

"Yes. I mean, no." Man, I really needed to get the lying thing down if I was going to keep doing stupid stuff. "I was looking for my friend, Brooke."

"In the cat door?"

"I thought maybe she was home but didn't want to answer the front door unless she knew who it was. So I thought I'd try to call her through the cat door."

"You're Brooke's friend?" He didn't look like he bought that one.

"We work together. You know her?"

He shrugged. "She's the Ligners' kid. Asked me last week if I could get catnip she could grow for her cat." He had an accent. Hard to place exactly, but he wasn't from the South.

"Have you seen her around?"

"Not for a few days. Why?"

"I just need to talk to her. You know. Work stuff. We're applying for a grant for enrichment supplies. Trying to get Boomer Balls."

Stop babbling, Grace.

I had to get my head on straight. I didn't think the yard guy was going to call the cops on me, but if he'd been around much, he might know something useful.

I needed to chat with him. Engage in small talk that would reveal a clue.

"So—uh . . . what kind of catnip did you get?"

"What?"

"The variety—there are a few, right?"

"Riiight." He drew out the word and studied me for several seconds.

I returned his scrutiny. His hair was cropped military-short, but looked like it would be blond if allowed to grow out. Sculpted cheekbones, chiseled jaw, and a muscular build rounded off the stud-muffin package.

Yard Guy was a fox. And though he was closer to my age than Brooke's I wondered if his looks hadn't contributed to her request for catnip.

"How well do you know Brooke?" I asked.

"Like I said, she's the Ligners' kid. Look, I've got to get to work."

He turned away and I hesitated, not knowing how to get him talking. I cast a quick glare at the cat door. I hated talking to people. Even foxy guys—no, *especially* foxy guys.

Yard Guy was walking toward the gate and I hurried to catch up.

"Do you always work on Sunday?" I asked as I followed him into the side yard.

"My boss expects a lot."

I read the logo on the pickup we were approaching: GREEN'S LAWN AND LANDSCAPING. "Mr. Green's a slave driver, huh?"

Yard Guy didn't answer.

"Do you happen to know when the Ligners will be home?"

"Sometime after noon, I guess."

"Does Brooke usually go with them to church?"

He shrugged and slipped on a pair of sunglasses he'd had clipped to the front of his shirt.

"Is that your Suburban?"

"Yes." I smiled. I could talk vintage cars—no problem.

"Can you move it? I need to back this load of mulch into the drive."

I left the Ligners' feeling frustrated and a little dejected. Not knowing what else to do, I decided to try my luck finding Brooke's boyfriend, Stefan, again. I cruised down Merrill Road, scanning the mini-marts and fast-food joints on my way to the mall.

I spotted a likely group of wayward teens loitering on a street corner near a Burger King. One of the boys had longish hair but was too far away to tell if he looked like the TV bad boy Emma had shown me.

As I pulled into the lot, the realization struck that I would have to get Stefan alone if I wanted to get any information out of him.

I wished I'd thought to bring Moss with me. To some, he was big and scary, but for whatever reason, most teenagers got a kick out of the great white wolf.

Moss was home guarding his kitten so I tried to think of another in with the group. I was still squinting through my windshield at the teenagers when my phone rang.

"Hi, Grace," Ozeal's voice crackled across the line. "Is there a chance you can come by later? Boris didn't eat much of his dinner and he didn't touch his breakfast. I was hoping you could take a look at him."

My heart sank at the words, and I couldn't help but feel a flare of anger. Boris, the *tiger,* was more affected by the disappearance of this girl than her own parents.

I huffed out a breath and muttered, "This is so frustrating."

"Sorry, Grace, I would have called Hugh, but I was afraid seeing him would add to Boris's stress."

"I understand and I'm happy to check on Boris. It's just sad; this girl has gone missing and the one who's most upset is a tiger."

"I take it Brooke's parents didn't want to file a missing person report?"

I gave her a summary of my conversation with them. "They seem convinced Brooke ran away. Well, her stepdad is, anyway. Brooke's mom seemed a little out of it."

"You spoke to Brooke's mother?"

"Yes. Why?"

"I've never met or spoken to her, even over the phone. I got the feeling she's not very . . ." Ozeal paused, seeming to search for the right word. "I guess you could say she wasn't interested in Brooke's life."

"What made you think that?"

"Brooke never mentioned her mother and, mostly, it was her stepfather who would pick her up or drop her off."

"Who else would Brooke get rides with?"

"Friends. Occasionally."

"No one in particular? Maybe someone named Stefan?" I asked as I watched the band of teenagers split into two smaller groups. The boy with the long hair came closer to Bluebell and as I got a better look, I knew I didn't have the right guy.

"I never asked for names," Ozeal said. "I wish I could think of something to help . . ." She breathed out a heavy sigh and I could almost feel the weight of her worry.

The mention of Brooke getting a ride sparked a memory.

"Ozeal, you said you let Brooke drive to the feed and seed store, right? Did she go on Wednesday?"

"Now that you mention it, she did. I sent her for some weekly supplies right after we got everyone fed that morning. Do you think her going to the store could have something to do with what happened?"

"I don't know, but I'm going to check it out."

CHAPTER 6

Ozeal gave me directions to the feed and seed, which, as I'd guessed, was close to Happy Asses, off Cedar Point Road. The mall was only a five-minute drive from where I was on Merrill, so I headed there first. As soon as I turned into the nearly vacant lot, I knew my aversion to shopping had finally caught up with me.

Most people would know the mall didn't open this early on Sunday.

With a muttered grumble of irritation, I hauled Bluebell around, jumped onto the expressway, and headed north. Twenty minutes later, I was pulling into Billy's Feed and Seed.

A demure chime heralded my entrance to the store, and I was immediately greeted by the malty scent of sweet feed, dried grain, and . . . goat?

I got a mental bead on the creature and turned to my left.

The aisle was empty.

Confused, it took me a moment to realize I needed to look up.

A solid-white goat stood on a stack of fifty-pound bags

of birdseed. The goat cocked its head and regarded me with its strange, goat eyes.

Billy, I presume?

He gave me an affirmative bleat.

I was about to ask Billy if he had seen Brooke the day she went missing when a man said, "He's harmless, you know."

I turned to see an older, paunchy man wearing a Billy's Feed and Seed T-shirt and a pair of honest-to-goodness overalls.

"Who?" I asked.

"Billy. The way you were looking at 'im, I thought maybe he'd spooked you. Can I help you find something?"

The idea of being spooked by a goat made me smile. "Actually, I was wondering if you were working last Wednesday morning."

"Billy and me work every morning," he said, returning my smile. "I'm Doc Riggins . . . This is my place. Don't tell Billy, though, he thinks he's the sole proprietor," Doc said with a wink.

"My name is Grace Wilde. There was a girl here last Wednesday—dark hair, a little taller than me, maybe around ten o'clock. Do you remember her?"

"Teenager?"

"She's sixteen."

"Yep. She's come in a few times with Ozeal Mallory. Works at Happy Asses, right?"

I nodded. "Her name is Brooke. She's missing."

His salt-and-pepper brows shot up. "Missing?"

"She disappeared last Wednesday. Do you recall if there was anyone else in the store around the same time she was here?"

"Are you a cop?"

"I'm helping Brooke's family look for her." Not really a lie—I considered Boris family, of sorts. "Brooke got into some trouble not long ago, so the police have been a little slow on the uptake."

He nodded thoughtfully. "We've been awful busy lately. You know, the old farm and fishing supply out by Fort

George got shut down. Foreclosed. It's a damn shame what the economy is doing to people."

"So you've had more customers recently?" I prompted, not wanting to get into a discussion about the state of the union.

"Yes, ma'am. As I recall, there were a few other customers in here that morning."

"Anyone seem to be paying attention to Brooke?"

"Most everyone—she was so upset, it was hard not to notice."

"Upset?"

"Crying so hard, she could barely give me her order. And, come to think of it, there was a young fella that seemed to notice her, just as she was leaving."

"Really?" I couldn't believe I was finally getting a lead. "What do you mean by *notice*? He didn't speak to her?"

Doc squinted at the door, as if trying to picture what had happened. Finally he shook his head. "No, she was on her cell phone and getting upset again."

"What did he look like?"

"Oh, I don't know." Doc removed his ball cap to rub his nonexistent hairline with the back of his hand. "Average build, I guess. Maybe in his early twenties, maybe a little younger."

"Race? Hair color? Eyes?"

"He was white. Didn't notice his eyes and he had on a hat."

"What kind of a hat?"

"A ball cap. Brown, or navy blue, maybe."

"Did he buy anything?"

"I think so. Though I don't remember offhand. I was on the phone a good bit that morning taking orders."

"Can you check your sales records? Maybe give me a name from a check or credit card?"

The chime on the door rang as a customer walked in.

Doc gave the tall man a wave in greeting, looked back at me, and said quietly, "I'd like to help, but I can't give out my customers' information. You understand."

"Sure."

I thanked Doc and decided to have a look around. I wanted to talk to Billy, but I sensed other animal brains in the store as well. I figured I could ask Kai to look into the store's records when we met at the gun range . . .

Uh-oh. I glanced at my watch. I was going to be late for our lesson.

Again.

Crap!

I rushed out of Billy's and barreled toward the range. I had to slam on my brakes halfway up the 295 on-ramp, thanks to some fool who'd run out of gas and was trying to push his car into the emergency lane. Traffic was crawling around him. I'd never make it to the firing range in time.

Kai wouldn't hear his phone, so, with a mental cringe, I sent him a text to let him know I wasn't coming, then turned back toward Happy Asses.

Time to check on a troubled tiger.

• • •

Boris paced in a long oval near the center of the enclosure. His path encompassed three things: the spindly tree so recently occupied by Hugh, a large log that ran diagonally across the pen, and a thatch of newly planted pampas grass.

It was almost noon and the sun gleamed off the tiger's coat. Muscles rippled under his shining fur as he padded rhythmically along on huge, silent paws. He moved with fierce, mesmerizing elegance, a living testament of raw power and grace.

I should have been awed by the sight. I wasn't.

I looked at Ozeal, and could tell from her frown she was thinking the same thing I was.

Boris was beautiful, but he was zombified. Stereotypical pacing is neurotic behavior and it was a bad sign.

The only thing I'd picked up when I'd extended my mind to his was the dull, driving need to walk.

And walk he did. Round and round, unaware of the two humans watching him.

"How long has he been at it?" I asked.

"I'm not sure. At least an hour."

"You said he didn't eat last night. Did something happen yesterday afternoon to upset him?"

She shook her head. "He seemed fine all day. A little reluctant to go into his house when it was time, but nothing other than that."

"Did you have to feed him at an odd time?"

Routines were established fairly quickly with intelligent animals and could cause a problem if interrupted.

"Started at five, same as always."

"What about Brooke? Did she ever give him treats?"

"The cats aren't allowed to have anything out of their specified diet."

That didn't mean Brooke didn't sneak in a little bit here and there. I remembered something Yard Guy had said.

"What about catnip?"

Ozeal gave me a startled look.

"The Ligners' landscaper mentioned Brooke wanted some plants," I explained.

"Boris and Larry are the only ones who like it." Ozeal hooked her thumb toward the lion in the adjacent enclosure. "Brooke gave them catnip on Saturdays. I can't believe I didn't think about it. We should have some in the commissary. Do you think it will help?"

"Can't hurt."

She nodded and trundled off, returning a few minutes later with a paper lunch bag filled with a tiger-sized portion of catnip. She shook the bag and called out to Boris.

Come here, Boris. I added a mental summons, gently urging him to come to where we stood.

Nothing.

What was it with cats today? Was every feline determined to ignore me?

I glanced over my shoulder at the lion, who lounged in his enclosure, dozing at the corner closest to us.

Psst! Larry.

The lion lifted his head, yawned, and pinned me with an inquisitive gaze.

Yes?

I mentally waved him off.

Never mind. Nap on.

He glanced at the bag Ozeal was shaking and his interest spiked.

You'll get some, too.

Promise?

I promise.

Satisfied, he lowered his great, maned head to rest on his paws and returned to his slumber. I turned back to Boris.

Ozeal had given up on calling Boris. She rolled the bag into a tight ball, took a few steps back, and lobbed it over the fence. It made it a good way into the pen, landing a half a dozen feet away from the tiger. He didn't break his stride.

"He doesn't seem interested," Ozeal said with a sigh.

I agreed with her. But I'm nothing if not determined.

Emma would call it stubborn—but it's the same thing, right?

"Do you mind if I go in with him?"

"Be my guest," Ozeal said, to my surprise. Boris's welfare obviously trumped any worry she might have for me.

We walked to the small access gate and as she unlocked it, I mentally scanned the tiger again, checking for any signs of aggression or anger.

Though I found nothing menacing, I entered the enclosure slowly and spoke to Boris in a soft monotone.

"Hey, Boris. Let's stop that pacing, okay?"

He didn't acknowledge me.

I eased over to where the bag of catnip lay in the grass. Keeping my movements careful, I retrieved the bag and watched the tiger stalk past. I waited until he was at the far side of the oval near the pampas grass before walking to stand at the opposite end of the log, at the base of the sapling.

I glanced down as I stepped over the log to place myself in Boris's path. Gouges an inch deep sliced into the wood— a reminder of just how lethal a tiger's claws could be. Not that I was worried about it.

Nope, not at all.

Boris rounded the clumps of grass and headed straight for me.

"Come on, handsome. Want some catnip?"

The tiger seemed to look right through me as he stalked closer.

I bent at the waist and rolled the bag toward his legs like a bowling ball. It tumbled forward and bounced off his paw.

That caught his attention.

His eyes snapped into focus, gaze locking on to the rolling bag. With lightning speed, Boris struck, crushing it under a paw.

A moment later, the scent of the herb reached his nose and he plopped down to pin the bag between both massive front paws. After a couple of quick, assessing sniffs, he began pulling the paper apart with his teeth.

"You're a fan, huh?" I asked softly as I approached. The cat welcomed my presence, or at least he didn't object to it.

I felt the effects of the catnip as the first wave flowed over him.

Nip—good, he affirmed and began rolling on the bag.

I bet.

I extended my senses out to him like an invisible hand, assessing his mood as I searched his thoughts.

The catnip seemed to have done the trick. Boris was no longer *Panthera zombis.*

I didn't want to delve too deeply into the cat's brain while he was blitzed out, so I simply skimmed over his thoughts.

"Is this your scratching post?" I lowered myself onto the log and settled in to watch him for a few more minutes.

I noticed something in the dirt next to the log. A dark green baseball cap. I reached down and retrieved it. The cap was embroidered with a stylized, circular design similar to a yin and yang symbol, with the head of an elephant on one side and a fish on the other.

I recognized the logo for the World Association of Zoos and Aquariums. A smile tugged at my lips.

Hugh must have lost the hat in his mad scramble up the tree.

I stuffed the dusty hat in my back pocket and turned my attention to the tiger rolling around in front of me. In his zeal to spread as much catnip over his body as possible, he had decided to flip on his back, smacking me with his tail as he went.

"Hey!"

Watch it, goofball, I chided.

My voice seemed to break his focus and he shifted to look at me. All four paws were in the air. Bits of paper bag and flecks of catnip clung to his face and whiskers.

"You look ridiculous."

He sneezed, twisted toward me, flopped over, and sat up. Plopping one paw on my foot he butted his head against my cheek.

That's when things got weird.

CHAPTER 7

"What do you mean, you saw Brooke?" Kai asked as he opened the box of doughnuts on his desk.

I'd taken a detour through the Krispy Kreme drive-through on my way to the sheriff's office, deciding a token of apology was necessary for missing my lesson. A box of assorted tokens, actually.

"I mean I saw her standing by the fence, plain as day."

"How?"

"Catnip."

He raised his brows and I explained Boris's affinity for the stuff.

"So your vision of Brooke was what? A hallucination?"

"Well, it wasn't a memory. It was different—too vivid and . . . alive. More than alive, actually."

It was hard to explain what I'd seen. Brooke hadn't looked like a normal girl. She'd been—*more*. Her face was beatific. With light eyes that shone with love and a radiant smile.

"I think I was seeing her as Boris does. She was absolutely beautiful."

"Interesting. What happened?" Kai asked.

"Brooke was there, smiling at us, then she was gone."

"Did that upset him?"

"Not really. But I got the feeling he was trying to tell me something."

"About Brooke?"

"Yes. And maybe about the last time he saw her, but all I got from him was the word *hide*."

"Hide? Like he was telling her to hide?"

"I'm not sure. I've told you before, animals communicate differently—"

" 'According to their intelligence, vocabulary, and ability to express emotions.' " Kai quoted my explanation from over two months ago.

"Um . . . right." I wasn't sure how I felt about the fact that Kai had paid such close attention to what I'd said.

"But because Boris was blitzed, you couldn't get a clear read," he surmised.

"Sort of. What Boris showed me was clear, it just wasn't what he meant. None of what I saw knit together. It was like having a bunch of puzzle pieces but they all went to different puzzles."

"Welcome to Criminology 101."

"Seriously?"

"Yep."

"There's something else, too." I told Kai about my trip to Billy's Feed and Seed and what Doc Riggins had seen.

"He didn't know why Brooke was crying?"

"Just that she'd been on the phone. He couldn't give me the name of the man who was watching her. I was hoping you could call and get the sales records of the people who were there at the same time as Brooke. Maybe get a name off a credit card or something?"

"Maybe. That sort of thing might mean acquiring a warrant, which I can't ask for."

"Someone took this girl and no one cares. Not her parents, not the cops, no one. It's just not right, Kai."

There was a long pause as he regarded me. "What was the name of the store?"

"Billy's Feed and Seed."

"I'll see what I can do," he said as he scrawled on a note-pad. "By the way," he continued, "I put in a call to a contact at the Department of Juvenile Justice. She's supposed to look into Brooke's case and get back to me. Until then, since you're so gung ho about it, work on figuring out a timeline."

"Where do I start?"

"With the last person to see Brooke. Then work backward from there. Make a note of anything significant."

"Like what?"

"Like arguments or odd behavior. Anything out of the ordinary. The best way to figure out what happened to her is to look at what might have led to it. If we can find out what triggered her disappearance, we'll be closer to finding her."

"Arguments?" I told him that Brooke and her mother had argued not long before she went missing.

"Could have just been regular mother-daughter tension," he said. "But it's good to know, anyway."

"Right." I glanced away, reluctant to tell him about the other argument I'd learned about. He noticed my hesitation and I could almost feel his investigator's brain zero in on me.

"And?"

"Brooke also had a disagreement with Ozeal." I explained that she'd caught Brooke in the clinic.

He pinned me with his gaze. "You didn't want to tell me. Why?"

"I don't know. It looks bad. Like Brooke was trying to get drugs or something."

"And you still don't think I'm taking you seriously."

"I do. It's just . . ."

Kai waited for me to continue. Which was bad, because I didn't know what to say.

After a few moments, he said, "I can't help you if you don't tell me what you know."

I nodded.

He leaned back in his chair and gazed at the ceiling. Maybe he was counting to ten or something.

"Kai?"

He finally looked at me, his expression unreadable. "Brooke might have been looking for drugs or she might not have. There are a hundred scenarios. I'm trying not to jump to conclusions and keep an open mind. If you want to find her, you should, too."

"Do I smell Krispy Kreme?" Jake asked as he ambled into Kai's office.

Without waiting for an invitation, he opened the box of doughnuts and plucked out a cream-filled with sprinkles.

Detective Jake Nocera's years in homicide showed in the deep lines of his brow and the rough edge of his humor. I knew he had a soft spot for dogs, and over the last couple of months I'd come to learn he was a softy in other areas, too.

He caught me staring and grunted, "What are you smirking at?"

I lifted a shoulder. "Didn't figure you for a sprinkles guy, Jake."

"There's a lot you don't know about me. I'm a man of mystery."

On the contrary, I'd found Jake to be more of a what-you-see-is-what-you-get man, which was one reason I liked him.

"The only mystery is why you delude yourself into believing Mary won't find out you're cheating on your diet. Blood sugar doesn't lie."

"It's one friggin' doughnut." He motioned with it.

"Yeah, but the sprinkles put it over the top," I said, straight-faced.

Like any good cop, he ignored my comment and turned the tables on me by changing the subject. "What's the word on the playdate?"

"Moss might be a little busy for a few days. He's babysitting a new kitten for me. If you want, you can drop Jax by the condo. I'll take him for a run on the beach and wear him out."

"Wearin' him out sounds perfect. I'll bring him by on Wednesday." He made the declaration around a mouthful of doughnut and hooked a thumb at Kai. "Me and your boy here got a date with a dead guy."

"A rosy thought," I said.

"That's Jake—a ray of sunshine," Kai commented.

Jake brushed his thick fingers together to dust off any incriminating sprinkles. "Not all of us get to play with puppies and kitties all day."

He knew my job was never that easy, but it had become a joke between us.

"Actually, I'm headed to the mall," I informed him with a lighthearted sigh.

"Hell, in that case, I feel sorry for you," he grunted as we filed out of Kai's office. "I'd take a dead guy over the mall any day."

I glanced at Kai and grinned.

"Ray of sunshine," he said.

"With sprinkles."

"I got your sprinkles," Jake muttered.

• • •

By a little after one o'clock, I'd made it back to the condo. Moss had moved Voodoo from my bed to his spot on the couch and was busily fleabiting the kitten's head.

"Aw, man. Do you have fleas, little girl?" I sat on the couch next to Moss and ran my hand from the kitten's tail to her head, ruffling her fur. "It's hard to tell with all this black fluff."

If Emma saw a flea . . . Armageddon.

I called my friend Sonja Brown, who worked as an animal behaviorist at the ASPCA. I knew it was her day off, but I wanted to set up a time to take Voodoo to the clinic.

Sonja wasn't a vet, but I knew she'd babysit Voodoo until Dr. Patrick or one of the other veterinarians could fit her in.

"You can bring her in whenever," Sonja said. "If you bring my handsome guy with you."

"Don't worry, Moss will not be separated from his kitten. He's been carrying Voodoo around and giving her baths."

"Aw! That's so cute."

"You won't think so when you see her. She's covered in Moss slobber."

Sonja chuckled; the sound was rich and warm and reminded me of melted caramel.

"What are you doing the rest of the afternoon?" she asked.

"Actually, I was thinking about going to the mall."

There was a long pause.

"Sonja?"

"You're going shopping?" I wasn't sure how I felt about her incredulous tone.

"Not exactly."

"Good enough for me." I could hear her smile through the phone. "I'll see you there."

Before reaching the food court where Sonja had suggested we meet, my phone began playing "Hot Blooded."

Apparently Emma had, once again, hijacked my phone and programmed a new ring tone for someone. A glance at the screen told me who.

I answered, silently vowing to figure out how to delete every ring tone except one that sounded like an actual phone.

"Hey, Kai. What's up?" I asked, stopping before the noisy food court made it impossible to hear.

"I heard back from my contact at the DJJ. Brooke was on probation for stealing and drugs."

Not what I wanted to hear. "Okay."

"The good news is, it looks like she's not so much a real user as a victim of bad timing and poor taste in boyfriends."

"You mean Stefan?"

"AKA Butter. Last name's Nebb. Seventeen. And he's not a wangster. He's a dealer. Nothing hard-core, yet, but he seems to be going that way. He's been in a lot more trouble than Brooke."

I glanced around. "What kind of trouble?"

"Mostly drugs, but he's been involved in altercations with some other baby thugs."

"So he could have something to do with Brooke's disappearance."

"Anything's possible." He paused. "I've got to run; I just wanted to let you know."

"Thanks."

I hung up wondering if going on a hunt for Stefan was really the best plan. Then I reminded myself the mall was crowded, I wasn't a cop, and all I wanted to do was talk to him.

A few minutes later, I'd found my preferred vantage point and was scanning groups of teens as they filtered past.

I spotted Sonja easily in the busy food court. Tall and striking, she had a flair for color. Sonja knew how to play up the warm tones of her dark skin with bold hues and chunky, gold jewelry.

Seeing my eyes were scanning people and not much else, Sonja sidled up next to me and asked, "So, who are we spying on?"

"No one. Yet. I'm looking for a kid who looks like the bad boy from *Pretty Little Liars*."

"Caleb."

I glanced at her, surprised. "You know who I'm talking about?"

"My niece is obsessed with that show." Sonja joined me in my search and after a few moments asked, "Why are we looking for him?"

I sighed. Sonja was one of the few people who knew about my ability, so I explained the situation as briefly as I could.

"And you think Brooke's boyfriend, the Caleb look-alike, might have done something to her?"

"I don't know. Someone took her. Kai said I should come up with a timeline. I've got most of her day at work figured out. And I know she had a fight with her mom the day before. I'm not sure what happened in between."

"Maybe Brooke contacted her boyfriend. What's his name?"

"Stefan."

"Maybe she called Stefan after the fight with her mother."

"That's what I was thinking. Also, according to Kai's contact, Stefan is bad news. So it's possible he could have done something to her."

"What kind of bad news?"

"Drugs, mostly. And he's been in some fights."

"But why hurt Brooke?"

"I don't know—when we find him, I'll ask."

We didn't find him.

After almost an hour, Sonja finally insisted we take a break and actually shop. It was more fun than I thought it would be. Sonja wasn't as bent on forcing me to try on impractical outfits as Emma, who was usually my shopping partner. Though *partner* wasn't really the right word.

Dictator was probably more accurate.

We'd made our way into a hip store with thrumming music and dim lighting. But despite my reservations and the fact that the staff seemed to be an average age of seventeen, I found a pair of ladies' cargo pants that were both stylish and had enough pockets to house the menagerie of animal-related stuff I had a tendency to carry. While I was in the dressing room tugging off the pants, Sonja tossed a sweater over the door.

"Here—try on this sweaterdress. It will look amazing with your eyes."

The sweater was a deep royal blue. The color did look good on me. The only problem was it did not qualify as a dress.

"Um . . . it's a little short."

"You're supposed to wear it with jeggings."

"Jeggings?"

"You know, jean leggings."

"Uh—no."

She sighed. "Hang on."

I waited. After a few minutes, it seemed like she'd been on a quest for jeggings for longer than necessary.

"Sonja?"

The store was arranged so that the dressing rooms were located in the back along the side wall and close to the cash registers.

I poked my head out of the dressing room. I had a clear view of most of the store, but didn't see my friend.

Just as I was about to retreat to continue my wait, I saw

something that made me pause. A teenage boy with long hair stood flipping through a stack of jeans.

No way.

"Stefan?"

He turned and met my gaze. Without thinking, I stepped out of the dressing room.

Stefan's eyes widened and he began to back away.

"No, wait. I just want to talk to you."

As I moved toward him, he turned and bolted, still clutching a pair of jeans. As soon as he crossed the threshold into the mall, the security alarm began to wail. I chased after him, realizing after only a few steps I was still wearing the sweater . . . and not much else.

"Crap!"

I spun in a circle, simultaneously wanting to go after Stefan and dive for cover. I compromised by grabbing the hem of the sweater and yanking it down. Not the greatest improvement but it was better than subjecting my fellow mall-goers to an unsolicited view of my . . . assets.

Shopping with a Streaker—the new mall experience.

"Grace?" Sonja appeared with an armful of jeggings and looked me over with eyes as wide and bulging as a gecko's. "Girl, where are your pants?"

"It's him, Sonja." I had to shout to be heard over the blaring alarm. "I saw Stefan. Go after him!"

"Do what?"

"Stefan." I had to let go of the hem to point, and the sweater sprang up.

I grabbed the article of clothing closest to me, which happened to be a pair of men's jeans, and started to put them on, still trying to keep my eye on Stefan.

By then, people had stopped to watch and I decided it would be better to wrap the jeans around my waist like a sarong rather than bend over to step into them.

"What's going on?" a male voice asked.

I turned and nearly bumped into the belly of a security guard who was almost as round as he was tall.

"That kid stole my jeans!"

I don't know what possessed me to say it. The words popped out of my mouth like a startled armadillo.

The security guard turned and we both looked in the direction I'd gestured.

Stefan was nowhere in sight.

• • •

Once the commotion died down, Sonja and I had scoured the mall in search of Stefan. After what seemed like hours, Sonja had given in and wished me luck before heading home.

I decided to do the same.

Moss had a problem with howling anytime I left the condo for an extended period, and our neighbor Mr. Cavanaugh—a circa-1925 fuddy-duddy—let us know by pasting nasty sticky notes on the door.

His running tally of complaints, some warranted, most not, kept the condo association busy.

So far, Moss had been too consumed with his new kitten to lament my absence—but I didn't want to push it.

"That is just . . . gross," I heard Emma say as I stepped through the front door.

I walked into the kitchen and saw the cause of her disgust. Moss sat looking up at my sister with a slobber-covered kitten hanging out of his mouth. His tail swished back and forth on the floor when he saw me.

"Your dog is revolt—" Emma paused, narrowing her eyes when she saw the shopping bag in my hand. "You went to the mall without me?"

"It was a reconnaissance mission." I filled her in on my search and near apprehension of Stefan. Once she was able to breathe again after her fit of hysteria, she asked, "So you chased him with no pants on?" Emma's expression was a mix of horror and glee.

"I had on underwear."

"Oh, well, in that case . . ."

"Whatever. He got away." I decided to change the subject. "What's for dinner?"

"Your turn to make dinner," Emma said, still wiping tears from her eyes. "Penance for going shopping without me," she added before turning and heading toward her bedroom.

I walked to the pantry to peruse the shelves. Moss followed, the kitten dangling from his mouth like an old dog toy.

"Put her down, she can walk."

Moss plopped the kitten on the tile floor, gave her a lick, and looked up at me with a hopeful wag of his tail.

Treat?

I glanced at his bowl. Full.

"Not till you eat your dinner."

I opened the fridge and stood staring at the contents. Although I knew the packages and containers held food, for some reason I was unable to come up with a cohesive meal plan.

Cheese, Moss suggested, helpfully.

I glanced down at him. His nose twitched and he let out a hopeful grunt.

"How about a panini?"

Emma had scored a real sandwich press from a caterer and we'd paninied every possible food item we could layer onto Italian bread.

I grabbed a tomato, some nifty basil spread Emma had concocted, and cheese.

Moss sat and watched, rapt, as I constructed the sandwich. If the smallest crumb hit the floor, he'd take care of it.

Voodoo mewed and pawed at Moss's tail.

I looked at the kitten and worried, like I always did, about raising a kitten with a large canine. Not that Moss would hurt Voodoo, but if the kitten encountered other dogs, she might be conditioned to think they were all like Moss—safe.

I cut a few slices of mozzarella and laid them on the tomato and bread and closed the lid to the press.

I turned back to Voodoo, who had flattened herself on the tile. Ears pricked, she watched, body twitching, waiting to pounce if Moss's tail moved.

"He could eat you in one bite, you know," I told the kitten as I opened the cabinet and set plates on the counter.

"Basically, he's the Grim Reaper. You're stalking the Grim Reaper's tail."

Voodoo ignored me completely.

A minute later I lifted a perfect panini onto each plate.

"We're going to have to get one of these presses for the new house."

Moss wagged his tail in agreement.

Ha! Voodoo's excitement had reached overload and seeing Moss's tail move sent her over the edge. She leapt forward onto the tip of his tail.

Bite! Bite! She attacked then hopped up, sat on her back legs, swiped at a long strand of his tail fur, lost her balance, toppled over, and simultaneously tried to snag more tail as she squirmed to her feet.

Voodoo was in full manic-kitten mode. Eyes wide, pupils dilated, brain a tangle of impulse and reaction.

A psychotic ninja on speed. Or acid. Or speed and acid.

She was oblivious to the fact that the tail she was gnawing on was attached to a predator a hundred times her size.

"You're courting death," I told her. "Or worse. This is Beelzebub, get it?"

Be-el-ze-bub. I mentally sounded it out.

The kitten reflected the word back to me but it came out garbled.

Bubba!

I froze mid-chew.

"What?" my sister asked as she entered the kitchen. "Grace, you look like you're choking on your panini."

When I still didn't respond, my sister placed her hands around her own neck.

"Use the international sign for choking if you need help."

I swallowed. "I just . . ."

"What?"

"Voodoo just called Moss 'Bubba.'"

Bubba! Voodoo punctuated the word with a meow.

"Bubba?"

"I was trying to explain that Moss was Beelzebub but she didn't get it. Oh my God!"

"Come on, there are worse nicknames." Emma grabbed a napkin. "I had a crush on Bubba Jenkins in junior high."

"No. It's Boris. He said the word *hide* today when I went to check on him. Clear as a bell. Everything was—it's hard to explain."

"Good, because my eyes are starting to glaze over."

I waved off her comment.

"I thought he meant Brooke had needed to hide. But what if he shortened a longer or different word and came up with something else, like Voodoo did?"

Emma set down her panini, grabbed a pen and paper, and wrote *HIDE* in all caps. Both of us stared at the paper as we ate, trying to come up with alternatives.

"Maybe he meant outside? She was standing outside the fence, right?" Emma asked.

"Yes. But I don't know how that helps. I already know where she was when she was taken."

"What about hide, like animal hide?"

"Meaning what? The person who took her was dressed up in a gorilla costume?"

"I don't know. I'm just tossing out ideas."

"Let's stick to something reasonable."

"Yes, because your life is so often burdened with reason. Hang on." Emma brushed panini crumbs off her fingers and went to grab her laptop out of her bag. We did a search of words containing H-I-D-E, writing down everything remotely plausible.

I read through the list but nothing clicked.

"Well, it was worth a shot," Emma said.

I blew out a sigh.

"This is making me crazy, Em."

"Is that what's doing it?" she teased.

"I've got nothing."

"Not true," Emma said. "You know about Stefan. About

Brooke's fight with her mother and her argument with Ozeal. More importantly, you know she was crying while talking on the phone the day she went missing."

"So she was upset," I added without much enthusiasm. "Teenage girls tend to be on the dramatic side."

"Yes, but she was so upset that the owner of the store, a man busy with new customers, noticed. Given the circumstances, that's more than a girl having a bad day."

"It's a clue," I said, feeling a spark of interest at the thought.

Emma nodded. "The question is—who was she talking to?"

CHAPTER 8

The next morning, Emma dragged me into the dojo at an unholy hour with the promise that training would help clear my head, or at the very least, take my mind off Brooke for a while.

We worked on a technique called *hamni-handachi*. Which, after a few minutes, I decided probably meant *impossibly painful and difficult* in Japanese.

Basically, I was supposed to stay on my knees while my sister attacked from a standing position. The idea was to use the aikido moves I'd learned to toss her around. The problem was, I'd learned those techniques while *on my feet*.

"Keep the center of your body over your ankles," Emma instructed when I tottered off-balance . . . again.

"I'm not sure I understand the point here. Why would I fight someone on my knees?"

"You never know when you might get knocked down. If you are, it's better to be comfortable moving on your knees. Plus, *hamni-handachi* is a good way to learn how to take advantage of your size."

"Em, I'm on the ground. I'm not seeing much of an

advantage." Even if I'd been standing, my sister was a good four inches taller than me.

"That's my point. Being shorter can be an advantage. It means a bigger person has to lean over to get to you—"

"Which puts them off-balance." I finished her thought. "Cool concept, but I'm kinda sucking at putting theory into practice."

"Here." She pulled up the voluminous legs of her black *hakama* and knelt. "Watch how my feet stay under my center. I can go forward, back, and pivot."

I watched her glide over the mat like she was doing the waltz and shook my head. Only my sister could make martial arts look like ballroom dancing.

She sailed back to me and started her step-by-step instructions. I'd almost managed to pull off a pivot when the door opened and Takeda Sensei walked in.

Emma and I stood, bowed, and said, "Good morning, Sensei."

Takeda Sensei inclined his head in greeting then focused on me.

"Today, you test. Okay?"

He turned and went into the dressing room without waiting for my answer.

"Test? What test?" I asked my sister, alarmed.

"It must be time for your *rokyu* test," she said, clearly as surprised as I was.

I didn't even know what a *rokyu* was—except that I wasn't ready to become one. "But I'm not really a student. Takeda Sensei knows that, right?"

Most of the time he and Emma trained alone or with one or two of Emma's high-ranking martial arts buddies. Sometimes, I trained with them—usually fumbling through class like a drunken water buffalo.

"I don't think I'm ready," I whispered to Emma when Takeda Sensei emerged from the dressing area.

"You can tell Sensei that. Just remember he's very traditional. He might think you're being disrespectful by questioning his judgment."

"Crap."

I wanted to avoid offending Takeda Sensei. Not that I was afraid of him—well, actually, I was. Kind of. He looked like a sweet little Japanese grandfather, but there was something about him that intimidated the hell out of me. Maybe it was the memory of the time I'd seen him slam a much larger opponent face-first into the mat. Yeah, that was probably it.

Crap!

"Okay, give me a quick refresher—what am I supposed to know?"

Emma whispered a review as we stretched and, unbelievably, I kicked major ass on my test.

Okay, so having my sister as my partner helped. Especially when I blanked out a few times when Sensei asked me to demonstrate a technique. But still, I was pretty amazing.

Grinning at my success, I turned to my sister to give her a hug when the door to the dojo opened and three men walked in. I only recognized one of them.

Kevin was at least six-two and one of Emma's favorite aikido boys. I thought there might be some chemistry between them, but being such a crappy judge of romancey-type stuff, I wasn't sure. After all, just about everyone had chemistry with Emma.

Usually my sister would have been happy to see them. Today, though, I couldn't tell what she was feeling, because the second they walked in, her face had become a mask of complete calm.

"Emma?" I wasn't sure what was going on, but if something weird was about to happen I wanted to be ready.

"Looks like you're not the only one being tested today," she said, one corner of her mouth lifting as she locked her gaze on Kevin.

Emma had earned her black belt a couple of years ago. She trained relentlessly. Kevin and the boys were in for a treat, and by the looks on their faces they knew it.

I watched my sister's second-degree black belt test with a mixture of awe and excitement.

She was spectacular.

Even when faced with simultaneous attacks from multiple opponents, she didn't crack. Graceful, calm, and absolutely merciless.

I started clapping when she finished, which earned a stern look from Sensei.

"Sorry."

He pointed to the mat, and I scurried to take the place next to my sister.

Takeda Sensei studied our faces for a moment.

"To learn, you must challenge yourself. Always. *Ne?*"

We nodded.

"You are beginner," he said looking at me. Then to Emma, he continued, "You are now *nidan*. Both are the same. Important to have new mind. *Shoshin*. Very important. *Ne?*"

We nodded.

I tried to pay attention as Takeda Sensei continued his lecture, certain that a large amount of wisdom was being imparted to us. But within the first few minutes the combination of his accent and the Japanese phrases threw me, and I glazed over.

My mind wandered to thoughts of Brooke. My sister had told me numerous times that the majority of attacks on women come from behind. In the snippet Boris had shown me, Brooke had been turning. I couldn't help but wonder if knowing a martial art would have changed things—given her time to call out for help or scream.

As if reading my mind, Takeda Sensei said, "Aikido is not here." He tapped his biceps. "It is here." He placed his index finger at his temple.

"Strong body—good. Strong mind—essential."

Something in his words sparked a vague idea, but it was too fleeting for me to grasp.

When he finally dismissed us, I gave my sister a congratulatory hug and hurried up to the condo to grab a shower, hoping I wouldn't be late for my first appointment.

Just as I was rushing past the kitchen, my phone belted

out the "Hot Blooded" chorus. I did an about-face, unhooked it from the charger, and answered.

"Kai, what's up?" I asked, a bit breathless.

"Hey. Moss taking you for a run again?"

"That only happened once when he thought I needed motivation."

"Uh-huh."

"Actually, I'll have you know I just passed my—" What was it called? Q-something . . . I decided not to bore him with the specifics. "My first official aikido test."

"Really?"

"Yep, I kicked butt."

"I'm sure you did." Was that sarcasm I heard in his tone? "I talked to Doc at Billy's Feed and Seed. The guy who followed Brooke paid with cash, so we don't have a name, but I found out what he bought. Do you have a pen?"

I snagged one off the counter and grabbed the notepad Emma kept in the kitchen.

"Go ahead."

He rattled off a list, which consisted of a canister of bug powder, three bags of garden soil, and a bag of cat litter.

"Does that tell you anything?" he asked.

"That we're looking for a gardener with a cat?"

"Yeah, me either."

Damn, I was so sure it would be a good lead. "Maybe I'll go back to Billy's and talk to the goat. I saw some bunnies, too. They didn't have a great view of the store, but that doesn't mean they didn't see something."

There was a long pause.

"Kai?"

"Sorry." I could almost hear him grinning. "I'm still not used to hearing someone say they're going to talk to bunnies."

"You'd be surprised. Some bunnies can be very loquacious."

He chuckled. The sound warmed me to my toes. "I'll bet. Have you worked any more on the timeline?"

"A little. I have to talk to one more person who was

working at Happy Asses the day Brooke disappeared. And I really want to track down her boyfriend, Stefan. I think he might have been the one on the phone with her when she was crying."

"Good luck with Bugs Bunny. And don't go poking around the wrong side of Cesery without the wolf-mutt."

• • •

Thankfully, my first appointment was with Mrs. Keane. As a septuagenarian with a philosophical view of time, she didn't grumble and grouse when I arrived at her home almost thirty minutes late.

I apologized anyway as I followed her into her foyer then stopped, surprised to see a lean, elderly man standing there.

"This is Rick. He came to help, but you know how clever Dew can be."

"He is that." Dewberry, or Dew, was her standard poodle and was smart as a whip. I looked at Rick and said, "Nice to meet you."

Rick gave me a nod and a critical once-over. I recognized the signs of someone who didn't believe I'd be able to solve the problem. I'd seen the look plenty of times. It didn't bother me anymore.

"So," he said in a pleasant baritone, "what's your plan?"

"Oh, I have my ways," I said as I moved past him into the living room, where I sensed the canine. I'd worked with Mrs. Keane and Dewberry on several occasions, and as soon as the dog saw me, his head drooped.

Dewberry sorry.

Not enough to stop, I scolded. Mentally expressing as much ire as I could.

The poodle flicked his woeful gaze up at me then collapsed and rolled onto his back—tail tucked, belly exposed.

Utterly pitiful.

"Don't apologize to me, Dew. You know better."

"Do you think you can find them this time?" Mrs. Keane asked.

I nodded. Dewberry was already projecting the location of his stolen prize.

"Let's head to the backyard. I'm going to need a small garden shovel, if you have one handy."

Mrs. Keane retrieved one from a potting bench and we began our search.

Plenty of dogs ran off with something belonging to their owners—usually a sock or the occasional shoe. Dewberry, on the other hand, had an obsession with Mrs. Keane's dentures. Thankfully, I was only summoned to hunt for her dental appliances once every few months.

Rick followed close behind me as I walked across the yard, as if looking for the bait and switch.

I stopped near a large oakleaf hydrangea, spread the thick branches of the bush, and found what I was looking for. I knelt and gently worked the shovel through the newly turned earth.

"Here we go," I said as I lifted the small shovel, shaking it to make the dirt settle around the dentures.

I wasn't terribly squeamish—I had gone through veterinary school, after all. Once you've done a necropsy on a horse you've met the quota on ick. But there was something about dentures that completely grossed me out.

I swallowed hard and plastered a smile on my face before turning to hold out the shovel to Mrs. Keane.

She plucked the dentures out of the soil and held them up to Rick. "I told you she could find them."

Despite what I'd told Kai about how seldom I was asked to explain my methods, I had a feeling Rick was going to ask me how I managed to zero in on the location of Mrs. Keane's dentures.

I gave him an expectant look and he surprised me by grinning wide enough to see he, too, had dental augmentation.

"Well, doesn't that just beat all?"

Mrs. Keane looked at me with a wink and said, "He didn't believe me."

Rick draped his arm around Mrs. Keane's shoulder and said, "I guess seeing is believing."

As soon as he said the words, an idea popped into my head.

A few minutes later, I was on my way to the Ligners' house. My search for Stefan would have to wait, because I had a theory I wanted to try. It was midday and I assumed the Ligners would both be at work. Which was fine—I didn't want to talk to Brooke's parents this time.

Rick's comment about seeing and believing made me realize I would be far more successful with Brooke's cat using a mental picture of her rather than just her name. Thanks to Boris, I now had a vivid image to call upon.

The cat would not ignore me today.

I managed to abstain as I passed the Krispy Kreme, although my mouth watered in a Pavlovian response when I spotted the flashing, neon HOT DOUGHNUTS NOW sign.

I parked across the street from the Ligners' and strolled up the walkway ready to repeat the routine from the day before. This time I didn't have to cast out my mental net to get a bead on the cat's location. I felt the hum of the animal's mind just as something brushed against my leg. I glanced down.

"Really?"

"Meow." Brooke's cat rubbed the length of his body against my shin, then sidled up to a pot of chrysanthemums to give the terra-cotta the same treatment.

"Cats." I shook my head and bent to stroke my clearly bipolar new friend.

You going to talk to me today?

Talk. "Meow," he added, in case I was on the slow side.

"Perfect." I gave the cat another pat and glanced around. I'd been expecting to have to go into the backyard again. Standing out in the open on the front porch seemed a bit too exposed for a one-on-one with the cat. Before I could decide my next step, the cat's attention was snared by something at the edge of the property. I followed the cat's gaze and heard a rustling sound coming from where a cluster of aza-leas loosely ringed a large sweet gum tree.

A thrasher bird was noisily sifting through the fallen leaves in search of a snack.

Brooke's cat was thinking about having a snack, too. It slinked over the grass toward the sound. I followed it into the side yard. Better to chat with the great white hunter around the side of the house than out front.

"You have no chance," I told the cat. "That bird has you on its radar."

The cat flicked its tail, and I got the message loud and clear.

Quiet. Hunting!

Suit yourself. I'm just saying—

Hunting!

I could take a hint so I followed without another word or thought until the bird finally cast the cat a cockeyed glare and flew away.

"See?"

Ignoring me, the cat swiveled its head to follow the bird's escape, and when I came into its line of sight I said, "Shall we?" and motioned toward the area close to the side gate.

I led the way past the wooden screen that hid the trash cans, stopping at the privacy fence. It was a good spot to talk. Shady, and not too visible.

I called the cat and it blinked at me for a long moment before finally walking toward me.

"First things first. I'm Grace, and you are?"

The cat didn't answer. There were a few ways to discover an animal's name when straightforward didn't work. I tried another method.

I scratched the cat under the chin and asked . . . *like?* Leaving a nice blank spot before the question.

Yes, Felix like.

"Man, I'm good."

I conjured the image of Brooke in my mind and projected it to the cat. *Okay, Felix, let's talk about Brooke.*

Brooke nice. He purred and kneaded the ground as he thought of her. *Stupid bitch nice, too.*

My fingers stilled, causing the cat to urge me on by meowing and rubbing his face in my hand.

Stupid bitch? Though the question had been to myself, Felix answered. An image flashed before me. A woman's legs, then a few stuttering snapshots of the same woman, bent to pour food into Felix's bowl.

Brooke's mother, Anne.

I lifted my hand from the cat so I could focus more on my own thoughts. I was reminded of an old Bill Cosby routine, though there was nothing funny about it. Someone had called Anne Ligner a stupid bitch enough times that the cat thought it was her name. Who? Brooke or Mr. Ligner? I was betting I knew the answer.

When I placed my hand back on the cat, I became aware of something I hadn't noticed before—hunger.

The reason Felix was being so nice was because he hadn't been fed since I'd seen him the morning before.

I'd get him a snack from Bluebell before I left, but first . . .

Can you tell me about—I drew an image in my mind of Mr. Ligner.

Felix's purring ceased instantly. He lowered into a crouch.

Smokeman bad. The thought was accompanied by a flash of Ligner, scowling as he drew on a cigarette.

I didn't have to ask for much more clarification than that, but I wanted to know more. Before I could urge the cat to continue, a scene began to play in my mind. Like a stop-motion film, the perspective was at ground level. It took me a second to realize Felix was looking out from under a table. At first, all I could see was a pair of legs, but I could hear Ligner screaming at his wife. She came into view, collapsing against the wall.

Weeping. Pleading. Saying she was sorry.

Ligner grabbed her by the hair and slammed her head against the wall. Cracks splintered out from the point of impact on the drywall.

A jolt of emotion hit me—a mix of my own outrage and Felix's residual fear. Having seen more than enough, I gently coaxed the cat to let go of the memory.

Okay, you're okay. I tried to reassure him. But Felix wasn't buying it. He'd actually grown more tense. His pupils had expanded so that his eyes appeared almost black.

A shiver of fear surged through me.

Felix let out a spitting hiss, and I turned to look over my shoulder. A dark shadow loomed over me.

Bob Ligner.

Crap.

CHAPTER 9

In one hand Ligner held a fast-food drink cup. The other was by his side, balled into a fist.

"Miss Wilde? What are you doing here? Is everything all right?"

The false concern in his voice set my teeth on edge. I'd known men like Ligner. My sister had married one. They masked their cruelty with charm and false sincerity.

The cat remained crouched, motionless, but I knew if Ligner made the slightest move Felix would bolt.

I had something different in mind.

"What did you do to Brooke?"

His eyes narrowed, and I caught a glimpse of the darkness inside him.

"My stepdaughter is a little tramp. Whatever happened to her, she deserved it."

A spike of cold rage shot through me.

"I guess your wife deserves it too, right?" My hands clenched into fists. The memory of my sister's battered face as she clung to life in a hospital spurred me to take a step forward. "You like hitting women, don't you?"

"You don't know anything about me."

"On the contrary. I know everything about you. You like to drink. And you like to beat your wife because it makes you feel powerful. And that makes you pathetic."

"I don't know who the hell you think you are—"

"I'll tell you who I'm not. I'm not your wife. And I'm not your stepdaughter. That means I'm not afraid of you." Like most men who batter women, Ligner was a coward. He wasn't going to touch me, at least not out in the open where someone could see.

His eyes bulged. Color crept up his neck into his face. His nostrils flared. He looked like an angry bull, mindless in his need to charge.

But unlike an animal that was driven by the need to survive, this man was motivated by something far darker.

"Get off my property."

"Or what?" I asked softly as I leaned toward him. "What will you do? Call the cops? Go ahead. I'll just tell them how you slammed your wife against the wall hard enough to break the Sheetrock."

His eyes widened, twitching at the comment.

"You have a very vivid imagination," he said stiffly.

I took a step closer to him, getting in his space. It might not have been the smartest move—the guy was at least six-two. But I was feeling all Dirty Harry from my aikido test and, in that moment, I was almost hoping he'd do something.

Make my day, asshole.

When he didn't move, I locked my gaze on his and said, "I want you to listen, because I'm only going to say this once. If you did something to Brooke, I'm going to find out. And if I ever hear that you've hurt your wife again, you'll get to see how creative my imagination can be."

I brushed past him and said over my shoulder, "Oh—and feed your cat."

Though I strolled to Bluebell with complete nonchalance, by the time I pulled myself behind the wheel I was beginning to shake. Whether from fear or anger, I wasn't sure.

I started Bluebell and made a beeline for the Krispy

Kreme. Nothing like a cup of afternoon coffee and a half a dozen glazed to calm the nerves, right?

I pulled through the drive-through and parked in the shade of a large oak tree. My mind was in overdrive. Why had Ligner come home in the middle of the day? Had he done something to Brooke? What about Anne Ligner? The cat hadn't been fed in over twenty-four hours—what had happened to Anne? What could I do about any of it?

Despite my threat, I wasn't sure I could do much of anything to Bob Ligner, no matter how much he deserved it.

After polishing off my second doughnut, I decided the best thing to do was to call Kai.

The call went straight to his voice mail, which meant he was probably in the middle of some geeky crime lab thing.

I thought about calling Jake, but what would I tell him? Jake Nocera was not a member of Grace's Wacky Roundtable. He had no clue I could communicate with animals and would want to know how I knew Bob Ligner beat his wife.

I was wondering if I should make a list of potential inductees to my "in the know" group and come up with a plan to indoctrinate them, when I saw Bob Ligner's Lexus drive past.

Maybe I'd spooked him. On impulse and with hopes of discovering something useful, I cranked Bluebell's engine, roared through the parking lot onto the street, and followed the Lexus. Thankfully, there was enough traffic that I could blend in.

Okay, who was I kidding? I was in a Skyline Blue 1975 Suburban with lots of chrome and an engine loud enough to rattle coconuts out of a palm tree.

I hung back as far as I could anyway. As it turned out, all my efforts at stealth were wasted. Ligner pulled into a small parking lot next to a building. The sign by the door read LIGNER AND HERSH ACCOUNTING.

"Dang." I'd gotten worked up and the creep was just going to his office?

I huffed out a breath as I rolled past the building and decided I'd stake him out anyway. Aside from trying to track down Stefan, I didn't have anything else to do until my appointment later that evening and I had to wait for Kai to call me back.

I did a U-turn, no small feat in Bluebell, and pulled into the parking area adjacent to Ligner's business. A row of cherry laurels divided the parking lots. I pulled as close to the bushy trees as I could and stopped alongside them. Cutting the engine, I slid across my bench seat to crank down the passenger-side window.

I didn't expect to overhear anything, and my tree-filtered view of the office was spotty at best, but at least with the window down I could hear if anyone came or went.

I sat back and waited for something to happen. I took a sip of coffee and grabbed a third doughnut.

At least I had the right supplies. I almost felt like a real cop.

I glanced at the clock, took another sip of coffee, and squinted through the leaves.

After what seemed like an hour, I checked the clock, saw it had only been fifteen minutes, and decided stakeouts sucked.

Another fifteen minutes crawled by. I was considering calling in a bomb threat to Ligner and Hersh's just to get something to happen when a sleek new silver Mercedes parked in front of the office. A familiar figure emerged from the luxury coupe.

"Yard Guy, what are you up to?" I murmured to myself.

Just because he drove an expensive car didn't mean anything. But I had a feeling something was off. I remembered how he ignored my question about the catnip and evaded my questions the longer I asked about Brooke.

But if he wasn't a real yard guy, who was he? Why go to the trouble of making a shirt and sign for a fake business?

I had a better view of the Mercedes than the building so I rummaged through my purse for a pen and wrote the license plate number on the top of the Krispy Kreme box.

With that, I had exhausted all my sleuthing ideas, which left my imagination free to conjure up several crazy scenarios.

Dozens of possibilities started zipping through my head. What if Brooke was buried in the backyard, under all that new mulch?

"You're getting way ahead of yourself, Grace," I muttered.

I had no idea why Ligner and Yard Guy were meeting. And I had no way to know what they were talking about in there.

An idea struck. Maybe I could find out.

I slid out of Bluebell and eased the door shut. Creeping silently to the end of the tree line, I peered around at the business.

The office building was small and looked like it had been built in the 1950s. There were plenty of windows, which meant I might be able to find Ligner's office and overhear something of value.

I crouched, ready to dart to a spot between an azalea bush and an air-conditioning unit when my phone screamed the beginning of "Crazy Train." I jerked it out of my pocket and sprinted back to Bluebell.

"Grace?" My sister's voice sounded overly loud as I scrambled back behind the wheel.

"Hang on," I hissed.

"Why are you whispering?"

"Shhhhh. Just—hang on." I scooted across the front seat and rolled up the passenger window. "Okay. Sorry, I'm on a stakeout."

"You're on a what?"

"I think Brooke's stepdad might have done something to her."

"Why?"

I didn't want to go into a lengthy explanation about Bob Ligner beating his wife—plus I was hoping my sister would validate my gut feeling about something else.

"Remember the yard guy who caught me trying to talk to the Ligners' cat? Well, now, he's driving a sporty little Mercedes SLS." I squinted at the car through the trees and let out a low whistle when I spotted a second logo above the bumper. Both Emma and I had learned about cars growing up—it was inevitable when your father lived and breathed all things auto. My interest was in vintage models. Emma knew luxury. "It's an AMG. What do they go for?"

"New? A hundred grand, at least," Emma said, then added, "Not the car of a poor landscaper whose boss makes him work on Sunday."

"Exactly!"

Emma started to say something else, but Yard Guy emerged from the office building and got into his car.

"Crap! Yard Guy is leaving. What do I do? Stay at the office to watch Ligner or follow Yard Guy?"

"Yard Guy. But hang back or he'll spot you in that blue monstrosity."

"I'll call you back." I tried to be discreet, but I was too busy hoping he'd lead me to a clue—or maybe even Brooke herself—to worry much about how unsuited Bluebell was to being a surveillance vehicle.

"Hot Blooded" began to play from my phone, which had slid all the way to the passenger seat. Kai was returning my call. I tried to keep one eye on the Mercedes, but by the time I managed to retrieve the phone and answer, the sports car was out of sight.

"Dammit!"

"Grace?"

"Sorry. I just lost Yard Guy."

"You what?"

"Yard Guy. I was staking out Ligner and he showed up—" I stopped, realizing I hadn't told Kai about meeting the mystery landscaper at the Ligners' the day before. I'd omitted that detail, knowing how Kai would feel if he knew I'd been trespassing.

"Grace—what's going on?"

I winced at the thought of telling the truth but knew I had to if I wanted his help. "You remember I told you about going to see Brooke's parents yesterday? Well I sort of went into the backyard to try to talk to their cat. And their yard guy caught me. Only he isn't who he says he is."

"Wait a second, back up. You went onto their property without permission?"

"Yes."

"Grace, please tell me you didn't try to break in."

"I didn't. All I did was stick my head through the cat door. The cat ignored me, by the way—but that's not important. Listen, I went back to the Ligners' house today and I think Bob Ligner might have had something to do with Brooke's disappearance. He beats his wife, Kai. And there's something shady going on with the yard guy. He didn't know what variety of catnip is the most effective and he's driving a hundred-thousand-dollar Mercedes."

"Hang on, Grace. Just slow down."

"Sorry. I'm just a little worked up." I took a breath and tried to clarify while I drove back to Ligner's office.

"Did the cat say anything about Ligner hurting Brooke?"

I had to smile at the question—not because the subject was funny, but because there was no hesitation in Kai's voice in asking.

"No. The cat only showed me the one incident. But that was enough. Bob Ligner is a big man, Kai. If he hit Brooke, he could have killed her."

"I believe you. But we're going to need more to go on."

"I got the make, model, and license plate number of the car Yard Guy was driving."

"That's a start. Give me the info and we'll know more in a minute."

I read the number off the box and as we waited for the information to run through the system I asked, "Do you think Ligner could have hired Yard Guy to cover up something he did to Brooke? I mean, hit men are pretty wealthy, right? The good ones?"

"In theory. But what would motivate Ligner to have his own stepdaughter kidnapped or killed? It's one thing for him to have hit her during one of his rages. But hiring someone to take her? Why?"

"I don't know. There has to be more going on here, right?"

"Maybe not." I could hear computer keys being tapped

in the background. "The car is registered to a company named IntraCorp. So, in theory, Yard Guy could really be just that—a landscaper."

"Driving a Mercedes AMG?"

"Which isn't his."

I huffed out a sigh. "What's going on here, Kai? Am I the only one who sees the dots but can't connect them?"

"We can't connect the dots until we have them all."

"So I should be trying to *collect* the dots instead of connecting them?"

"Bingo."

• • •

I had to put my dot-collecting efforts on hold and focus on my next appointment, which proved more challenging than I'd anticipated.

My evaluation of the cats was simple. Explaining the issue to their owner would not be. It wasn't that the problem between Baby Face and Fancy Pants was especially uncommon or complex, but Mrs. Wiggins seemed to be a little on the neurotic side.

She'd thrown open her door when I'd arrived and exclaimed, "Thank heavens! This has been the worst week of my life!"

As I'd worked, she'd paced, intermittently twisting her fingers together, biting her nails, and brushing away tears.

Her histrionics were starting to make my eye twitch.

It's not in my nature to be patient. With people, anyway.

But I pasted a gentle smile on my face, turned to her, and said, "What happened is something called *misdirected aggression*. Fancy Pants saw or perceived a threat and, with no outlet, he turned on the only viable target."

"Baby Face?"

I nodded. "Most of the time when something like this happens, it's pretty isolated. Once the actual threat is gone, the aggression abates."

"But not always."

"No, not always."

"So what can we do?"

"It will take time, but I think we'll be able to remind them they were friends." I explained to Mrs. Wiggins the strategy for their gradual reintroduction, then turned my attention to Fancy Pants.

Usually, it would take weeks to get the cats reacquainted. But this duo had something most cats didn't—me. I had a talk with the felines and explained the situation.

As I'd hoped, Baby Face and Fancy Pants understood. If Mrs. Wiggins followed my instructions, the two cats should be fine within a week or so.

"I'll come back in a few days to check on how things are going. Call me if you have questions."

"Thank you! Thank you so much." Her tear-stained face crumpled and she snatched me into a suffocating hug. I gave her an awkward pat and tried to extract myself from her arms.

"Ah . . . you're welcome."

She stepped back but kept her hands on my shoulders. "You don't know what this means to me. You've given us a chance to be a family again."

"I'm just glad I could help."

She turned her watery gaze to the lounging Himalayan. He blinked his Prussian blue eyes at us.

"I didn't know what to do—Fancy has always been so sweet." She looked back at me and dropped her voice. "This misdirected aggression . . . can it happen again?"

"It can. Usually, a cat is more susceptible if there are extra stressors going on. A move or if someone new enters or leaves the family—"

A lightbulb flipped on in my head.

Boris.

Caitlyn said the maintenance worker had been standing with her, watching Hugh, just before Boris snapped. Could that have been the trigger?

"Ms. Wilde? Are you all right?"

I blinked at my client's worried face. "Yes. Yes, I'm fine. I just remembered something. I've got to go."

My mind bounced around like a pinball as I rushed to Bluebell.

The maintenance man had arrived at Happy Asses after Brooke was kidnapped—but that didn't mean he had nothing to do with it.

I called Ozeal.

"Your maintenance man, what's his name?"

"Paul McGee."

"He was there the night Boris turned on Hugh?"

"He was."

"I don't remember seeing him."

"You told me the fewer people there the better, so I asked him to go. He left just before you got here."

"Is he still on vacation?"

"No. He got back today. He's working on the donkey pen right now."

"I'd like to talk to him. I can be there in twenty minutes—will he still be around?"

"He's rebuilding the covering that houses the irrigation pump. Somehow the top collapsed. I imagine he'll still be working on it when you get here."

• • •

I could hear the metallic whine of a saw as I parked, and assumed Paul was, indeed, still working. Ozeal stepped out of the office and walked with me to my favorite miniature donkey's pen, pausing to shake her head at the herd.

"I'm not sure what's gotten into them."

"What do you mean?" They seemed fine to me, though they didn't approach us seeking attention and treats as we walked through the gate.

"They've just been distant. Especially Jack-Jack."

"Hummm." Jack-Jack was keeping to himself because he was up to something—but I couldn't explain that to Ozeal. "Maybe it's the noise of the saw."

She eyed the herd one last time before turning away. "Maybe."

Paul looked up from the sawhorses as we approached.

He was a rangy man with glasses and a scraggly mustache. A lump of tobacco was stuffed in his bottom lip, making his worn face seem lopsided. A web of burst blood vessels spidered over his nose, the telltale sign of a heavy drinker.

"Paul, this is Grace Wilde," Ozeal said. "She'd like to talk to you, if you have a minute."

"You're the boss—I have as many minutes as you'll give me."

Ozeal looked like she might comment but her phone buzzed. She answered and nodded a farewell to us before heading out of the pen.

"I just have a couple of questions about Brooke, the girl who works here."

"I know Brooke. She's one of the strays."

"Strays?"

He smiled. Flecks of chaw clung to his yellowed teeth. It wasn't a pleasant sight. "You know. Ozeal likes to take in charity cases. Like me."

"You?"

"Yep. I used to be pretty hopeless. Too much booze and not enough sense. One day I thought it would be a good idea to sit by the road with a sign: WILL WORK FOR FOOD. That was a lie. It should have been WILL WORK FOR BOOZE but like I said, I didn't have much sense. You know what happened?"

"No."

"A woman in a pickup stopped and asked me if I thought I could lift a fifty-pound bag of feed. I told her I figured I could. She hired me. You know who that woman was?"

"Um . . . Ozeal?"

"Yes, ma'am. Ozeal Mallory hired me off the street. Paid me fifty dollars that day and told me I could come back the next if I was sober. You know what happened?"

"You came to work and have been here ever since?"

"Nope. I showed up drunk as a skunk. Ozeal tossed me out fast as green grass through a goose. But she gave my sorry ass another chance when I finally did come back sober.

Just like a stray. Me, Brooke, Caitlyn, all these critters. We was in the same boat. Till we met Ozeal."

"Uh . . ." I didn't know what to say. I hadn't expected the guy to tell me his life story. For a few seconds, I lost track of what I'd asked to prompt the man's monologue.

Finally, it clicked. "So, you know Brooke. Okay. Good. I wanted to ask you about last Wednesday. Brooke thought there was a problem with the fence?"

"Ozeal asked me to check it. Said there might be a loose spot, but I pulled on it and it seemed fine."

"Did you see Brooke that day?"

"Yep. She asked me if I had an extra spring clip." He motioned to a set of keys hooked to his belt with a brass clip.

"For her keys?"

He nodded. "Said she was going to need something sturdy if she was going to have a collection like Ozeal's."

I wasn't sure if that was relevant but I mentally filed the information for later.

"Does anyone else work with you?" I asked. "If you have a bigger job than this to do?"

"Sometimes. But not in a while. My uncle, Dave, he's a contractor. Taught me everything I know—he came out with one of his guys when we enlarged the lion house. A guy named Joe. He was a hard worker. I had him help with a couple of other things around here."

"Joe?"

"I don't remember his last name. I haven't seen him since his mom died a few months ago."

"Do you have his contact info?"

"I'd have to dig it up."

I handed him a card. "Call me when you find it."

It was a long shot—more than a long shot, actually, that this Joe would know anything. But I was desperate. My hopes that the maintenance man would provide any leads were sinking fast.

Paul seemed open and honest and his only outside help hadn't been around for months. Even so, I wasn't ready to give up.

After all, I still had one witness I could ask, but it meant I'd have to get Paul to the tiger enclosure.

"Could you do me a favor and show me where you checked the fence?" I asked him.

He agreed and we walked to the spot.

Boris chuffed out a friendly hello when he saw me. I zeroed in on the tiger's mind, ready to pick up any indication that seeing Paul upset him, but Boris just gave a groaning yowl and rubbed his body along the fence.

Still keeping my mind focused on the cat, I turned to Paul.

"Brooke said it was loose right along here." Paul pointed to an area of the perimeter fence. He clamped his fingers through the chain-link and tugged. The fence didn't move.

"See? Tight as can be."

I nodded. But my attention was trained on Boris. The tiger was watching us and, though I scoured his mind for any sign he mistrusted or disliked Paul, I found only curiosity.

I glanced over my shoulder at the tiger.

Hide?

Boris didn't react to the word. He blinked at me then pressed his head against the wire.

Pet.

In a second, I promised.

I thanked Paul and as he walked away, I called Kai. I gave him a brief overview of what I'd learned—including the misplaced-aggression theory.

"So you think Boris attacked Hugh because he couldn't get to his real target."

"I thought so, but Boris didn't react when he saw Paul—not even a blip of emotion."

There was a pause and Kai said, "That doesn't mean the misplaced-aggression theory is wrong. Maybe you just haven't found the real target."

"Maybe." I walked to the enclosure where the tiger was waiting and did my best to scratch him between the ears through the wire.

"I'll run a check on the maintenance worker. Paul McGee? See if anything shakes out."

"Thanks, Kai. I really appreciate it." I hung up and reached out again to Boris. His mind was calm, radiating contentment. The big cat was happy to get a bit of attention from his new friend.

With my index finger, I traced the black fur that formed a curved, upside-down V between his ears and was reminded of the William Blake poem.

Tyger Tyger, burning bright . . .

I quoted the last line aloud. " 'What immortal hand or eye dare frame thy fearful symmetry?' "

And what was I missing?

CHAPTER 10

Feeling restless and unsettled, I decided to head back to the condo and take a walk on the beach.

The water, sand, and sound of the sea always soothed me and helped clear my mind.

But as I sat idling at a traffic light at Heckscher Drive, I saw something that made me change my mind.

On the passenger seat, next to the empty doughnut box, was Hugh's hat. I picked it up and studied the worn brim and faded threads of the logo.

If Hugh had been wearing the hat, Boris could have equated it with the person who'd taken Brooke. Which meant two things—my misplaced-aggression idea was still viable, and the kidnapper had been wearing a baseball cap when he'd taken Brooke.

I tried to call Hugh, but didn't reach him.

Being less than five minutes away from the zoo, I decided to track him down at work.

The Jacksonville Zoo had always been one of my favorite places to decompress.

You might think the multitude of animal brains buzzing around would give me a headache, but in reality, all those minds run together into a soothing white noise.

I parked and nodded to the ticket taker as I passed. It had been a couple of months since I'd been banned from the zoo for disobeying a senior staff member's direct order, but, since I had yet to let that stop me from visiting, the woman recognized me.

As I walked along one of the zoo's shady paths, I felt the tension begin to slide from my shoulders.

A howler monkey let out a whooping call—probably spotting one of the keepers—and I heard a chorus of birds echo the sound.

I passed one of the zookeepers I'd worked with before and asked for Hugh's location. She raised him on the radio. He was on his way to the clinic, so I headed that way, finding him just outside the door.

He wore a zoo-issue khaki button-down shirt tucked into jeans. The tips of his sandy-colored hair stood out at odd angles and I noticed his face was dusted with a bit more stubble than usual.

"Everything okay?" I asked.

He glanced at me and nodded, letting out a long breath. "We had an issue with the rhino calf. She's okay now."

"Here all night?"

"Since yesterday morning. I'm off tomorrow—I'm going to sleep till noon."

"I found something of yours." I handed him the hat.

Hugh looked it over with a tired smile. "I thought Boris might have eaten it."

Much as I had done the day before, Hugh tucked it into his back pocket.

"Do you do that a lot?"

"What?"

"Keep it in your pocket rather than on your head."

"Depends. Why?"

"I was thinking Boris might have gone after you because of your hat."

"Misplaced aggression?"

I nodded. "Were you wearing it that night?"

Hugh ran his hand over his stubble thoughtfully. "Actually, yeah. In fact, I'd had it in my pocket but when I squatted down, it started to slip out, so I put it on."

"And that's when Boris went for you."

"Damn. I didn't even consider the hat could have been what set him on me. Who do you think the real target was?"

That was the million-dollar question. "I don't know."

The radio clipped to his belt blared to life.

Hugh adjusted the volume with a grimace but not before I recognized the voice. Karen Lynch, the woman who'd declared me persona non grata. Needless to say, she was not my biggest fan. The feeling was mutual.

Karen asked Hugh for his location and informed him she required his cooperation with pest control.

"Pest control?" I asked.

Hugh shot me an apologetic look and raked his fingers through his already tousled hair.

"She's talking about me, isn't she?"

He didn't answer, which was answer enough.

"She can't make you leave, Grace."

She couldn't—which was one of the reasons she hated me. But she could make Hugh's life difficult for associating with me.

I shrugged.

"I just came by to return your hat. I've got to run, anyway. I have an appointment across town."

It was true, if you counted going to the condo to let Moss have a potty break as an appointment.

I said good-bye to Hugh and left, making sure to stay out of Karen's way.

As I pulled out of the zoo parking lot I took a moment to marvel at the fact that I'd made the effort to avoid conflict. Maybe my aikido training was sinking in.

"Strong body—good. Strong mind—essential."

Takeda Sensei's words from earlier popped into my head,

bringing with them the same, nebulous seed of an idea I'd had when I'd first heard them.

Try as I might, I couldn't latch on to it.

• • •

Mondays are my sister's night off, a lull between the crazy weekend events and upcoming bookings, when she often met up with friends for a more laid-back evening than her usual posh parties. Emma never failed to invite me to come along.

I, of course, never did.

Yes, I'd gotten better at dealing with people in social settings, but I still had a habit of being closed off, even cold, to those I didn't know or like.

It bothered Emma and usually prompted her to pontificate on the difference between being fake and being friendly. Something I could never quite grasp.

Why pretend to like someone?

I'd decided long ago to spare Emma and myself from arguments by avoiding Monday evenings altogether.

But that night I was going to accept her invitation—not because I had suddenly morphed into Miss Congeniality. I was going to accept because of Bob Ligner.

Emma had married a man like him. Anthony Ortega was charming, wealthy, and violent.

He had almost taken my sister from me.

For a while after what happened, I had been her shadow. I didn't hover like my mother, who gently brushed Emma's hair out of her swollen face, or snarl and pace around the hospital room like my father.

I stood to the side and watched. And waited. I held myself still, like a leopard poised for an ambush.

For weeks, even after Emma was out of the hospital, I stayed close, but not so close that I might miss my opportunity.

But Ortega, the spineless worm, had never come near Emma again. He'd sent his lawyers. Wes dealt with them as quickly as a falcon plucks a pigeon from the sky. He eviscerated Ortega legally—Emma had gotten a huge settlement of both cash and municipal bonds worth a small fortune.

It wasn't enough for me.

I had wanted to punish Ortega. But in the end, I'd only punished myself.

And Emma.

After, I'd pulled away from her. My fear at seeing her hurt made me look away. My anger made me distant.

Ligner had rekindled some of that anger, and I finally realized what an idiot I'd been.

"Hey—" Emma paused two steps into my room when she saw I was dressed and ready to go. "Where are you headed?" she asked.

"You tell me. I figured I'd hang out with you tonight."

Her brows rose in surprise. "Really? Why's that?"

"Moss is being a mother hen. I don't have anything else to do."

"Hummmmm . . . Okay."

"Really. And I'm tired of thinking about Brooke and Boris. I need a break."

"So, Kai's busy?"

"He was busy earlier when I called. I'm sure he's on a case."

"You know," Emma mused as she flopped down on the bed, "they have a saying about assuming too much."

"When you assume, you make an *ass* out of *u* and *me*." It was one of our father's favorites. "Yeah, we grew up in the same house, remember?"

"So why do you *assume* Kai is working? Call him and tell him he can meet us if he gets a chance."

"I don't want to bug him if he's busy."

Emma sat up and regarded me the way she had so many times before when trying to bestow a bit of Emma-wisdom.

"Okay, let me break it down like this. Call. Him." She grabbed my phone off the nightstand and tossed it to me. "Tell him we're going to Drop Shots."

Drop Shots was a sports bar with an overload of video and arcade games. Even for a laid-back Monday, it was a stretch for Emma.

"You want to go to Drop Shots?"

"Kevin and the other guys from the dojo want to redeem themselves after I creamed them this morning."

"By doing what? Beating you at pinball?"

"Sad, I know. But they've promised to pay for every round of drinks if they lose."

An hour later, I found myself with a belly full of fried pickles and cheese sticks, sipping a beer and playing Skee-Ball, a game at which, for some mystical reason, I excelled.

Emma high-fived me when I made yet another perfect score, leaving Kevin and his friends no hope of catching up.

After some smack talk about cheating and being hustled they went to the bar to fetch the drinks as promised.

"You're a Skee-Ball ace. Who knew?" Emma said.

"Not me," I laughed, marveling at the fact that I was actually having a good time.

I'd called Kai to invite him but, as I predicted, he'd had to work. So I was surprised when Emma nudged me and said, "Look who's here. Good job, little sister."

I glanced over my shoulder and spotted Kai weaving through the crowd toward us. He saw me and smiled, making my stomach do that odd swooping thing. I looked away.

"All I did was call him," I told Emma.

"See how easy it is?" She grinned and turned to say hello to Kai before moving past him to add another beer to the tab.

"I thought you had to work."

"Finished up early." He assessed the scoreboard. "Looks like you're the reigning Skee-Ball champion."

"One of my many hidden talents."

"How are you at pool?" he asked, motioning to a free table.

"Let's find out."

We staked our claim on the table and I quickly realized two things: One—I was really bad at pool. Two—I had no desire to improve.

Not that the game was boring—it wasn't. In fact, my heart rate was increasing steadily the longer we played.

This was due more to Kai's teaching method than the

game. Every time I went to line up a shot he would lean in behind me. The solid muscles of his chest brushed against my back as he covered my hands with his and guided the cue.

Occasionally, his lips grazed my ear as he explained the whys and hows of the game, sending a thrill of goose bumps fluttering down my neck.

It completely wrecked my concentration. Which was not a problem in the least.

Truth be told, I didn't care much about learning how to hit the little white ball into the other balls. But I certainly didn't want Kai to stop trying to explain it to me.

Eventually, the inevitable happened. Kai sank the eight ball and the game, and my lesson, were over.

We yielded the table to the next players and made our way back to where Emma and her crew were.

Introductions were made and Emma said, "We're going to do Big Game Hunter next. You two want to join us?"

"Yes, because I so enjoy shooting animals."

"Virtual animals," Emma corrected.

"I'll pass."

"I have to do enough shooting for work," Kai said and Emma turned to join her posse, which had already moved on to the game.

"That reminds me," Kai said. "I ran a background check on Paul McGee. Ozeal's maintenance guy has never been arrested or in any kind of trouble."

"That's surprising. Paul admitted to having a drinking problem. I assumed he'd at least been ticketed for public intoxication or something."

"Nope. Not a spot on his record. Not that it means much. The BTK killer had never even gotten a speeding ticket, and all the while he was happily murdering people."

"A cheerful thought."

"Maybe this will perk you up—I may have found something on Bob Ligner."

"Consider me perked."

"It's nothing solid. A domestic disturbance back in the days before they were taken seriously. I'm trying to track down his ex wife—one of three, by the way—to get more details."

"Bob Ligner has been married four times?"

"Must be his animal magnetism."

I made a face.

Kai lifted a shoulder. "He has to have some sort of charm."

"He's a narcissistic batterer—of course he's charming. Men like Ligner are masters at hiding the truth. They manipulate. The world never suspects how twisted they are." My eyes automatically tracked to Emma. "Their victims never see it until it's too late."

"I'm sorry."

I yanked my gaze away from my sister, but Kai had known I was talking about her.

"It doesn't matter. Emma survived." Barely. "Right now, I'm worried about Brooke and her mother."

"I might be able to come up with a reason to bring Ligner in."

"Really?"

"Not related to Brooke or even his wife, but I can see if there's anything shady going on with his business. Dig a little deeper into his past relationships."

"Shake the tree and see what falls out?"

"Why not?"

"Can you do that?"

"Officially, no." He grinned, a rebellious gleam sparking in his eyes. "But I will. On one condition."

"What's that?"

His smile faded as he locked his gaze on mine. "You have to promise to stay away from Bob Ligner. No more tailing. No more trespassing."

"Deal."

• • •

I didn't keep my promise.

I'd wanted to, but the next morning as I sat on the balcony overlooking the ocean, I remembered Felix.

The cat might have more to worry about than missing a few meals. Pets could be used as a tool to hurt the people who cared about them. Refusing to feed the cat was a bad sign. I wouldn't put it past Ligner to take Felix to the pound, or worse.

"Don't do it."

My sister's voice snatched me out of my dark thoughts.

"What?" I asked as she sat at the patio table next to me.

"Whatever you're making that face over."

"I wasn't making a face."

"Yes you were. You were making this face." She squinted her eyes and pressed her lips together until they formed a bloodless line.

"Attractive."

"It's your plotting face." She did it again.

"You look constipated."

"No, that's different. See the eyebrow?" She made the face and pointed at one arched brow. "It means you're thinking about doing something you shouldn't."

I shrugged.

Emma leaned back and took a sip of her tea.

Waiting me out.

I avoided discussing domestic violence with Emma, even though it didn't bother or upset her. I couldn't say the same for myself.

"Bob Ligner is an abuser. The cat told me."

Emma took another sip of tea. "You think he did something to Brooke?"

"Maybe. He's capable, without a doubt."

"And you're planning to . . . what? Sic Moss on him and make him talk?"

"Not a bad idea. But, no. I'm not planning on doing anything to Ligner."

"Then why were you making the face?"

"Because I told Kai I'd stay away from the jerk."

"So stay away from him."

"I'm worried about Felix, the cat."

"Oookay."

"You remember my client with the Houdini dogs?"

"Not offhand."

"Nice guy. Single. He had twin boys. He thought his dogs were somehow climbing over his fence because the gate was locked and they'd be loose."

"The guy with the crazy ex?"

"Right. The crazy ex was the one opening the gate."

"I guess that answers that question."

"What question?"

"Who let the dogs out?"

"She did."

"Come on—I'm talking about the song."

"What song?"

Emma sang a few bars of a hip-hop song I vaguely remembered hearing in college.

"I'm trying to make a point here, Em. The crazy ex wanted to hurt those dogs. They could have been lost or hit by a car."

"And you want to rescue Felix the cat before something happens to him?"

"Yes."

She angled her head and studied me. "I'm not buying it."

"What do you mean? The cat hasn't eaten—"

"That may be true and you may have a good reason to be worried but that's not really the reason you want to break your word to Kai. You want to snoop."

"I . . ." Crap, she was right. "Okay. Maybe I do, but so what? I might find something useful."

"Or, you might get caught."

"Ligner's a coward. He wouldn't do anything to me."

"That might be the stupidest thing I have heard you say in a long time."

"He already caught me once, and he didn't do anything then."

"Because you made up a good excuse and apologized, right?"

I didn't answer.

"Great. Perfect." She set her teacup down with deliberate care then leaned over the table, propping her weight on her elbows. "You're telling me you called him out? Challenged him?"

"It's not like I went all Lisbeth Salander on him and tattooed 'I'm an abusive asshole' on his forehead."

"Oh, well, in that case, it's no big deal." After her fit of sarcasm, Emma leaned closer. Emotion sparked like fire in her dark eyes. "People like Ligner have to be in control. It means everything to them. *Everything.* Anyone who can't be controlled is the enemy."

"Works for me."

"I'm serious, Grace."

"So am I. Ligner can think I'm the queen of England for all I care."

"You're underestimating him. Don't." She raised her hand to stop me when I tried to counter her argument. "I know you think Ligner's a coward. And you're right. But he's not stupid. You played your hand. Called his bluff and upped the ante. If you think he's not stewing over how he can win back the upper hand, you're wrong."

"Okay, fine. I'll be careful. I'll go pick up Felix and that's all. No snooping. I won't even trespass."

Emma looked dubious, so I lifted my hand and offered what had always been the most solemn oath between us.

"Pinky swear."

Emma's lips twitched into a smile and she hooked her little finger to mine.

• • •

I pulled into the Ligners' neighborhood an hour later. I knew Bob Ligner was at work—I'd called his office moments before and was told he was meeting with clients—but, keeping to the pinky promise, I cruised past his house and turned into the next driveway on the street.

The FOR SALE sign was still out front, there was a lockbox affixed to the front door, and there weren't any window treatments or other signs of occupancy. The home was vacant. Perfect.

I hopped out of Bluebell and headed to the side of the house closest to the Ligners' property. Through the thicket of oleanders, I caught a glimpse of the spot near the trash cans where Bob Ligner and I had had our little heart-to-heart, but could see little else.

Which was fine. I was here for Felix, not to snoop.

The gate leading to the vacant backyard was propped open so I strolled through—just another potential home buyer taking a look around.

Feeling supremely clever, I walked to the privacy fence bordering the Ligners' property and cast out my mental feelers in search of Felix.

I found him quickly enough, but not where I'd expected.

Felix wasn't in the Ligners' house or yard. And he wasn't hungry or frightened. In fact, Felix was sending out super-happy vibes. Waves of contentment rolled through him, and though I couldn't hear it, I recognized the familiar feline signature.

Purring.

Curious, I tried to pinpoint Felix's location and began moving along the fence toward the far end of the backyard. It was my ears rather than my mind that led me to him.

"Oh, all right," a reedy voice said from the other side of the back fence. "I'll give you a lap for a few minutes."

"Meow!"

I peeked through the space between fence boards to see an elderly woman set her watering can on the ground then ease herself onto a large garden bench. Felix sprang up and into the woman's ample lap.

Soft. Nice. His mind was a thrumming ball of happiness.

I watched Felix settle down into a comfortable ball. The woman scratched him under his chin and his eyes closed in utter bliss.

Cats.

My view of the woman's house was limited, but I could see a small bowl sitting by the back door. I could tell from the full feeling of his belly that Felix had been fed.

When the woman stopped petting him, Felix opened his eyes to gaze up adoringly at her then gently patted at her arm with a paw.

"I can't sit here all day, you know," the woman chided. "I have daylilies to divide."

As only cats and contortionists can, Felix twisted his upper half until his front feet pointed skyward. He continued to make eyes at the woman and began pawing the air.

Charmer.

Like so many cats before him, Felix had found the secret to survival: Find a sucker willing to take you in.

Being a card-carrying member of the Sucker Club, I had to smile.

I pushed away from the fence, hoping my impending house hunt would yield a place with a nice cat lady next door instead of someone like Emma's crazed animal-hating neighbor, Mr. Cavanaugh.

Or worse, a man like Bob Ligner.

No longer worried about Felix, I turned to head back to Bluebell. I'd make sure to tell Brooke where her cat was when I found her.

If I found her.

That sobering thought made me pause as I reached the open gate.

Temptation bubbled up inside me to take a quick peek over the fence into the Ligners' backyard and look for . . . for what?

I would probably do more harm than good snooping around. Kai was looking hard at Ligner. I had to trust he'd find something.

Plus, I'd pinky sworn.

My resolve restored, I started through the gate and froze. A sound drifted from next door. Footsteps through the grass and something being dragged. I heard the metallic scrape of the gate latch and the groan of hinges. More dragging, the garbage can lid being opened, something heavy being dumped in the trash, and then . . . a small sob.

I crept forward and peered through the oleanders.

Anne Ligner stood with her back to me, facing the open can. I could just make out the top of the black plastic trash bag she'd deposited. Her shoulders shook and, as she slowly closed the lid, I heard her whisper something that chilled me to my core.

"I'm sorry, Brooke."

Then she turned, walked through the gate, and into her backyard. A moment later, I heard the back door slide closed.

I was surprised I could hear anything with my pulse pounding so hard in my ears. Heart hammering, I stood there for a moment, staring at the trash can.

Was it possible that Anne Ligner had just dumped her daughter's body in that can?

All thoughts of promises gone, I took a deep breath, let it out slowly, crouched, and pushed through the spindly lower limbs of the bushes.

Scrambling up, I stepped to the can, lifted the lid, and stared down at the thick black plastic.

Fingers trembling, I reached out and unwound the twist tie that had been used to secure the bag.

I stopped, hands poised to pull the bag open.

My breaths came in little ragged puffs. Squeezing my eyes shut, I fisted my hands and tried to get a handle on my breathing.

I really didn't want to open the bag.

I had to open the bag.

"Okay," I whispered to myself. "Just do it."

Forcing myself to obey, I opened my eyes, grabbed the bag, and jerked it open.

CHAPTER 11

I did not find a body in the Ligners' trash.

The wave of relief threatened to turn my knees to Jell-O, but my curiosity soon had me straightening to reach into the bag.

It was filled with stuffed animals and other toys. Was this a sign that Anne Ligner knew her daughter was never coming home? I picked up a teddy bear with the words MR. SNUFFLES LOVES YOU! embroidered on his chest and noticed something odd.

The bear had been sliced open, and his stuffing, or what was left of it, spilled out of a long gash on his back.

I lifted another plush doll—it, too, had been cut open. A rubber pony was missing its head. The bag was filled with mutilated toys.

A chill crept over me.

I retied the bag and got out of there as quickly and quietly as I could.

Once safely inside Bluebell and on my way out of the neighborhood, I let the litany of curses and questions I'd been stifling spill out.

"Holy shit! What the hell was that?" I asked aloud.

"Creepy," I answered myself. "That was friggin' creepy."

So creepy I decided I needed to grab a doughnut to calm my nerves. I had just taken the first warm bite of my Krispy Kreme chocolate glazed when my phone began singing "Crazy Train."

It was Emma calling to check on me. I relayed the story, talking around a mouthful of doughnut.

"That's pretty damn creepy," she said.

"I know, right? They were murdered, Emma. It was a toy massacre. Who does that?"

"People who are losing control and want to take it out on something. I think you need to call Kai and tell him about this."

I paused to swallow. I didn't really want to admit to Kai that I'd been to the Ligners'.

"Just explain that you wanted to check on Felix," Emma said, reading my mind. "He'll understand."

I wasn't certain that was true, but I would call him anyway.

"Hey, Em, we're looking at houses tomorrow, right?"

"Yep, the Realtor is supposed to be e-mailing a list of properties in the morning."

"Is there a way to do a neighbor check? A screening or something for nutcases?"

My sister laughed, but I was completely serious.

"I'm not kidding. I'd hate to end up next to another Cavanaugh, but he's better than someone who would eviscerate a teddy bear."

"That reminds me, Moss howled after you left."

"And Cavan-ass left you a sticky note?"

"Of course, but that's not what I was going to say. When Moss howled, Voodoo jumped up and ran to him like she'd been summoned. What's that about?"

"Who knows?"

There was a pause. "Um . . . you?"

"I don't know everything about animals," I said.

"And here I've been telling people that was your job."

"Speaking of jobs, I've got to go. I have a bunny that needs me."

• • •

When I finished up with Patches, the aforementioned bunny, I called Kai.

"Hey, can I bring you an early lunch?"

I wasn't really that hungry, but I wanted to talk to him face-to-face if I was going to admit to breaking my promise to stay away from the Ligners'.

"Actually, how about I meet you at Farah's? I could stand to get away from this place for a little while."

We agreed on a time and as soon as I walked into Farah's, the scent of spanakopita washed over me, obliterating the memory of my earlier zillion-calorie snack.

I found a booth, slid in, and ordered drinks while I waited for Kai. He walked in a few minutes later and slipped in to sit across from me. The waiter came by to take our orders and bustled away.

Kai slid his phone across the table. I picked it up and studied the image on the screen. It was a photo of Brooke. A mug shot, actually.

"What's this?" I asked, trying not to sound angry. Was he trying to remind me that Brooke had been in trouble?

"Brooke's record. I can't legally send it to you, but I thought you might want to take a look at it. Stefan's is there, too."

"Oh," I said, feeling sheepish for jumping to the wrong conclusion—again. "Thank you."

I looked over the files for a minute, not seeing anything I didn't already know.

"So, how's your day been?" I asked as I handed him back his phone.

As he often did, he waved my question away.

"Busy. Tell me how things are going with you."

"Well, I just helped a champion jumping bunny get his mojo back."

"Champion jumping bunny?"

"You've never heard of bunny show jumping?" I asked deadpan.

"I have to admit, I haven't. Is it taking the sports world by storm?"

"Not sure Patches and his crew are there, yet. But you never know."

"Now that he's got his mojo back?"

"Yep. It turns out Patches hadn't really lost his passion for the hurdles. He just disliked the foul-smelling paint job his owners had given his obstacle course. I took two terra-cotta pots, flipped them over, and put a stick across them and he hopped over that sucker like the champion he is."

Kai leaned back to study me—my loquaciousness seemed to have triggered his cop radar.

Crap. Might as well get it over with.

"I went to the Ligners'," I said just as the waiter appeared with our lunch.

Kai never took his eyes off me as the waiter placed the plates on the table and asked if we needed anything else.

I thanked him and, once he'd hustled off, said to Kai, "I was worried about Felix."

"Felix?"

"The cat. I was afraid Bob Ligner might do something to Felix, so I went to get him. I even went to the house next door, so I wouldn't have to trespass, but—"

"Get him?" Kai interrupted. "Let me get this straight; your interpretation of staying away from the Ligners' is to go to the house *next door* and steal their property?"

"Felix is not property. And I didn't steal him. He's fine, but I can't say the same for Mr. Snuffles."

"Who?"

"Brooke's teddy bear." I explained what I'd seen, starting with Felix being safe and putting a lot of emphasis on the fact that I had been leaving when I'd seen Anne Ligner acting odd.

Kai didn't look pleased at my justification.

"I couldn't just leave."

"Yes, Grace, you could have. Or you could have called me."

"But it might have been nothing."

"Or it might have been a body. And you could have contaminated the crime scene."

"Seriously? You're playing the *CSI* card?"

"I'm not playing at all."

The waiter popped by to check on us, probably noticing that neither of us had touched our lunch and wanting to be sure there wasn't something wrong. There was, of course, but it wasn't the food.

Kai handed the waiter his plate and asked if he could take it to go. I did the same and then glared at Kai.

"This isn't a damn game, Grace," he said in a low tone.

"We're talking about a guy who decapitated a My Little Pony," I said. "Believe me, I understand it's not a game."

Kai shook his head. "You don't even know if Bob Ligner is the person who tore up the toys. It could have been his wife. You said she apologized out loud when she threw them away, right?"

"I can't see her taking out her anger on her daughter's stuff."

"You don't know that's the reason the toys were ripped apart."

"Why else would someone do it?"

"Maybe Ligner or his wife was looking for something."

"Like what?"

He shrugged. "I can think of several things a teenager on probation might want to hide from her parents."

"You're talking about drugs again."

"Brooke's boyfriend is a drug dealer."

"So?"

"He might have asked Brooke to hold on to his stash."

"Brooke was turning her life around."

"You don't know that."

"Yes, I do."

The waiter deposited our lunches and the check. I picked it up before Kai could.

"I asked you to come—I'll get it." I rummaged around in my purse, knowing I had a twenty somewhere, and tried not to be upset. I'd known Kai wouldn't be happy with me but I hadn't expected to be just as irritated with him.

Finding the crumpled twenty, I smoothed it out on the table and laid it over the check.

When I looked up at Kai, I saw the lines around his eyes had softened.

"I'm just trying to stay objective, Grace. We know Brooke and her mother recently had a fight about something. Maybe Anne Ligner was going through Brooke's things, even started to cut open her toys."

I hated to admit it made sense, but . . . "According to Ozeal, Anne Ligner wasn't involved in Brooke's life. I got the same feeling when I met her. She hadn't noticed Brooke was missing."

"Learning Brooke was gone could have goaded her into looking through her daughter's things. We don't know."

"You're right, we don't. We don't know enough about any of this because you can only poke around a little and I'm not supposed to poke around at all."

"I'm sorry. I got upset because I worry about you. I don't like the idea of you anywhere near Bob Ligner."

"And you don't want me to mess up a crime scene."

"That, too." He flashed me that heart-stopping smile and I returned it with one of my own.

"Does that mean we can sit here and eat lunch?"

A beep sounded from his phone. He checked the display and frowned. "I've got to get back. It's been a . . ." He trailed off as his gaze met mine, then he let out a slow breath. "Let's just say I haven't had time to do much checking on Bob Ligner's finances or his past relationships."

An emotion I couldn't name suddenly stirred in my chest. Kai was doing this for me. Taking extra time out of long days because he wanted to help *me*.

I didn't know what to say, so I nodded. He must have taken my silence as disappointment on his lack of progress because his manner turned brusque as we gathered our lunches and headed outside.

"I'll call you if I find something," Kai said.

When he started to turn away, I reached out and touched his forearm to stop him. There were a dozen things I could have said, detailing how much his help meant to me, but all I managed was, "Thank you."

"You can thank me by staying safe."

"I tangle with crazy animals every day and, so far, I'm in one piece," I said, trying to lighten the mood.

But he only nodded and walked away.

• • •

I debated my next move as I walked to Bluebell.

I could try to find Stefan again. Or see if I could dig up more on Yard/Mercedes Guy—though how I'd go about doing so was a mystery.

As I was climbing behind the wheel I got a text that made the decision for me.

The message was from my sister. It read: Issue with important clients. Need help. ASAP.

At first I thought she might have sent me the text by accident until the follow-up message beeped onto the screen: And be nice!

I sent a message back asking where she was. She replied with an address that turned out to be . . .

A cemetery?

Ooookay.

After parking, I wandered toward the iron gates. I found Emma a few yards past the entrance, standing with a man and woman in the shade of a stately oak.

The couple was dressed in all black and both had raven hair that contrasted sharply with the very pale skin of their faces.

Emma smiled as I approached. "Eddie, Lilith, this is my sister, Grace."

Eddie, like Eddie Munster? I couldn't help but see a resemblance.

We shook hands. I glanced at my sister and plastered a smile on my face before saying, "Nice to meet you both. What can I do for you?"

"We're having problems with the bats," Eddie said in a low baritone I hadn't expected from such a thin man.

"Bats?"

"They're for our wedding, but there's something wrong." Lilith's large doe eyes misted over, her voice quavering with concern.

"Bats. For your wedding," I repeated just to make sure I wasn't hearing things.

"To release instead of doves," Emma clarified. "Sunday night, at the rehearsal, they didn't seem to want to leave their cage."

"Lilith loves animals and she's worried that something might be wrong with them." Eddie placed his narrow fingers on his betrothed's shoulder with a comforting pat.

"Your sister says you are not only an animal expert, you're also licensed as a veterinarian," Lilith said. "We were hoping you could take a look at Vlad and Mina just to make sure they're okay."

Vlad and Mina?

I glanced at my sister. Her smile had become stretched and strained into something closer to a grimace. Not the typical Emma face. I wasn't sure what was going on, but it was clear my sister needed me to smile and nod, so that was exactly what I did.

As I fell into step behind the couple, I noticed Lilith's hair flowed almost to her waist and was tipped with red the color of, you guessed it, blood.

I tried to catch my sister's eye, but she'd edged forward to answer some question Eddie had posed.

Before long, the path angled to the right and we passed through a short wall into a private plot. A massive mausoleum dominated the center. Its steep roof and pointed arches reminded me of a mini–Gothic cathedral. Which, given the company, was fitting.

In front of the tomb was a tall, intricate birdcage sitting on a marble pillar.

I stepped up to the cage and leaned down to look at the bats. Large and furry, with fox-like faces and big brown eyes, their small ears flicked around with interest. One of them yawned and stretched, displaying a dark, leathery wing as long as my forearm.

I took a moment to assess the bats. They were a little restless and hungry. With a bit of prodding I learned that they were used to eating by now, which meant one thing.

Stifling a sigh, I reminded myself to *be nice*.

"Well," I said, turning back to Eddie and Lilith. "Vlad and Mina seem healthy but I don't think they're going to work for your wedding."

"Why?" my sister asked.

I struggled to keep my tone friendly and said, "These are a type of giant fruit bat also known as flying foxes. Samoan flying foxes to be exact—which happen to be one of the few species of diurnal bats."

"Diurnal?" Eddie squinted at the bats then cast me a quizzical glance.

"That's the opposite of nocturnal, right?" Emma asked.

"Right. In the wild, they typically forage in the midmorning and sleep at night. Which means they're probably hungry. Also, these guys are from the tropics. If you released them here they wouldn't survive long—it gets too cold."

Lilith pressed her dainty hand over her black-lipped mouth.

"Oh no! Eddie, we can't. There must be another way."

She turned those big, doe eyes to me and I looked at my sister for help.

"Maybe we could find some local bats to use," Emma said.

"Would that work?" Lilith asked, eyes wide and hopeful.

"Um . . . I don't . . ." I blinked at my sister, but she was doing the smile/grimace thing again so I trailed off.

"Please," Lilith said. "We just can't have the ceremony without the bats."

"Money is no object," Eddie added, setting my teeth on edge.

"Emma." I pinned my sister with my gaze. "Can I talk to you for a minute?"

I did an about-face and walked through the gate, down the lane, and out of earshot.

When my sister caught up to me I spun to face her.

"Have you lost your mind?"

"Come on, Grace, you can do this, can't you?"

"Do what?"

"Get a couple of local bats."

"From where? The 7-Eleven?"

"Can't you have them come to you like you used to do with the birds?"

"Emma, talking a few birds into coming to eat out of my hand and capturing wild bats isn't the same thing."

"Why not?"

"I'd have to find a colony, for starters, and I am not kidnapping bats just so these weirdos can get their Goth on."

I blinked at her in utter confusion. "How is it possible that you neglected to consult the animal telepath—who you live with—about this?"

She pinched the bridge of her nose, a gesture that reminded me so much of our mother I almost smiled.

"I didn't know about the bats," Emma said. "Eddie gave them to Lilith Sunday night as a surprise—*after* I'd gone to deal with a major catering issue at another event."

I eyed my sister. She actually looked harried. Emma didn't get harried. She was Emma.

"Are you okay, Em?"

She nodded. "I've got to hire an assistant. Sometimes people are—"

"Really stupid?" I supplied in a helpful tone.

"Unpredictable."

"I'm going with *stupid*. Do you know that most flying foxes are endangered?"

Her shoulders slumped. "Oh no."

"Yep—and you know what that means?"

"You're going to confiscate the bats."

"You're damn skippy."

"This is a nightmare," she muttered. "Can you find some local bats or not?"

"Honestly, Emma, no, I can't." I waved away her scowl. "I'm not just being stubborn. Tonight is a full moon, right?"

She nodded. "That's why we're doing the wedding on a Tuesday night."

"Well, bats don't like to fly during the full moon."

She groaned. "You've got to be kidding me."

I shook my head, but talking about the full moon sparked an idea.

"I tell you what: I might be able to coax Vlad and Mina to fly tonight if we make some major adjustments to their cage. And provided Eddie and Lilith agree to donate the bats to the zoo and give me the info on who they were purchased from."

Relief flooded Emma's face and she yanked me into a hug.

"You're my favorite sister, ever!"

"I'm your only sister."

"You'd still be my favorite sister—even if we had lots of sisters."

"Tell me that after we pull this off."

• • •

Operation Bat Wing was a surprising success.

I'd been able to sweet-talk Vlad and Mina into leaving their roost to fly by the light of the moon with the promise of their favorite snack. Kiwi for her. Bananas for him.

The giant bats had awed the guests as they'd swooped overhead then circled around to the back of the mausoleum where Hugh and I waited. I handed the bats and the information on who had sold them over to Hugh and even managed to snag a plate of cheese-and-mushroom tortellini from the caterers before heading home.

Moss sat at my feet and gazed longingly up as I finished off the tortellini.

Have bite? he asked with a whine.

"No."

One bite?

"If I fed you every time you asked me for a bite you'd have a belly like a nanny goat."

This earned me an indignant snort.

Moss was a canine in his prime and he knew it.

He also knew I was a sucker, so he followed me into the kitchen and showered me with exuberant admiration when I set the plate on the floor for him to prewash.

I even left a few tortellini.

Pouring a glass of wine, my mind drifted to thoughts of Brooke and Boris. I tried to mentally sum up what I'd learned about Brooke's disappearance, but once again, wound up with a bunch of unconnected dots.

Out of everything I'd discovered, Yard Guy's role in what had happened to Brooke puzzled me the most.

He could be a landscaper simply doing a job for the Ligners, as Kai had suggested. But my gut told me otherwise.

I unplugged my laptop from its place on the kitchen counter and wandered into the living room to sit on the couch. On a whim, I Googled the landscaping company name I'd seen on Yard Guy's shirt. Not surprisingly, I found no listing for Green's Lawn and Landscaping.

Next, I tried looking up IntraCorp, the company to which the Mercedes AMG was registered. A nondescript website popped up. I navigated through the site for a few minutes, but could only ascertain that IntraCorp dealt with distribution of goods. Nothing more specific.

A mewing cry made me look down.

Voodoo stared up at me with wide blue kitten eyes then meowed again, clamped her claws on my bare shin, and began to scale Mount Grace.

"Ouch!"

I scooped her into my lap before her needlelike claws gained much purchase.

Up!

No. I encouraged her to settle down for a nap by giving her a few slow strokes and some gentle, calming thoughts.

With a happy squeak, she began kneading and purring as she tottered around in a slow circle on my lap.

Moss came up to give Voodoo a sniff and a lick before flopping down with a sigh.

"She's wearing you out, now, huh?"

Tired, he agreed. Then raised his head and looked at me with droopy eyes and asked, *Kitty?*

I've got her. Take a break, big guy.

He let out a second, longer sigh and drifted off to sleep.

I tried to think of another search I could do to divine the identity of the mysterious Yard Guy. But after a few minutes of staring at the laptop's screen, I knew I was getting nowhere. There was no way my tired brain could fend off all the bliss and contentment floating through the air. I gave in, closed my laptop and my eyes, and leaned back, hoping inspiration would come to me if I relaxed.

I was on the edge of sleep when my phone rang. I was so used to hearing the crazy ring tones Emma had programmed, the normal ring threw me off for a few seconds. I'm sure I sounded half asleep and confused when I finally managed to answer. Not that it mattered.

A recorded voice announced the call's origin. "Union Correctional Institution."

Suddenly, I was wide-awake. Who would be calling me from a high-security penitentiary?

There was a pause, and I realized I had to press ONE to accept the call. I managed to bring up my keypad and hit the number.

"Hello?"

"Grace Wilde?"

"Yes. Who is this?"

"This is Charles Sartori."

Sartori? The name was vaguely familiar, but I couldn't place it.

"I'm sorry, who?"

"You're looking for a Brooke Ligner. I want to know why." His tone was calm, almost conversational, but it carried the weight of someone who was used to having people do what they asked. Usually, this attitude would have earned Sartori an earful of dial tone, but I thought he might have useful information about Brooke and, I have to admit, I was curious.

"Why do you care about Brooke?"

"She's my daughter."

Daughter?

Brooke's biological father was in prison? I was too surprised to comment, and after several seconds, Sartori asked, "Why are you looking for Brooke?"

"I think something happened to her," I told him, shaking off my shock.

"What, exactly?"

"I'm not sure."

"Don't play games, Miss Wilde. My daughter is missing."

"You don't think she ran away?"

"No, I don't. Brooke always contacts me when she leaves her mother's house. I haven't heard from her."

"Okay. To start with, I think she was kidnapped from where she worked. No one has seen her since last Wednesday."

Silence.

"When's the last time you talked to her?"

He didn't answer my question, instead saying, "Tomorrow morning, you will meet with my associates and tell them everything you know."

"I don't know anything. Just that she's gone."

"You know enough to be looking. My people will be in touch. You'll be meeting them before noon."

Not a request.

He hung up and I held the phone out and stared at it for several moments, as if it would offer an explanation for the bizarre turn my search for Brooke had just taken.

How had I gone from calling it an early night to setting up a meeting with some felon's "associates"?

I opened my laptop, this time searching for Charles Sartori. After scanning a few results, I remembered who he was—one of the biggest mobsters to have ever moved into North Florida.

Crap.

CHAPTER 12

I didn't get much sleep. And not just because Voodoo had discovered the joys of attacking my feet at two o'clock in the morning.

My head had been spinning with questions and theories. Did the fact that Brooke was the daughter of a made man play into her kidnapping? It seemed likely. But what about Bob Ligner? His violent temperament couldn't be discounted. I'd debated calling Kai, but knew he'd be less than thrilled to learn of my planned rendezvous with the mob.

I awoke bright and early certain of one thing.

If I was going to meet up with gangsters, I needed to know who I was dealing with.

I thought about asking Emma if she knew anything about Charles Sartori, but though my sister knew just about anyone who was anyone within a two-hundred-mile radius, I had a feeling Wes, who'd worked at the State Attorney's Office before moving to Savannah, might know more.

I tried his cell then his office, where his assistant, Claudio, informed me Wes was flying back from meeting with clients in Atlanta.

"I can make sure he gets a message as soon as he lands," Claudio offered. He had been working with Wes for a few years. I'd met him on a handful of occasions, and he knew how close I was to his boss. I wondered if he could help me out with a little four-one-one.

"I was actually calling to get some information on a man by the name of Charles Sartori. I know he's serving time at Union Correctional, but I was hoping to learn more."

I could hear computer keys clicking over the phone line.

"Give me just a sec," Claudio said. "Yep. Charles Angelino Sartori—doing time for fraud. Looks like he has been implicated in a lot of shady stuff, but nothing definitive."

"I heard he was some sort of mob boss."

"You heard right."

"Do you have any information on his known associates? People who work for him or with him?"

"Let's see . . . that might take a minute. Anyone specific?"

"No. Just see if he has, you know, a right-hand man or something."

"I'll get back to you as soon as I find something."

I thanked Claudio and hung up, hoping he would call me back before the meeting was set.

I checked the time—just past seven.

Waiting around to be summoned by criminals was not my idea of a relaxing morning. To take my mind off the prospect of the impending meeting, I decided to take Moss for a quick walk on the beach.

As I'd hoped, my wolf-dog was much less concerned about Voodoo now that the kitten had become more energetic.

Moss questioned me about the whereabouts of his kitten a few times as we walked along the water's edge. I assured him everything was fine, and he eventually relaxed. He trusted me enough to let go of his worry, which was good, because I had no intention of attending my clandestine meeting without backup—and few things worked as well for backup as a giant, white wolf-dog.

My phone rang just as Moss and I were walking up the steps to the condo.

"Grace Wilde?"

"Yes?"

"I was told you would be available this morning for a meeting."

I didn't bother to ask who I was talking to—I could almost hear the tune from *The Godfather* playing as he spoke.

"I'm sure you were. Though I don't believe I can tell you any more than I told your boss."

"Then it should be a brief discussion. I can have a car come for you or give you the address. Either way, we'll be expecting you as soon as possible."

A car? Um—no. "The address will be fine, thank you."

"Are you sure? It's a bit out of the way."

No way was I getting picked up by the mob. How dumb did this guy think I was?

"I'll drive myself, if it's all the same."

He gave me an address and I jotted it down on the back of a piece of junk mail. Once Moss had checked on Voodoo, we headed out the door. Thirty minutes later, I was no closer to meeting with the mob—because I was lost.

Emma called just as I realized the road I'd been following was a dead end.

"Hey, where are you?" she asked.

"Lost north of nowhere, somewhere off Cedar Point Road." I tried not to sound as rushed and nervous as I felt.

"I assume that means you won't be home anytime soon?"

"Not likely. Why, what's up?"

"Oh, not much. I'd just walked in from the dojo when a man arrived with a strangely familiar-looking Doberman pinscher."

Jax.

I'd forgotten my playdate appointment with Jake.

"Crap. Tell Jake I'm sorry, but we'll have to reschedule."

"I would, but he already left."

"You're kidding."

"He said he'd just gotten a call to go to a crime scene. I said it would be fine, but then I remembered something . . ."

"Voodoo." I wanted to bang my head on the steering wheel.

"Is it okay to leave Jax here when I go to work or will he eat the kitten?"

"Honestly, I don't know. Let me call Sonja and see if she can take care of Jax for a little while."

I didn't think Jax would hurt Voodoo on purpose, but I didn't want to chance it. I negotiated a three-point turn while I made the call, grumbling to myself when she didn't answer. I could think of only one other person who not only had experience handling large animals but also owed me a favor.

I found the number and dialed as I headed back down the road.

"Hey, beautiful."

"Hugh, are you busy right now?"

"You know I always have time for you."

"Good, because I have a really big favor to ask."

"How big?"

"About the size of a Doberman pinscher."

He chuckled. And after I explained the situation, he promised to pick up Jax at the condo.

"Oh, and while you're there, I've got a new kitten who needs her boosters. She's probably pretty wormy, too."

"I'll take care of it."

"Thanks, Hugh."

"Not a problem. I owe you more than this for all the times you've helped me out. Have you learned anything else about Brooke? Ozeal says she hasn't turned up."

"Some." I spotted a street I'd missed the first time down the road and headed toward it, hoping I was finally on the right track. "Listen, I've got to run. Thanks again."

I called Emma back and gave her Hugh's number so they could negotiate the exchange.

"Are you still lost?" she asked.

"Pretty much."

She sighed. "You know you have a GPS on your phone."

"I do?"

Emma told me where to find the app and then said, "Don't forget, we're meeting the Realtor today. And I have a surprise for you, so don't get hung up."

"I'll do my best." I could imagine what being hung up by the mob might entail.

Moss growled from the backseat. My overactive imagination was making him wary.

"It's okay, big guy. I'll let you know if there's going to be a rumble."

He let out a doubtful snort.

I had envisioned the meeting taking place in some remote warehouse or equally sinister place, so I was surprised when the GPS led me to a small, homey restaurant nestled along the edge of a large creek.

Cooper's Catch looked more like a fish camp than a Mafia den. Which, I suppose, was the point.

I parked, and Moss and I traipsed over the crushed-oyster-shell lot to the rough, wood-clad structure. The sign on the door indicated that the restaurant was closed until eleven. I knocked, and within a few moments, the door creaked partly open. A tall man with dark hair and eyes peered at me.

"Yes?"

"I'm here to see . . ." I wasn't sure who I was there to see. "Charles Sartori sent me."

With a subtle nod, he started to step back and open the door fully—then he caught sight of Moss.

His eyes widened and he moved so that his body was partly shielded by the door. Then his brow furrowed and he scowled. I knew the look. I'd seen it countless times. He was afraid of dogs and that fear embarrassed him.

"No dogs in the restaurant," he snapped.

"Understandable. But I'm not coming in without him."

His scowl deepened, but he finally nodded and ushered us in.

The interior was a welcoming blend of fisherman's cottage and sailor's retreat. Exposed wood beams, warm, earth-tone walls, and hardwood floors gave the place an inviting glow. The back wall was composed entirely of windows, divided in the center by a set of French doors. Beyond the glass, a deck overlooked the water.

Not surprisingly, we were led through the restaurant to the doors and onto the outside deck.

Fine by me. It was a beautiful, mild day and I was far more comfortable out in the open than inside the restaurant—no matter how charming.

I chose a table close to the water and sat, like I'd seen in spy movies, facing the French doors.

Moss's attention was caught by something in the water, and I peered through the railing to see a large alligator cruise by.

Great. I'd led us to the disposal site for the Jacksonville Mafia.

I shook off the thought, reminding myself I was there to help a man find his daughter. For all I knew, Charles Sartori had gone straight. Gotten into the restaurant business and his associates were a butcher, a baker, and a candlestick maker.

Well, I could hope, right?

Just then my phone began playing a salsa tune. I answered, recognizing Wes's office number.

"I'm sorry I wasn't able to get back to you any sooner, Grace," Claudio said. "It's like the minute Wes leaves town, everyone calls wanting something. Oh! I didn't mean you, sweetie."

"I know. I appreciate you looking into it for me."

"Not a problem—really. You want the quick-and-dirty version or an e-mail with detailed documents, or both?"

I glanced at the closed doors leading into the restaurant. "Let's go with quick and dirty. You can send the rest later."

"Okay. First up—Charles Sartori. Very traditional. I found a lot about him; you can look over all of it in the e-mail file. Basically, he's old school. 'Honor among thieves' sort of thing. When he went to jail four years ago, Frank Ferretto took over running the business. Ferretto has worked for Sartori forever. Sharp when it comes to business—he's the right-hand man you asked about."

My gaze was glued to the doors. "Okay, anyone else?"

"A couple of names popped up, but the scariest is a guy named Vincent Mancini. AKA Machete Mancini. I'm sure you can guess why."

"Dear Lord."

"Yeah. Oh, and there's another one I thought was interesting. The Ghost."

"Ghost?" As in . . . what?

"No one really knows who he is. There isn't even a photo of him."

"Great," I muttered under my breath. So much for the butcher and baker—well, the butcher might be right.

There was a pause, then Claudio asked, "Grace, why are you asking about these guys? You're not thinking of taking one of them on as a client, are you? Because these are not nice people."

That moment, the French doors opened and a trio of men stepped into the bright, midmorning sun.

"Nope. Listen, I've got to run. Thanks." I hung up on another round of Claudio's warnings and stood to face the men.

Thankfully, years of dealing with the sometimes chaotic thoughts of animals had gifted me with a strong rein on my own emotions. So when I recognized one of the men, I was fairly sure I kept my shock under wraps.

"Miss Wilde." The tall, lean man at the front of the group smiled and offered his hand. "I'm Frank Ferretto."

Though I didn't relish the thought, I took his hand. The drive to be polite overrode my wariness.

Southern is as Southern does.

"Thank you for coming out here to talk with me."

As we took our seats on opposite sides of the table, the other men moved to flank Ferretto in traditional bodyguard style.

Yard Guy wore dark sunglasses, so I couldn't tell if he was looking at me or not. The second man, who was slightly smaller, with a wiry frame, flicked his gaze over me, gave me a creepy half smile, then he locked his eyes on Moss.

I inclined my head at Ferretto. It was the only response I could manage, given that Moss was radiating aggression like an angry badger.

I knew without a doubt that Mr. Creepy Smile was Vincent Mancini. The fact that he had locked eyes with Moss meant he was either stupid or crazy.

Bad. Moss let out a low growl.

I know. It's okay.

Not okay. Bad.

I clinched my teeth then forced a calm breath. Encountering a sociopath had not been on my to-do list for the day. Mancini was triggering a searing protectiveness in Moss. It vibrated through me like an electric current. I wasn't sure I was up to the task of shielding myself from thoughts of massive violence while keeping a reasonable line of communication open.

"Could you ask your friend to stop challenging my dog? He's sensitive." I placed my hand on Moss's head and he peeled his lips back to show Mancini who had the bigger, sharper teeth.

Ferretto glanced from me to Moss. Until that moment, I don't think he'd given Moss much notice—which made him either arrogant or a fool.

I was betting on arrogant.

"Vince," Ferretto snapped, "go grab us some coffee or something."

Mancini hesitated, then moved away, still holding that creepy little smile.

"My apologies, Miss Wilde." Ferretto plucked a piece of lint from the knee of his trousers and flicked it away. "I'm afraid my associate gets excited easily."

I didn't really want to think about what excited Mr. Machete, so I said, "I'm not sure what your boss thinks I can contribute. I told him everything last night."

"Mr. Sartori would prefer you tell me firsthand."

I shrugged and explained my concerns about Brooke,

leaving out the part where the witness to her kidnapping was a tiger.

"And how do you know Brooke?" Ferretto asked.

"I don't. Not really. All I know is that she cared about the animals at the rescue facility. She wouldn't have left them. Not without word. Your boss must agree with me, otherwise I wouldn't be here, right?"

"Mr. Sartori loves his daughter very much. It would be devastating if anything were to happen to her."

"Well, then, I suggest you guys start looking for her."

"We are, Miss Wilde. You can be certain of that." He gave me an expectant look.

The young man who'd opened the door earlier appeared and, keeping as far away from Moss as he could, set two mugs of coffee on the wood table.

"Thanks, Jimmy."

"No problem, sir." Jimmy kept his gaze downcast, but I could tell he was focused on my dog. I had a feeling if Moss sneezed, Jimmy would faint.

Usually, I tried to reassure people who were uncomfortable around Moss. I didn't bother in this case—a little fear on their side was probably a good thing.

Mancini didn't reappear, and that made me uncomfortable. It's always good to know where the psychos are so you can avoid them.

"Listen," I said to Ferretto, "I've told you everything I know. I'm not sure how I can help you."

"That's just it, Miss Wilde," Ferretto said and took a sip from his mug. "I am not sure you have told us everything you know." He studied me over his cup of coffee.

"What reason could I possibly have to lie to you? We want the same thing."

"If that's the case, then you won't have a problem working with us to find Brooke."

"Work with you?"

"Yes. And, as you might imagine, we ask that you keep the police out of it."

"Excuse me?"

He held up his hand to stop me, as if sensing I was about to tell him to go jump in the river.

"All I ask is you promise to contact us first if you learn anything. This is my direct line." He set a business card on the table between us. I picked it up, recognizing the Intra-Corp logo.

It wasn't as if he was asking me to whack somebody, but there was no way I was making that deal—not that he had to know that.

"Okay, sure. If I find out anything else about Brooke, I'll let you know."

I could rationalize agreeing to help all I wanted—I still felt like I was making a deal with the devil. Or, the devil's right-hand man, as the case may be.

The thought made me want to get out of there as quickly as possible. I stood, shot Yard/Mob Guy a curt nod as I passed, and, with an eye out for where Mancini might be lurking, hightailed it through the restaurant and out the front door.

The sky was darkening in the distance and the wind rustled the reeds along the inlet. Moss sniffed the air.

Rain, he informed me.

"I noticed." Even without a dog's sense of smell, I could figure some stuff out.

The thought gave me a sudden idea. What if Moss could find and follow Brooke's trail through the woods? It might lead nowhere, but it was worth a shot.

I fished my phone out of my purse and after a quick scan of the map, I decided I could be at Happy Asses in less than ten minutes.

The storm was probably a good half hour from hitting. I cranked Bluebell and said to Moss, "Warm that sniffer up, buddy. We're going to look for clues."

CHAPTER 13

I called Ozeal, explained my idea, and asked her to look for something that might work as a scent article for Brooke.

Before the first rumble of thunder had boomed its warning, I was standing in the building that housed the commissary and clinic, in what might be considered a locker room, only there were no lockers. Instead, the tiny room had a row of cubbyholes lining one wall.

The cubbies held a hodgepodge of clothing, including a hat with the Happy Asses logo embroidered on it, a hooded sweatshirt, and a pair of dusty leather gloves.

"This is the cubby she usually used." Ozeal said, pointing. "So that might be her hat. The rest is probably either Caitlyn's or Ben's."

I picked up the ball cap to look for initials or something else to determine ownership. Moss could tell the difference between my scent and someone else's so touching it wouldn't be an issue. There was a problem however—it didn't belong to Brooke.

I showed the initials marked on the tag to Ozeal. "C. M. Caitlyn's?"

Ozeal nodded. "Okay, well, let's see if we can find something else."

We poked around for a minute but came up empty.

Frustrated that my almost-great idea had been so quickly thwarted, I tried to think of another way to direct Moss to find her scent. Inspiration remained elusive, however, and, defeated, I followed Ozeal out of the cubby room and down the hall.

I paused as we started past a door labeled CLINIC.

"You said you caught Brooke in here. What's the protocol for the clinic?"

"No one is allowed inside unsupervised but me."

I tried the handle. Locked.

"How did she get in? Did Brooke have a key?"

"Everyone who has any contact with the animals has a key," Ozeal said. "The door locks automatically. Which is an extra deterrent. On the off chance someone was to break into the building, they'd have to get through this door"—she unclipped her sea-anemone cluster of keys, unlocked the door, and pushed it open—"then, to get to anything worth having, they'd have to get into that cabinet."

She pointed to the opposite wall, where a large metal cabinet stood. I'd seen similar drug safes. Though it looked like a typical metal locker, the steel was thick and the locks heavy-duty. I noticed this one needed two keys to open it.

"Who has the second key?"

"I carry them both."

I nodded, wondering why Brooke would have been in this room. She had to have known it would have taken two separate keys to unlock the drug safe.

I looked around, hoping the answer would present itself.

The small room was clean and orderly. A shallow cabinet ran along one wall. A microscope sat on the counter next to a small stainless steel sink, along with a box of latex gloves, a red biohazard container, and other typical equipment for basic veterinary exams. The scent of antiseptic and animal fur would have made me smile if I hadn't been so frustrated.

Just as I was about to turn and head back out the door, I heard a low chime.

"What was that?"

"I don't know," Ozeal said, frowning.

"You don't have any timers or anything set?"

"No."

We both looked around for several seconds. "It almost sounded like my phone. It makes that noise when the battery is about to die."

Ozeal and I exchanged a look, then began the hunt in earnest.

You'd have thought we were searching for earthquake survivors the way we tore into the place.

After less than a minute, I heard Ozeal suck in a breath. I turned to see her staring into an open cardboard box.

"What is it?" I asked, stepping toward her.

She answered by reaching into the box and pulling out a small, light blue purse. Ozeal met my gaze and I knew what she was going to say.

"It's Brooke's."

We were thinking the same thing. Any hope that Brooke had simply run away vaporized with the discovery. No sixteen-year-old girl would run off and leave her purse and her phone behind.

"What's it doing in here?"

"I don't know—" She broke off, caught by a sudden thought.

"What?"

"When Brooke first started working for me, she had trust issues. I let her keep her purse in here. She hasn't asked to do that in months."

"But if she just wanted to lock up her purse, why not tell you? Why make up a story about pliers?"

"Only thing I can figure is she was trying not to stir the pot."

"You mean if she'd told you she didn't feel comfortable leaving her purse out anymore you'd have wanted to know why. You think she was protecting Caitlyn?"

"Damned if I know what she was thinking."

I remembered what Kai had said about kids ratting on each other. Would the fear of being labeled a snitch have trumped getting caught and telling the truth? Probably.

I opened the purse and pulled out the phone. It was an iPhone like mine. I desperately wanted to scroll through and see what calls she'd made but knew the battery wouldn't last that long.

"I've got a charger for this," I told Ozeal. "I'm going to plug it in, then I'll use the purse to see if we can pick up her trail. Okay?"

Ozeal gave me a grim nod. "Let me know if you find anything."

I jogged back to Bluebell, where Moss was waiting. After making sure the phone was charging, I grabbed Moss's leash.

We made our way around the perimeter, staying close to the fence line. When we finally reached the section closest to Boris's enclosure, I stopped and scanned the area. The first time I'd come back here, I'd determined the most likely spot Brooke would have been standing when she was grabbed.

I tried to find it again by peering through the chain-link, shuffling to the side until I had a clear shot of the tiger house. Boris had heard us and was staring back intently. I didn't want him to worry so I sent him a few reassuring thoughts.

Remembering Brooke had claimed to need pliers to tighten the fence, I threaded my fingers through the chain-link and tugged. It seemed secure.

Stepping back, I was getting ready to present Moss with Brooke's purse to sniff and ask him to find her scent when I noticed something I hadn't seen before.

About a foot from the bottom of the metal post, poking out from a thatch of shriveled weeds, was a brass clip. I crouched and studied the clump of dead grass and weeds. They weren't rooted into the ground—rather they had been placed along the bottom of the fence.

I brushed them away and discovered why.

The fence had been cut.

The brass clasp was actually holding the fence together.

I sat back on my haunches, perplexed.

It looked as if someone had tried to break in by cutting the fence. Had Brooke used the clip as a temporary fix until she could get a set of pliers? If so, why wouldn't she tell Ozeal? Could her discovery be the reason she'd been kidnapped?

I looked back through the fence, wondering what would motivate someone to break into an animal rescue facility.

It wasn't like the animals could be stolen. Drugs? Always a possibility.

I sat there mulling it over so long that Moss finally got bored and nudged my chin with his muzzle.

Go?

A not-so-distant rumble of thunder punctuated his question.

I'd have to think about the fence later.

"Come on, big guy, let's see what that wolf-nose can do."

• • •

It turned out the wolf-nose was not all it was cracked up to be.

As much as I loved him, Moss was not a bloodhound. And I was not a tracking-dog handler.

As we'd zigzagged through the woods, Moss would occasionally stop and tell me he recognized Brooke's scent. But within moments he would lose the trail, wander off track, and become distracted by the odoriferous wonders the woods had in store.

By the third time he stopped to inspect squirrel scat, I was ready to give up. Then I heard something that sparked my interest.

It was the rumbling noise of a truck engine. I started toward the sound and remembered Happy Asses was bordered on two sides by roads.

I'd brought my phone with me, and thanks to what was turning out to be an exceptionally handy GPS app, I was able to determine the most direct route.

We emerged from the woods and stopped at a muddy culvert separating us from the shoulder of a two-lane road.

Moss cleared the ditch in one graceful leap. I landed with a splat, a foot shy of dry ground. Teetering off-balance, I finally heaved myself forward onto my hands and knees in the weeds.

Okay?

I could feel the amusement in the question and glared at my dog as I picked up the end of his leash and got to my feet. "Stellar, thanks for asking."

Though the traffic was intermittent, it was hardly deserted enough to drag a teenaged girl into a vehicle without the possibility of being seen.

I led Moss up and down along the shoulder anyway.

While Moss sniffed, I scanned the ground. Weathered bits of trash and more cigarette butts than I could count dotted the shoulder.

"Don't people know these things don't decompose?"

We reached a turnout made of broken oyster shells and sand.

I spotted something iridescent glowing in the light and bent to pick it up. It was a large piece of shell with a real pearl protruding like a blister from the nacre.

I ran my thumb over the pearl, suddenly feeling dejected. I had managed to find a pearl on the side of the road, but I couldn't find any trace of Brooke.

I shoved the shell into my pocket and urged Moss to keep going. We walked a few more yards and he paused.

"What is it?"

Possum!

Eew! Dead possum.

"Leave it, Moss."

I tugged on his leash but I might as well have been pulling on an elephant.

"Moss. Leave. It."

Thunder rumbled overhead.

Come on, or we're going to get soaked.

I looked around, noticed a billboard I'd passed that morning, and realized we were on the same street we'd taken to Cooper's Catch.

I wasn't sure that fact was significant, especially since Moss had yet to find a trace of Brooke along the road.

Plus, as sinister as her connection to the mob might be, Brooke was the boss's daughter. They'd made it clear they wanted to find her as much as I did.

So why did I get a weird prickle of unease as I'd made the connection?

I heard the hum of a car engine and turned to see a silver Mercedes roll to a stop on the shoulder.

Oh, that's why.

I watched as the man formerly known as Yard Guy gracefully unfolded himself from the coupe.

Moss finally turned his attention from the flattened remains of the possum and faced the man walking toward us.

"Did your car break down?"

"Bluebell doesn't break down."

"That's what you call it? Bluebell?"

"Do you have a name for your car? Let me guess—The Compensator?"

He laughed and the genuine warmth of the sound surprised me.

"I guess I deserved that. I'm Logan, by the way. I couldn't be completely honest with you when we first met."

"Why the landscaper act?"

"Mr. Sartori was concerned about Brooke, so he asked me to keep an eye on her."

"Why was he so worried?"

"She missed a scheduled visitation about a month ago. She said she forgot, but Mr. Sartori thought she might be hanging out with the wrong people again, so . . ." Logan shrugged.

"So you got to dress up in cargo shorts and spread mulch?"

"Pretty much."

"What did Brooke think of having a babysitter?"

"Brooke doesn't know I work for her father." Logan glanced down at the light blue purse I had slung over my shoulder.

"Brooke's?"

I thought about denying it, but I had a feeling Logan would smell a lie. And, honestly, what were the chances I'd carry a bag exactly like Brooke's?

"I'm using it as a scent device to try and track her movements."

"You found her trail in the woods?"

"Bits of it."

"So whatever happened, she left or was taken from work and came this way." Logan's face became set in grim lines as he scanned the trees then looked up and down the road.

"It's hard to tell. The trail is old. We need more time, but it doesn't look like we're going to get it."

In that moment, a few light drops of rain began to fall. Logan glanced at the sky.

"Come on, I'll give you a ride."

I followed him to the car, my curiosity overriding my good sense. I wanted to know more about Logan and ask what he'd learned about the Ligners. And I wanted to know why Mancini had fixated on Moss.

I only questioned my logic when Logan opened the passenger door.

"A two-seater?" I asked.

His lips twitched in what might have been the beginning of a smirk. "Guess you two will have to ride double."

It took some maneuvering but I managed to get Moss settled on my lap. Not the most comfortable position, given that Moss weighs as much as I do and has a bony butt.

"So," I huffed out as we pulled off the shoulder onto the road, "who was the nutcase with you and Frank?"

Logan shook his head. "No one you need to worry about."

I wasn't at all sure about that but moved on to my next question.

"Have you been watching the Ligners, too, or just Brooke?"

"Both."

"So you know about Bob Ligner."

To my surprise, Logan nodded.

"When I first started watching them, I noticed Brooke's mother had been calling in sick. I reported this to Mr. Sartori, and he asked Brooke about it. She said it was the flu."

"It wasn't the flu."

"No, it wasn't. Bob Ligner has had domestic violence issues. This was back when you could talk your way out of getting arrested for beating your wife." He paused and a muscle in his jaw tightened. "I didn't find out until the day Brooke went missing."

"Do you think Bob Ligner did something to Brooke?"

Logan shook his head. "If he did, he's a walking corpse."

His tone was calm, but something in his words held enough menace to force a growl from Moss.

"He going to bite me?" Logan asked without taking his eyes off the road.

"Not as long as you're nice to me."

"Then we should be fine."

His lips twitched into the almost-smile I'd seen before but vanished when I said, "You seem to care a lot about a girl you've only known a few weeks."

He shook his head. "I've known Brooke since she was a baby. I hadn't seen her in a long time, which is why Mr. Sartori asked me to look out for her. He knew she wouldn't recognize me."

"Anne Ligner didn't recognize you either?"

"The last time I saw Mrs. Sartori, I was a scrawny seventeen-year-old with long hair."

He certainly wasn't scrawny anymore. Even in the tailored shirt, his shoulder muscles strained against the fabric as he drove.

I studied him for a moment, wondering if he'd honed his physique in prison, then I remembered the way he'd stood next to Frank Ferretto. Something about his stance said military.

"What branch?" I asked.

Logan cast me a questioning glance as he turned into the drive leading to Happy Asses. It was tour day so he was able to drive through the open gate and park next to Bluebell.

"Of the military," I clarified.

"Guys like me don't do well in the military."

Not much of an answer, but it wasn't important enough to pursue.

"Well, thanks for the ride," I said and reached around Moss to grope for the door handle.

"Here—" Logan reached into his shirt pocket, pulled out a card, and handed it to me. "If you can't reach Frank for some reason and you need anything, call me. I'll do what I can. In fact, call me even if you do reach Frank."

"Dissension in the ranks?"

"I just have a faster reaction time. And I want to make sure Brooke is safe."

I took the card and Moss and I tumbled out of the car into what had become a light drizzle. After we climbed into Bluebell, I glanced at the card.

Except for a phone number printed in black ink, it was completely blank. I flipped the card over, but there was nothing on the other side.

I glanced out my rearview mirror and caught sight of the Mercedes taillights disappearing in a swirl of mist and remembered what Claudio had told me about the main players in Sartori's organization. Frank Ferretto, Vincent Mancini, and the mystery man no one knew . . .

"Hey, Moss, do you believe in ghosts?"

CHAPTER 14

I tapped the card on the steering wheel, letting my mind wander as I flipped it over and over between my fingertips.

Could Logan really be the Ghost?

What would it mean if he was?

As I wondered, another mysterious character caught my eye.

Jack-Jack.

The miniature donkey was frolicking with one of his pasture-mates. Both animals were having a great time jumping and playing chase.

If Jack-Jack sensed I was trying to get into his head, he'd clam up again. I'd have to settle for subtle eavesdropping—or would it be mind-dropping?—on his thoughts. What I learned was both intriguing and perplexing.

It became obvious that as much as he was enjoying playing with his friend, Jack-Jack was filled with anticipation. He was looking forward to something that would come later.

Not mealtime. It was almost as if he'd come up with something he wanted to try.

I focused a little more intently on his thoughts and discovered he was hopeful the new step would hold.

Step? I pondered that, then made a sudden connection. The broken housing for the water pump. When Paul was repairing it, he'd commented that the damage looked like something heavy had caused it to give way.

"I know what you're up to, little donkey." Smiling, I pushed the driver's-side door open. The rain had picked up again but not enough to stop me. Leaving Moss in Bluebell to snooze, I walked to the fence and whistled. Jack-Jack and his friends all turned their attention to me.

Jack-Jack immediately tried to tune me out of his head.

No need to hide anymore, buddy. I've got your number. With as much detail as possible, I imagined step by step what the donkey had planned.

Escape.

He had been able to climb onto the wooden box housing the water pump, balance on the trough, and make a leap over the fence.

Jack-Jack let out a quiet snort of denial. But I knew I had him.

I opened the gate and stepped forward.

"You've been sneaking out of your pen, haven't you?"

No sneaking.

"Really?" I strolled to the new wooden box covering the water pump. "Would you like me to demonstrate?"

I climbed onto the top of the box, then balanced on the side of the trough. I noticed, from this height, I could see over the thicket of palmettos into the woods where Brooke had been.

I turned back to the mini-donkey. "Jack-Jack, do you climb up here every night?"

No climb.

"Come on, buddy, I'm just trying to connect the dots here." Or was I still collecting dots? I wasn't sure. "Besides, you can't lie to me. I can read your mind."

There was a long pause as Jack-Jack tried to think of a way to weasel out of his predicament. He knew he wasn't allowed out of his pen, especially at night, but he liked to wander around. He was curious about the animals who were hidden from view the rest of the day.

He couldn't see all of them, of course, just the smaller cats whose houses opened into large, rounded cages.

Visit Muffin, Jack-Jack finally said. And an image of a female bobcat was broadcast into my mind from his.

Muffin was the kitten you found?

Muffin likes Jack-Jack.

I twisted my upper body and scanned the property, then crouched so I was more at the donkey's height. Not as much of a view, but maybe that wasn't as important as the fact that Jack-Jack had been out roving the facility when every other possible witness was confined.

Brooke had been kidnapped in the same place someone had cut the fence. Maybe he'd seen who.

As soon as the thought entered my mind, I got a quick series of memories from the little donkey.

Night.

The scent of rain in the distance.

A rustle of movement—out of place.

Curiosity.

Investigate.

Deserted pine-straw path beneath silent hooves.

More sounds—footsteps.

Caution.

Pausing to continue more carefully.

A shadowy figure. Crouching near the fence. Then a surge of something I hadn't expected.

Protect.

Just as Jack-Jack had readied to charge, the intruder slipped through the hole in the fence and disappeared.

"Grace, what in the world are you doing?"

Startled out of my reverie, I nearly lost my footing and ended up in the water trough.

Arms outstretched for balance, I turned to see Ozeal, hands firmly planted on her ample hips, looking up at me.

"I, uh, well . . . I was just trying to get my bearings." When caught looking like an idiot, misdirect.

"I found something," I told her.

"Up there?"

"No." I stepped over the fence onto the other side of the trough and hopped down. "In the woods."

I told her about my discovery at the base of the fence and we walked in that direction.

"Why wouldn't she tell me the fence had been cut?" Ozeal asked.

"I don't know. Unless maybe she thought she knew who was trying to break in." I thought about Stefan. "Maybe she thought she could repair the fence and talk whoever had cut it out of whatever they had planned."

Ozeal nodded thoughtfully. "Brooke would know better than anyone how hard it would be to get anything of value."

"So you don't keep cash here?"

"We do the deposit every night."

Ozeal and I had already talked about the drugs. And I knew they were as safe as she could make them.

I gazed over to the apartment above the commissary, where Ozeal lived.

"What about something personal? Do you have anything valuable up at your place?"

Ozeal placed her hands on her hips. "Yes, I have a whole collection of Fabergé eggs. I keep them lined up on a shelf right under the Rembrandt."

I lifted my hands in a gesture of surrender. "Look, I'm just trying to figure out why discovering the breach in the fence might get Brooke kidnapped."

Ozeal huffed out a breath and nodded. "I get what you're saying. But aside from my animals, I don't have anything worth kidnapping someone over."

"Unless . . . what if the hole in the fence wasn't to take something? Do you have any enemies who would want to hurt you? Break in and start a fire or something?"

She shook her head. "We've had a couple of crazy e-mails. Nuts cursing us six ways from Sunday because we're holding the wild animals captive."

"But you're a rescue. None of these animals could be released into the wild."

"Well, that little nugget of logic seems to escape some people. But none of the e-mails we've ever gotten have been threatening. Basically, they're just rants. And again, why take Brooke?"

"Crazy people don't need a reason. That's why they're crazy."

My phone beeped and I knew it would be a text message from Emma about house hunting. Ozeal and I had exhausted the discussion regarding the fence, so we said our good-byes and I hurried to Bluebell and tried to muster up some enthusiasm.

My spirits lifted some when I opened the text and realized the first house on the list was on Jax Beach not far from where Emma and I had grown up.

It had turned into a blustery day and I could tell from the crisp tinge to the air that by dusk, I would regret my choice of shorts and a T-shirt. We didn't have fall in North Florida—we had plummets. One second you'd be cranking your AC, the next digging under your bed for the storage box of scarves and gloves.

I parked in the driveway next to Emma's sleek Jaguar and left Moss to guard Bluebell, though he didn't appreciate being left behind.

The rain had blown over and I took time to look around as I walked up the drive toward the front door of the first house.

The yard was tiny but nicely landscaped, with a small patch of lawn flanked by sago palms. A row of hibiscus ran along the front wall under a large picture window.

The place had been painted dove gray with crisp white trim.

As I stepped up to the door, I felt a sudden thrill of nerves. This was my first real leap into the real estate ring and I wasn't sure what to expect.

I took a slow breath, but before I could knock the door

opened and I blinked in surprise at the person standing in front of me.

"Wes!"

He grinned and pulled me into a hug.

"Surprise."

I smiled up at my oldest friend, so handsome in his designer shirt and slacks.

"Claudio told me you were on your way home from Atlanta."

"I am. With one small detour." He angled his head and asked, "Checking up on me?"

"Just calling to say hi."

Wes would find out I'd been asking about the Mafia, but I didn't want to broach the subject of my interest in Sartori. Not while house hunting, anyway, so I changed the subject.

"My mom always dreamed we'd be looking for a house together someday."

Wes laughed. "She always had high hopes for us, didn't she?"

"Especially after the prom incident."

"That was brilliant, if I do say so myself."

"Devious, was what it was."

Wes and Emma had conspired against me. Emma bribing me to "model" a dress for her so when Wes showed up at the door in a tux, I was ready to go. My mother had been thrilled. I couldn't burst her bubble by not going, and they knew it.

Much as he had then, Wes linked his arm with mine and guided me through the door. He patted my hand and muttered, "Deep breaths, Grace, this is supposed to be fun."

I don't know if I would call it fun, but I enjoyed the next two hours looking at homes. I'd always fetch Moss to evaluate the yards, his opinion being paramount in that department.

We were touring the final property of the day when it hit me.

As I followed my sister and Wes from room to room and we laughed and joked, I realized, as much as I wanted my own place, I didn't want to lose the connection I'd established with my sister.

I'd lived alone for years. I'd liked it. I only moved in with Emma because my old landlady realized her insurance didn't cover wolf-dogs and booted us without warning.

The idea of cohabitation with another human, even my own sister, had filled me with dread. It was a shock to discover I'd gotten used to it.

No, I *liked* it.

"Grace." Emma had noticed my sudden silence. "You okay?"

"Yeah. I . . . It's getting late. I need to relieve Hugh of dog-and-kitty-sitting duty. And I'm supposed to meet Jake at the JSO at four and drop off Jax."

I gave Wes and my sister quick hugs and fled.

Not sure what to make of my latest revelation, I pushed it out of my mind and I headed back toward town on Atlantic Boulevard.

I'd never been to Hugh's house, so I plugged his address into my GPS app—which I was growing pretty enamored with—and followed its directions to a street off Tallulah Avenue and a tidy brick house across the street from the river.

Drawing from my new real estate knowledge, I guessed the house was built sometime in the thirties. It reminded me of an old English cottage with its steep roof, huge chimney, and arched door.

It looked more like somewhere a sweet old lady who liked to garden would live than the rugged bachelor pad I'd imagined.

I double-checked the address, and finding it was correct, parked along the curb.

"Okay." I turned in the front seat to face Moss. "I'll be back in a minute."

Go. He stood and let out a low *woof.*

Moss had let me know repeatedly that he had grown tired of being banished to the car while I looked at houses.

"Sorry, big guy. This will be a quick stop, I promise."

I wasn't sure how Moss would act around Voodoo in someone else's territory. I'd hate for Hugh to lose a limb just for making a sudden movement toward the kitten.

No stay. Go.

He moved to jump into the front seat and I placed my hand on his chest firmly.

"Stay." I put a little extra force of my own will behind the word. Just a touch of alpha energy. It would have worked on most dogs. Moss was not most dogs.

Go.

"Stay. Or no treats."

Moss grumbled, turned in a circle, and flopped down with a grunt.

"Getting grumpy won't make me move any faster."

He let out a disdainful snort and gazed out the window, completely ignoring me.

Only a canine like Moss could pout and look regal at the same time.

I rolled my eyes, leaving him to sulk as I made my way down the brick path to the door. The knocker was fashioned not in the traditional lion's head, but in the shape of an elephant holding a ring in its trunk.

Elephants were one of Hugh's favorite animals. Maybe he did live here.

My theory was confirmed when I rang the bell. A familiar eruption of barks sounded and a moment later, the door swung open.

Hugh smiled and released the hold he'd taken on Jax's thick leather collar.

I turned my attention to the dog, who was quivering with excitement and pure joy at the sight of me.

Grace!

"Hey, Jax." I squatted in front of him to give him a hug.

Grace here. Grace. Grace. The Doberman's ode to Grace was redirected when he caught Moss's scent. He let out a high, excited whine. *Moss? Where's Moss?*

You'll see him in a minute.

I looked up at Hugh. "Thanks again for taking care of him."

"It wasn't a problem. He's a good boy," Hugh said, and gave Jax a hardy pat.

Giving the Doberman another hug, I murmured, "Yes, he is."

Jax, good boy.

"I also took care of the kitten, um . . . Voodoo? Interesting name."

"My sister's idea," I said as I stood.

"Emma."

Something about the way he said her name had me arching my brows.

He understood my silent query and grinned. "Your sister is . . . very nice."

Another one bites the dust. "I hear that a lot."

"Come on in and we'll get everybody ready to go."

I followed him into a large living area. The cottage-style house might have surprised me, but the decor did not. I was no expert, but I'd categorize it as a bachelor's version of safari chic.

With a little too much safari and not quite enough chic.

"I treated Voodoo for the usual," Hugh said as he scooped the kitten off the floor and placed her in the carrier. "Rubbed some flea treatment on her, too."

"Thanks. So Jax was okay with her?"

"Jax didn't know what to think. A tiny, crazy fluff ball that leapt at him from under the couch? He seemed a little scared of her, to be honest."

We both laughed at the idea of a trained protection dog shying away from a two-pound kitten.

I lifted the carrier and as we started out the door I turned and asked, "Hugh, do you like living alone?"

"I'm not alone that often," he said with a wicked grin.

"Sorry, I forgot—you live with your inflated ego."

He chuckled, unaffected by my jab.

"Seriously. Do you get—" I almost said *lonely.* "Bored?"

"Nah. If I do, I just have a cookout or have the guys over to watch the game or something. You know."

"Yeah."

Actually, I didn't know. I'd never hosted a get-together. I didn't have enough friends. Human ones, anyway.

For some reason, the thought bothered me. I thanked Hugh again and, after a happy reunion between Jax and Moss, I drove toward the sheriff's office.

I was running late and Jake would be waiting. I imagined the gruff detective shaking his head and grousing about my tardiness. The thought made me smile.

Jake was like a cheese panini—crusty on the outside but warm and gooey in the center.

"Hey." I glanced over my shoulder at Jax, who was warily eyeing Voodoo's paw as it clawed the air through the carrier's door. "I could put you and Jake on the invite list if I ever had a cookout, right? Mary, too."

And Kai, I thought, my smile stretching into a grin. On impulse, I snagged my phone and called his cell, frowning when it went straight to voice mail once again.

I figured there had to be a big case going on for him not to have returned my call by now.

I called Jake earlier and he'd given me a short "Let me call you back."

Which, of course, he hadn't done. I could have taken Jax home with me, but I needed to talk to Kai and tell him what I'd learned. I knew he wouldn't be happy with me. Meeting with mobsters didn't really fall under the category of staying safe.

But Brooke's connection to the mob was too important to keep from him. And there was the breach in the fence at Happy Asses.

And, if I was honest with myself, I just wanted to see him.

"You are getting soft, Grace."

I pulled into the JSO parking garage at a little after four, left the dogs in the car with the window cracked, and headed inside.

The door to Kai's office was closed. I started to knock but heard someone say, "He's not in there."

I turned and recognized Charlie Yamada, one of Kai's fellow investigators.

I smiled. "Let me guess, he's geeking out with a microscope somewhere?"

The usually gregarious Charlie didn't return my smile. "No, he's—" He broke off as if debating what to say. "In a meeting."

"Okay, do you know how long he'll be?"

He pursed his lips together and glanced away. "I don't . . . I'm not sure. I don't think it's a good idea for you to be here, Grace."

"Why? What do you mean?"

Charlie met my gaze and I noticed worry lines marred his typically smooth face.

He stepped forward and said in a low voice, "You should go."

Without another word, he sidestepped around me and walked away.

What the hell?

I stood there for a moment, too confused to do more than blink at Charlie's retreating back. A ripple of anxiety snapped me out of my stupor. I turned toward the elevators and made a beeline for the homicide unit to track down Jake.

In true detective fashion, he found me before I found him.

"Grace, what are you doing here?"

"Coming to bring you your dog, for starters."

He glanced at his watch and cursed.

"What the hell is going on, Jake? I ran into Charlie and he told me I should leave. Where's Kai?"

"Come here." He gripped my elbow, led me into an empty interview room, and closed the door. "Kai is in trouble. Some muckety-mucks from internal affairs have been inter-rogating him all day."

"What?" I asked utterly shocked. "Why?"

"It would seem that he's been askin' questions about the daughter of a certain crime boss named Charles Sartori." His gaze zeroed in on mine. "You wouldn't know anything about that, would you?"

"Kai is in trouble because he asked around about Brooke?"

"You know her?"

"Yes—I mean no."

"Which is it, Grace?"

"No, I don't know her—but I'm trying to find her."

"Why?"

"She disappeared from work over a week ago."

"No missing person report has been filed."

"That's because her parents think she ran away."

"But you don't."

"Obviously. That's why I'm trying to find her." I held up my hand to stop him before he got on a roll with the questions, especially since there were several I didn't want to answer. This wasn't the time or place to tell Jake about my telepathic ability. "Look, here's the deal: I told Kai about Brooke and he explained there was nothing the police could do until her parents reported her missing, so I asked him for a few favors. If anyone should be in trouble, it's me."

"What kind of trouble?"

I wasn't sure what he meant. "I'm just saying Kai didn't do anything wrong."

"There are some who think he might have some connection to Sartori."

"That's ridiculous. Kai doesn't even know Sartori's Brooke's father."

"Why don't you start from the beginning, Grace, and explain."

I shook my head. "I'll explain it to the idiots who are stupid enough to think Kai could be involved with the mob." I turned to leave, but Jake placed his meaty hand on the door before I could open it.

"No so fast. So far, Kai hasn't mentioned you. I'm gonna assume it's for a reason."

He gave me his cop eyes and I stepped back, folded my arms over my chest, and glared at him.

"And that would be what, exactly? You think I'm in league with the Mafia? Come on, Jake."

Jake was giving me a hard stare. I'd known him awhile, and though he'd often shook his head, bewildered by my "knack" with animals, he'd never looked at me with utter suspicion.

Something else was going on.

"What aren't you telling me, Jake?"

"I'd ask you the same question."

My eyes narrowed as I studied him. I have a low tolerance for BS, especially from someone I consider a friend. "Take your hand off the door, Detective."

"No."

"Am I under arrest?"

He scowled.

"Then open the door."

He lowered his voice to a low growl. "You need to tell me what's goin' on, Grace."

"You're harassing me, that's what's going on."

"Why were you at the Ligners' house?"

"I—what?" How did Jake know I'd gone to the Ligners'? Had Kai told him? He answered my question before I could ask.

"An old, light blue Suburban was seen parked in front of their house, not once, but twice in the last few days."

"So?"

"What were you doin' there?"

"Why does it matter?" I was starting to get a bad feeling about the questions he was asking.

"Do you know Bob Ligner?"

"We've met."

Jake's faced darkened.

"Why are you asking about Bob Ligner?" I had to ask, though I had the feeling I already knew the answer.

There was only one reason a homicide detective would be grilling me about being at the Ligners' house.

"Oh my God. He's dead, isn't he."

"Have a seat, Grace. We need to talk."

CHAPTER 15

Bob Ligner was dead.

"This is a new dot," I muttered as I settled into the bleak-looking chair Jake had indicated.

"What?" he asked.

"Nothing."

"Grace, I don't know what's goin' on, but you need to come clean with me." Jake leaned forward, placing his palms on the table between us. "Your vehicle was seen parked adjacent to the Ligners' house the same day he was murdered. Why were you there?"

"I . . ."

What could I say? I wanted to check on Brooke's cat? That answer would only lead to impossible questions.

"I was looking for clues."

"Clues?"

"To what might have happened to Brooke."

"Why?"

"Because no one else was."

"And?"

"And what?"

"Find any?"

Had I? The mangled toys were a clue, but if I told him about them I'd have to admit to snooping in the trash. Wasn't that a federal offense? No—I was confusing the trash with the mail. Which was about right these days . . .

"Grace."

Jake's gruff voice yanked my train of thought back in line like a cowboy jerking the reins of a shying horse.

"What?"

"I asked you where you were Tuesday night."

"Operation Bat Wing," I muttered.

"What?"

"I had to work. Then I went home."

"What time?"

"I'm not sure. Sometime after nine."

"Did you leave?"

I shook my head.

"Can anyone verify that?"

Sure, my dog.

A realization hit me like a slap in the face.

"You're asking me for an alibi?"

"You got one?"

I stood without answering and headed for the door. Jake moved to stand in my way.

My temper spiked, and a rush of cold anger settled over me. Opening my purse, I took out my cell phone and began scrolling through my contacts.

"What are you doing?" Jake asked.

"Calling my attorney."

My phone began playing what sounded like a sea chantey before I could call Wes.

When I saw who was calling I actually wanted to smile, but current circumstances short-circuited the urge.

"Hey, Uncle Wiley. What's up?" I frowned at the answer. "Okay. I can be there in twenty minutes."

Jake scowled. "Grace. . ."

"I have to help my uncle. If you want your dog I suggest you come get him."

Jake loomed behind me like a black cloud all the way to Bluebell.

"Later, me and you are gonna talk," he said as I handed him Jax's leash.

"I'm sure we will, Jake."

When I got into Bluebell, Moss nudged me under my chin. *Okay?*

I patted him and said, "I'm fine."

We both knew it was a lie. My mind was whirling.

Bob Ligner was dead.

Jake, someone I considered my friend, suspected me of being involved with the murder, and Kai was in trouble because I'd asked for his help.

Part of me wanted to scream in frustration, but mostly I didn't know what to think.

I blew out a sigh as I headed over the Hart Bridge. Maybe friendly cookouts weren't in my future after all.

• • •

"What do you think, Gracie? Can you get him out?"

I glanced at my uncle Wiley. Like always, he wore a beret. Tufts of hair puffed out from under it like white cotton candy. His mustache, an impeccably groomed handlebar, was as white as his hair. At least it would have been, if not for the speckles of mud all over his face.

And his shirt.

And his pants.

"Yeah, I think so."

I didn't ask why my uncle had dug the three-foot-wide, eight-foot-long pit on his property. I knew.

He was nuts.

Wiley was *that* uncle. The weirdo. The eccentric. The oddball who was whispered about and made fun of. The one children adore until they no longer believe an old man's stories of high seas adventure, pirates, and buried treasure.

I still adored Wiley. Which was why I was standing by his side, staring at the animal caught in one of his excavations.

This is going to get ugly.

In the pit, chest deep in thick, brown mud, was a white-tailed deer. Judging from the large rack of antlers, a mature male of at least three years. What the big guy was doing on my uncle's island, I didn't know. Though a bridge connected the seven-acre lump of land to the rest of Neptune Beach, I doubted the buck had walked the long, narrow road. Deer could swim—maybe the buck had decided to take a break before traversing the rest of the Intercoastal.

Honestly, I didn't care how he'd ended up in the pit. I needed to get Bambi's daddy out of the mire and on his way. Somehow.

In the distance, thunder rumbled.

Crap.

The last thing I needed right now was another downpour.

"I tried to get him to back up," Wiley told me softly.

"What do you mean?" I asked in a soft monotone.

"Well, I'm not a young man anymore," he said. "I have to make an easier way in and out when I'm digging. There are a couple of steps."

I suspected my uncle—great-uncle, actually—could dig circles around me.

"So, there are some sort of steps on this side?" If there were, they weren't visible through the opaque brown water.

"Just two. I guess that's how he got down there. Do you think he could use them to climb out?"

"Let's find out." Bold words for a tricky situation. First, I'd have to convince the buck to turn around. Then, I'd somehow have to explain the concept of the steps.

I'd already done a preliminary scan of the deer's mind—he was tired, trapped, and terrified.

The trifecta of imminent failure.

Sighing, I handed my uncle my phone, a few business cards, and anything else in my pockets. Then I bent over and started unlacing my boots.

"What are you doing?"

"Taking my boots off. I don't want to lose them in the mud." I tugged the first one off.

"You're going to get in there with him?"

"Yep." I peeled off my socks. As I straightened, I felt cool mud ooze up between my toes.

"Is that safe, Gracie?"

"It will be fine," I assured him. In truth, I wasn't sure it would be fine. The buck's hooves and antlers had the capacity to inflict serious damage.

I walked slowly to the edge of the pit, directly behind the deer. He craned his majestic head around to watch me as I lowered myself to the ground. I gritted my teeth as I dipped first my right foot, then my left, into the muck.

I closed my eyes and concentrated all my efforts on the deer.

I'm your friend. I'm not going to hurt you.

I extended my leg lower, felt the top step, and slid off the edge of the pit to stand thigh-deep in the mud.

A surge of his emotions prompted me to still.

Fear and wariness.

Exhaustion.

Pain.

I pulled these feelings in, drawing on the connection between us. Legs unsteady, I waded forward, down to the next step, and slowly reached out. Finally, my fingertips brushed his flank. I felt a little rush at the contact and it took all my control not to jerk away.

My heart began to beat in tandem with the buck's. My legs and arms burned and trembled as they took in his exhaustion.

I took a long, calming breath and saw the deer's chest expand with mine.

Houston, we have a link!

Now all I had to do was get him to turn around and guide him up the steps.

It took what seemed like eternity, but we finally managed a U-turn.

Climb.

I felt him shuffle, uncertain.

Up?

That's right. Up.

Trembling with unsteadiness and fatigue, the buck wrenched his front hooves onto the first step.

I forced a steadying breath as the buck struggled to maintain his footing. Finally, he was still.

Now, if he could just take one big step and get his hind legs free, he could jump out of the mud.

I prodded him forward.

Just a little more.

My hand was still on his back, and I eased farther along his side, thinking I'd show him how to climb.

A sudden clap of thunder rocketed through the air.

The buck started. His sharp hooves slipped in the mud. Then, in a flurry of kicks, he was free.

And I landed face-first in the muck.

I gasped as I surfaced, sputtering.

Mud clogged my eyes and I felt a hand snag my upper arm and haul me out of the pit.

"Here we go." My uncle chuckled. "Great job, Gracie."

I shivered, telling myself it was from the coolness of the muck rather than the residual stress I'd gleaned from the deer.

"You must be freezing. Come on inside."

Too unsteady to protest, I let my uncle lead me to his house, onto the oversized deck, and inside.

As soon as I stepped through the door, the spicy scent of gumbo wafted around me. I hadn't realized I was hungry, but my stomach let me know with a loud rumble. The tantalizing aroma of onions, pepper, and dark roux seemed to beckon me, and I started forward only to stop when I looked down.

"I'm ge-getting mud everywhere," I sputtered.

"These floors have seen worse. Go on and get cleaned up." He motioned toward the hall bath, and I slopped toward it.

"I still have some things of your aunt Marabelle's," Wiley said once I'd made it into the bathroom.

Wiley's wife, Marabelle, had died sometime in the seventies. I didn't want to imagine what kind of outfits he could supply me with.

"That's okay, Uncle Wiley, I can just—" I cut myself off

when I caught sight of a mirror. One look at my reflection and I knew I'd be leaving in bell-bottoms.

Wishful thinking.

I'm not sure who designed the wide-legged, plunging-halter-top jumpsuit, but they took things a bit too far when they chose gold lamé in *leopard print* for the fabric. I couldn't bring myself to look in the mirror once I had it on—it was that bad. At least I wouldn't be seen in public with the getup on. I'd rinsed my clothes out and tossed them into the dryer.

Then, gleaming like a disco ball, I walked down the hallway and into the kitchen. Wiley had retrieved Moss and Voodoo from Bluebell and they both sat looking up at my uncle as he stood at the stove, stirring a large pot.

He glanced over his shoulder at me and grinned. I placed my hands on my hips and said, "This is all you could find?"

"What do you mean? You look funkadelic!" Wiley's grin widened. "That was one of Marabelle's favorite disco outfits."

"I bet."

He chuckled and turned back to the stove.

"Set the table, I'll make us some bowls."

I fetched spoons and napkins as Wiley ladled the gumbo over rice and scooped a few oysters out to give Moss.

I set the table then flopped down onto one of the old ladder-back chairs at the kitchen table.

"Don't call me if the next critter you accidentally trap is a gator," I told Wiley as he placed the bowls on the table and settled in across from me. "They can climb perfectly well on their own."

"I usually cover my excavations with plywood. It started raining so hard the other day, I didn't have time."

"Find anything good?"

"Just a bit here and there."

Wiley was convinced he'd found a pirate camp when he'd acquired the little island forever ago.

He took a bite of gumbo, then pointed to a grimy bottle on a nearby shelf. I'd seen many like it in his collection.

"Rum bottle?" I asked.

"Wine. Still had a little liquid inside," he told me,
bright.

I sincerely hoped he hadn't drunk whatever was i
bottle, but I wouldn't put it past him.

We made short work of the gumbo and I was fe
pretty fat and happy, and growing more tired by the se
I listened, and could still hear the dryer going.

"Grace?"

"Sorry, what?"

"I was saying this is a nice piece of tabby." My unc
up the shell I'd found earlier that day.

"Of what?"

"Tabby. Do you keep it for luck?"

"No, I just found it today on the side of the road

"That's odd."

"Why?"

"Tabby wasn't used in roads. It was used to build ouses
and other structures."

"You've lost me, Uncle Wiley. The only kind tabby
I'm familiar with is the cat."

"Tabby is a mix of lime, sand, and oyster shell . Aside

"It just looks like a regular piece of shell to n
from the pearl."

"It's not. Look—you can still see traces of the ime that
made the cement." He flipped the shell over and ge of the tip
of a weathered finger over a rough line along the e
back.

"Tabby was used by the first Europeans who settled the
southeast coast."

"So you wouldn't find this in a modern struc ure?"

"I wouldn't think so, no."

I studied the piece of tabby, wondering what the heck it
was doing on the roadside behind Ozeal's place ed.

I posed this question to my uncle. He shrug d it."

"It shouldn't have—unless someone droppe king me bolt

A flare of excitement zipped through me, ma
upright.

"What? What is it?" Wiley asked.

"It's...

"Ch...

"I've ... Uncle Wiley. Thanks for the gumbo." I brushed ... his cheek, called Moss, scooped up the kitten, and ...cern over my outfit forgotten, hurried out the door.

In a rush ...were on our way, zooming over the little bridge and ...the road. I pulled out my phone to call Kai—maybe ...ould look at the tabby under a microscope and ... then I ...membered.

I couldn't ...ntact Kai.

Jake had m... quite clear. As a possible suspect in the murder of Bob...ner, it was best if I kept my distance, unless I wanted ...o make things worse.

Guilt exting...ished my excitement. My shoulders slumped under the weight of reality.

By the time I ...pulled into my spot at the condo, I was beyond bummed.

Moss nudged my cheek from the backseat, sending a wave of love to envelop me like a warm hug. I sighed, looped my arm around his neck, and roughed his ear.

"Thanks, big guy."

I grabbed both my and Brooke's purses from the front seat, swinging them onto my shoulder as I sluggishly opened the door and slid to the ground.

The temperature had dropped like a stone and I shivered in the crisp night air. The gold lamé did zero to ward off the chill.

Why did fall in North Florida have to be so bipolar? Hadn't it been seventy that morning?

I started to reach for the back door handle to let Moss out and froze.

A gun barrel was pressed against the back of my head.

CHAPTER 16

"Don't move."

It was a redundant order. I was pretty sure it would have taken a herd of rabid elephants to make me move at that point.

"Don't make a sound." The male voice was no more than a raspy whisper. "And if you think about siccing that mutt on me, I'll blow your head off."

I had a flashback to a month ago when I desperately needed to open the same door in order to save my life. My hand rested on the handle. Moss was silent, teeth bared, ready for action, but I knew my hand wasn't faster than a bullet.

"Take your hand off the door."

I did.

"Now take a step backward. Good. Keep moving."

The farther we moved away from Bluebell, the harder my heart pounded. Panic bubbled up inside me. Suddenly, my mind shifted from compliance mode to hell-no-you-will-not-be-taking-me-anywhere mode.

I stopped.

"What do you want?" I asked.

"Your purse."

"Fine, here—" I started to peel the straps off my shoulder but he jabbed the gun into the base of my skull.

"Don't move unless I tell you."

I froze.

"If you want my purse just take it." I'd been trying for calm and reasonable, but the words had come out rushed.

"Relax. I'm just putting some distance between me and your mutt. Now, keep moving."

We'd reached the edge of the lot. "Isn't this far enough?"

"Sure . . ." The sly sarcasm in his voice sent a chill through me. "Get on your knees."

On my knees?

"No." The word snapped out of my mouth before my brain could think of something better.

"There is a silencer on this gun," he informed me. "Get on your knees or I'll shoot you." As motivation, he jabbed the middle of my back with the gun.

The pavement bit into my skin through the thin fabric as I knelt.

Hamni-handachi. The aikido technique I'd practiced with Emma popped into my head. I had scoffed at the idea of fighting on my knees, but she'd told me it was about more than that. What had she said?

It was about balance. Making my attacker overextend. But this wasn't hand-to-hand. The guy had a gun, which he'd once again pressed to my head.

What could I do? If I screamed, he'd shoot me. If I tried to run, he'd shoot me.

I thought about Moss and had a sudden flash of inspiration. I couldn't scream. But Moss could howl.

A wolf's howl can be heard miles away. My assailant seemed concerned with keeping quiet—maybe he'd run if Moss raised the alarm. It wasn't a great plan, but it was all I had.

I could see my dog from my position and realized my attacker also had a clear line of sight. If Moss started making noise, he might shoot him. I focused as much as I could and sent out the mental order.

Get down on the floor. Now, Moss! Down.

Moss slipped to the floorboards. The thick steel of Bluebell's door would shield him from being seen or shot.

Howl!

Moss belted out a deep, menacing howl. The sound was enough to raise the hairs on the back of my neck. I hoped it would be enough to scare off my mugger.

Relief flooded me when the pressure of the gun was lifted from my skull.

It worked!

I turned my head slightly and out of my peripheral vision saw the man's arm come up as he aimed the gun toward Moss.

The bastard was going to try to shoot my dog.

Something in me snapped. It was one thing to mug me and even try to kill me, but my dog?

Unacceptable. In a fit of what I can only assume was insanity, I spun on my knees, ignoring the sandpaper effect the pavement had on my skin, reached up, grabbed the gun, and yanked.

There was a loud *pfft* sound and concrete exploded into shards next to me.

The gun had gone off.

Okay, pulling was not such a good idea.

My attacker jerked his hand and twisted, trying to dislodge me. But I had clamped my fingers over his wrist and was clinging to him like a barnacle on steroids.

I knew I should have been focusing on my attacker, not the weapon, but it was a lot easier said than done.

"Let go!" he growled.

"Right, so you can shoot me?"

Just then, I heard a familiar voice calling from the front door of our building.

"Hey! What's going on out there?"

Mr. Cavanaugh.

I never thought I'd be happy to hear his voice.

Before I could call out for help, my attacker grabbed a handful of my hair and tried to pry me off. I bared my teeth and made a sound that was part growl, part scream.

"What—what are you two doing out there? Decent people don't have to stand for these sort of perverted S and M shenanigans!"

We struggled a beat longer then paused.

S and M?

I glanced up at my attacker. I couldn't see his expression because his face was covered with a ski mask, but I had a feeling he was as stunned as I was.

"I'm calling the police!" My neighbor punctuated the statement by slamming his door.

I couldn't believe it—Mr. Cavanaugh had seen me struggling on my knees with a masked assailant and he'd assumed I was engaged in a sadomasochistic romp in our parking lot.

What. An. Ass.

My attacker recovered before me, twisted the gun away, stripped the purses off my arm, and sprinted into the night.

It took me several long moments to get my heart rate under control. Once I managed that, I staggered to my feet and limped to Bluebell.

I stopped at the rear door. Moss was beside himself with the need to chase down my assailant and tear him into little, tiny pieces.

I was in no condition to stop him physically, so I gave him the only command that had any hope of working.

Moss, guard.

For once, he obeyed, and when I opened the door he anchored himself to my side, still snarling like a rabid, well, wolf, of course—some things can't be helped.

Leaving the carrier for later, I scooped up Voodoo and, what seemed like a decade later, made it up the stairs and into the condo.

My legs didn't give out until I'd turned into the kitchen. I collapsed with my back against the fridge, shaking like an idiot.

Moss whined and moved to inspect my wounds. He sniffed at my bloody knees and I just managed to set the kitten down and raise my hands to block him before his tongue made contact with my skin.

"I understand you want to help, but that's just gross."

Moss let out a long, grumbling sigh and glanced at Voodoo. The kitten had rediscovered the water bowl and was batting at the liquid with the uniquely feline combination of curiosity, confusion, wariness, and excitement. Moss lowered himself to the floor and laid his head on my lap.

Okay?

"Yeah, I'm okay. I just need a minute." Or twenty.

The adrenaline rush long gone, I sat there in a daze, as if my mind had lost the power to function along with my body.

Sometimes, when I'm asleep or even just overly tired, the door to a deeper side of my mind slides open, letting the thoughts of the closest animal slip inside. It can be confusing to wake up with an odd desire to chew on a tennis ball or feel the urge to run as fast as possible down the beach. Confusing, but pretty mundane—most of the time.

Then, there are the other times . . .

Moss lifted his head. A rush of tension and hostility erupted from him, sending a wave of pinpricks over my skin. If I'd had hackles, they'd have been raised.

Guard. Moss's low growl was followed by a loud knock at the door.

He sprang to his feet.

Before I knew it, I, too, was standing, ready to fight. To protect . . . someone. It took me a moment to realize what had happened and a few more to wrench my mind free.

One bonus, the shockwave of pure aggression had kick-started my system, and I no longer felt an ounce of fatigue.

The knock sounded again. "Sheriff's office. Open up."

At the sound of the man's voice, Moss's growl evolved into a snarl.

"It's okay, Moss." *Easy.* I urged him to calm down. The last thing I needed was my dog sinking his teeth into a cop. But even as I tried to soothe him, I knew it was pointless.

"Just a second," I called out. Then, to Moss I said, "Sorry, big guy," before looping his leash through both refrigerator handles and clasping it to his collar. Emma's appliances were commercial-grade stainless steel. It would hold, right?

"I've got to get the door. I'll be back in a minute."

Moss tried to accompany me out of the kitchen but quickly reached the end of his tether. He glanced back at the leash, then shot me a look.

"I'll be fine."

He let out a vehement snort of disagreement. I left him with a pat on the head and made my way through the foyer. I opened the front door to find a deputy waiting—not all that patiently.

His brow furrowed as he took in my gleaming gold outfit. "Have you been drinking, ma'am?"

"What? No!"

"Your neighbor, Mr.—" He glanced at the little notebook in his hand.

"Cavanaugh," I supplied, already knowing where this was headed. "Who, for the record, is an idiot."

"Mr. Cavanaugh claims he witnessed you—"

I raised my hand. "In the midst of shenanigans. Yes, I know."

"So that's not the case?"

"Of course not. Do I look like that type of person?" Indignant, I crossed my arms, belatedly realizing the movement enhanced my already exposed cleavage.

Great. Perfect.

My weariness returned in a rush. I suddenly had no desire to explain what had happened. I wanted to forget about the attack, crawl into bed, and sleep for a week.

"You know what?" I said with a sigh. "You're right. I'm a shenaniganist. I'm sorry to have disturbed the peace. It won't happen again. Good night."

I started to close the door in his face, but he caught it with the toe of his shoe.

"Ma'am—"

I glared at him, but his gaze was not on my face. He was focused on my torn pant legs and bloody knees.

He lifted his eyes to meet mine and said, "Tell me what happened."

I told him everything I could remember—even managed to summon enough energy to accompany him to the parking area to walk him through it. He dutifully took notes and scanned the area with his Maglite.

The glint of metal sparked in the beam. The deputy bent down and studied the object. I moved closer and saw what it was.

"A bullet casing?" I asked.

"Yep. I'll collect it and log it as evidence."

His radio squalled to life. I listened as he updated the dispatcher, and though I'm not up to speed in police codes, I gathered my status had gone from perpetrator to victim.

Thankfully, Ponte Vedra Beach is part of Saint Johns County, so neither Kai nor Jake would hear about my drama.

"There was a robbery at a convenience store off Third Street a couple of nights ago," the deputy said as he walked me back to the door of the condo. "Guy had on a ski mask. It could be related. We have some leads on that case—it's only a matter of time before we catch the guy."

I thanked the deputy and dragged myself back into the condo.

In the kitchen, I found Moss had managed to drag the fridge a good two feet into the room. He looked up at me and hacked out a cough.

"Well that's what you get for trying to pull a refrigerator around with your neck."

Loose. Now.

I was too tired to reprimand him for his demand or try to shove the fridge back in place. With a sigh I freed the very perturbed Moss from his restraint and was shuffling toward my room when I heard the front door open behind me.

"Mr. Cavanaugh called," my sister announced from the foyer. She tossed her keys on the entry table, flipping on the light as she walked toward me. "So, you're turning tricks—"

She froze mid-sentence. "What are you . . . Is that gold lamé?"

I turned to face her and Emma's eyes went wide with alarm.

"What the hell?" My sister rushed forward. Moss, who was still on edge, let out a snarl that would have made grown men wet themselves.

Emma only paused for a moment then continued forward more slowly.

"You're bleeding."

"I know."

"What happened?"

"You know that knee-walking technique? It's not so good on cement."

"No. I would think not." Emma guided me into her bathroom. "Come on. Sit on the edge of the tub and let's have a look."

Though my medical training definitely trumped my sister's, I obeyed passively, comforted by the way she went into big-sister mode. She fumbled with the large, shredded pant legs but managed to push them up over my knees. "Tell me what happened," Emma said as she dabbed at my scrapes with a washcloth.

"Mugged." I explained everything, starting from the moment I felt the gun pressing against my head. By the time I'd finished, we had moved to the living room, my wounds were clean and dry, I'd changed into cutoff sweats and a long-sleeved T-shirt, and my sister had gone into Terminator mode.

Most days, I was her personal pain in the ass. But mess with me, and I became her baby sister. Like a tiger anxious to sink its teeth into its next meal, she prowled in front of where I sat on the couch.

"Criminals can't just come here and mug people. This is Ponte Vedra."

I rolled my eyes at my sister's indignant tone. Our posh little enclave wasn't immune to crime. Nowhere was.

"I'm fine, Emma."

"Why didn't you have Moss with you?"

I'd already answered her once; I didn't bother to do it again. My sister's questions had become rhetorical.

"I still think you should call Kai. No matter how much trouble he's in at work."

"Because of me."

"He would want to know, Grace."

"I told the deputy everything I could remember. They'll handle it."

"That's not what I meant."

I knew what she meant. But I didn't think I could handle any more emotional turbulence. Between my sister's reaction and Moss's, I'd met my quota on that already.

Voodoo, of course, was unfazed by my brush with death. As my sister paced, the kitten watched from her favorite ambush spot—which was anywhere near Moss.

At first, I thought she was missing the point of the concept, then I realized the little cat was a genius. Next to Moss, who would notice a two-pound kitten?

Voodoo's eyes were fixed on Emma's bare feet. The kitten crouched lower, wiggled her butt, and sprang onto my sister's foot, landing for a millisecond before tumbling off. She raced in a circle and came back for round two.

Emma had become used to Voodoo's kitty insanity, and put a stop to the mania by scooping the kitten up into her arms and scratching her under her chin. Voodoo instantly melted into a puddle of relaxed kitty bliss. She was purring so loudly I had to wonder how such a small creature could possibly produce such a sound.

"The condo needs better security," Emma said.

There was a knock at the door. Emma's gaze narrowed as she turned toward the entrance. She took two steps toward me and deposited the semicomatose kitten in my lap.

"Stay here," she ordered and headed toward the door.

I glanced down at Voodoo. She hadn't moved. She looked boneless. I would love to be able to sleep like that. A voice from the foyer made my head snap up.

Kai walked into the room straight toward me. My sister

was conspicuously absent. I stood, thankful I'd changed out of the gilded disco outfit.

Voodoo started to slide out of my hand and I had to tuck her into the crook of my arm as I moved to face him.

Kai's intense gaze searched my face. "Are you okay?"

I nodded. Moss, who had been drooling on a custom-made silk cushion, was roused by Kai's presence and sat up with a growl.

I glanced at him. *Leave it alone.*

Guard. Moss blinked at me and fixed his attention on Kai.

I was too tired to argue.

"I'm okay," I told Kai.

He gave me a second once-over, pausing at my bandaged knees. A muscle worked in his jaw.

Kai's anger drew another growl from Moss.

"I'm fine. The asshole wanted my purse—I gave it to him. I didn't see his face. But you know this already somehow, right?"

"I have a friend at Saint Johns dispatch who heard your name come across the radio and called me."

I wasn't sure what to make of that. Before I could decide if I was offended or flattered, Kai hooked his finger under my chin and kissed me.

And I mean *kissed.*

It was a real chart topper that left my body warm and my brain numb. When he eased back, I opened my eyes and blinked up at him as I tried to collect my senses.

"Uh . . ." was all I managed.

His lips quirked into a smug half smile. "That good?"

"It's Voodoo. Her happy-cat brain waves are bleeding into me."

Kai looked down at the kitten. "She looks dead."

"No. Just in a bliss-induced stupor." We both regarded the kitten for a moment, then Kai said, "I'm going to look around outside. I'll be back in a few minutes. Stay here."

I shook my head as I watched him walk away. What was it with people telling me to stay put? Did I look like I was getting ready to run a marathon?

Still holding the kitten, I sat on the couch to wait. Voodoo's happy oblivion rippled over me with each purr, making my eyelids droop.

Kai returned after a few minutes, sat on the block of cut driftwood that served as our coffee table, and studied my face the way that always made me feel as if he was trying to uncover some bit of evidence he'd missed.

"What?"

"I'm tempted to ask you to walk me through what happened but you look tired."

"I am." I set the kitten on the floor next to Moss. "Besides, I already told the deputy from Saint Johns everything and you—" I stopped, not sure what to say.

Kai raised his brows and waited.

"You—Jake said you're in trouble at work."

"Suspended at the moment."

"Because you were helping me look for Brooke?"

"It's just a lot of bureaucratic BS. Everything will get sorted out. Listen, Grace, there's something you need to know. Brooke is the daughter of a very dangerous man."

I nodded. I really didn't want to tell Kai I'd spoken to Sartori but I wasn't a liar and I wasn't a coward.

Usually.

"I'm not talking about Bob Ligner," Kai said. "Brooke's real father is a man named—"

"Charles Sartori. I know."

Kai's brows drew together, then his eyes narrowed.

Oh boy, here goes.

"He called me."

"Called you." Kai didn't phrase the words as a question, which made them seem more angry.

"He found out I was looking for Brooke and called because he's worried about her, too."

"When was this?"

"Last night."

"What else did he say?"

"Nothing. Just that he was worried about Brooke and . . ."

Oh man, I didn't want to tell him this part.

"And . . ." he prompted.

"He wanted me to meet with some of his . . . people to tell them what I knew."

"And you agreed."

"It wasn't really a request."

He blew out a sigh and tilted his head back to stare at the ceiling.

"Look, it wasn't a big deal," I said.

He leveled his gaze on me.

"Yes, Grace, it is a big deal. You're telling me you met with mobsters."

"They're trying to find Brooke."

"I don't care if they're trying to find a cure for cancer. These men are dangerous."

I opened my mouth to defend myself but he talked over me.

"Has it occurred to you that Brooke might have been taken by one of Sartori's enemies? And by associating with Sartori's *people* you put yourself on their radar?"

"But—"

"You think you were mugged tonight at random?"

"I—"

"How many average thugs use a gun with a silencer?"

It was a good point.

"You think my mugging is connected to Sartori?"

"I'm not sure it was a mugging at all. Bob Ligner was executed. Forced to his knees and shot."

"Oh, God." I felt the color drain from my face. Moss rolled to his feet with a sudden growl in response. I reached out with a shaking hand to clamp my fingers in the fur of his coat.

Guard.

I'm okay. I forced a steadying breath.

"I think you might have been a target, Grace."

"But why? Why would someone want to kill me?"

"I don't know. Maybe you've gotten close to finding something someone doesn't want you to find."

"Like what? I'm looking for a teenage girl."

"All I know is Sartori is getting out of prison in a few

days. Bob Ligner was murdered. Brooke is missing. None of this is good, and you being in the middle of it is making me crazy."

I looked away, heat scorching my cheeks. Why couldn't I process the idea that Kai cared about me without feeling like a fool?

"I want to talk to your supervisor," I said, desperate to change the subject.

Kai leaned back and regarded me.

"Why?"

"You're suspended because I asked for your help. That isn't right."

"Don't worry about me," he said and stood. "I'm going to make a few calls. See if I can talk someone from Saint Johns into coming out and looking more closely at what happened tonight."

"They have the shell casing," I said.

"Which is good. We—*they*—might be able to match it to evidence from the Ligners' house. But it can't hurt to have another look around. There could be more evidence the deputy missed."

I walked him to the door. "You're sure there's nothing I can do?"

"You can stay safe. I'd hate to have to kill someone. Then I'd really lose my job."

CHAPTER 17

I nudged the piece of broken glass with the toe of my tennis shoe.

Kai had called to let me know he hadn't been able to convince anyone from the Saint Johns CSU that my mugging could be linked to the Ligner murder. They were working the convenience store robbery angle and didn't want Kai's input.

Apparently, he was being blacklisted because of the investigation into his involvement with Sartori, which was continuing during the day with more meetings and depositions.

I felt a surge of guilt and anger at the thought, but pushed the feelings aside. Kai might not be able to look for evidence, but I could.

Instead of our usual walk on the beach, I had decided to take Moss through the parking lot where the mugging had taken place the night before. Two pairs of eyes are better than one.

We'd stopped under the large security light that usually illuminated the section of the parking lot from where my mugger had come. Glass littered the ground and sparkled like diamonds in the morning sun. I looked up at the light.

Shattered.

I thought of the silencer on the gun and a shiver ran through me. Had my attacker planned this? Had he been lurking in the dark waiting for me? The idea of being watched gave me the heebie-jeebies, and I looked over my shoulder just as Moss tugged the leash to drag me away from the parking lot to the line of hawthorn bushes that separated our condominium from the next property. He let out a soft *woof,* lowered himself onto his belly, and squirmed under one of the thick bushes.

I squatted down, wincing as the unyielding denim of my jeans pressed against my injured knees. I squinted through the leaves and spotted what Moss had discovered.

"My purse."

"Woof," he agreed.

I reached past my dog and grabbed the strap, dragging it out from where it had obviously been discarded.

I opened it—keys, wallet, phone. Nothing seemed to be missing. If it had been a robbery, why wasn't anything taken?

Unless Kai was right, and I had been targeted for more than a random mugging.

Maybe it was wishful thinking, but my gut was telling me I hadn't been. Slinging the strap over my shoulder, I followed as Moss sniffed around a bit more.

As we walked, another idea started taking shape. One that made more sense than a random mugging or planned hit. I wanted to talk to Kai and get his input but would have to wait. He'd told me he would call when he got the chance, and who knew when that would be.

Our earlier conversation had been rushed and I'd been so tired the night before, I'd forgotten to tell him about my hunt through the woods behind Happy Asses for Brooke's scent trail, and about finding the tabby and getting a ride with Logan—a man who may or may not be the elusive Ghost.

I grimaced inwardly. I had a feeling Kai wasn't going to like that last part.

Satisfied there was nothing more to discover in the parking lot, Moss and I headed inside.

Moss trotted off to check on Voodoo as I set my bag on the counter and poured myself a cup of coffee.

"Hey, you found your purse." My sister paused as she walked into the kitchen. Her hair was pulled back in a fashionable twist that showed off the sapphire earrings she wore.

"Moss did, actually."

I told her about the broken light and the location of my bag.

"But I'm starting to think this isn't about me or my purse."

"Then why were you mugged?"

"Because I wasn't just carrying my purse. I had Brooke's, too. I found it at Happy Asses and unsuccessfully tried to use it to locate her trail in the woods."

"I'm not following you, Grace. You think someone mugged you because they wanted Brooke's purse? Why?"

"That's just it, I don't know. There wasn't anything unusual in it. At least not that I remember. Her wallet, a brush, keys—"

"Keys? To what? I thought you said she didn't have a car."

"Her house key, I guess, and . . ."

Emma arched her brows. "And?"

"What if that's what they wanted? A way into Brooke's house?"

"Someone eviscerated those poor stuffed animals looking for something."

"Kai thinks Brooke might have hidden Stefan's stash for him."

"If she did, he, or someone he knows, could be after it," Emma said.

"I don't know. Stefan didn't seem like the type of guy to commit armed robbery. He ran from me in the mall, remember?"

"Well, you were pant-less."

"Not going to let that go, are you?"

She shook her head. "If I could get my hands on that security footage . . ."

"You would be a good sister and burn it."

"After uploading it to YouTube."

"You wouldn't."

"You're right. But it would still be incentive to stay on my good side." Emma looked at my purse and asked, "You're sure nothing's missing?"

I opened my purse and dumped the contents onto the kitchen counter. The piece of tabby tumbled out. I caught it before it could go over the edge and held up the shell. Once again I was struck with the feeling that it was some sort of clue.

"What's that?" Emma asked.

"A piece of tabby."

"Of what?" I relayed what I learned from Uncle Wiley about the shell.

"And you found it near where Brooke went missing?"

I nodded. "It has to mean something, right?"

"Maybe. What did Kai think?"

"I haven't told him yet. I was going to ask him to examine it with his fancy *CSI* stuff. But thanks to me he's been suspended."

"Well, that's . . . unfortunate."

Understatement.

"Why don't you ask Uncle Wiley? Maybe he can tell you more about this stuff. Where it comes from or something?"

It was a good idea. I called Wiley, who was more than happy to meet me for breakfast and tell me all he knew about tabby, which turned out to be quite a bit.

• • •

"Look here, see?" Wiley held up the shell. "This is fossilized. You can tell by the color. A fresh oyster shell will be bleached white by the sun. This one is gray and kind of lustrous, which means it came from some of the prehistoric middens that the native Americans had left behind."

"So you think this came from a specific place?" I asked before downing the last bite of my hash browns cooked with onions and jalapeños and covered in cheese. Delicious.

"Stands to reason. There aren't that many old tabby structures in the area."

"Do you know where they are?"

"Well," he said. "The Kingsley Plantation on Fort George Island, for starters."

Fort George? Hadn't I just talked to someone about Fort George? My mind tried to shake the memory loose but it didn't come.

"And people used tabby for other things, too," Wiley continued. "There are even some tabby grave markers up around Fernandina Beach."

"Grave markers?"

"Yep. I know of one cemetery with a tabby wall around it."

"Can you tell me where it is?"

"Well . . ."

I narrowed my eyes. "What? It's on private property, isn't it?"

"Yes. But I know the woman who owns the place."

"I don't need to get arrested for trespassing." Especially since I'd trespassed at the Ligners' and Bob Ligner was dead. I shook off the thought.

One thing at a time, Grace.

"Why don't we split up?" Wiley asked. "I'll take a look around the cemetery and you can go to Fort George."

I agreed, and as I climbed into Bluebell it hit me.

Doc at Billy's Feed and Seed had mentioned a farm and fishing supply store near Fort George. It had gone out of business, which was why he'd gotten so many new customers.

New customers—like the young man in the dark ball cap who'd followed Brooke.

Had I found a clue after all?

I cranked Bluebell's engine and headed north to find out.

Half an hour later, I located what used to be the farm and fishing supply off Heckscher Drive, less than a mile past the bridge leading to Fort George Island. I pulled into the drive and parked, getting out and crouching to examine the oyster-shell-and-gravel lot. Just as my uncle had said, there was a marked difference between the shell I had found and these cracked and dusty modern oysters.

Though it reaffirmed his claim that my shell was tabby, it also meant the shell hadn't come from the parking lot.

Not the most encouraging start.

The store looked more like an old farmhouse than a farm supply business. But as I stepped up onto the wraparound porch, I knew I was in the right place.

Cupping my hand against the glass, I peered through the front window, surprised to find the shelves remained fairly well stocked for a place that had gone out of business.

Had the bank foreclosed that quickly?

I started around the side of the porch and paused at the sound of a low voice. A man's voice, actually, echoed from behind the building.

I crept to the corner and listened.

"I know it's not much, but till I get paid, this is all I can do."

He paused.

"Next week will be better, I promise."

Another pause.

"Well, I've got to get back to work, now."

I slowly peered around the corner, expecting to see the man talking on a cell phone. Instead, I saw him standing near the opposite side of the building with his back to me. He hummed as he dipped a brush into a can of paint and brought it up to sweep over the wood siding.

For a moment, I thought he'd been talking to himself, but then I registered the presence of a feline. I turned and spotted the cat huddled under a small carport. It was completely focused on the small tray of dry cat food on the ground in front of it. I homed in on the cat's thoughts. It was happy and relieved to have food. I began to draw my attention back to the man when I sensed more cats nearby.

I scanned the area, noting the full-size tan pickup truck and what appeared to be a long, narrow storage shed. The door to the shed was open and after a moment several more cats scurried from their hiding places to get their share of the food.

Before long, five more cats surrounded the tray, including

a heavily pregnant female. Within seconds, the food was gone.

The first cat licked its chops and walked to the man to begin rubbing against his leg, begging for a second helping.

"Go on now, Buddy, you know I don't have any more."

Buddy persisted with some plaintive mews then gave up. He stalked back to the empty food tray, sniffed it, then wandered off to find a sunny spot for a bath.

I hadn't expected to run into anyone at the store, let alone a fellow animal lover. Hopefully, the man would be able to tell me where I could find the previous owner.

I stepped around the corner and said, "That's nice, feeding the strays."

The man turned to me, surprised. He was young and muscled in a way that hinted more toward physical labor than time in the gym.

"The what?"

"The cats."

"Oh. Those are Mr. Reedy's cats. He can't get around too well so I help out some."

"Mr. Reedy?"

"His family owned this place for a hundred years. He asked me to paint it for him but I haven't had much luck lately with all the rain." He sighed, shoulders slumping, as if his failure was a measure of his character.

"Can't do anything about the weather."

He brightened at my words. "No, ma'am. That's up to the Lord. 'God is in heaven, he hath done as he pleases.' That's what the Bible says."

I smiled and nodded. I'd have to take his word for it. I only knew one quote from the Bible—the one Sonja had had engraved on the back of a Saint Francis medal for me. It was hard not to memorize something that dangled around your neck every day.

"Do you know where I could find Mr. Reedy?" I asked.

"If he's not here I'd try his house. Just head up Fort George Road then make your first left. He's up about a half mile on your left. You can't miss it. Just look for the BEWARE OF THE DOG sign."

"Thank you. I'm sorry—what's your name?"

"Josiah."

"I'm Grace."

"A pleasure, Miss Grace. Oh, and don't worry about those old dogs of his, their bark is worse than their bite."

· · ·

I hadn't been to Fort George Island in a while. The area was heavily wooded with live oaks and a thick undergrowth of palmettos. I had doubts I'd find Reedy's place as easily as Josiah had promised but my concern proved unwarranted.

I pulled into a dirt driveway with signs posted on either side depicting vicious-looking canines and the word BEWARE!

Everything Josiah described in his directions was accurate— with one exception. Those "old dogs" happened to be four lean, exceptionally disgruntled pit bulls.

As I rolled to a stop at the fence, they barked like mad and eyed me with silent menace as I approached.

I could smell brine and knew the salt marsh must be close, but I couldn't see through the thicket of surrounding palmettos to discern a direction.

Spanish moss hung heavily in the trees, so thick that even the bright morning sun couldn't pierce the gray-green curtain.

I scanned the area for a tabby ruin, but saw nothing more than a small dilapidated shed.

The house, too, was run-down. The cedar planks making up the exterior had warped and faded to a moldering gray. One of the front porch posts was missing, making the corner droop. It reminded me of a partial frown. Dogs aside, Reedy's house had to be one of the most forbidding places I'd ever seen.

It was a creepy kidnapper's lair if there ever was one.

I turned my attention back to the dogs and was just about

to ask about a dark-haired girl when the front door opened and, after a moment, a man emerged from the shadows.

I knew two things instantly.

One—I'd found Mr. Reedy. And two—he was not a kidnapper. That is, unless he'd found a way to use his portable oxygen tank to subdue his victims.

"What do you want?" he gasped. Two of the dogs trotted to him as he spoke; the other two remained in their positions, watching me.

"Mr. Reedy? I'd like to speak to you for a few minutes if you have the time."

"You go back to the bank and tell them they can kiss—"

"I'm not here from the bank," I said, cutting him off. "I have a question about one of your old customers. Please. It's important."

"Oh, I'm sure it is," he muttered and began to turn away.

"Wait." I put my hand on the gate and the dog closest to me let out a warning growl.

"I wouldn't do that if I were you. They don't let anyone in the gate unless I say the word."

"Oh? And what's the word?"

"Wouldn't you like to know."

And with that, he wheeled his oxygen tank around and shuffled inside.

I sighed and looked down at the brindle dog. "So, who wants to tell me the magic word?"

It turned out to be fizzlesticks. And once I uttered it, accompanied by a heavy dose of calming, confident energy, the dogs became their goofy, grinning selves.

To say Mr. Reedy was shocked to find me standing at his front door, flanked by two happily panting pit bulls, would have been an understatement.

"How the hell did you do that?"

"Wouldn't you like to know?" I parroted his words and thought I saw his lips quirk under his grizzly facial hair. "How about this? Ask me in and I'll tell you."

Clearly intrigued, he opened the door and ushered me

inside. I was greeted with the odor of stale cigarette smoke and wet dog.

Not exactly pleasant, but bearable.

I followed him to a small living room, where he lowered himself onto a blue corduroy recliner. He motioned to an adjacent blue plaid couch.

Once I sat, he asked, "Okay, how did you get past my dogs, Ms. . . ."

"Wilde. Grace Wilde. I'm an animal behaviorist. I know all the tricks."

He made a skeptical grunt then took a pack of cigarettes from his breast pocket and tapped one out. Mr. Reedy looked like he needed a shave, a shower, and a break in life.

"Please don't," I said.

"Don't worry about me, sweetheart. My lungs are shot."

"Mine aren't."

He paused to regard me as he raised the cigarette toward his lips. "You telling me not to smoke in my own house?"

"No. I'm *asking* you not to smoke in your own house."

He blinked at me, stunned, then let out a bark of laughter that devolved into a hacking cough.

"I like you. Even if you are from the bank," he proclaimed when he could catch his breath. Then he lifted a can of beer from the side table and raised it in salute. "You've got spunk."

"I'm not from the bank."

"Right, you're an animal whatever it was."

"Behaviorist." I dug a card out of my back pocket and handed it to him.

"Why would an animal behaviorist want to know about my customers?"

I gave him the shortest version I could. Explaining that the man at Billy's Feed and Seed who seemed to have followed Brooke might be an old customer.

"You think one of my customers kidnapped this girl?"

"I don't know, but I'd at least like to find him." I described the young man and added, "He bought three fifty-pound bags of garden soil and a twenty-five-pound bag of cat litter."

Reedy shook his head. "I don't—" The rest of what he was going to say was lost in another fit of coughing.

He tipped back the beer, finished off the last gulp, and dabbed at his tearing eyes with a handkerchief he pulled from the same pocket that housed the cigarettes.

He held out the can. "Mind getting me another one?"

I took the can, walked into the tiny, cluttered kitchen, and dropped it in the trash. I found a clean glass in a cabinet and as I filled the glass at the sink, something caught my attention.

The weak presence of a canine nearby. Hurting.

Turning to glance around, I noticed a laundry room off the kitchen. I poked my head through the door to find a dog curled in a ball on a pile of old blankets.

I knew instantly the dog had been injured in some way.

The animal slowly lifted its head and blinked at me with bleary eyes.

"Hey, girl." I squatted down and, though I didn't touch her, I offered as much comfort as I could with my thoughts as I assessed her injuries.

I felt soreness and fatigue. And a hint of wooziness that went along with pain medication.

A quick glance at the prescription bottles on the washing machine told me what I needed to know.

"I noticed you have an injured dog," I said to Reedy as I handed him the glass of water.

"What's this?" he asked, staring at the glass.

"You're welcome."

He set the glass aside with a snort.

"If you agree to look into your old customer files for me, I'll make sure she gets the medicine she needs. I'll also come back and take the sutures out so you don't have to make a trip to the vet."

"Really—and how are you going to do that?"

"I'm a veterinarian."

"You a ventriloquist, too?"

"Smart ass."

He coughed out a laugh. "All right, you've got a deal. I'll

just have to figure out how to get to the files—they're in storage and they weigh a ton."

I thought about the fit and eager painter I'd met.

"There was a man at your place working—he said his name was Josiah. Maybe he could help."

"That boy." Reedy *tsk*ed with a shake of his head. "I haven't been out much in the last few months. I guess I need to try to get it through his head to stop trying to take care of the place."

"He seemed a little . . . slow."

"Wasn't always." He tapped a finger to his head. "Had an accident a while back. Made him simple. He's always been softhearted, though. Trying to take care of everyone."

"He was feeding your cats."

"Cats? There shouldn't be more than one—Buddy."

"Well, word has spread. You've got a colony going now."

"Peachy."

"I have a friend at the ASPCA. If you don't mind giving up the cats, I might be able to find them homes."

"That sounds good to me. Hell, I can't bring them here," Reedy said. "Rhett would probably kill one of them, the way he goes after the squirrels. And now, with Scarlett hurt, I don't know how I'd pay to feed them."

"Rhett and Scarlett?"

"I've got Melanie, Ashley, and Belle, too." He grinned.

• • •

I called Sonja. Miraculously the ASPCA had room for the cats. She agreed to meet me with extra carriers and a couple of nets. I was pretty good at cat wrangling, but felines could be, well, feline, and refuse to cooperate despite my proclamations of good intentions.

Uncle Wiley called as I was pulling into the old farm supply store.

"You aren't in jail, are you?" I asked.

"Nope," he said with a chuckle. "That's the good news. The bad news is I don't think your piece of tabby came from up here. The color of the shell's different."

I told him I hadn't done much better in my search and he promised to keep looking and call if he found a possible location.

I pushed the tabby out of my head as I drove around the building and stopped.

The tan truck was gone, as was Josiah.

Just as well—I didn't want to upset him.

Sonja arrived not long after I'd climbed out of Bluebell and cast my mental feelers out for a head count.

"Hey," she said, stepping up to stand next to me.

I muttered a distracted greeting, too focused on my task to offer more.

A few of the more curious cats stepped out of the shed to peer at us. I homed in on each animal. Though I couldn't be a hundred percent sure of how many cats were in the area, I was able to gauge how skittish or tame they were.

I sensed a mixture of hopefulness, hunger, and wariness, but none of the animals was plagued by the bone-deep fear of humans that would indicate a feral.

"I'm counting somewhere between five and six," I told Sonja. As I said the words, my mind caught the trace of something . . . else. I focused on the quick, panicked thoughts. One of the cats had caught a rodent. I closed my mind off to that particular circle-of-life moment with a grimace.

"What is it?"

"One of the cats is making a meal out of a mouse."

"Eew." She made a face.

"Yeah."

"Feral?"

"Not that I can tell. Skittish, but they're hungry. They'll come once they smell the food."

"The oldest trick in the book," she mused.

"Whatever works," I said and shook the bag of cat food Sonja handed me.

She popped open a can of cat food and called out, "Who's hungry?"

Buddy was the first to succumb to temptation, trotting over with a happy *meow* to ribbon through my legs. Sonja was able to coax him into a carrier with a bit of mental encouragement from me and a dollop of wet cat food.

We rounded up the rest in similar fashion—five in all— and were loading the carriers into the ASPCA van when Josiah's tan truck pulled around the side of the building.

"Crap."

"What?" Sonja asked.

"This guy is kind of mentally challenged—he's been feeding the cats. I was hoping to avoid having to explain where we're taking them."

"Miss Grace? What are you—" His eyes went wide in alarm when he saw the cat carrier I held and the stack already in the van. "What are you doing?"

"We're taking them to find new homes. It's okay, Mr. Reedy said so."

"But this is their home."

"Josiah, I'm sorry, but they need—"

"And—and Mr. Reedy said I could look after them."

"I'm going to look after them now, okay?"

"No! They are my responsibility." He snatched the carrier out of my hands. The jostled cat let out an alarmed yowl, which only seemed to upset Josiah more.

"Josiah." I spoke in a calm, stern voice, the one I reserved for overexcited elephants. "Put the cat carrier down. Now."

"The Bible says to rescue the weak and the needy; deliver them from the hand of the wicked."

I would have been offended if it hadn't been for the tears threatening to spill from his wide eyes. I looked at Sonja for help. She eased closer to him.

"That's right, Josiah," she said. "We who are strong have an obligation to bear the infirmities of the weak, don't we?"

Josiah's wild, roving gaze swiveled to focus on her.

"And the Bible also says that you who are younger be subject to the elders. So we should respect Mr. Reedy's wishes."

"He asked me to take care of them. He wants me to."

"I know. But things are different now. The cats aren't getting enough food, are they?"

Josiah's eyes became dark pools of utter despair. Tears began to fall in wide streams.

"I'm sorry. I'm so sorry."

"I know you are, Josiah." Sonja's voice was low and lulling. She eased the carrier out of his arms and handed it to me, then led Josiah to sit on the nearby steps.

I slid the carrier, with its irritated but unharmed occupant, into place next to his comrades and shut the van's door.

As I walked to where Sonja and Josiah stood, I could hear her talking to him in a soft, reassuring voice.

"I told my sister I'd bring her a kitten," Josiah said. He was no longer crying but he seemed miserable.

"You can still have a kitten. I promise," Sonja assured him. "You and your sister can come pick one out once they're old enough. That way, she can get whichever one she wants. How does that sound?"

He swallowed hard and nodded.

Without looking at me, she said, "You go ahead, Grace. I'll meet you at the center."

Something in her tone made me pause. The way she said my name. Terse and angry.

I blinked at her, baffled at what I'd done to raise her ire. Sonja was understanding and lighthearted—I rarely saw her angry.

She continued to talk to Josiah and shooed me away with one hand. I did as she asked, bewildered.

My problem, in a nutshell: I could soothe a panicking polar bear but when it came to people I was clueless.

• • •

"What was I supposed to do, Sonja? You saw how upset he was."

"Which is why you should have waited and talked to him *before* we'd packed up his cats to zoom off with them."

"They aren't his cats."

"Doesn't matter whose cats they are," she said as we toted the last two cat carriers into the ASPCA.

She let out a long, heavy breath, set the carrier down with the others, and turned to me.

"He cared about them. It just about broke his heart thinking he'd failed to care for these cats."

"Sonja, he's had a brain injury—the guy isn't all there."

"And that makes it okay?"

"No—"

"I do *not* like hurting people, Grace." Sonja's dark eyes bored into me. "And I do not like picking on people."

"What are you talking about, Sonja? You calmed Josiah down."

"By making him believe he'd done wrong." Her expression was one I'd never seen on her smooth, dark face. A mix of anger and regret. I realized I was the person who put it there and my eyes watered, stinging with unshed tears. I swallowed them back.

"I'm sorry, Sonja," I said around the lump in my throat. Her face softened abruptly.

"Oh, now. Don't you start, too."

"I wasn't thinking."

"It's not your fault. It's natural to focus on what you're good at and ignore the rest."

"I don't mean to."

"I know," she said softly. "Come on, let's get these guys settled in. It might be a while before one of the docs will be able to take a look at them."

We worked side by side, and after a while, I started feeling a little less like a bad friend.

"That's enough moping," Sonja said, as if she were the one who could read minds. "You're making me feel like I kicked a puppy."

"Sorry."

"You can make it up to me by bringing that handsome mutt of yours to see me. How're Moss and his kitty?"

"Moss is still acting like a mother hen—he likes to carry the kitten around. Poor Voodoo, she's constantly coated in dog spit."

"You named the kitten Voodoo?"

I told Sonja the story behind the kitten's name and the tension between us dissolved like mist in the sunshine. I was lucky to have her as a friend. Lucky to have my sister and . . . I had a sudden flash of Kai's face.

I thought about how warm his lips had been when he'd kissed me.

Heat flushed into my cheeks when I thought about that kiss, prompting Sonja to ask, "What is it? Why are you looking all dreamy?"

"I don't know what you're talking about."

"I'm talking about that goofy look on your face."

I changed the subject. "Hey, way to bust out with the scripture earlier. Should I start calling you Sister Sonja?"

She crossed her arms and flicked her gaze over me. "Nice try."

I gave her a wide-eyed shrug. "What?"

"Please, girl. I can see you blush. Start talkin'."

I shook my head with a smile. I didn't want to get into the mugging so I said, "Kai kissed me last night. It was . . . nice."

"Nice? That's it? Nice?"

"More than nice."

"I guess so, judging from that look."

I waved the subject off as I went to get the last two cats and settle them into cages.

The cats were wary of their new surroundings—all except one. Buddy made it clear he wasn't interested in where he was as long as food would be provided.

The cat's hunger reminded me of Felix. I hoped Brooke's cat was still charming the lady next door, because I certainly couldn't drive over there and check on him.

My thoughts jumped to Bob Ligner's murder. Chances were, whoever killed him had something to do with Brooke's kidnapping.

But why? Was this really all about Sartori? Brooke was only sixteen. It seemed logical that between a mob boss and his daughter, he would be the more likely catalyst. But what about the man who'd followed her at the feed and seed?

I brought Buddy some food, and thought about the mug shot Kai had shown me of Brooke and how different that girl seemed from the fresh-faced, dark-haired beauty of Boris's memory.

As I absently ran my hand down Buddy's back, an image popped into my mind.

A girl with dark hair calling to the cat as she poured food on a small tray.

Brooke?

What the . . . ? I stared at the cat, realizing he had shown me a memory. Had Buddy seen Brooke with Josiah?

"Grace? Are you okay? What is it?" Sonja returned from her phone call and was looking at me with concern.

"I've got to check on something," I told her as I headed past her toward the door.

I sped to the farm and fishing supply, skidded around the building, and ground Bluebell to a stop at an angle behind Josiah's pickup truck.

I sat there for a moment, breathing hard. Josiah had taken up his painting duties and stood on a ladder he'd propped against the side of the building. He'd looked over his shoulder at me, puzzled. I gave him what I hoped was a friendly smile and a wave. He returned both and began to climb down the ladder.

Suddenly, I was both relieved and slightly panicked to discover he was still there. Of all the stupid things to do, I had driven out here alone to confront the man who might have kidnapped Brooke.

I sent Emma a text message on the off chance I disappeared, too.

Talking to a guy named Josiah at the old farm and fishing supply. Heckscher Dr. RE: Brooke. Don't call me but if I don't send you another message in ten minutes send the police.

I put the phone on vibrate, knowing Emma would flip when she saw the message and call me anyway.

Climbing out of Bluebell, I stuffed my phone in my back pocket and walked slowly toward Josiah. After my dramatic arrival my cautious approach probably seemed odd. He was regarding me with the curious, confused expression I'd seen before.

"Miss Grace. What are you doing back here?"

"I'm looking for someone. A girl named Brooke."

He had no discernible reaction to the name.

"Brooke? I don't know anyone named Brooke."

"So you haven't seen anyone else here?"

"No, I sure haven't."

My phone vibrated in my pocket. I pulled it out and glanced at the screen. Emma.

I ignored the call and paused, trying to come up with a way to show Josiah a photo of Brooke so I could gauge his reaction.

"Actually," I said, "I've asked around about her and no one seems to know where she is. If I show you a picture of her can you tell me if you've seen her anywhere?"

I pulled up the photo I'd gotten of her and held it out to him.

This time, there was a reaction.

"Mercy. She looks a lot like my sister."

"Your sister?"

"Abigail. Remember? You said we could come pick out a kitten?"

I flinched when he moved to extract his wallet from his back pocket. Must still be jumpy from my mugging *shenanigans*.

Josiah flipped the worn wallet open and showed me a school photo of a girl who looked enough like Brooke to be her sister.

The photo on the opposite side was a family portrait showing a younger, grinning Abigail, Josiah, and a woman I presumed was their mother.

A mixture of relief and disappointment settled over me.

I didn't want to believe Josiah, the sweet, simple guy who spent his paycheck on food for needy cats was a kidnapper, but eliminating him as a suspect left me with nothing.

"The girl you're looking for, is she from around here? 'Cause I know everybody around here, just about. My mama says, a good Christian should be selfless and help others when they can. Maybe I can help you find her."

"That's okay, I think I've looked as much as I can." A fact I was going to have to face, whether I liked it or not.

"Well, I'll keep my eye out, anyway," he said with a solemn nod.

"Thanks, Josiah."

My phone buzzed again, vibrating in my hand as I walked to Bluebell.

"Hey, Em. Sorry."

"Sorry? I was three seconds from calling the police. What's going on?"

"Nothing." I climbed into Bluebell and started the engine. "Dead end."

So far, I'd slogged through the muddy woods, streaked through the mall in pursuit of a juvenile delinquent, struck a deal with the mob, staked out a misogynist, and questioned a cougar, a tiger, a tabby cat, and a donkey.

There was only one thing left to do.

CHAPTER 18

As it was lunchtime, I had a good idea where I would find Detective Jake Nocera.

Casa Dora was popular, so I had to park a couple of blocks away and walk to the little Italian restaurant.

As soon as I pushed the glass door open, the aroma of fresh bread, garlic, and spices wrapped around me, comforting as an old bathrobe.

I paused for a moment to enjoy the homey, cheerful ambience of the place before turning to scan the area for Jake. I spotted him at a table next to the brick archway that led to the other side of the restaurant.

I walked to his table and said, "I have a feeling that's not on your diet."

Jake glanced up from his huge plate of lasagna, eyes going cool at the sight of me. He gave the man seated across from him a curt nod, which must have been some unspoken gesture of dismissal because the guy slid out of his chair, leaving the seat empty for me. I took his place and set the oyster shell fragment on the table between us.

"What's this?" he asked, gesturing at the piece of tabby with his fork.

"It's a clue."

"A clue to what?"

"Brooke's disappearance. I found it close to where she went missing. According to my uncle, it's a piece of tabby."

"Of what?"

I gave him a brief explanation, then told him about the man seen following Brooke out of Billy's Feed and Seed, the connection I'd made to Fort George Island, and the old farm supply store.

"I thought it would pan out, but it was a dead end."

"You telling me you took evidence from a potential crime scene? What? You like making Kai's job hard?"

That stung, but not wanting it to show, I met his sarcasm with my own.

"Yes, Jake, I intentionally contaminated a crime scene to make trouble for the cops. I do that in my spare time when I'm not killing people."

"You think this is a joke?" he asked, eyes hard and narrow.

"No. I know it isn't a joke, which is why I'm bringing this to you." I gestured to the tabby.

"What the hell am I supposed to do with a piece of shell given to me by a person of interest in a murder investigation? Ever heard of chain of custody? This ain't the way it works."

"First of all, I picked this up because I thought it was pretty. I had no idea it might be significant until I showed it to my uncle. And second, what the hell, Jake? Person of interest? Do you actually believe I had something to do with Ligner's murder?"

"I believe in the facts, and the fact is your car was at the murder scene earlier the same day Ligner was killed and you won't explain what you were doin' there."

"I told you, Jake, I've been trying to find Ligner's step-daughter, Brooke."

"Yeah? Then why did one of the neighbors report hearing Ligner having an argument with a woman around the same time your Suburban was seen in the neighborhood? You trying to find Brooke then, too?"

I pressed my lips together and glared at him.

He took a bite of lasagna, glaring right back as he chewed. Finally, he asked, "Are you a vigilante, Grace?"

"What?"

"See—I've been thinking." He paused to swipe a napkin over his mouth. "I heard Ligner liked to beat his wife."

"Yeah? I've heard the same thing."

"I also heard you've had some personal experience with men like him."

I felt my jaw clinch but managed to feign surprised interest. "Really?"

"I'm talking about Anthony Ortega."

"Who is—and you can quote me on this—a world-class asshole."

"It must've made you mad. Knowing he was getting away with putting your sister in the hospital."

A cold wave of anger swept over me.

Line. Crossed.

"What are you doing, Jake?" I kept my voice low, but the chill it carried was palpable.

"My job."

"No." Something occurred to me as I sat there looking at him. "This doesn't make sense. Why even consider me as a suspect when the victim had connections to a crime ring? You've got a guy like Machete Mancini running around and you're coming down on me? Why?"

"Just because I'm your friend doesn't mean I won't do my job."

"Good. Then take that—" I pointed to the shell, momentarily tempted to tell him where he could shove it, and said, "Find out where it came from. Brooke disappeared a week before her stepfather was murdered. I was targeted because someone wanted her purse."

The lines in his brow deepened at my words, but he remained silent.

"Find Brooke and you'll find your answers."

I got up and left without another word.

Jake thought I was capable of murder. I knew he was a cop and his job was to be suspicious of everyone but still . . .

And why bring up my sister's scum-ball ex-husband?

Anthony Ortega. Self-made millionaire. Handsome and charming, he was every girl's dream. But dreams can so easily become nightmares.

Remembering the charm, the ease with which he'd slithered into Emma's life—and the coldness he'd shown when he almost ended it—made me want to kick something.

Actually, in that moment, what I wanted to do was *shoot* something. More specifically, a target fashioned from a photo of Tony Ortega's face.

Okay, maybe that would have been taking it a bit too far. But it wouldn't hurt to put in some time at the firing range.

Oddly enough, shooting had a calming effect on me. Something about the focus and control needed to hit the target—which I only managed to do about half the time.

Before I knew it, I'd turned Bluebell toward the range and called Kai.

"I'm in the mood to shoot something," I said when he picked up.

"It sounds like you're in the mood to shoot *someone*."

"So, you talked to Jake."

There was a pause. "No. Why?"

"He thinks I had something to do with Bob Ligner's murder."

Silence.

"Kai?"

After a moment he said, "Were you serious about shooting?"

"Come on, you don't think—"

"I mean, at the range."

"Oh, yeah. I was."

"Meet me there in thirty minutes."

• • •

I was only a little late. Kai was already in one of the shooting lanes we usually used. Interesting how people do that.

The whole place could have been empty, almost was, actually, and we'd have still picked the same spot.

Kai was loading ammunition into a gun I hadn't seen him shoot before. Some type of revolver.

"Where's your Glock?"

"At the JSO."

"Oh, right."

A fresh wave of guilt washed through me.

"If you're going to learn to shoot, you should practice with as many firearms as you can. This is a Smith & Wesson .38 Special."

I nodded, happy to let the subject of his suspension drop.

He went over the basics of the revolver—some I already knew, just from watching reruns of cop shows and by using deductive reasoning—but I paid close attention, anyway. Not just for the sake of firearms proficiency. I enjoyed listening to Kai. I could even forget about missing girls and monsters and suspicious detectives.

"So," Kai said as we set up our targets, "what exactly did Jake tell you about Bob Ligner's murder?"

Or not.

"Just that he knows I was there and suspects I had words with Ligner."

"Did you?"

Crap.

I hadn't told Kai about my not-so-friendly chat with Ligner. I lifted a shoulder in what I hoped was a casual gesture.

"Please tell me you didn't threaten him, Grace."

"If I did, no one heard me."

"Jesus."

Kai shook his head and aimed at his target. Like always, the grouping of shots was tight. Less than an inch between each bullet hole.

Mine, not so much.

I scowled at the target.

"It doesn't matter if I put an ad in the paper declaring: 'I hate Bob Ligner!'" I said with frustration as I reloaded the gun. "What are the chances I'm guilty of murder when there are gangsters running around?"

"Not very good. Especially with that aim."

I gave him a narrow-eyed glare but he just motioned for me to try again. I took a calming breath and managed to hit the target for the rest of the session, mostly, but I never got close to the bull's-eye. A fact I blame entirely on Kai.

I wasn't sure if it was the revolver or our Monday night billiards lesson, but something had inspired him to take a more hands-on approach to teaching.

Instead of telling me to correct my stance, he would physically move me into the right position. Sometimes, he'd pause to watch, standing close enough that I could feel the heat from his body along my back.

It was all I could do to remember how to pull the trigger, much less aim.

"Better," Kai declared when I'd emptied the revolver.

"I like my Glock. I don't have to worry about a safety, or pull the trigger as hard. But thank you for showing me how to use the Smith & Wesson."

He nodded and as we started packing up, asked, "Did Jake say anything to you about Anne Ligner?"

"No, why? You think she killed her husband?"

"I think it would be interesting if Jake didn't. The statistics are clear when it comes to murder and married couples."

"Here's to being single."

"Maybe you just haven't found the right guy." He smiled and my heart did the sudden stop, drop, and roll thing it liked to do when he looked at me like that.

Out of nowhere, I remembered his kiss from the night before. The intensity. The heat. He'd tasted *good*.

I licked my lips and his gaze dropped to my mouth.

"Yeah, well . . . I've got to run." I backed out of the booth as my face grew hot. "I have to help out with a hyperactive kitten."

"Aren't all kittens hyperactive?" Kai asked, seeming amused.

"Actually, I've known some kittens who are pretty chill, but this little girl is bouncing off the walls—literally—and driving her owners crazy. So, I'll talk to you later."

I hightailed it out of there before I did something really embarrassing. I was pretty sure Kai had been teasing me with the "right guy" comment, but I wasn't very astute when it came to people. Especially in the relationship department.

It wasn't that I never wanted to find the right guy; I just didn't want to think about it.

It was safer to tune in my thoughts elsewhere, so I moved on to something relevant to my next task. Overactive kittens.

• • •

It didn't take me long to evaluate the kitty, Molly, who it turned out was not abnormally excitable. The couple who had adopted her had one other pet, an older, very relaxed cat who, by comparison, made Molly look like a whirling dervish.

After leaving the harried kitty parents with a cornucopia of toys, a laser pointer, and some recommendations on burning off kitten energy, I headed home. I had my own kitty to take care of. Not that I had to worry about Voodoo with Moss on duty.

It wasn't dinnertime yet—maybe Moss and I could take a jog on the beach before dark.

I had turned onto Beach Boulevard, headed home, when Kai's comment drifted into my mind.

Not the one about finding the right guy. I had decided to forget that remark. But why hadn't Jake mentioned anything about Anne Ligner? Had something happened to her?

At a stoplight, I snagged my purse, dug out my phone, and called Jake's number. Instead of answering with his typical, if gruff, "Yo," Jake snapped, "What?"

"Is Anne Ligner dead?" Two could play the abrupt game.

"Excuse me?"

"I figure she has to be. If I'm your best suspect."

"Anne Ligner ain't dead."

"Well, she must have a rock-solid alibi because—"

"She's in the hospital."

"Hospital? You're saying he . . ." I trailed off, caught by a sudden memory.

Emma. Surrounded by beeping monitors and machines in the hospital. Her beautiful face made unrecognizable from all the bruises and swelling.

My hand tightened on the phone. Jake was saying something about drugs. I forced myself to listen.

". . . a cocktail of painkillers and sleeping pills. She was unconscious, and had been, according to her doc, for most of the day. So, yeah, she's got a pretty good alibi. Now, unless you're calling to tell me something useful, or explain why you were stalking my victim, I gotta go."

"Jake—" I hesitated, unsure.

A horn blared behind me. The traffic light had changed.

Jake said, "Didn't think so." And hung up.

I blew out a sigh and wondered how long Jake was going to be mad at me.

I also wondered about Anne Ligner. She had seemed a bit glazed over the day I'd met her—had she been taking something then, too?

I wondered if, without her controlling husband to stop her, she would be willing to report Brooke missing.

The closest hospital to the Ligners' house was downtown. I put on my blinker, did a U-turn, and headed to have a talk with Anne Ligner.

• • •

The woman lying in the bed at Baptist Memorial Hospital bore little resemblance to the polished woman I'd met only a few days before.

Anne Ligner's hair was limp and tangled, her cheeks and eyes hollowed. Though there was a plate of food in front of her and an empty saltine wrapper on the tray beside it, she looked like she hadn't eaten in a week.

Her gaze was fixed on a television set high on the wall, but she didn't seem to really be watching.

"Mrs. Ligner?" I said her name quietly as I stepped into the room.

She blinked and turned her head slowly toward me.

"Do you remember me? My name is Grace Wilde."

"We've met?" she asked, a crease forming between her eyebrows.

"Once, a few days ago."

"You're the woman who came to the house looking for Brooke."

"That's right."

She moved to sit up straighter then stopped and eased back. She squeezed her eyes shut. It looked like she was going to lose what little she'd eaten.

After a few moments, she reached out and lifted the little paper cup that sat next to her plate. With trembling fingers, she brought it to her lips and took a tiny sip.

"My head," she said. "I thought the nurse was bringing me something. I'm just so dizzy." She took a breath and focused on me. "Can you ask the nurse to come? I need something for my head."

"Sure. But first I wanted to ask you about Brooke."

"Did you find her?"

"Not yet."

"Probably with her boyfriend."

"Stefan?"

She nodded and I was surprised to see a small smile play on her lips.

"She sneaks out to see him all the time. Brooke thinks I don't know, but I do. I remember what it was like to be young and in love."

Her face crumpled suddenly and she started crying. Like always, I was out of my element. I wanted to pat her on the shoulder but she looked too frail to touch.

"Bob," she said, her voice catching. "They told me Bob's dead."

"Yes."

"I don't know how any of this happened. Everything is so fuzzy. I can't—I don't remember."

"You were unconscious."

"But . . ." She trailed off, looking utterly confused.

"You took a dose of pain medication along with sleeping pills."

"No." She shook her head. "I took the pills my doctor gave me. That's it. They're for depression."

"Antidepressants don't knock you out."

She shook her head again and winced. "My head. Why won't anyone bring me something for my head?" Her voice rose with every word until she was shouting.

A nurse hurried in.

"Mrs. Ligner—" the nurse started in a soothing voice, but Anne Ligner was not in a soothable mood. She grabbed the nurse's arm.

"My head! I need—" Her eyes had widened as she looked at the nurse. "It hurts."

"I understand, ma'am. But you know we can't give you any more. You're in withdrawal."

"No! I'm not! I'm telling you! Why won't you help me?"

A second nurse rushed into the room. I stepped out of the way, and made a quick exit just as the tray of food clattered to the floor.

CHAPTER 19

My phone jolted me out of sleep at 2:00 a.m.

"Grace?" The female voice was barely audible over the loud music blaring in the background.

"Yes?"

"It's Caitlyn. Look, I know it's late, but if you still want to talk to Stefan, I just saw him."

"Um . . ." It took a moment for her words to penetrate my still-slumbering brain. "Okay, where are you?"

"At a party. On the west side." She named an intersection I was fairly sure I could find.

"I'm on my way."

I started to hang up but Caitlyn said, "Wait. You have to wear a costume."

"What?"

"A costume," she repeated. "Otherwise, they won't let you in."

Crap.

I hung up, shoved my sheets aside, and rolled out of bed. Still half asleep, I stumbled over Moss, who grunted out a rebuke.

Tail!

"Sorry."

Okay?

Yeah, I'm fine. Go back to sleep.

I shuffled to my sister's room—the door was open. By the light of the nearly full moon, I could see her bed was still made and unoccupied.

I flipped on the light and squinted in the sudden brightness.

Blinking, I made my way into my sister's huge, walk-in closet, stopping in front of a section she reserved for costumes. Emma and I are not the same size—she's tall and lithe where I'm short and curvy—but I'd make it work.

Hopefully.

Bleary eyed, I pawed through the costumes looking for something simple.

My hands brushed over a half a dozen corsets, elaborate dresses, and several wigs.

Two things became obvious fairly quickly.

First, simple was not going be an option and second, if I wanted the top to fit, I was going to have to find something stretchy.

"Spandex," I muttered as I flipped through the costumes. "I need spandex or—aha!"

I spotted a sleeveless white leotard with a fluffy, pink ball attached to the back and a set of bunny ears dangling from a clothes hanger.

Bingo.

I pulled off my sleep shirt and started to maneuver into the bunny costume when I realized I was still wearing a pair of cutoff sweatpants.

"Wake up, Grace," I told myself.

If I didn't get moving, I'd miss my chance to talk to Stefan.

With a growl of frustration, I peeled off the leotard and kicked out of the sweats. Snatching the leotard off the floor, I yanked it on as quickly as possible.

I turned to reach for the bunny ears and noticed something else clipped to the hanger—a pair of pink satin opera gloves. Seeing them reminded me of how cold it had been the night before. I pulled on the gloves and started searching through the costumes for a warm, bunny-appropriate accessory. Mere seconds into the hunt I gave up and grabbed my sister's red, down-filled jacket.

I'd made it two steps out of the closet when I realized my feet were bare.

"This thing is a black hole," I declared to the empty room as I did an about-face and marched back into the closet.

Glancing over my sister's multitude of shoes I spotted a pair of suede over-the-knee boots.

Perfect. I snagged a pair of thick socks both for warmth and to help pad the boots, which, like all Emma's shoes, were a size too big for me. I pulled them on, vaguely noticing the bright red sole. The signature of some designer whose name eluded my sleepy brain.

Probably expensive. But it wasn't like I was going to a pig farm. I'd only be wearing them long enough to talk to Stefan. It would be fine.

By the time I left, I was too frazzled to focus on much more than finding the address Caitlyn had given me. I'd forgotten my cell phone, so I couldn't use my GPS.

I also couldn't call Kai.

I could have gone home and gotten it, but, in all honesty, I didn't want to involve him any more than I had—and I didn't want Stefan to slip away again.

Besides, I was relatively sure Stefan wasn't the one who'd mugged me. There was something in the way my attacker had spoken—with such menace, such cold intent—that didn't jibe with the kid who'd run from me in the mall. No matter what my sister said.

Of course, a little voice in my head warned that Stefan could have put someone else up to it, gotten a friend to ambush me. But why? Why would Stefan have wanted Brooke's purse?

Only one way to find out.

·   ·   ·

I hadn't felt the need to bring backup to a costume party but I regretted not having Moss with me when I neared the address Caitlyn had supplied.

The area was an unfortunate mix of low-rent apartments and decaying industrial buildings. The few working street-lights were dim and provided just enough light to see it was not a place I'd like to visit during the day. Weeds sprouted tall and unchecked in every crevice and corner not clogged with litter. A stained mattress sagged partly into the street, draped over what might have once been a couch.

The only indication of the party Caitlyn had described was the rows of cars lining the otherwise deserted street.

I finally spotted bright lights and a cluster of people a couple of blocks ahead and started scanning the area for a place to park. A Bluebell-sized opening was unlikely with this crowd, so I turned onto a side street. After circling the block and crossing over to another side street with no luck, I decided I'd have to make my own parking space.

Circling back to the main street, I spotted the discarded mattress and made a wide turn so that Bluebell was in position. There was just enough space between the cars for me to pull in, nose-first.

I had to gun the engine a little to get onto the mattress, and Bluebell sat at an awkward angle, but she could handle it.

"That's why we have four-wheel drive, right?"

I gave Bluebell's dash an affectionate pat, climbed out, and said, "Don't worry, Bell, I'll take you through the car wash tomorrow."

The wind whistled, cold and cutting, down the bleak street. I hunkered down into the quilted jacket and tried to see the bright side—at least I was no longer tired. In fact, I'd become hyperaware of a couple of things. Bunny ears are not aerodynamic and heels higher than three inches should come with a warning label and a walker. I tottered along the crumbling sidewalk toward the party, trying hard not to look like a wounded gazelle to any lions stalking the night. Hope-fully, anyone witnessing my parking job and promise to Bluebell would think I was crazy and give me a wide berth.

I was only a block away from the building when a hand shot out of the darkness and clamped on to my arm.

I stifled a shriek and snapped my head around. Caitlyn

stood with her back to the wind, huddling in the meager shelter of the scraggly bushes.

"Jesus!"

The girl had almost gotten a taste of my newly tested aikido skills.

"Sorry!" Caitlyn said, shivering. She was sporting a bright pink, furry hoodie with purple horns over a pink miniskirt and a tube top the size of an ACE bandage.

"What are you supposed to be, aside from freezing?"

"A monster. Here"—she held out a Day-Glo orange strip of plastic—"you need a wristband to get inside."

She snapped the band in place and we made our way toward the entrance line.

As we waited, I couldn't help but notice several people drinking beer near the entrance as they shared a cigarette. I glanced at my underage companion.

She didn't seem tipsy.

"Have you been drinking?"

She shook her head.

"Can't. I'm on antibiotics." She angled her head and pointed at her eyebrow. A silver ring looped over the far corner. "Just got this, but it started getting red. I have to take them till it heals."

A frigid blast of wind made her turn into me. She hugged herself and goose bumps pebbled over her slim arms.

"Here." I slid the jacket off and draped it on her shoulders.

She blinked at me, surprised. "Thanks."

"I'll have to find Stefan on my own if you die of hypothermia."

"Of what?"

"Never mind."

The line moved more quickly than I'd anticipated and we were through the door and out of the cold before I had time to regret giving away my coat.

Inside, music thrummed through the cavernous space, vibrating in my chest like a giant's heartbeat. Strobes flashed. Laser lights swirled. I spotted a disco ball and smiled, remembering Marabelle's golden jumpsuit.

I got a couple of odd looks as we cut a path through the throng of costumed partygoers, though I wasn't sure why. Was a bunny costume too retro for this crowd? I shrugged it off and Caitlyn led me up a set of metal stairs to a catwalk overlooking a teeming dance floor. We stood at the balcony and my hopes waned as I took in the number of painted, masked, and otherwise disguised faces filling the space.

"There," Caitlyn called out and pointed.

"Where?" I blinked, blinded for a moment by a burst of strobing light.

"You see the guy all in green?"

I squinted and saw who she was talking about. To say he was all in green was an understatement. Every inch of his body, including his face, was swathed in neon green spandex.

"He's hard to miss," I almost had to shout over the music.

"The guy next to him—in the pirate costume—that's Stefan."

I nodded and headed down the steps. At the bottom I paused before throwing myself on the mercy of the throng.

I noticed there was a door marked with an exit sign near Stefan. I didn't think he would notice me in the crowd, but I didn't want to take the chance he'd recognize me and make a break for it.

I hesitated at the edge of the dance floor, looking for something I could use as a makeshift disguise.

"Hey," a deep voice said from beside me, "I like your costume."

I didn't think he was talking to me until he said, "You're a bunny, right? Where's your tail?"

How drunk was this guy?

I turned to give him one of my signature "back off" looks but came face-to-face with a massive, utterly bare, male chest.

I looked up . . . and up a little more, finding his square chin and finally, his eyes. The back-off-or-lose-an-appendage glare lost a little of its punch when I had to crane my neck to make eye contact. But I made a valiant effort.

The beefcake looking down at me smiled and said, "Oh, there it is."

Was this guy stoned or something? Bewildered, I followed his gaze along the front of my body and there, three inches below my navel, was a pink bunny tail.

I closed my eyes and shook my head. In my flurry to dress, I'd managed to put the damn thing on backward.

Stellar, Grace.

"Do you want to dance?" the giant asked.

I glanced up at him. My first instinct was to tell him to get lost, but then, I was struck with an idea.

"Sure, let's go to the other side of the dance floor. It's quieter."

"What?"

"Other. Side." I motioned.

"The bar?" he asked.

Close enough. I nodded and he moved to lead me through the crowd by grabbing my wrist with a polar-bear-sized hand.

Honest to God, he could have played tennis with those things.

I let Goliath part the seas for me, peeking around him a couple of times to make sure the green bean and the pirate hadn't moved.

Once we got close, I tried to extract myself from the giant's grip, but his hand didn't budge.

After being mugged, I probably should have been alarmed but I felt not the least bit threatened by Goliath.

I will hug him and squeeze him and call him George.

I tapped his beefy shoulder and he turned.

"I have to talk to my friends. You go ahead, I'll be there in a minute."

As I'd hoped, he released me. Not as I'd hoped, he stood there waiting. I decided to ignore Goliath and turned to zigzag back toward Stefan.

"Hey," I shouted at Stefan as I pulled off his tricorne hat. He whirled to face me, his eyes going wide.

"We need to talk."

"About what?"

"Your girlfriend."

"Hey, who's the babeasaurus rex?" the green bean asked.

He started to look me up and down, caught sight of my bunny appendage, and let out a "Whoa!"

"Eyes up, buddy," I said, still focused on Stefan.

He was staring at the same spot his buddy was. "Is that supposed to be—"

"It's my pet tribble. I'm a Trek Bunny."

He started to back away from me but the crowd was thick and he didn't get far.

"Look, there's nowhere to run. I just want to talk. Really."

"You're crazy."

"Maybe. But"—I hooked my thumb over my shoulder toward Goliath—"he's crazier and if you try to run, he'll stop you." I lied so smoothly, I almost believed it myself.

I could see I had him before he said, "Fine. Whatever. What do you want?"

What I really wanted was the music to stop so I could hear myself think. I knew that wasn't going to happen so I turned to Goliath and gave him the one finger back-in-a-minute signal.

He frowned. I wanted to avoid a scene with Goliath so I placed two fingers to my lips and mimed smoking an imaginary cigarette. When he started toward me I shook my head, pointed at him, then at the bar then repeated the fingers-to-lips smoking gesture, and pointed to the exit door.

The frown eased a bit and he nodded.

I turned back to Stefan. "Outside," I said, pointing to the door. Stefan and I wound around a few people, pushed the lever on the door, and slipped out into a dimly lit alleyway.

Though it was warmer in the alley than on the windy street, I could still see my breath fogging the air and was glad I'd opted for the knee-high boots and gloves. At least I was capable of getting that much right.

"What do you want?" Stefan asked.

"To ask you about Brooke."

"What about her?"

"When's the last time you saw her?"

"I don't know, a couple of weeks ago, I guess. We aren't supposed to see each other."

"Did she seem upset about anything?"

He shrugged.

I tried a different angle. "What about the last time you talked to her?"

"What about it?"

"What did you talk about?"

"Seriously?"

"Yeah, seriously."

Another shrug.

"Come on, Brooke could be in trouble. I'm trying to help her."

"I don't remember. Usually she just talked about how much she missed me and that kind of crap."

"So Brooke called you to babble about how great you are?"

He smirked. "What can I say—the ladies love me."

I gave him a cold, unimpressed stare.

"Whatever, lady. I'm done talking to you." Stefan turned to go inside but the door had no handle on the outside.

"Looks like you're not."

He scowled over his shoulder at me and pounded on the door.

"Her stepfather is dead. Did you know that?"

Stefan turned to face me with an expression that told me he didn't.

"He was murdered."

"Murdered?" Stefan blinked at me for several seconds before saying, "Okay, listen, Brooke was planning on getting away."

"From what?"

"I don't know—she wouldn't tell me. All I know is she told me to be careful. She was scared. For real."

"Scared of who? Her stepdad?"

"Yeah, of him. But someone else, too—"

Music flooded the space around us as the door opened. The green bean guy stuck his amorphic head out and said, "Come on, man. They're getting ready to start the foam."

"Foam?" I asked.

"It's the last thing they do before the party ends," Stefan

explained, catching the door before it closed. "They turn on the foam machines and fill up the whole place. You know."

I didn't, and had no desire to become acquainted with the process. Besides, I was pretty sure foam and suede would not mix well. Emma would kill me if I ruined her designer boots.

"Are you coming?"

"I think I'm going to pass."

He shrugged then paused halfway through the door. "Listen," he said when his friend was out of earshot. "I don't know where Brooke is. I hope she's okay. If you find her, tell her to call me. Okay?"

I nodded, the door *thunk*ed closed, and I turned and started down the alley toward the street. I hadn't made it far when a figure materialized out of the darkness to block my path.

He moved toward me and I took a step back.

"Stop!" I shouted.

He did, just as he stepped fully into the light.

Mancini.

Great.

My heart began to hammer hard against my rib cage. I was trapped in the alley with a man known as the Machete.

"I'm sorry, Miss Wilde. I didn't mean to startle you."

"What are you doing here?"

He angled his head. "The same thing you are. Trying to find our Brooke."

The way he said "our Brooke" shot a chill through me.

Could this guy get any more creepy?

"You look a little like her, you know," he murmured in a soft voice.

Apparently, he could.

I tried to talk myself into remaining calm.

Be cool, Grace. Everything is okay.

Just chatting with a complete psychopath in a dark alley. Totally normal. Not alarming in any way . . .

All the while, my heart raced as I tried to come up with an exit strategy.

I could scream. I was pretty sure the front door was close enough that someone might hear me. Whether or not they'd come to my rescue was another question.

Mancini stepped closer and I shifted my weight, ready for the attack.

"Back off, Mancini, I'm not in the mood." My voice wasn't as calm as I'd hoped and he responded to my fear like a shark sensing blood. Smile widening, he slid closer.

Get a grip, Grace.

If I wanted to make it out of the alley I was going to have to stay calm and . . . what?

Retreat wasn't my goal but I took a step away from him anyway. I needed room to move, although where I would go was unclear.

I was seriously regretting my decision to leave my Glock in Bluebell and beginning to feel the first cresting wave of panic when the door opened with a bang that made me choke back a scream.

Goliath.

He was covered from the waist down in puffs of white suds.

"The foam party started," he informed me with a frown.

"Well, wouldn't want to miss that."

Thanking the powers that be, I turned my back on Mancini, and without so much as a backward glance, linked my arm with Goliath and waded into the froth.

• • •

By the time I made it to the condo, the sun was rising over the Atlantic in a burst of fiery colors. I would have been awed if I hadn't been so tired.

I'd only had one drink with Goliath at the party, but I was beat. Not wanting to have to worry about another missing girl, I'd insisted on taking Caitlyn home, which turned out to be a half-hour drive out of the way.

Rather than spurring me awake, the chilly morning air brought on a wave of longing for a bed prewarmed by an oversized canine. Fatigue made my eyelids feel like they were made of sandpaper. I had a hollow ringing in my ears from the music.

I was so focused on making it to my bed, I didn't notice the man standing next to the stairs until he spoke.

"I didn't figure you for the party-till-the-break-of-dawn type."

I whirled around.

"Logan." I glared at him. "First Mancini, now you? You guys are like cockroaches."

"Mancini? You saw Vincent?"

"Oh please, you know you're tag-teaming me."

Logan's brows arched and he gave me what might have been a smile—which for Logan was a slight quirk of his lips.

He slipped his gaze over me and said, "I don't share."

Oookay.

"What do you want, Logan? Or are you here to mug me again?"

The hint of amusement I'd seen on his face vanished.

"Mug?"

"Yep. By one of your buddies. Unless, of course, it was you."

His eyes narrowed.

"Look, sweetness," he said, "I don't pick on little girls."

"Sweetness?" I'd been called a lot of things, but sweetness certainly was not one of them.

Ignoring my frosty tone he said, "Why don't you tell me what happened?"

"Someone came here to snatch Brooke's purse while holding a gun to my head. That's what happened. And you know what? You and Ozeal were the only people who knew I had her purse. I'll let you draw your own conclusions."

As I spoke, his expression became darker. Finally, he said, "I came here to warn you."

"Well, in that case, you're a little late."

"No. I'm not. You need to stop looking for Brooke. There're things happening in our . . . organization. Frank has been making subtle moves to try to take over."

"Ratting on your boss? Isn't that frowned upon in your business?"

"I don't work for Frank Ferretto." Though his voice was soft, anger rumbled through the words. A warning. Logan's face was cold but those golden eyes burned with ferocity.

Wolf eyes.

Usually, I know better than to poke at angry, wild things, but I was cold, irritated, and too tired to think straight.

"That's right," I said. "Sartori asked you to keep an eye on Brooke. Too bad she got kidnapped on your watch."

Instead of reacting to my barb, Logan asked something that caught me off guard.

"Why are you doing this?"

"What?"

"You've been running around like crazy looking for Brooke—why? Why go to the trouble for a girl you've never met?"

What could I say? The truth was I wasn't really sure.

"I don't know. I guess I would want someone to do the same for me."

"Look for you if you went missing?"

"Give me the benefit of the doubt. Without passing judgment based on what someone thinks they know about me."

He regarded me for a long moment, his expression unreadable.

"Frank has given Vincent permission to do whatever it takes to find Brooke. If you keep looking for her, you're going to cross paths with him again, which would be a bad thing."

"Why does Frank want to find her? To use as leverage against Sartori?"

"I don't know."

"Why come here and snatch her purse?"

"I don't know."

"Really?" I wasn't buying it.

"Really," he said. "I don't know what Frank is after or why he wants Brooke. But I can tell you one thing. You're in over your head, sweetness. Time to get out of the water."

Before turning to leave, he flicked his gaze over me.

"Nice outfit, by the way."

I stood and watched him for a moment before climbing the stairs and heading inside.

I wasn't sure I trusted Logan. If Frank and his goons were holding Brooke somewhere, Logan could have been sent to issue a warning so I'd back off. Which would mean I was getting close.

So was that why both Mancini and Logan were following me? To make sure I didn't figure out where Brooke was and get her into protective custody before they could get their hands on her?

Moss lifted his head as I entered my room. He and Voodoo were snuggled together on the bed. Moss watched me for a moment as I struggled to pull off the damp boots. Then he yawned, stretched all four legs out with a trembling groan, and relaxed with a sigh before drifting back off to sleep.

Somehow, even with all the questions zooming around my head like a hive of bumblebees, I managed to fall asleep, too.

What seemed like a millisecond later, my sister's voice was snatching me from my sleep.

"Wake up, sleepyhead. It's almost noon."

I grunted and rolled over, stuffing my head under my pillow.

"Come on, your phone has been ringing like crazy for the last half hour. Did you have an appointment this morning?"

I was having a hard time remembering what day it was, much less if I'd missed an appointment.

With a sigh, I eased the pillow off my head and blinked up at my sister. The scent of fresh coffee hit me at the same moment I spotted the mug in her hand.

Locking eyes on the coffee, I let out a pathetic whimper, and she handed me the mug.

Emma eyed me as I sat up to take a sip.

"I noticed you were gone when I got in around three. I also noticed you raided my costumes. And is that a wristband?"

I glanced at the plastic band. "Costume—foam party."

"And I was not invited to participate for what reason?"

I explained Caitlyn's phone call and gave my sister a rundown of my night.

"So, this Mancini guy, do you think he was there because he's been following you or Stefan?"

It was a good question, reminding me of Logan's warning. "I don't know. I'm pretty sure he wanted to chop me into little pieces."

"I thought you and the mob flunkies were on the same side."

"Not according to Logan."

"Who?"

"Yard Guy."

"Right. He's mob flunky number two."

"I don't know what he is, aside from scary."

"Scarier than a guy who's known as the Machete?"

"Logan's an unknown quantity. At least I know Mancini's nuts. I'm not sure about Logan."

Emma's gaze flicked to a spot at the foot of my bed and froze.

"Are those my Louboutin boots?"

I glanced at the floor, where the boots lay in a heap.

"Um . . . I didn't have a choice. It was either walk into the foam with Goliath or get hacked into bits by a psycho. I took them off as soon as I could. They didn't get too foamy."

Emma didn't respond; she just stared at the boots.

I followed her gaze. There were some splotches here and there but it didn't look too bad.

"I can have them cleaned," I said.

Silence.

"Emma?"

Just when I feared I'd signed my death warrant by choosing to wear her boots, my sister said, "What if the same thing happened to Brooke?"

"What?"

"Maybe she was faced with a choice—like you were. Staying at Happy Asses was dangerous, so she took off."

"She didn't run away, Emma. Boris—"

"I know, he said she was taken. But what if she had to make the choice suddenly? She was on the outside of the fence, right? Maybe she saw someone and knew she had to run? Boris sensed her fear and that's what stuck with him."

I thought about the flash of memory I'd gotten from the tiger that first night. Brooke had been turning to look back, as if someone was behind her.

"I don't think that's what happened. But even if she had decided to run, why leave her purse?"

"Maybe she didn't have time to grab it. Or she knew she'd be safer without it—look what happened to you."

"So she just runs, no money, no phone . . . holy crap!"

A thought struck me like lightning and I bolted out of bed.

"What?"

"I'm an idiot!"

"Okay—and?"

"Her phone!" I said, shoving my mug into Emma's hand. "I have her phone. I plugged it into Bluebell to charge. I can't believe I forgot about it."

My excitement had caused Moss to let out a short, confused howl as I charged through the condo and out the door.

When I returned a minute later he was trotting around Emma in the kitchen, woofing up at her.

Grace? Grace! Moss out.

"Sorry, I don't speak mutt," she told him.

"It's okay," I said to him, breathless.

He scrambled to me with a little hop. Then threw back his head and let out a longer howl just to let me know he didn't appreciate being startled into thinking something was wrong.

"Meeooooooooowoooo!" The kitten's cry, as drawn out as the howl, sounded from the living room and a moment later Voodoo came bounding into the room and tumbled to a stop at Moss's feet.

"Great—she thinks she's a mini-Moss, doesn't she?"

"Looks like it." I shrugged. At the moment I was not worried about an interspecies identity crisis.

I held up the phone, then frowned when the screen remained blank.

"I charged it—why won't it work?"

"Here, let me see." Emma held out her hand and I gave her the phone. "It wasn't on, genius."

"Oh."

Emma powered up the iPhone and soon we were viewing Brooke's phone log. Not surprisingly, there were several calls to and from Stefan. The last call received was marked as being from home.

"Could have been a call from her mom or her stepdad," Emma said.

"Check her texts," I said.

She scrolled through them, but they were nothing more than chats with Stefan and some friends.

"Damn—I thought for sure this is what they were after." By *they* I'd meant my mugger and his associates, but I didn't have to explain that to my sister.

"Maybe it was. Let's see what else she has stored on here," Emma said as she tapped the screen.

I watched over her shoulder as she searched.

Finally, my sister shook her head. "I only see a few documents. They look like some sort of essays about the animals she works with. And there's some other paperwork. Applications and that sort of thing. Didn't you say she was trying to get a grant?"

"Yeah. But I think the deadline has passed."

"Well, all of these are either short Word documents or pdf files."

"So, nothing worth kidnapping for?"

Emma was still scanning the contents of the phone.

"There are a zillion pictures," she said after hitting the photo icon.

"What's that?" I pointed to a dark square with a symbol and some numbers across the bottom.

"A video." Emma hit the image and we watched in silence. My heart began hammering harder against my ster-

num the longer it played. After the abrupt ending my sister
and I exchanged glances.

"Call Kai," she said.

I was already reaching for my phone.

CHAPTER 20

I called Jake, too, then hit the PLAY icon and watched the video again.

In fact, I managed to view it six times before Jake arrived. My sister let him in and excused herself to make a phone call.

Jake nodded to her and ambled into the kitchen, where I'd situated myself in order to have easy access to coffee.

The detective's sharp gaze flicked over me, swept the room, and finally fixed on the phone I held.

I handed it to him. He watched the video, brows knit, then looked up at me.

"Where did you get this?"

"The phone was in Brooke's purse, which she'd hidden at work. You can ask Ozeal Mallory for verification. She was with me when I found it."

"When?"

I had to think about it—the last week had started to blur.

"It was the same day I was mugged. So, Tuesday, I think."

"Mugged? What the hell are you talking about?"

"Didn't Kai tell you?"

"Kai hasn't had much to say to me lately."

The doorbell rang before I could ask for an explanation. As Emma breezed by on her way to answer the door, I realized I'd neglected to tell Jake that Kai was coming to look at the video. Nor had I mentioned to Kai my intention to call Jake.

I hadn't thought it would be a problem.

I was wrong.

As soon as Kai walked into the room, Jake's expression changed from irritated to downright pugnacious.

"What the hell are you doing here?"

"I assume I'm here for the same reason you are."

"This is regarding an open murder case—"

"Hang on, Jake," I said. "Kai's just trying to help."

"Really? He hasn't been much help so far."

Kai held Jake's gaze for a moment, then set a case on the counter.

"I have a program on my laptop that enhances video quality. Do you want to use it or not?"

In less than five minutes we were watching the video on a larger screen.

The image was blurred and unsteady at first, then it zeroed in on the figure of a woman standing in a kitchen. I recognized her and the house. The video had been recorded at night from the Ligners' backyard looking in.

Brooke's mother stood leaning against the kitchen counter. She looked dazed. A dark stain of what might have been blood marred the corner of her mouth.

Bob Ligner was pacing back and forth. Finally, shooting his wife a disgusted look, he snatched a pack of cigarettes off the counter and turned toward the back door.

"Shit!"

The curse was a panicked whisper and the image was jostled as Brooke, or whoever was holding the camera, scrambled out of sight. Only darkness and rapid but muted breaths followed until Bob Ligner spoke.

"It's me. She says she doesn't have it."

There was a pause and then the image of Ligner entered the frame. He was pacing and smoking as he talked into a cell phone.

"No," he said. "She gave it to Brooke as some sort of stupid sweet-sixteen gift."

He took a long drag then blew out a stream of smoke. "Look, don't worry about it. I can handle that little slut. What? No. Not like that. I'm not stupid. I know nothing can happen to her until her dad is locked up for good."

There was another long pause as he paced and smoked.

"I'll get it, okay?" I thought I heard a trace of fear in his voice. "Listen, you want me to make sure she doesn't miss it and go running to Daddy, right?" He paused. "Well, I'm going to swap it out or something." Another pause. "She's just a stupid kid, she won't even notice. Yeah, okay."

Ligner turned off his phone and flicked his cigarette butt in the direction of the camera. There was a gasp and the video cut off. We stood in silence for a moment.

"So," I said. "Who was Ligner talking to?"

"And what is the 'it' he was supposed to get from Brooke?" my sister said.

"And why would whoever he was talking to want whatever 'it' is?" I added.

"More importantly," Kai said, "if Ligner's murder is connected to this . . . thing, how does it tie in? Does it mean they got it and killed him to shut him up or that he didn't deliver?"

We all stood silently for a minute.

"Obviously," I said, "Brooke knew she was the target, which goes along with what Stefan told me. She was planning on running away with this, this . . . whatever it was, until her dad was out of jail."

"So why not ask for help?" Jake asked.

"From who?" I countered. "Her mother?"

We all knew Anne Ligner was in no position to help Brooke.

"Why not contact Sartori?"

Kai had a good answer to my sister's question.

"The phones at the prison are monitored. Chances are Brooke knew that. And she couldn't trust anyone working for her father to get him a message."

"Hang on. How would she even know Ferretto was betraying her father?"

"Maybe she didn't. Brooke may not have known who Ligner was talking to, which meant she couldn't trust anyone."

"What about Yard Guy? What's his name?" my sister asked.

"Logan." I shook my head. "Brooke didn't know he'd been sent to look after her by her dad. And it's good that she didn't go to him. I'm not sure whose side he's really on."

"So Brooke knows someone is after her. She doesn't have anyone to turn to, and she runs off," Jake said definitively and turned toward the door.

"Where you going?" I asked.

"To ask Anne Ligner what was so important it got her husband killed."

"Who cares about Bob Ligner? What about Brooke?"

"I'm trying to solve a murder here, Grace."

"When are the police going to do something to help this girl?" I looked from Jake to Kai.

"The way I see it," Jake said, "Charles Sartori is scheduled to be released in a couple of days. I got a dollar says she'll show then."

"She didn't run off, Jake."

Jake shook his head. "Where the hell are you gettin' that from? You just told me her boyfriend said she was planning on hiding out. We know the mob is still looking for her—which means they haven't found her. Ergo, she ran off."

I shook my head. "That was what she was planning, but it didn't work out that way."

Three sets of eyes found me. There was a long moment of silence.

Kai cleared his throat and arched his brows at me expectantly.

"You might as well tell him while you have us here to back you up," Emma said.

"Back you up how?" When no one answered, Jake turned to Kai. "What the hell are they talking about?"

Kai didn't answer. Keeping his eyes on mine, he said, "It's not my secret to tell."

"Okay." I sighed. "I guess if you already think I'm capable of murder it won't bruise my ego much more if you decide I'm crazy, too."

"Grace, I never thought you were capable of murder."

"Then why come down so hard on me?"

"Because I knew you weren't telling me everything. I didn't know what to think. Kai's not talking. You're not talking. And I'm left wondering what the hell's goin' on."

There were several beats of silence.

"I—I'm a . . ." Wow, this wasn't as easy as I thought it would be. "The thing is, I have this ability—with animals, not people—I can . . ."

"She's a telepath," Emma said when I trailed off again.

I gaped at her.

"What? We don't have all day." She defended herself with a shrug.

"A telepath," Jake repeated, looking from me to Emma before finally stopping at Kai. "Really?"

Kai nodded, his face serious.

"Do I look like an idiot?" He snorted out a laugh. When no one joined him, he said, "Come on. You're tellin' me all that stuff with Jax and LaBryce's leopard—"

"Jaguar," I corrected.

"Whatever. You're sayin' that you can—what?"

"Talk to animals. Yep." It felt ridiculous saying it like that. Especially to Jake.

Jake studied me for a long moment. "So, you could call your dog without turning around or looking at him?"

"Yes. But Moss is—"

"A pain in the butt," my sister said.

"He can be difficult. But I'll give it a try if it will prove I'm telling the truth."

Moss! Come in here.

Nothing.

Want a treat?

I knew he was on his way before I heard the jingle of his

tags. He nudged his way between Kai and Jake and sat looking up at me expectantly.

Treat?

"Em, will you give him a treat?"

Jake's eyes narrowed at that and I knew he was wondering if Emma had somehow signaled to Moss.

"It's not a trick," Kai said.

"What? You psychic now, too?" Jake turned to my sister. "And what about you? What's your superpower?"

She tossed Moss the treat she'd gotten out of the pantry and flashed a brilliant smile.

"I'm, well . . . *me*."

I rolled my eyes and realized why Emma and Moss so often butted heads. They were too much alike.

"Back to the original question," I said. "The reason I know Brooke was kidnapped is because Boris, the tiger at the rescue facility where she works, saw it happen."

"So you know who took her," Jake said.

"It's not that easy. He didn't see everything that happened. Or at least he hasn't shown me everything."

"I'm not following you."

I sighed—feeling my head begin to throb. "It's complicated."

"Grace can't simply access an animal's memories," Kai explained. "She can understand what they're thinking and feeling and see a memory if it enters their mind, but she can't force it. Right?"

I nodded. "Boris told me Brooke was taken. He didn't show me how it happened exactly."

"So you don't really know," Jake said. "According to you, she was taken, but if that's the case, why are Ferretto and his guys still looking for her?"

I didn't have a ready answer to that.

"Maybe she got away," Kai said. "What if she was kidnapped but managed to escape?"

Which meant Mancini had been following Stefan instead of me.

It made perfect sense.

"We have to find her, Jake," I said. "We have to find her before they do."

"We?" Jake snorted. "*We* don't have to do anything. You are not a cop."

"But—"

"No. I'll handle this."

"She hasn't been reported missing."

"No, but her stepfather was murdered. Now that I know she's in trouble I can make the call to look for her." He paused and held my gaze. "You should have told me sooner."

I felt a stab of guilt. What if something happened to Brooke because I'd been too much of a coward to tell Jake the truth?

"You wouldn't have believed her," Kai said. "I didn't."

"Maybe not." He fixed his eyes on Kai. "But I would have believed you. Both of you are on my shit list."

He turned to leave and I thought I heard him grumble something about Dr. Dolittle as he walked out the door.

"What do we do now?"

"Let Jake handle it."

I nodded and my phone rang. I picked it up to glance at the screen and recognized the number as the one I'd missed several calls from earlier, so I answered.

"You said you'd be here to check on Scarlett."

"Hello to you, too, Reedy."

"I got my files."

"Find anything?"

"Not yet. You coming out here?"

"Yes."

"Good. Bring a six-pack of Bud with you."

"No."

"Prude," he said and hung up.

I sighed and turned to Kai and Emma. "Duty calls."

• • •

True to form, the weather had once again shifted. By the time I parked in Reedy's drive at a little past three, all trace of the chill from that morning was gone, smothered by a muggy warmth.

Still bleary eyed, it took me a minute to locate my first aid kit, which, like so much of the necessary junk I hauled around with me, was buried in Bluebell's cargo area.

As expected, the dogs greeted me with a cacophony of barks, and by the time I'd walked to the gate, my headache had returned with a vengeance.

"Fizzlesticks! Fizzlesticks, already, jeez."

They quieted immediately but my head didn't seem to notice.

I managed to greet the dogs as I walked past them toward the front porch. The door swung open before I could knock.

"Took you long enough."

"No, I don't mind supplying your animals with free medical care. But your gratitude is heartwarming."

His lips quirked up into a half smile and he coughed out a short laugh.

"Spunk," he said, still grinning.

"Not today, old man," I muttered as I followed him inside.

"Late night?"

I grunted an affirmative.

"Hope it was worth it."

"Well, I survived. And believe it or not, that's saying something."

As we walked toward the kitchen, I asked, "How's our patient today?"

"Better. She still seems tired, but she's eating."

I was surprised to find the washing machine busily sloshing when I walked into the laundry room. And Scarlett had a fresh, albeit ratty, blanket.

I spoke softly to Scarlett while I checked her sutures, and finding them to be healing well, started slowly removing them. Scarlett was a stellar patient, never so much as flinching even when a couple of the sutures pulled. She even thumped her tail on the blanket as I worked. Typical pit bull—stoic and sweet.

I wished more people understood that.

"There you go. All done."

I gave the dog a pat on her blocky head.

Better?

Better. She sighed, gave her tail a couple of more thumps to express her gratitude, then settled down for a nap.

"She's healing well," I told Reedy as I packed up.

"How are the cats doing?"

"The cats are fine—Josiah was the one who lost it."

"He's been getting worse lately. Ever since his mama passed away a month or so ago."

Something about what he said stirred a thought, but I couldn't hold on to it long enough for it to solidify.

"Now that she's gone," Reedy continued as I followed him into the living room, "I don't know that he keeps up with his meds like he needs to."

"Is there someone at his church that can help out?"

He gave me a questioning look. "How did you know he went to church?"

"Josiah started quoting scripture when he got agitated. I assumed he was a member somewhere."

Reedy nodded. "I'll make some calls. Mrs. Belleview looked in on him a time or two, but he frightened her off the last time. Said he would only talk to the angels, or some nonsense."

That surprised me. Though Josiah had been upset when we'd taken the cats, I hadn't sensed he would become violent.

"What types of medications is he taking?" I asked Reedy.

"Hell, I don't know. Gets confused if he doesn't take them, though. Like his mind wants to go back to when his sister was alive."

"When his . . . Josiah's sister is dead?"

He nodded. "Abby was killed in the accident."

"Oh my God."

The words were barely a whisper but Reedy must have read my expression because he asked, "What is it?"

"I think Josiah kidnapped Brooke."

"What? Why?"

"I'm not sure, but yesterday he told me his sister was alive. And I think he was the man at Billy's Feed and Seed who bought the garden soil and the cat litter."

"What in the Sam Hill are you talking about?"

Understanding flooded me in a rush. "The paint. Cat litter. Josiah was painting the back of your old store."

"So?"

"You can mix cat litter into paint to make it a solid. He needed the litter to dispose of the old paint."

"You're jumping to a lot of conclusions based on cat litter. I've known Josiah since he was knee-high to a grasshopper. And I'm telling you, there is no way he'd kidnap a girl."

"Okay, what about the other things on the list? The man at the feed and seed bought litter, and three bags of soil. Does Josiah have a garden?"

The old man's lips thinned. "That doesn't mean anything. A lot of folks around here have gardens."

"Do a lot of folks around here also have to take medication to keep in touch with reality?"

"No, but I can think of a couple who probably should." Reedy glowered at me for a moment then said, "I already told you, before his mama passed—"

"His mother . . ." I trailed off as another piece fell into place. "The maintenance worker at Ozeal's place said he'd had a helper named Joe. But he hadn't been around since his mother died. Which is why I didn't follow up on it. I can't believe it—Joe has to be Josiah."

"No, he does *not*!" Reedy said the last word with enough force to send him into a coughing fit so violent he had to sit down.

Reedy didn't want to believe Josiah was capable of kidnapping, but I needed to look into the possibility—starting with having a look around Josiah's house.

"Reedy, I'm not saying Josiah's a bad person. But like you said, he's confused. Here"—I showed him the photo of Brooke—"she looks a lot like Abby, doesn't she?"

"Gracious sakes," he whispered as his rheumy eyes flicked over the picture. "She does."

"All I want to do is go by his place and look around. That's it. I'm not calling the police or accusing him of anything."

"Grace, that boy has been through so much . . ."

"I know. I just want to look around. Okay?"

He nodded then met my gaze. "But I'm going with you."

• • •

Despite my protests, Reedy managed to climb into Bluebell, oxygen tank in tow, and sat stony faced as we drove north, deeper onto the island.

"There—take a left up ahead," he said, voice gruff.

The thicket of palmettos was so dense, I couldn't see much of a left to take until we'd almost passed the drive.

Reedy let out a garbled curse that may have been an insult to my driving ability as I negotiated the sudden turn. I wasn't listening.

I slammed on the brakes and stared out the windshield.

"What in holy Moses are you doing?" he exclaimed, planting both hands on the dashboard to brace himself. "Why'd you stop?" When I didn't answer, he went on, "We aren't even close. The house is all the way down the drive."

"Tabby."

"What?"

I put Bluebell in park and opened the door. I stepped down onto the sandy lane and walked to the small, square clump of oyster shells. Not what I would call a ruin, but certainly not a pile of trash either.

I scanned the drive and saw that several pieces of tabby had settled into the ruts.

Squatting, I lifted a piece. The shell had the same sheen and grayish tint as the one I'd found.

I still didn't know why Josiah would take Brooke, but I knew I was on the right track. I wanted to call Kai, or even Jake, but I'd promised Reedy I wouldn't involve the police.

I also didn't want to risk upsetting Josiah. I'd seen how quickly he could become agitated. Despite Reedy's insistence he wasn't dangerous, I didn't believe that was entirely true.

Josiah knew Reedy. If we were going to find anything useful, trust would work better than force.

I climbed back into Bluebell and handed Reedy the piece

of tabby. I explained that I'd found a similar piece on the roadside close to where Brooke had last been seen. I left out the bit about the witness being a tiger.

"I know it isn't proof," I said, "but you have to admit it's possible that a chunk of this stuff got wedged into one of Josiah's truck tires and came loose when he parked on the side of the road before he went through the woods to get Brooke."

"But why? If Josiah's confused into thinking Brooke is Abby, why would he sneak through the woods to get her? Wouldn't he just go in through the front gate and say, 'Let's go, sis'?"

It was a good question.

"Look, I don't have all the answers. But I can't ignore this. If Josiah is living in some delusion where his sister is still alive, we need to find out whether or not he has Brooke. All right?"

Reedy's lips thinned but he nodded.

"He trusts you, Reedy. If we're going to have any hope of understanding what's going on, we'll need to look around. Which means you're going to have to play along. If he jumps back and forth from now to sometime in the past, just go with it. But we need to get inside the house."

"What if he's not home?"

"If he's not home we move to plan B."

"What's plan B?"

"I don't know yet."

I put Bluebell in gear and rolled along the shaded drive, parking in front of a small, tidy house painted a cheerful buttery yellow. A set of rocking chairs sat on the wide porch flanking the door. I helped Reedy out of Bluebell and up the front steps.

My heart had started running double-time when I'd caught sight of the tabby earlier. It increased to triple-speed as soon as I pressed my finger to the doorbell.

The jolly *ding-dong* of the chime and the sunny paint color only added to my sense of foreboding. I thought of Brooke's mother, Anne, and her immaculate house and perfect appearance.

Things are so often not what they seem.

"I don't think he's here," Reedy wheezed. "Truck's gone, too."

I let out the breath I'd been holding and looked over at the old man. His skin had paled and he was leaning heavily on his oxygen tank. He was more sick than I'd realized, and our outing was costing him.

"Here." I led him to one of the rocking chairs. "Take a breather while I look around."

He nodded and reached into his breast pocket, making a disgruntled sound when he came up empty.

"Damn. You made me forget my cigarettes."

I rolled my eyes and stepped off the porch to make my way around the side of the house.

The air was still and quiet, except for a small flock of sparrows flitting around a birdbath with a statue of Saint Francis in the center. The birds took flight as I approached and began fluttering in the trees, trying to decide what branch would make the best roost.

Unlike Reedy's place, which was shrouded in oaks and Spanish moss, here the trees opened up, providing a large area free of shade. Josiah, or possibly his mother, had taken advantage of the sunny spot and planted a sizable vegetable garden.

Rows of corn grew lush and tall and squash ripened on the ground in a tangled heap next to the green, feathery tops of what looked like carrots. There was a variety of large-leafed plants, of which I could only positively identify collard greens. I had to admire the bounty. I had what most would call a black thumb.

"Don't worry," I told the plants, "I'm not here for you."

I started to turn to continue my exploration, when I heard . . . something.

A gasp?

I froze, straining to listen. I thought the sound might have come from the patch of corn.

"Hello?" I leaned toward the cornstalks.

After a minute I shook my head. "Talking to animals is bad enough—don't start hearing plants, too."

I'd only taken a few steps when something rustled in the corn. Something big.

Pausing, I focused my mind on the garden. I picked up the zinging hum of a tiny animal.

Digging-digging-digging.

A shrew.

Whatever hid in the greenery was much bigger than a shrew and it wasn't an animal.

"Josiah?"

I inched closer to the corn, though in the back of my mind I had to wonder why he would be hiding in a vegetable patch.

Of course, I'd never studied the effects of a brain injury on a human being in veterinary school but I knew people could revert back in time. Josiah had seemed very childlike during his tantrum over the cats—maybe he was playing hide-and-seek.

"Are you playing a game?"

I turned my head to listen as I crept around the corner of the plot. I inched closer to the end of the corn row and peered around the leaves—no one was hiding between the first and second row.

I continued past the next. Empty. Then the next—

A wave of shock rooted me in place.

A dark-haired girl stood between the rows, looking at me with large blue eyes. She wore a long denim skirt and long-sleeved white blouse. I almost didn't recognize her in the plain clothes with her hair pulled up into a modest bun, but I knew.

I'd found Brooke.

CHAPTER 21

Part of me had expected to find her, maybe locked in a closet or imprisoned in some way, but certainly not harvesting corn.

"Brooke?"

Her eyes widened as I spoke her name and she stumbled back.

"No," she said. "My name is Abby."

"Brooke, it's okay." I stepped toward her but she scrambled away, shaking her head.

"You have the wrong girl. Go away."

She turned and fled, sprinting toward the barn.

"Brooke. Stop!" It occurred to me as I took off after her that the scenario was all wrong. She shouldn't be running away from me—I was there to rescue her, dammit.

Had she been brainwashed? No, it hadn't been long enough, had it?

Brooke darted through the open barn door. I followed on her heels into what turned out to be not so much a barn as a workshop. A pile of lumber was stacked chest-high in the center of the large space. Brooke ran around one side. I tried to catch her by going around the other and she reversed directions.

I mirrored her movement and we were soon eyeing each other over the wood, playing a back-and-forth game of cat and mouse.

"Why are you running from me?" I panted.

"Why are you chasing me?" she countered, not nearly as out of breath.

I was going to have to start running with Moss again if I was going to keep doing stuff like this.

"And what the hell were you doing? Picking corn?" I asked. "Don't tell me you've gone all Patty Hearst."

"Who's Patty Hearst?"

I waved off the comment. "Never mind. Listen, I'm here to take you home."

I knew as soon as the words left my mouth I'd made a mistake. Brooke spun around and snatched a pitchfork from where it hung on the wall behind her.

I raised my hands and stepped back when she pointed the tines at me.

"You're not taking me anywhere." She hissed the words like a feral cat.

"Okay. Okay."

I was so baffled, I was having a hard time thinking straight. Obviously, Brooke was not being held prisoner. She was clearly afraid of something and it didn't seem to be Josiah. But what?

That would be you, genius.

Did she think I was one of Frank Ferretto's flunkies? If so, how could I convince her otherwise?

"Brooke, I want you to listen to me. I don't want to hurt you."

"Oh, I know what you're after and you're not going to get it. Keep your hands up and walk slowly to the door."

I hesitated but the steely look in her eyes reminded me that despite the farm-girl clothes, Brooke had spent time running the streets.

Turning, I did as she asked.

As we walked out into the late afternoon sun, I tried to

think of something that would get me out of the fine mess I'd stepped into. Brooke was Charles Sartori's daughter. I wasn't stupid enough to underestimate her.

The thought of the mob boss sparked an idea. "Your dad has been worried about you."

She didn't respond, so I tried again.

"He called me from prison and asked me to help look for you." Not exactly true but close enough.

"Sure he did."

"It's true."

"My father doesn't need help finding people—that's why I had to stay here. I knew no one would look for me here."

"So Josiah didn't kidnap you? Who did?"

"No one."

Puzzled, I paused, then turned to face her. She lifted the pitchfork and held it at the ready.

"Keep moving."

But I was too distracted to follow the order.

"That can't be right. Someone *took* you. Taken. That's what—" I caught myself before I said the words that hovered just on the tip of my tongue. She'd skewer me for sure if I tried to tell her about Boris.

Unless . . .

"I know you think I work for Ferretto but I don't. Ozeal called me. A couple of days after you went missing Boris tried to attack Dr. Hugh Murray. You've met him?"

"Boris did what? No. Boris wouldn't hurt anyone." Though she said the words with vehemence, the look on her face told me she wasn't sure.

"Tigers are wild animals and, like any wild animal, they can be unpredictable when they're agitated. Boris went after Hugh—Dr. Murray—and I came to help. I'm an animal behaviorist. In my back pocket, I have one of my business cards. I'm going to take it out and show it to you, okay?"

"Slow," she commanded.

Moving at a snail's pace, I pulled out the card and held it up. She extended the pitchfork forward and said. "Stick it on here." I impaled the card on one of the tines. She stepped back and pulled the card free.

"My name is Grace. I specialize in dealing with animals who have issues. After you left, Boris began suffering from separation anxiety."

The pitchfork lowered a fraction and her eyes widened. "Is he okay?"

"He'll be happy to see you. He missed his catnip. But he missed you more."

Brooke's shoulders finally relaxed and she lowered the pitchfork.

I let out a relieved sigh when the points were no longer aimed at me.

"I don't understand," she said. "You were looking for me because of Boris?"

"Yes. And because of Ozeal. But none of that matters right now. We have to go." If I could get her to the police she'd be safe. Jake would see to it.

"Wait. What about Josiah?"

"What about him?"

"I can't just leave. He wouldn't understand. Listen, he . . . it . . . it's complicated."

"I understand that he has issues. He gets confused and upset."

"He needs help," Brooke said. "I've been trying to get him to take his meds but it's hard to keep up with all of them. I'm not sure he has everything he needs."

"We'll get him some help, I promise."

I remembered Reedy sitting on the front porch of the house in the rocking chair and had a flash of inspiration. I quickly explained my idea to Brooke. We could leave Reedy to wait for Josiah, and he could explain.

"Josiah trusts Reedy. He'll listen to him."

"I have to at least say good-bye. He won't understand."

I thought about what Sonja had said about the cats. Josiah had been devastated when we'd taken them. But this was different. Brooke was in real danger. I didn't have a choice.

"Listen, if I managed to find you, Ferretto, or one of the creeps who work for him, will be able to find you, too."

She still looked uncertain.

I hadn't wanted to tell her in this way but I needed something to goad her into coming with me.

"Brooke, your stepfather is dead. He was murdered. The police think it was Ferretto or one of his cronies."

She blinked at me in shock. "Dead? But . . . Oh my God! My mom?"

"She's fine." Not exactly true. But I wasn't sure telling Brooke that her mom was headed to rehab would help convince her to come with me.

Brooke must have picked up on the subtle subterfuge because she frowned and asked, "What happened?"

I waved off the question. "I'll explain later. Right now, we need to get you somewhere safe."

Brooke shook her head. "I'm better off staying here with Josiah."

"You being here puts Josiah in jeopardy."

Tears welled in her eyes but she was still shaking her head. I had to get through to her.

"You know what these people are like. Mancini? They would kill him, Brooke."

At those words Brooke finally nodded. She walked to the garden plot, stabbed the pitchfork into the ground, and said, "Let's go."

"Stop!"

Brooke and I turned. Josiah walked toward us from the rear of the house, glaring at me. In one hand, he held a gun, which was pointed squarely at my chest.

"You!" he said. "You devil. You will not take my sister!"

Crap!

"Josiah, it's okay." Brooke stepped toward him but her words only seemed to upset him.

"No! No, Abby. I won't let this wolf take you."

My mind whirred as I tried to reason a way out of this.

"Josiah, do you remember me?" I said with a gentle smile, hoping I could get him to recognize me. "I'm Grace—you met me yesterday. You're confused. But it's going to be okay."

"Quiet! Speak not with your lying tongue."

Okay, so I'd have to try a different tactic. I couldn't think of Josiah as the confused, mentally challenged, softhearted boy who fed stray cats. In that moment, he was a delusional, unstable man pointing a gun at me.

Reasoning would not work. Sonja had said something to calm him down, something biblical. I tried to recall but drew a complete blank.

"Josiah," I said as my desperate brain latched on to something Reedy had told me. "I'm here as a messenger. An angel."

His eyes narrowed. "I don't believe you. The angels promised not to take my sister again! You're a false prophet! That's what you are!" His eyes had gone wild, chest heaving. "But I know. I see you. You come in sheep's clothing but you're a ravening wolf!"

Not the reaction I had hoped for, but there was no turning back now. Josiah thought he spoke to angels; I had to make him believe I was one.

I straightened and with what I hoped was angelic authority said, "Do not question me, Josiah. You would question one of God's messengers?"

He glared at me with wide eyes for a long moment. "Prove to me you are who you say you are."

Okay, that was bad. I had a feeling Josiah was going to shoot me if I didn't conjure a halo.

Brooke continued to try to reason with Josiah, pleading with him to put down the gun. But I knew from the frenetic look in his eyes it was going to take more than that.

"Thou shalt not kill, Josiah," I reminded him in what I hoped was a gentle, but firm seraphic voice.

"The wicked will be revealed. The enemy of the righteous will be slain."

Oh shit.

Okay, even I had to admit I wouldn't make a very good angel, but I was pretty sure I was going to get to meet some if I didn't do something awe-inspiring.

I had to think. There had to be something . . .

Out of the corner of my eye I noticed the Saint Francis birdbath.

Suddenly, I had a plan. I looked up at the flock of sparrows and cast my mind over the roosting birds, searching. I zeroed in on my target, and though I hadn't done it in years, connected to the dominant bird.

I closed my eyes, raised my hands out to the side, and quoted the only bit of scripture I'd ever memorized.

" 'Ask now the beasts and they shall tell thee.' " I opened my eyes to meet Josiah's and spoke with as much divine might as I could manage. " 'And the birds of the air and they shall *show thee*!' "

I urged the lead bird from his perch and, as he took flight, the entire flock lifted from the branches to sweep overhead in a fluttering, chirping cloud. I focused every ounce of my brainpower on guiding the bird down, down . . . calling him to me.

Come here, little one.

The bird, bless him, answered my summons, landing with a flutter in the palm of my raised hand. I lowered my hand and the rest of the birds settled around us in a noisy rush.

Brooke gasped. Josiah stared at me, slack-jawed. Then, he collapsed to his knees and began to weep.

"What the hell was that about?" Reedy shuffled toward us, wheezing. At the sound of his voice, the birds started and took flight. I had nothing to offer the little bird but my gratitude, but I sent it to him in waves.

How many people can say they owe their life to a sparrow?

He chirped in acknowledgment and flitted off to join the others in the trees.

I helped Brooke get Josiah into the house and coaxed him to take a dose of diazepam. We got him settled on the couch in the living room, and Reedy agreed to stay there and look after him for a while.

Brooke met us in the hall as Reedy and his oxygen were making their way into the room.

"Josiah's asleep. He'll probably be upset when he wakes up and I'm not here. But you should be okay." She gave Reedy a small smile. "I hid the gun."

"Peachy."

●　●　●

Brooke and I climbed into Bluebell. We'd barely made it out of the drive when she turned to me and asked, "How did you do it?"

"Do what?"

"That thing with the birds."

I lifted a shoulder. "It's something I learned how to do when I was a kid."

Not a lie. But I wasn't keen on telling Brooke the truth. I knew she wouldn't believe me and the tenuous trust we had developed would weaken.

"That's not much of an answer."

"Well, it's all you're going to get."

She let out a dramatic sigh, punctuating it with a grumpy "Whatever."

"Forget about the birds," I told her. "How did you end up out here with Josiah?"

I glanced over and she shrugged.

When it became obvious she wasn't going to answer, I tried prompting her with: "I talked to the guy who owns Billy's Feed and Seed, what's his name?"

"Doc Riggins?"

"That's it—Doc. He said Josiah was in the store the same time you were, but you didn't talk."

"I didn't even really notice him. But he followed me."

"Why?"

"I was upset. Crying, you know, and I think Josiah, well, you saw how he is. He started to think I was his sister, Abby."

"He wanted to protect you."

"Yeah."

It made sense except for one thing. Boris hadn't seen a protective brotherly figure offer Brooke help—he'd seen her being taken.

"I don't understand. You were on the other side of the fence. Right where the . . ." I trailed off as understanding dawned. "It was you. You were the one who cut the hole in the chain-link. That's what you were doing," I said, looking over at her.

She glanced at me sharply. "No, I wasn't."

"Yes, you were," I stated. "Why would you cut a hole in the fence?"

Brooke didn't answer. She sat and stared out the windshield, her lips pressed tightly together. A perfect example of the term *clammed up*. Once you disturb a clam or, more apropos, an oyster, its single adductor muscle flexes, clamping the shell closed like a vise. You can't force it open. You just have to wait.

Unless, of course, you have an oyster knife and you know how to use it.

What tool could I use to make her open up?

I thought about this as we rumbled along. Waiting Brooke out didn't appeal to me. I'd spent the last week looking for this girl. I'd risked my neck, my friendships, and—thanks to my aunt Marabelle's gold lamé—a good portion of my dignity. But Brooke didn't know any of that.

I had a feeling that a do-you-know-what-I've-been-through-to-find-you lecture would roll off her like water off a duck's back. If I wanted answers—and I very much did— I was going to have to try a different tactic.

A sudden and surprising thought hit me.

She'd asked about what I'd done with the sparrows. What if I told her the truth? I weighed the options and was a bit shocked to discover that a part of me actually wanted to share.

Everything I'd learned about Brooke—her devotion to the animals she helped care for, even her stubbornness— made me think of her as somewhat of a kindred spirit. To gain her trust, I had to get her to view me in the same way.

"Listen, I know you don't want to open up to me. I get it. You don't trust people. Believe me, I understand. More than you know." I paused, then added, "But I also know it's not easy keeping secrets."

"Yeah," Brooke said sarcastically. "Like you have so much to hide."

"You might be surprised. How about this. I'll make you a deal—a secret for a secret. You wanted to know about the birds, right?"

"Yeah."

"I'll tell you how I did the trick with the birds if you promise to answer some questions."

"And you'll teach me how to do it?" she asked, her eagerness trumping her wariness.

"I didn't say that. It's not really something I can teach." I could feel her eyeing me as she considered, but I kept my focus on the road.

"Okay, deal. But you have to tell me first."

"You'll probably think I'm crazy."

"Crazy?" she scoffed. "I know crazy and I'm not talking about Josiah. You met Mancini, right? That guy is completely whacked. As far as I can tell, you're not."

We'd see about that. "I have the ability to communicate with animals. It's something I was born with. I don't know exactly how it works or why but that's how I knew you'd been taken at the fence. Boris saw what happened and when he went after Hugh—Dr. Murray—he showed me a snippet of that memory."

"Seriously?"

I couldn't tell by her tone if she was being sarcastic or not.

I glanced over at her. "He says you smell like peppermint."

Her eyes widened and a smile spread slowly across her face.

"Oh, wow. That is seriously the most awesome thing I have ever heard."

"It can be a real pain in the ass, actually."

"Come on. It's got to be so sweet to be able to talk to animals."

"It has its moments."

"Can you like, talk to everything? I mean, birds, obviously. But can you talk to fish? What about beetles?"

"Beetles don't have a lot going on in the brain department."

"This is so awesome. What happens? You said Boris showed you a memory; is it like a movie? Or do you hear voices?"

I raised my hand to stop the onslaught of questions. She was worse than Kai.

"Enough. Now it's my turn. I want to know what happened. Boris was sure you'd been taken, as in kidnapped. He was afraid for you. Afraid and angry."

"I guess it's because of the way it all went down. Josiah came up behind me and grabbed my arm. I almost screamed but he put his hand over my mouth. Totally freaked me out. But then I saw why. There was someone else in the woods."

"Who?"

"Mancini."

"What was Mancini doing in the woods? Looking for you, obviously, but how did he know where you were?"

"I don't know. I guess he saw me when I stopped on the back road."

"The one that runs behind Happy Asses?"

"Right."

"Why did you stop?"

"I needed to mark the way through the woods. So I took a bag of birdseed and left a trail."

"A trail? I walked all over those woods. I didn't see—" Then I remembered. "The storms. All the seed would have washed into the ditch."

"Probably got eaten, too—that's why I used birdseed. I just needed to find my way on one night. After that, it didn't matter."

"So you *did* cut the hole in the fence. Why?"

She hesitated for a long moment.

Finally, she said, "I needed to get inside after hours."

Not a very complete answer, but I let it go for the moment.

"Why cut the fence? Ozeal told me you have the gate code."

"I couldn't use it. An alarm goes off at her place when the gate is opened."

"Okay," I said, piecing together with some difficulty what I'd learned. "Josiah sees you at the feed and seed. He follows you. You stop to lay your birdie bread crumbs and cut the hole in the fence. Then what? Ozeal's truck didn't go missing. You had to have gone back to work."

"I did."

"But you went back into the woods."

"When I cut the fence, it kind of pulled the chain-link apart, like a curtain. It wouldn't stay together."

"So you went to close it with a brass clip. Like the one Ozeal uses for her keys."

"Yeah. That's when Josiah grabbed me. Once I saw Mancini, I knew I had to get out of there, so I went with Josiah. He told me he saw Mancini watching me. I don't know when or where. It's hard to understand Josiah when he gets upset sometimes."

"I noticed."

"It's not like he's stupid," she said defensively. "He was smart enough to know Mancini was bad news."

"Even a beetle is smart enough to pick up on that." I smiled at my own joke, and glanced at Brooke. She glared at me.

"What?"

"You don't have to make fun of him."

"I wasn't," I said, confused. Weren't we just talking about beetle brains?

"He can't help it."

"I know that." People rarely got my sense of humor, which was why I usually didn't employ it. "I was talking about Mancini's creepiness, not Josiah's intellect."

"Well, anyway, I think Josiah saw Mancini go into the woods where I left the trail, and followed him."

I mulled it over as we drove down the long, two-lane road. "Maybe . . ." I said as my thoughts came together. "There's a restaurant, Cooper's or whatever it's called. It's right down the road. Mancini could have been headed there and spotted you."

"Cooper's Catch?"

"That's it."

"I forgot it was down that way. It's one of my dad's places. He used to take me there for fried catfish when I was little. He said I was a picky eater, but I loved the stuff at Cooper's Catch."

The emotion in her voice became more palpable the longer she talked about her father. Whatever kind of criminal enterprise he ran, she loved him.

"I didn't get a chance to try the food when I was there."

"They have banana splits, too. I haven't been there since . . ." She trailed off.

I glanced at Brooke. From the way her voice had grown soft and thick, I expected to see tears, but she'd kept them at bay. Practice makes perfect.

"What are they after? Mancini and Ferretto," I asked, to steer the subject into less sentimental waters.

"Why do you want to know so bad?"

"Because whatever it is, I got mugged because they thought I had it."

"Mugged?"

"At gunpoint," I added. "And the jerk threatened to shoot my dog."

"What?" she asked, anger coloring her voice.

"Yeah, so, I deserve to know."

"It's a key."

"A key? To what, a car?"

"To a safety deposit box. My mom gave it to me. She told me my dad would want me to have what's in the box for my sixteenth birthday. She said when he got out of jail, we could go together and open it."

Out of nowhere, understanding hit me. "You wanted to hide the key. That's why you cut the hole in the fence."

"I put it in Boris's enclosure."

"Which you could only get into after he'd been put in his house for the night." I nodded, impressed. It was pretty smart. Who would think to look in the tiger cage?

"What would Ferretto want with a sweet-sixteen gift?" I asked. "Do you know what's in the box?"

She shook her head.

I didn't believe Charles Sartori would endanger his daughter by giving her something his enemies would kill for. It didn't make sense. And no one other than Sartori would have been able to gain access to the box anyway. Nothing was adding up.

"Are you sure they were after the key?" I asked.

"I can't think of anything else."

"It doesn't matter, the police will sort everything out. We've just got to get you—"

"Police? You can't take me to the cops."

"Brooke, these guys are after you. You need to be in protective custody. I have a friend—"

"No. You don't understand. Frank has snitches everywhere—even with the cops."

I wasn't going to argue with her. She was going to the JSO whether she liked it or not. My resolve must have been clear because she unbuckled her seat belt and started to open the door.

I slammed on the brakes. A horn blared behind us and I had to hit the gas.

"Are you crazy? What the hell are you doing?"

"I'm not going to the cops."

"So you jump out of a moving car? We're going sixty miles an hour! You'd be roadkill."

"You take me to the cops, and I'll be just as dead." She inched the door open.

"Okay! I won't take you to the cops. Close the door! And put your seat belt back on," I added.

She complied but said, "I know where the sheriff's office is; I've been there enough times. If you go anywhere near it, I'll get out and run."

"I said I wouldn't take you to the police and I meant it."

"So, where are we going?"

"To the only other person I know who's capable of protecting you."

CHAPTER 22

"Emma?" I called out my sister's name as I opened the door to the condo. "We have company."

"Who's Emma?"

"My sister."

Moss trotted into the foyer to welcome me home and assess our visitor.

As expected, Brooke was impressed with my dog.

"Whoa, you have a wolf?"

"He's a hybrid. Moss, this is Brooke. Brooke, Moss."

I said my introductions as I walked past them, tossed my keys on the foyer table, and went into the kitchen.

"Hi, Moss." I could hear Brooke cooing from the entry-way. "You're beautiful, aren't you?"

Smug satisfaction radiated from my dog. Moss loved to be told he was pretty.

Handsome. Moss.

I rolled my eyes.

Okay, everyone knows you're the best-looking mutt around.

Handsome.

Without compare, I agreed. Then decided to change the subject before he got too carried away. *Where's Emma?*

Beach.

I checked for a note on the counter and found one that said she was headed for a run.

I opened the fridge to grab something to drink. The sound spurred Moss to abandon his new admirer for the prospect of food.

"Emma went for a run without you," I told him as he trotted into the kitchen.

Bad Emma.

"Well, she probably thought you would be a brat and yank her around like you did the last time."

Dinner.

"She didn't feed you, either?"

Bad Emma.

I went to fill his bowl and noticed Brooke standing at the entrance to the kitchen staring at me.

"What?"

"Are you . . . like, talking to him?"

"Yes. Can't you hear me talking to him?"

"I mean—is he, like, talking back?"

I knew what she'd meant but I didn't feel comfortable with the odd look on her face. It occurred to me that I might have made a mistake telling her the truth. What were the chances a sixteen-year-old would be able to keep my secret?

Yes, I had revealed my ability to more people in the last few months than I had in the last ten years. But I didn't want to put it on a billboard.

I handed Brooke a can of soda and said, "Listen, I was being straight with you earlier when I told you that my ability is a secret. Actually, you're one of maybe ten people in the world who know what I can do. And I'd like to keep it that way."

"Why? What you do is awesome. It's like a superpower or something."

"Maybe. But the truth is, out of those few people I've told, one wanted to arrest me and another thought I was a freak and never spoke to me again. Those aren't very good odds."

"A freak? Come on. Whoever said that was a hater."

"Yeah, well, at the time, I thought he was pretty important and believed he felt the same about me. So . . ."

Brooke looked down at the can and fiddled with the tab. Finally, she popped the top and took a sip.

"You don't want me to talk about it," she said.

"That would be best."

I could tell she was disappointed. She'd probably envisioned all the ways I could save the world by chatting up chipmunks.

"You mean I can't ever talk to you about it?" She fiddled with the tab on her drink some more, pushing it left and right with her index finger. "Like, even if there isn't anyone else around?"

"We can talk about it privately."

"Okay." She pulled her gaze away from the can and looked at me. "Was Boris really upset when I left?"

"Yes. He missed you a lot."

"I would have come and visited him if I had known." She paused, then asked, "Is that why you were looking for me? Because of Boris?"

"And because no one else was looking. The police couldn't help because you hadn't been reported missing."

"So my mom . . ." She trailed off, shaking her head. "Never mind. Bob wouldn't have let her talk to the cops even if she wanted to. He—" Brooke's face darkened and Moss went over to lean against her leg, offering comfort. Brooke automatically reached out and curled her fingers into his ruff.

"You don't have to explain. I know how Ligner treated your mom."

"You do?"

"I talked to Felix."

Her lips curled up slightly at that. I hated to take away even such a tenuous smile but I knew it was time to tell her about her mother.

"Listen, there's something I need to tell you."

I explained what I'd learned from Jake and at the hospital.

"So my mom's a druggie? Great."

"I heard one of the nurses say she's going into rehab. So she's going to get help."

"This is so messed up," Brooke said. "My mom used to be, like, a real mom."

She absently stroked one of Moss's ears. My dog looked up at her, then at me.

Nice.

Yeah, she's a nice kid.

Okay?

She's tough. She'll be fine.

"For what it's worth," I said, "I think your mom was trying to stand up for you." Brooke looked up and met my eyes. "I saw the video you took on your phone."

I explained the discovery of her purse, the trek through the woods, and how I'd only remembered I had her phone that morning.

"Your stepdad was mad because your mom hadn't gotten the key back from you. She didn't want to take away the only thing you'd gotten from your father. She refused to give Ligner that."

"It was my birthday. That night, I mean. I'd snuck out to meet my boyfriend, Stefan, and when I got home, I went around back to go through my window. But the light was on. I heard Bob yelling at my mom . . ." She trailed off.

"I know—you don't have to go into that."

She shook her head. "But that's why I did it. I had my phone and I thought maybe if I got him on video I could make him stop, you know? Tell him I'd call the cops if he touched her again or something. So I got as close as I could but he'd already hit her, I think. And then, well, you heard what he said. I knew I'd have to get out of there until my dad was released."

"Your dad's worried about you."

"I know. I wanted to send him a message. Let him know I was okay. But I couldn't trust anyone."

That made me wonder.

"Brooke, do you remember someone named Logan from when you were younger?"

"Yeah." She cocked her head. "Why?"

"How did you know him?"

"I don't know. He was around a lot when I was a kid. I think he went off to fight in some war or something. I haven't seen him since."

"Yes, you have."

I told her about Yard Guy.

"No way! He like, grew up. I mean, majorly. And he's, like, smoking hot."

At least it confirmed part of Logan's story but I still wasn't sure I completely trusted him. As much as I wanted to let Sartori know Brooke was safe, I had no way to deliver that message.

Another question popped into my head, though I didn't expect an answer.

"Does the word *hide* mean anything to you?"

"Hide?"

"One of the times I was talking to Boris, he showed me you and said the word *hide*."

"Did you give him catnip?"

I blinked at her, surprised. "Yeah."

"The woman who used to own him trained Boris to do all sorts of stuff. You know, tricks."

"Hugh mentioned Boris was being trained for film production."

"Right. Ozeal told me he'd learned how to act, too, sort of. With hand signals and certain words. Not like you tell a dog to sit or roll over. Different words."

"And *hide* was one of them?"

"Yeah. I got a list from his old owner."

"What's he supposed to do?"

"Lie down and put his paws over his face. Like this." She set the drink on the counter and covered her eyes with her hands.

"I don't get it. Why would he tell me that?"

"It was the trick we'd been working on. I'd give him his catnip if he did it."

Now it made sense. "So you rewarded Boris with catnip if he responded to the command to hide. I gave him catnip. Which reminded him of both you and the trick you were working on with him."

Emma arrived a moment later, calling out something about running late as she came through the door. She stopped when she reached the kitchen and saw Brooke.

"Oh! Hey." Emma gave the girl a friendly smile. "Sorry, I didn't expect Grace to have company."

My sister looked from me to Brooke and sudden recognition widened her eyes. "Oh my God! You found her."

"Hiding in the bushes."

"It was corn."

"Corn?" Emma asked.

"It's a long story. What were you saying about being late?"

"I have to meet clients and I haven't had time to plan dinner. Do you want to order pizza?"

"I'm always up for pizza."

Pizza. Moss wagged his tail and let out a low *woof.*

"Moss is in favor of pizza, too," I told her.

"That is so cool," Brooke said, grinning.

My sister's brows rose in surprise. "Okay, I am going to have to hear this story. Order food while I hop in the shower and then you guys can fill me in."

Thirty minutes later we were seated at the dining room table, munching on pizza.

"So she did the bird thing, huh?" Emma asked.

"Yeah, it was wild."

Emma leaned back and took a sip of red wine. "So, you don't even know what's in the safe deposit box?"

"No," Brooke said. "My mom just gave me the key and said there was something from my dad in it for me."

"I don't get it," I said, looking at Brooke. "Ferretto's goal is to do a hostile takeover of your dad's organization. So whatever's in the box has to help him achieve that—it can't just be a gift for you."

"Maybe it's something that will keep Sartori in jail. Evidence," Emma said.

"What kind of evidence? He's not going to keep a bloody knife next to something he's saving as a gift for his daughter, is he?"

We both looked at Brooke.

"No! And my dad might be a criminal but he is not a murderer."

Emma and I shared a dubious glance.

"I mean it," Brooke said, affronted. "He isn't like Frank and those other guys. He has principles."

"I still don't get how Ligner figures into this." Emma changed the subject, setting her pizza on her plate and brushing her fingers on a napkin.

"I've been wondering about him, too," I said. "Even if he found out there was something incriminating in the box, he would have to have known about Ferretto's plans to betray Sartori for it to have been useful."

"Maybe not," she mused. "Ferretto might have approached Ligner. Asked him to get the key."

"True. But why not just take it from Brooke? Plan a mugging—something they're obviously more than capable of arranging."

"You're right. It would be pretty easy to steal it."

"Too risky," Brooke said. "Word would get back to my dad if I was mugged and the key was stolen. He'd know something was up for sure."

"And he'd know what they were after," Emma said. "Assuming there is more in the box than a birthday gift."

"The important thing is that Ferretto doesn't have the key," I said. "Which means Sartori will be released and Brooke will be safe."

"So, we've just got to keep you on lockdown for another day," Emma told Brooke.

The girl gave my sister an appraising look. "Grace said you were some sort of kung fu master."

"Something like that. Between me and fluff butt over there we got you covered."

"Hey, what about me?" I said. "I'm a certified haiku, remember?"

"Rokyu," Emma said.

"Whatever. I kicked butt on my aikido test."

"Yeah, you're so scary you had to ruin my boots running away from the crazy guy following Stefan. I will be expecting you to replace them, by the way. Try not to have a heart attack when you get the bill."

"Wait!" Brooke said. "Someone was following Stefan?"

"Mancini."

Her face paled and she grabbed my phone. "I need to call him and make sure he's okay."

"No"—I plucked the phone from her hands—"you don't. Brooke, listen to me, they were following Stefan because they were hoping you'd contact him. Doing that will only put him at risk."

She slumped her shoulders, completely dejected for a moment, then her face brightened.

"What if you call?"

I shook my head.

"Please? All you have to do is ask him if he's okay. You said you'd met him, right?"

"I did."

"Well, just call him. Ask if he's heard from me or something. You can even tell him that you saw some people around that could be dangerous. You could warn him."

I looked at my sister, silently pleading for backup.

"It can't hurt," Emma said. "Even if Ferretto's got eyes on Stefan, they don't know Brooke is with you and as long as you're sure to make it sound like you're still looking for her, it may even keep them off the right track."

"Right! Exactly."

I gave in and called Stefan, reminded him who I was, and asked if he'd heard from Brooke.

"How did you get my number?" he asked, voice heavy with wangster attitude.

"Devine intervention."

"Huh?"

"Listen, Stefan—"

"What the—" There was a sharp intake of breath. "No."

Something in the tone of his voice made me ask, "Stefan, is there something wrong?"

"Oh, no. No!" he cried.

"What is it?"

"Somebody trashed my car."

"Trashed?"

I had a feeling that he wasn't talking about simple vandalism.

"Yeah, trashed. They ripped the seats out and tore open the cushions. They even ripped off the inside door panel. I can't believe this! My mom is going to kill me."

Not if someone else did it first. "Stefan," I said, "I want you to listen to me. Wherever you are, find a big crowd of people and call the police. Stay in a group until they get there."

"I'm not calling the damn po-po."

"If you're smart, you will."

Stefan made a derisive sound.

"You know the people Brooke was so afraid of? They're the ones who did that to your car and if they find you, you'll look like one of your cushions." There was a long pause.

Brooke's face had gone utterly white as she listened to my end of the conversation. She'd fisted her hand in the fur of Moss's ruff.

Finally, Stefan said, "Okay, I'll call."

I hung up and turned to Brooke.

"What happened? Is he okay?" she asked.

"Stefan's fine. Someone tossed his car."

"They must have been looking for the key," Emma said.

"Why would they think it was in Stefan's car?"

"You left home the night you took the video. Where did you go?"

"Nowhere. I wanted to clear my head and think. So I sat at the Krispy Kreme by my house for a while."

"How did you get to Happy Asses the next day?"

"Stefan—" Her eyes went wide.

"They already searched your house," Emma said. "Then they hit Stefan's car. They're retracing your steps."

"Ozeal." Brooke and I said the name in tandem.

Brooke leapt to her feet. "We have to warn her."

I was already pulling up her number on my phone. I called, my trepidation growing with every unanswered ring. Ozeal's voice mail clicked on and I left a message for her to return my call as soon as possible.

"Feeding time is over, right?" I asked Brooke, knowing Ozeal didn't always answer her phone when she was tending to the meals and putting everyone up for the night.

"She should be finished by now," Brooke said with a nod.

"Maybe she's in the shower," Emma said.

We all exchanged a look.

"Okay. Let's not panic. Ozeal locks the gate at night, doesn't she?"

"As soon as it gets dark," Brooke said.

"So she should be all right."

"Unless they forced their way in," Emma said.

"We have to go make sure Ozeal's okay." Brooke looked from me to my sister.

"The only thing you have to do is stay here," I told her as I stood. "I'll go to Happy Asses."

"Not going to happen," Emma said. She got up and reached for the phone. "We call the police and have them check on Ozeal."

"There isn't time," Brooke said. "It will take too long to explain. I have the security code. We can get in."

"Okay, we can call Jake and Kai on the way," Emma said. "Tell them to meet us there."

"Emma—" She raised a finger to cut me off.

"I'm going with you. End of discussion."

If anyone other than my big sister had pointed their finger at me and spoken to me like I was five, there would have been more than a discussion. But it was Emma, so I nodded, then turned to Brooke.

"What's the code?"

"I'm coming with you," Brooke said.

I shook my head.

She raised her chin. "I'm not giving you the code unless you take me."

"I must be losing my mind," I muttered. "Fine. Let's go."

We started toward the door but Brooke paused.

"Aren't we taking Moss?"

I turned and looked at my dog.

"No. I can't always control him. If somebody is threatening me, he'll try to take them out."

"Why is that a problem?"

"Usually, it isn't. But these guys have guns. I won't risk it."

Emma and Brooke headed out the door. When Moss moved to follow, I knelt in front of him to block the way.

Go.

I shook my head. *No. You have to stay.*

Go.

"Stay here and take care of your kitten." I gave him a quick hug. "Don't worry, I'll be back soon."

At least I hoped I would.

CHAPTER 23

I cut Bluebell's headlights as I turned into the drive leading to Happy Asses.

"Stop here," Emma said. "And turn off the engine. They'll hear us coming if you get any closer."

"Hopefully *they* aren't here," I said as I shifted into park.

The sudden absence of Bluebell's rumbling engine was unsettling in the quiet.

We all stared through the windshield. The nearly full moon washed the landscape in silver light. Everything looked normal. The office windows were dark and there was no discernible movement.

The gate was illuminated by an overhead light, and I could see it was closed. There was no sign that anyone was there but us.

"Try to call Ozeal again," Brooke whispered from the backseat.

Again, no answer.

"Kai and Jake should be here soon," I said.

I hadn't explained the whole situation to Kai. Brooke had insisted I leave her and any specifics regarding the key out of it. Despite my vagueness, he promised to get in touch with Jake and ride to the rescue.

Another minute dragged by.

"Grace, can you get anything from the animals? See if something unusual is going on," Emma suggested.

"You can do that?" Brooke asked.

"In theory."

I sent out my mental feelers but only managed to pick up the faintest hum.

I shook my head. "Out of range."

"Let's walk closer," Brooke said. "If we stick to the shadows we could make it almost to the gate. Will that be close enough?"

"It's worth a try."

We climbed out of Bluebell and tiptoed along the drive. All the while, I was stretching my mind as far as I could toward the donkey pen. I was hoping to connect with one donkey in particular. Eventually, I found what I was looking for. Jack-Jack began to come into focus.

A hand snagged my arm.

"Stop," Emma said. "Any closer and you'll be in the light."

"I'm still too far away."

We stood in the balmy night listening to the crickets for what seemed like an hour.

Where the hell was Kai?

"Maybe we should go in," I said. "So far, we haven't heard anything. We may have beat Frank and his guys here."

"If they're coming," Emma whispered. "It looks like a pretty big place—they couldn't hope to search it all."

"Then why isn't Ozeal answering her phone?" Brooke asked, pointedly.

"Who knows, she could've dropped it in a water trough or the battery could've died."

We stood in silence. I strained my ears, listening for Kai's truck or, even better, police sirens.

"We could ring the bell," Brooke suggested.

I'd forgotten that there was a buzzer at the gate.

"Does it ring in Ozeal's apartment?"

"In the office, in her place, and in the commissary, too."

It was worth a try. I was sincerely hoping we'd ring the buzzer and a few minutes later an irritated Ozeal would appear, wearing a bathrobe, with her hair wrapped in a towel.

We all walked forward. Brooke stepped up to push the buzzer and froze. She reached out, but rather than ringing the bell, she gently pushed on the gate's rail.

It eased open with a whisper.

I'd promised Kai I'd wait for him, but it was looking like I was going to have to break that promise.

A crash echoed through the night, followed by a muffled cry, and my decision was made.

We shoved our way through the gate and sprinted over the grassy field toward the cover of a large oak tree. Before we reached the shadow an explosion of raw fear and panic struck me hard enough to make me stumble. Emma grabbed my arm to steady me.

"Grace?" She hissed out my name on a breath.

I swayed for a moment, then yanked my mental shields into place.

Emma pulled me, still wobbling, into the darkness

"I'm okay. I was too open and—" I waved off the explanation. "Something's happening in the barn. The donkeys are freaking out."

The covered picnic tables partially obscured our view, but I could see a sliver of light outlining the door.

Another crash sounded. "They must be tossing the barn."

"We might be able to get the drop on them," Emma whispered.

"And do what?"

"I don't know. Maybe we can lock them in or something." She looked at Brooke for confirmation of her plan.

"What about Ozeal?" Brooke asked. "We can't lock her in there with them."

"Good point."

We huddled together, thinking. Though all I could think about was how loud our breathing sounded in the still night.

"Wait!" Brooke's exclamation was more of a gasp. "The alarm!"

"There's a burglar alarm?"

"No. It's an escape alarm. For the big cats. If one escapes, we're supposed to hit the alarm. It flashes a red light and announces there's a code ninety-eight."

I knew some zoos used radio codes. Hearing "We have a code ninety-eight, *Panthera pardus*" over the radio didn't usually incite panic like "The leopard has escaped."

But I wasn't sure an alarm spouting codes would do much good. "How is setting off the alarm going to help?"

"Maybe they'll think they messed up and tripped it," Brooke whispered. "It doesn't notify the cops but they don't know that."

I looked at Emma.

"It could scare them off," she said.

It was worth a shot.

"Where's the closest alarm?"

"The office, but it's probably locked. There's the barn but . . ." She seemed to be going over the facility's layout in her head. "The next closest would be by the cougars. Between their enclosure and Boris."

I remembered the cougars' pen. It was just before the tiger enclosure, on the same side of the path.

We might even be able to hit the alarm and, if we needed to, make a break for it through Brooke's little rabbit hole in the fence.

"Okay, here's what we're going to do," I said. "Brooke, you know this place, you lead the way. Keep us in the shadows. I'll follow next and stay tuned in to the animals closest to us as we go. If they sense something, we'll hide. Em, you bring up the rear."

Edging around the tree, we ran to the wood fence that ringed the commissary and Ozeal's apartment above. The only light was on the corner of the building, flooding a section of the path leading toward the big cats. We'd have to pass under its beam, but if we were fast and lucky, we'd make it to the shadows on the other side in seconds.

An overgrown oleander draped over the fence near the path. We paused in its ragged shadow to listen—Emma and Brooke with their ears, and me with my mind.

I lowered my shield slowly, trying to partially block the donkeys' fear and remain open to everyone else. It wasn't easy. Boris was just outside my range; I could sense him but nothing more. The lion was closer and I picked up grumbling waves of agitation from him.

Hungry.

I moved over to the cougars, whose enclosure sat catty-corner to the lion's. They were pacing as well, bellies rumbling.

"Crap."

"What?" Emma breathed the word.

"I'm not getting a good read on the animals," I whispered. "Dinner's late and no one's happy. Food is what's on their minds and not much else."

"Keep the channel open anyway," Emma said.

"I will." I paused then said, "Okay—we make a run for the alarm on the count of three. If something happens, split up. One. Two. Three!"

We sprinted out of the dark, through the bright beam of the floodlight and down the pine-straw-covered path. Zipping past the cougars, who watched us with startled jerks of their heads, we hopped, one after the other, over the short wooden fence that separated the path from the enclosures.

Brooke reached the power pole, lifted the plastic cover on a little box, and pressed the button.

She looked up. I followed her gaze to the large, dark square jutting out above us. I assumed it would blink or flash. It didn't.

Brooke pressed the button again.

Nothing.

"What the hell?" She slammed her finger against the button.

"It's broken," Emma said.

"It can't be."

"It is," I said, remembering Ozeal mentioning an electrical issue caused by lightning. And, like a lightning strike, I remembered something else.

"Crap."

"What?"

"I left my Glock in Bluebell."

"Too late now," Emma whispered.

She was right, of course. But I still lamented the absence of the one thing that might save our skin.

Kai had encouraged me to get a concealed-carry permit for my gun, saying, "Better to have it and not need it, than need it and not have it."

Boy, wasn't that the truth.

Smart—real smart.

A sudden surge of excitement and joy rolled through me, cutting through the frustration I felt at my oversight. Boris had seen Brooke. He bounded to the fence and blew out a friendly chuff.

"Hi, Boris," she whispered and took a step toward the big cat, but there wasn't time for a reunion.

"Come on," I said. "We have to try another alarm. Is there one close by?"

Brooke turned away from Boris with some reluctance and nodded.

"Just past the commissary across from the bobcats."

"Lead the way."

I followed Brooke and Emma back toward the path. They scaled the small fence, but just as I'd made it to the other side, a bobcat whistled, quick and excited.

The sound made me pause. It took a few seconds to zero in on the cat. I felt a flutter of happiness, similar to what Boris had expressed at seeing Brooke, but this emotion was clearly aimed at someone else.

Ozeal.

Hungry!

The cat's jubilation was cut short, replaced by confusion and a dash of fear.

The bobcat had seen Ozeal, but she wasn't alone. She was with someone . . .

Someone who frightened the small cat.

I ran forward and started to call out a warning to Emma, but it was too late. She and Brooke had jogged ahead and had almost reached the corner of the commissary when Logan materialized out of the shadows, holding Ozeal at gunpoint.

Her hands were bound with duct tape and a piece had been pressed over her mouth. Logan had pushed the oversized roll of tape onto his wrist, like a giant bracelet.

Emma grabbed Brooke's arm and yanked her to a stop. They pivoted and bolted back toward me.

They'd only sprinted a few yards before skidding to a stop.

"Run!" Emma shouted.

It took me a moment to realize she was talking to me.

I looked over my shoulder. Two figures stepped into the floodlight.

Mancini and Ferretto.

Too late, I realized we were trapped, penned in on either side by enclosures—the lion's to our right, Boris's to our left.

There was nowhere for me to go but to join my sister and Brooke. I moved to where they stood. Emma and I instinctively positioned our backs to one another, shoving Brooke between us, like elephants protecting a calf from hungry hyenas.

Mancini held a gun pointed casually in our direction. Though Ferretto's hands were empty, I assumed he was armed as well.

"The police are on their way," I said. "Leave now and you might have time to get out of here before they show up."

"So sweet." Mancini stepped forward, his dark eyes bright as they focused on me. "Worrying about us?"

I felt my sister tense behind me. If Mancini got close enough, she'd be on him like a spider monkey. But I wasn't sure that was a good thing.

Brooke might be tough, but bullets cut through more than

street cred. As much confidence as I had in my sister, I knew she couldn't take on three armed men.

We only had one chance: stall.

I looked past Mancini to Ferretto.

"You're not going to get what you came for without our help, so call off the psycho."

"Oh? And what is it I want?" Ferretto asked in a cool tone.

"The key," I said.

His gaze shifted to Brooke.

"So, you did know I wanted the key."

"I guessed," Brooke said from over my shoulder.

"Why?" I took a step forward. "What's in the box?"

"The one thing that will give me the power I need to finally take control of this organization. A book. A detailed account of everyone who owes Charles and why."

"A little blackmail book?"

"That's funny, Miss Wilde. Yes. A little blackmail book. Though I'm told it's not little at all."

"But you can't open the box," I said. "Your name isn't on the account."

"True. But Anne's is. And I've made sure she's . . . malleable."

Suddenly, I realized why what Sensei had said about having a strong mind kept popping into my head. Anne Ligner had been pushed around physically but her mind was the greatest threat.

"You had Ligner drug her."

"That was Bob's doing, actually. He'd been replacing her antidepressants with narcotics for a while. It made her easier to handle, I suppose."

"Charming."

Ferretto shrugged at my remark. "Whatever works. He called me one evening with a proposition. He'd heard I was interested in a certain key and he felt he could get it for me."

"Ligner worked for you?"

"Not at first. I couldn't trust him not to say something

that might get back to Charles. But once he started gambling . . ."

"He needed money."

Ferretto smiled. "Odds are always on the house. Now, where's the key?"

I had two choices. Tell the truth and run the risk of them getting the key and promptly shooting us, or lie and if they caught on they'd shoot us on principle.

"It's in the tiger enclosure."

From behind me, Brooke sucked in a shocked breath.

"Really?" Ferretto glanced at Boris. The tiger growled. "Clever."

"I'll help you get it," I said. "But you have to let everyone else go."

"You're not really in a position to negotiate."

"Sure I am. Unless you want to get eaten."

"What if," Mancini said, almost to himself, "I just shoot the cat?"

He raised his gun and pointed it at Boris. My blood turned to ice at the sight, but I managed to force a short laugh.

"You shoot him and you're never going to get your stupid key."

He glanced at me, that creepy half smile widening into a grin that would make a hyena wince.

"What?" I asked, letting my voice drip with as much distain as I could manage. "You thought you could kill a tiger with that little thing? Shooting him will only piss him off."

"So you say." Mancini locked his gaze onto Boris. The tiger lowered his head and snarled.

Bad.

Boris was seething with the need to pounce on Mancini. The emotion rolled over me and I clinched my hands into fists.

Striving for calm, I pulled my mental shield into place and turned to Ferretto. If I was going to make him believe my lies, I didn't need the homicidal thoughts of a tiger muddying my mind.

"Listen," I said, "he could shoot until the gun is empty

and you know what you'd have? Six hundred pounds of wounded, angry tiger between you and what you want. Not the best idea, is it, Frankie?"

Ferretto's eye twitched at my use of his first name but he turned his attention to Mancini.

"Vincent," he snapped. When Mancini didn't lower the gun, Ferretto stepped forward and held out his hand to take it.

Mancini didn't respond. Just when I was sure he'd pull the trigger, he aimed the barrel skyward and said, almost meekly, "Sure, boss. No problem."

He handed the gun to Ferretto. Then, like a switch had been flipped, he locked his eyes on me and murmured, "I prefer my knives."

As he spoke, he raised his hand up and over his head to reach the back of his neck. I blinked in disbelief at what I was seeing. From what must have been a hidden sheath somewhere under the collar of his sports coat Mancini produced a sword.

No, not a sword. A *machete*.

Crap.

Then Mancini did something that would have been laughable—if it hadn't been so friggin' creepy.

Never releasing my gaze, he brought the machete to his lips and *licked* the blade.

It freaked me out so much I reflexively employed the only weapon I had available—sarcasm.

"Why, Vincent," I said in a breathy, Scarlett O'Hara drawl. "People will say we're in love."

Ignoring our little tête-à-tête, Ferretto turned to me, casually aiming the gun at my chest.

"The key."

I was more than happy to have an excuse to look away from Mancini.

Out of the corner of my eye, I could see my sister inch a step closer to Logan. She had a plan—I hoped. Maybe to get ahold of his gun or . . . it didn't matter, I didn't need to know.

The only way I could help was to keep everyone's attention focused on me.

I moved forward, away from where Brooke and Emma stood, and pointed to the small building at the rear of the enclosure.

"That's the tiger house. The best way to get the key is to put the tiger inside. Once he's secure, you're free to get what you want. No muss, no fuss."

Ferretto regarded me for several moments then turned abruptly and pointed the gun at my sister.

"You," he said to Emma, "tape the little bitch to big mama. Don't want her running off again."

Logan released Ozeal, stepped to the side, and tossed the giant roll of tape to Emma.

"Ankles first," Ferretto ordered.

Emma knelt, and with a rip, began unfurling the tape. She tore a piece off with her teeth and began binding Ozeal and Brooke together. She slid me a glance and flicked her gaze at the keys clipped to Ozeal's belt.

I wasn't sure what she was trying to tell me at first, but then she moved to reposition her weight. She was getting her feet under her so she could move fast.

"I need the keys," I said, hoping I'd read her right. "If I'm going to put the tiger up."

My sister's face was unreadable but the set of her jaw told me to be ready—though for what, I had no idea.

She unrolled another length of tape, this one much longer than the first, and paused.

"Vincent." Ferretto motioned for him to retrieve the key ring.

Before Mancini moved he flicked his wrist, making the machete's blade whir through the air between us like a propeller. He stopped the display as abruptly as he'd started it, then strolled past me, casually resting the machete on his shoulder.

Ozeal's eyes blazed at him as Mancini unclipped the keys, but he ignored her. Then he did something stupid. He turned his back on my sister.

Silly psychopath.

He'd only taken a few steps when Emma surged to her feet. Just as he was giving his machete another showy twirl, she swung the heavy roll of tape like a mace. It smashed into the side of Mancini's head.

He lurched sideways and crashed into the short fence. The machete kept moving, cartwheeling through the air in the opposite direction.

Never losing momentum, Emma whirled to face the second-nearest target, whipping the tape in an arc. The blow caught Logan squarely across the jaw.

He staggered back and Ozeal and Brooke charged him like contestants in a three-legged race for their lives. They plowed into Logan and the trio went down with a thud.

Mancini pushed himself away from the fence and squared off against my sister, hands raised like a boxer, ready for Emma to swing for his head.

She knew better.

My sister struck out with the tape, letting it whiz by Mancini before dropping to one knee. In the same instant, she swung the roll around again, aiming low. Momentum sent the tape winding around his ankles. Hobbled by the sticky straps, he stumbled, off-balance, and Emma had him. Like a cowboy roping a calf, she stood and yanked.

Mancini went down hard, his head bouncing back against the ground with a *thunk*.

Ferretto and I stood frozen and watched, too transfixed by my sister's Jackie Chan moves to react for the few seconds it had taken Emma to execute her attack.

We exchanged a glance and, in that moment, both of us seemed to realize one important point.

Ferretto still held a gun.

Swinging his arm, he lifted it to aim at Emma.

"Look out!" In utter panic, I lunged for the pistol and missed. My crazed leap slammed me into Ferretto's shoulder instead. He fumbled the weapon and it dropped to the ground.

Ferretto moved to grab the gun. I reacted in precisely the wrong way. I kicked it, sending the gun skidding out of sight.

This was wrong because I should have focused on my opponent instead of his weapon. It was a mistake I paid for.

Ferretto backhanded me hard enough to make my teeth rattle and send me sprawling to the ground.

"Gra—" Emma's cry was cut short. Mancini tripped her as she came at Ferretto. She landed on her hands and knees and was moving to stand when Mancini snagged one of her ankles.

Emma snapped her leg back like a whip, planting her foot in his face. He crumpled face-first into the ground and didn't move.

As this was happening, a glint of metal caught my eye.

The machete.

I scrambled toward it. Just as my fingers wrapped around the handle, something hit me. My breath exploded from my lungs in a painful *woosh*. It took a moment to realize what had happened. Ferretto had kicked me. Hard.

I collapsed on my side and he plucked the machete from my hand. I didn't fight to hold on to the weapon because suddenly, all thought focused on one thing—air.

I needed air.

But my lungs weren't working. Pain burned through my midsection as my diaphragm spasmed. I couldn't do more than draw in the tiniest sip of air.

Not enough.

Though my vision was blurred, I saw Ferretto turn to Emma. She was standing, Mancini unconscious on the ground behind her. Ferretto raised the machete and my sister assumed the relaxed and ready stance I'd seen so many times in the dojo.

Ferretto was toast.

I squeezed my eyes shut and tried to focus on bringing air into my lungs.

My pulse pounded in my ears, making my head throb.

I opened my watering eyes and saw something that made my already racing heart slam even harder in my chest.

Mancini lay on his side, silently cutting through the

tangle of tape that bound his legs. How many knives did he have?

Didn't matter. I had to warn Emma.

I tried to call out, but no sound escaped my lips.

Emma was focused on Ferretto, who was drawing her attention by feinting from one side to the other and keeping her back to Mancini, who began to slowly rise to his feet.

I tried again to shout a warning, but couldn't force more than a whisper from my lips.

I had to do something.

This was mind over matter. I was not dying, but my sister might if I didn't warn her. I opened my mouth, determination burning through me. But all I managed was a strangled "hem."

Tears leaked from the corner of my eyes as I watched Mancini stalk closer to my sister.

"Hem-a," I tried again. The sound was barely audible.

Emma, look out!

My mental plea was useless.

There had been times in the past when I'd wished my ability extended to human beings, but never as fervently as I did in that moment.

Then it hit me. I couldn't call out to Emma, but there were others who could be my voice.

I let my mental shield drop and reached out. One by one, starting with Boris, then Larry, the old lion, and finally the cougars.

Come on, everybody. Make some noise!

And they did.

Chest-rattling roars erupted in tandem from both the lion and the tiger. Coupled with the cougars' whining screams, it was an unearthly sound, startling everyone, including my sister.

Emma glanced around and caught sight of Mancini. He'd only broken stride for a moment but a moment was enough.

He lunged at her but she dodged, spinning away.

It was still two against one, but she'd at least managed to maneuver both men to where she could see them.

I glanced to where Ozeal and Brooke still struggled to hold Logan down. At least one bad guy was out of commission.

Drawing in a painful breath, I told myself it would be okay. This was like her aikido test. They would attack; Emma would handle it.

Then I saw the trickle of blood on her forearm.

Fear spiked through me. This wasn't a test. I would have to do more than lie on the ground as my sister took on two armed men.

Ignoring the shooting pains in my abdomen, I rolled to my knees and felt something bite into my shin.

Logan's gun.

I snatched it up and staggered to my feet.

"Stop!" I coughed out the word as I aimed the gun.

Ferretto glanced over his shoulder and froze.

"Drop it." The command was raspy but it was all I could manage. My chest burned with every breath. I felt like I was trying to force air into lead balloons.

Both men stared at me. Ferretto dropped the machete and slowly raised his hands.

Mancini didn't move.

"You, too."

For a moment, I didn't think he would obey, then that sly grin I'd come to despise slid into place and he opened his fingers to let the knife fall from his grasp. "Well, I guess you got me," he said.

If I could have breathed a sigh of relief I would have.

Mancini paused to regard me then stepped toward Ferretto, bent, and retrieved his machete.

"Stop!"

He took a step forward and I shuffled back, wanting to keep my distance from the blade.

"Don't move, Mancini."

"Or what? You'll shoot me?" He angled his head. "I don't think so."

I planted my feet like Kai had taught me and leveled the gun at his chest.

"Try me."

"I don't have to try you. I already know. Have you ever shot anyone? Killed another human being?"

I didn't answer.

"No?" A feverish glint lit his eyes and he breathed, "I have."

"Don't listen to him, Grace," Emma said. "If he takes another step, drop him where he stands."

I wanted to believe I could do it. "Spare me the psycho killer bit, okay? I don't care."

"Oh, I think you do."

I was good at freezing people out and pretending I didn't care. But it was a mask. Mancini wore the true face of a psychopath. I was outmatched and we both knew it. He took another step forward and when I didn't shoot him, his smile widened.

I was screwed.

Then it dawned on me.

I was there, surrounded by predators. I could use that. Use them to bolster my courage.

The heart of a lion was within my reach.

Admittedly, Larry was old and grumpy, but deep inside the link to the wild was there.

My hands had begun to shake, from either fatigue or fear or both. It didn't matter. Mancini could feel my desperation. It was now or never.

A dozen feet away, Boris paced and growled, and I decided the heart of a tiger was my best bet. I homed in on him. Instantly, his desire to tear into Mancini roared through me. The need to claw and bite. To rend flesh from bone.

I latched on to the primal spirit at the core of his need and let it burn into me. Welcomed the spark as it ignited the feral beast that lies dormant in us all.

It was more than lack of empathy or criminal insanity. The beast inside of me roared awake, savage and beautiful and blindingly pure.

Mancini's eyes met mine and he stilled.

"Drop. Your. Weapon." I growled the words slowly.

Mancini's eyes widened for an instant and I knew he'd

seen that beast rise within. His smug smile faltered and his gaze dropped—just for a moment, but it was enough.

If we had been wolves, he would have abased himself at my feet. But we weren't wolves and he wasn't sane.

A heartbeat after admitting defeat, he lunged. And I did what the beast wanted.

I pulled the trigger.

CHAPTER 24

Nothing happened.

I wasn't sure who was more surprised. Me, because there was no flash-bang, or Mancini, because he was still breathing.

The problem with linking to the inner wild—no pun intended—was that higher reason was trumped by instinct. I bared my teeth and hurled the gun at Mancini's head.

He ducked and it sailed past.

I felt my hold on the beast slip just as a blur of movement shot by me.

Jack-Jack.

The little donkey rammed Mancini's knees, flipping him like a pancake.

Jack-Jack brayed and stomped like a wild attack donkey. Within moments, Mancini was curled in a fetal position, whimpering, "Get it off! Get it off—please!"

"That's enough, Jack-Jack."

He let out a snort, turned away, and gave Mancini a departing kick for good measure. Mancini lay on his side, a pathetic, sobbing ball.

All his obsession over predators and he'd been taken out by Jack-Jack.

"Sheriff's Department!" I turned to the sound of Kai's voice. He was running down the path, gun drawn at his side.

He stopped short, taking in the scene when he saw our motley crew.

"You're late," I told him. "Again."

"You were supposed to wait." He frowned at Mancini. "Is that—"

"Vincent 'the Machete' Mancini? Yes. Don't worry about him—he just got his ass kicked by a miniature donkey."

Kai glanced at Jack-Jack, who stood over Mancini with his ears pinned back, eyeing the psychopath with open hostility.

Protect.

You did great, Jack-Jack.

The donkey gave me a snort of acknowledgment, but kept his attention on Mancini.

"That"—I pointed to Ferretto—"is wannabe mob boss and half-ass mastermind Frank Ferretto." He still stood with his hands raised and I soon realized why. Emma had snagged Mancini's knife and was holding it at the ready.

"And over here we have—" My jaw went slack as I turned to point out the third bad guy.

Logan was gone.

I vaguely recalled seeing the pile of limbs and grunts that was Ozeal, Brooke, and Logan as I faced off against Mancini. Out of my peripheral vision, I'd noticed Ozeal shift her ample weight to more effectively pin Logan to the ground while Brooke wrestled with his legs. I hadn't seen him get away. Apparently, Brooke and Ozeal hadn't either.

Still on the ground, they exchanged a dazed look.

"Where did he go?" I asked.

Ozeal started to answer my question, noticed the duct tape dangling from her jaw, and snatched it off before saying, "I don't know. When I heard Jack-Jack, I looked over at what was happening and then . . . I don't know."

She surveyed the ground under her as if she expected to find Logan still there.

Brooke seemed as confused as Ozeal.

"He—he was just here," the girl said. "It's like he disappeared. Like a . . . a . . ."

"Like a ghost," I finished.

There was shuffling behind us and Kai and I spun around. Jake huffed out of the shadows a moment later.

Before the detective could speak, Kai informed him that one suspect was still on the loose. In less than two minutes, Jake had cuffed both Ferretto and the still-moaning Mancini while Kai jogged off in the direction Logan would most likely have taken.

A flood of deputies arrived not long after. They searched, but Logan was nowhere to be found.

• • •

"Shouldn't you be out there looking for Logan, instead of asking me a bunch of questions?" Brooke asked Jake.

We were on our second round of questions. Jake had started round one moments after it became clear Logan had escaped, but Ozeal had cut him off before he got going. Hands planted on her hips, she informed him that the animals were hungry and upset and they'd be fed and settled before she'd be talking to the police.

Jake, being an intelligent man, conceded. Brooke and I had taken care of Boris and the cougars while Ozeal secured Jack-Jack and tended to Larry and the rest of the cats.

Brooke had become increasingly agitated the closer we'd come to finishing our task and therefore, to talking to the cops.

Now she stood with her arms crossed, doing her best to answer every question Jake posed with another question, much to his irritation.

He was giving her his hard, cop stare. Brooke, to her credit, seemed almost unfazed as she returned his glare.

I could almost hear the old western showdown theme whistle through the night air as I watched them.

I started to call a time-out, but Kai, who was standing next to Jake, beat me to it.

"Grace, why don't you take a minute and explain to Miss Ligner—"

"Don't call me that," Brooke snapped. "I never wanted to change my name. My mom did it because Bob wanted her to. I should still be Brooke Sartori."

"Give us a few minutes." I put my arm around Brooke's shoulder and steered her away from the two men.

We walked toward the parking area, which by then was clogged with emergency vehicles parked in a helter-skelter fashion. A few lights flashed, causing red and blue light to bounce at odd angles off every surface.

I spotted Emma sitting in the back of an open ambulance as a paramedic finished bandaging the cut on her arm. She was smiling and chatting with the handsome young man, and he seemed to be taking his time dressing her wound.

Emma.

"Why are you stonewalling?" I asked Brooke, turning to face her.

She didn't answer. Surprise, surprise.

"You're going to have to talk to the cops at some point. And so am I."

"Please—you can't tell them anything."

"Kai and Jake are the good guys."

"Yeah? What are they going to do if we tell them about Josiah? Or about what Ferretto was looking for? They'll take Josiah to jail or some nuthouse and my dad . . . if they find out about the key . . ."

"Josiah will be fine. Reedy will help look after him."

"And my dad?"

"They already know Ferretto was after something you had."

"But if we tell them, they'll find out about the safe deposit and the book and the blackmail. If the cops get the book, they'll use it to keep my dad in jail. My mom's a druggie. You want me to end up in a foster home?"

"Your mom is getting help. And you won't end up in a foster home."

"Yeah? You sure about that? Because I'm not."

"Jake is a homicide detective. He doesn't care about some little blackmail book, except that it was a motive for murder."

"Then it doesn't matter. We don't have to tell them."

"A lie of omission is still a lie."

"So when you *omit* the truth about your ability—is that a lie?"

She was right. I had lied countless times about what I could do, even to the police. Who was I to throw stones? Still . . .

"Look, can't we . . . can't we just wait?" she asked, her eyes pleading.

"For what?"

"For my dad to get out of jail."

"Your dad would just get rid of whatever's in the box."

"Not if I give it to you."

"Give what to me?"

"The book. We can go to the bank tomorrow and if there's a little black book or something, you take it with you and then give it to the cops later."

I shook my head but Brooke was on a roll.

"Please. You can go to the cops after my mom's out of rehab. That way, I can see my dad for a little while, too, maybe." Her voice caught and she swallowed back the emotion. Tears welled in her blue eyes. I watched as one spilled over.

Crap.

"How are we supposed to get access to the safe deposit box? The only people allowed in are your mom and dad."

"Well, then. I guess you'll have to be my mom."

•   •   •

I'd taken Brooke to visit her mother early the next morning and, in true delinquent fashion, she had swiped her mom's wallet while giving her a parting kiss on the cheek.

When Brooke handed me her score—her mother's old driver's license—I admit to being surprised.

"See? I told you."

"Your mom has blond hair."

"She colors it now."

I studied the license. Though Anne Ligner's hair was lighter than mine and styled differently, the photo was old and looked enough like me to pass at a glance. I just had to practice her signature.

"The name is still Sartori on here."

"Why do you think I wanted to use it?" she said with a sly grin. "Now, we just need the key."

We made the trip to Happy Asses and, with Ozeal's blessing, entered Boris's enclosure. The tiger was so happy to see Brooke and so intent on giving her loving head-butts and demanding she pet him, I had to be the one to retrieve the key. Which meant reaching past my elbow into the damp, dark, hollow end of the log.

Only brushed one spiderweb. Lovely.

Emma was thrilled to assist our covert endeavors by supplying me with a polished skirt and blazer along with a pair of oversized sunglasses. She slathered so much makeup on my face I felt like it would crack if I smiled too broadly.

Good thing I wasn't in a smiling mood.

I tucked the license in one of Emma's classy purses and we were on our way.

"Does your mom go inside the bank much?" I asked as we pulled into the lot and parked. I'd borrowed Emma's Jaguar just to complete the look and to assure the least amount of animal hair would affix itself to my clothes.

"No. Just the drive-through. Well, she used to. But Bob does all the money stuff now—or did."

"Okay. You ready?" I asked and donned the oversized glasses.

"Let's do it."

My nerves jangled with the little bell on the door and became more frayed the closer we got to the teller. It was silly. I'd faced a raging bull—I could handle a mundane, completely illegal visit to a safe deposit box.

Still, my heart continued to pound even after I managed to sign the card and Brooke and I were led into the safe. The attendant used both her key and Brooke's to open the door, smiled politely, and left.

Brooke and I looked at the box, then at each other. She nodded and I clasped the handle, slid the long box out of its drawer, and set it on the narrow table provided.

"Go ahead," Brooke whispered.

"It's your box," I replied, just as quietly. She reached out and slowly lifted the lid.

Along with a small, square jewelry box and a velvet pouch containing a pocket watch, there was, in fact, a book. Just not the book we had expected.

"A Bible?" I said, staring at the large, leather-bound book.

"It must be my grandma Sartori's," Brooke said after she'd opened the jewelry box. "This is her crucifix."

Baffled, I lifted the heavy book out and set it on the table with a *thunk*.

"But . . . it can't be just a Bible. There has to be more to it. I opened the book and flipped through the pages, expecting to find a cutout or some other hidden compartment.

The only thing I found was page after page of scripture.

"I don't get it. There's nothing here."

"Maybe Ferretto was wrong or maybe he knew there was a book in here, just not *the* book."

I shook my head. "He's desperate enough to work with Mancini but he's not stupid."

We searched the interior of the box, looking for a false bottom or something taped to the sides, but came up empty.

I glared at the Bible, picked it up, held it by the spine with both hands, and shook it. Nothing fell out.

"You've got to be kidding me." I started to place the book on the table when I heard something. A scraping, rattling sound.

I held the Bible by the spine and shook it again. And again when I began to turn the book right-side up I heard . . . something. Then it hit me.

"The binding."

"What?"

"In these old books the leather binding on the spine is loose—see?" I held the book in my palms and opened it. The spine separated from the leather, forming an oval cylinder. I tilted the Bible and heard a metallic tingle as something hit the tile floor.

"What was that?" Brooke asked, then bent to pick up the object.

"I don't—" I stopped, shocked when I saw what she held.

"It's another key."

"Why would my dad hide a key to the safe deposit box *in* the safe deposit box?"

I took the large, flat key from her and studied it. "Because it's not a key to this box. Look. The numbers are different."

"So that means there's another box?"

"Number 322."

We turned to the walls of safe deposit boxes and began scanning the numbers.

"Here!" Brooke pointed to a large square door at the bottom of the wall near the far corner of the room.

I grabbed the bank attendant's master key from the first box and knelt beside Brooke.

"This is a big box." I stated the obvious as I inserted the keys and turned them. The locks clicked and the door popped open.

Brooke clasped the handle but I put my hand over hers. "Hang on."

"What?"

"Maybe this isn't such a good idea." It had occurred to me that a box this big might contain more incriminating evidence than a sixteen-year-old needed to see.

"Why not?"

"Because there could be—" God only knew what in a box that size. "Too much stuff in here to take."

"Then you can just keep the key," she said simply, and slid the box out to rest it on the floor.

Before I could object further, she'd flipped open the lid.

"What the hell?"

I leaned over to look. The box was empty, except for one thing.

Brooke reached in and picked up the business card. It was blank, except for a ten-digit number.

"Logan."

Whatever had been in the box, the Ghost had gotten to it first.

CHAPTER 25

"Where's your costume?" Brooke demanded as soon as she brought the four-wheeler to a stop behind the tiger house and cut the puttering engine.

I looked at the teenager from where I was leaning on the concrete block wall. She was dressed in stereotypical safari khakis—shorts, brown boots, and a vest sporting a plethora of pockets. Around her neck hung a pair of binoculars. The only element that threw off the look was the large, lime green name tag with the word VOLUNTEER across the top.

"I was hoping to hide from Emma, so I wouldn't have to wear one."

"Come on! It's a masquerade."

"I'm aware—it's all I've heard about for a week."

After learning Brooke had missed the deadline to apply for grants, Emma decided to raise money for Happy Asses by putting on a last-minute "Feast with the Beast" event. From that moment on, life had been a party-prep whirlwind. Everyone who worked at the rescue facility had pitched in—Brooke more than anyone. She'd done everything from mailing invites to stringing lights.

I was contributing by donating my services to the silent auction—or so I'd been told.

"Don't be lame, Grace."

I ignored her statement. "How's Josiah?" I asked.

"Good. His docs got him the right meds now, and Reedy makes sure he takes them."

I straightened away from the wall. "And your mom? Did she get the okay to come tonight?"

"Yep. The rehab place let her out a day early." She looked away and asked, "Any word on Logan? From the cops, I mean."

I knew she wasn't asking because she was afraid of him. She was afraid *for* him. After talking to her father, Brooke had decided Logan was loyal to him and, by extension, to her. The fact that he'd cleared out the safe deposit box, including the blackmail book, protecting her father and his secrets, only made him more of a hero in her mind.

"Don't worry," I told her. "There are still no leads on the Ghost."

"My dad says the cops won't find Logan if he doesn't want to be found."

"I can believe that."

"Well, at least they got Ferretto and Mancini," she said brightly.

Both men had been arrested, hauled off to jail, and charged with a litany of offenses. Though Mancini had to be treated first for broken ribs and numerous small hoof-print-shaped contusions.

The thought still made me smile.

"What about the guy who mugged you?"

"That remains a mystery. None of the guns the cops found here matched the bullet casing from my mugging."

"I bet it was that psycho Mancini," she said and started walking around the building to the tiger enclosure.

I fell into step beside her and nodded. Though, looking back on the event, I had my doubts. "So sure it wasn't Logan?"

"Logan's not like that," she said, confident. "He wouldn't

hurt a girl. He didn't even really fight me and Ozeal when we tackled him. I told you, remember? He kept saying he was on our side, but we didn't listen. He wanted to help us."

"Hummm . . ." I wasn't sure I believed that. When it came to Logan, I wasn't sure about anything.

"Brooke, you'd tell me if you saw Logan, wouldn't you?"

Boris had been pacing, rubbing his head along the fence and making happy tiger sounds as we approached.

"Hey, Boris," Brooke said, ignoring my question. She cooed as she knelt by the fence. "How's my boy doing today?"

Boris pressed his head against the wire fence and chuffed. *Pet.*

Brooke glanced at me with raised brows.

I gave her a bland smile. "Oh, right . . . you need someone who speaks tiger to translate."

"Come on, Grace, you promised."

"You're right, but my services come with a price."

Brooke got to her feet and said, "I haven't seen him, okay?"

"What are you two doing? Grace, why aren't you dressed?" Emma materialized on the path to glower at us from the other side of the fence. She wore a tiger-print mini-dress and leather arm cuffs, more to hide the stitches on her biceps than as part of the outfit, but Emma made it work.

She looked like Jane of the Jungle—if Jane wore less clothes and had kitty cat ears.

"My greeter"—she pinned Brooke with her gaze—"is supposed to be in her place, ready to welcome the early arrivals."

Brooke scurried to the four-wheeler and popped a safari hat on her head. "Hey, I'm ready. See?"

Emma turned to me, arching a brow.

"As long as you promise me I won't have to put on a loincloth."

"Your costume is in the office. Sonja's waiting for you."

I hitched a ride on the four-wheeler with Brooke and found my costume hanging on the door of one of the offices. It wasn't a loincloth, but a dress. Black-on-black leopard print, whose pattern, much like a real black panther, was most discernible when caught by the light.

The fabric was beautiful—there just wasn't much of it.

I shimmied into the dress just as there was a knock at the door. Sonja, holding a black half mask, breezed into the room.

"Grace, you look amazing." She grinned. "Amazing Grace."

I rolled my eyes.

"Emma has decreed you must wear your hair down and put this on." She held out the mask.

It was made of black leather shaped into the upper part of a cat's face. Gold accents detailed the ears and outlined the eyes in a distinctly Egyptian style.

"Let me guess, Bastet?"

"You got it."

I pulled out the ballpoint pen that had been holding my bun in place and combed my fingers through my hair, then turned to let Sonja tie the mask.

"You make me sick the way you can just let your hair down and it looks all flowy and perfect."

"I'd cut it short, like you, but I don't have your bone structure. I'd look like a ten-year-old boy."

"With your body? Please, girl."

"What about you? Where's your mask?"

She flashed me a grin, the gap in her teeth winking as she said, "It wouldn't fit through the front door."

We left the offices and on the porch I saw what she meant. Sonja's mask, or headdress, rather, was shaped similarly to mine but in a tawny gold with a profusion of feathers fanning out like a lion's mane.

"Female lions don't have manes," I pointed out.

"Oh, who cares? It looks fantastic."

I helped her tie her mask and she asked, "Is Kai coming tonight?"

"Yep. I thought it was a bad idea since Sartori was going to be here, but he didn't care."

"I thought he was cleared of all that mob stuff."

"He was."

"You can't keep beating yourself up over all that, you know. Kai's a big boy. You didn't force him to help you. And it all turned out okay, anyway."

I nodded. Emma had said almost exactly the same thing, but I still felt bad about it. I'd promised myself not to get Kai involved again in anything that could ruin his career.

We stepped off the porch and walked toward the covered picnic area. A band was set up where the tables had been and a portable parquet dance floor was spread out in front. To one side, tables and chairs decked out in subtle animal prints and tropical centerpieces flowed out over the grass. To the other, there was a trio of long tables lined with goods for the silent auction.

I caught sight of Brooke. She was ushering a couple, both masked and dressed to the nines, to a table.

She was flushed and smiling.

Happy.

I found that as I watched her, I was smiling, too.

"You look—wow."

I glanced over and saw Kai, wearing a tux and carrying a small mask, striding toward me.

I turned, and his gaze slid over me slowly. I could almost feel the heat everywhere he looked.

Or maybe that was the blood rushing to my face . . . and other places.

Kai. In a tux. Looking at me with as much hunger as any of the big cats around us.

Heaven help me.

"Hi" was all I managed to say.

"Hey, Kai." Emma hurried toward us, grinning as she gave him the once-over. "You look delicious. My sister's a lucky girl."

"That's what I keep telling her."

"I'm going to leave it to you to make sure Grace mingles. We want someone to bid top dollar for her services and they won't do that unless they know what she has to offer."

"In that dress, I'm sure she could sell just about anything."

"You guys make it sound like I'm peddling more than a pet consult."

"Hey, whatever works," my sister said with a wink before heading off.

I watched her go and saw with surprise that she'd linked arms with Hugh. He leaned down to say something in her ear—knowing Hugh, it was probably scaldingly flirtatious—and Emma laughed, looking up at him with an expression I hadn't seen in a long time.

"She likes him," I muttered aloud.

"Is that a problem?" Kai asked.

"Not as long as he's nice to her."

"You're not jealous?"

"What?" I cast Kai an incredulous look and, seeing he was serious, said, "Listen, Kai, Hugh is just a friend."

"Good." His lips turned up into an almost feral grin and I flushed.

Kai did, in fact, make me mingle. So much so that an hour into the party I had to seek solace by sneaking off for a quick visit with Boris. I'd snagged a few pieces of sushi to share with the tiger. He dissected the first piece, daintily pulling out the bits of salmon and leaving chunks of rice and vegetables behind.

"Kind of picky, for a tiger."

More?

I gave him the last piece of tuna, shaking my head as I watched him repeat the process.

Boris heard it before I did. A whisper of movement followed by a *thump*.

I couldn't be sure in the twilight but I thought it was the sound of the door to the tiger house bumping open.

Had there been a breeze, I would have blamed the wind, but the night was still and quiet.

I stood and walked toward the rear of the enclosure to take a look. I'd almost reached the door when he stepped out in front of me.

The mask he wore did little to hide his identity. I recognized the close-cropped hair and those unmistakable eyes.

"Taking a break from the festivities?" he asked.

"What are you doing here, Logan?"

He glanced down at his tuxedo. "Isn't it obvious?"

"I don't usually ask questions I already know the answer to. So, no."

"I wanted to give you something." He reached into his jacket pocket and handed me a piece of paper.

"Another one of your notorious cards?"

"This one has something special on the back."

I flipped the card over.

"James Russo. Unit 35-D . . ." I read the rest of the address and looked up at Logan. "What's this?"

"You remember seeing a guy at Cooper's Catch the day you met with Frank? Younger than me and Mancini."

"The waiter?"

"More of a gofer. He did all sorts of things for Frank. Very eager to please the boss. That's where you can find him."

"You running a dating service now?"

He did that almost-smile thing and I had to wonder if I'd misplaced my brain in the last few minutes, because I wasn't afraid. Okay, I was a little bit afraid. But mostly I was confused. And curious.

"Depends," he said. "Are you into the type of guy who'd mug his own mother to get ahead in the business?"

"Mug . . . wait. This is the guy who mugged me?"

Logan inclined his head. "Jimmy will be at that address until someone unlocks the storage unit and unties him."

"You locked him in a storage unit?"

"Just to give him time to regret attacking a woman."

I stared at him, openmouthed. "Why are you doing this?"

"I told you, I don't like men who hit women."

"Is this supposed to make me believe you really aren't such a bad guy?"

"No. I'm definitely a bad guy."

"Grace?" I whirled around at the sound of my name in time to see Kai walk into view and stop at the fence.

I turned back.

Logan was gone.

"Emma asked me to round you up," Kai said. His smile dimmed when I turned back to face him. "What's wrong?"

"Why? Do I look like I've seen a ghost?"

He was over the fence in a flash and almost as quickly drew a gun from his ankle holster.

"He's gone," I said. "You know he is."

My words didn't stop Kai from checking the area.

"What happened?" he asked when he was sure Logan had once again vanished.

"He gave me this." I handed Kai the card and told him Logan's claim that James Russo was my mugger.

"I'll get a deputy to check out the storage unit." He frowned at me and asked, "Grace, have you been in contact with Logan?"

"You mean since the night he Houdinied on us? No. I would have told you, Kai."

He searched my face for a moment, then nodded. A few seconds later Brooke and Sonja appeared on the path.

"See?" Brooke said. "I told you she'd be over here with Boris."

"Come on, Grace," Sonja called. "They're about to announce the winners of the silent auction."

"Go on," Kai said. "I've got to make a few calls, then I'll join you."

I nodded and walked toward Sonja and Brooke, but stopped as I reached the fence. I'd come the long way around the back to avoid being spotted and because I didn't want to try to scale the small fence in a dress and heels.

"I'll have to go around." I turned, but before I made it more than a few steps, Kai scooped me up into his arms.

"This will be easier," he said, looking down at me with a smile as he leaned over the rail and gently set me down on the other side.

My heart was fluttering in surprise and from the sensation of being in his arms.

"Umm . . . thanks."

"I'll be there in a minute," he said, fishing his phone out of his pocket as he turned away.

"Lord!" Sonja let out a dreamy sigh as she watched him go. "A knight in a tuxedo."

We walked down the path, making it to the main area, where Emma was listing auction items and announcing the name of the corresponding winning bidder.

Kai appeared beside me a few minutes later as she said, "Next up, we have a complete Call of the Wilde pet consultation provided by my lovely sister, Grace. Wave, Grace, so everyone can see you."

Sonja elbowed me.

I plastered a smile on my face and waved.

"And the winning bid goes to . . ." Emma looked down at the bid card. "Mr. Anthony Or—" She broke off. Her gaze flew to meet mine. She didn't have to say his name, I knew.

Anthony Ortega.

Emma fumbled with the microphone for a moment. "We'll just move on to the next item," she said hastily.

"Wait a second," Sonja murmured. "Anthony. Like Anthony Ortega, Emma's ex-husband?"

I didn't answer. Anger, cold and sharp, stabbed at my gut. I could feel the weight of Kai's gaze as he looked down at me. He was a smart enough guy to judge our reactions and come to the conclusion that Ortega was the man who'd abused my sister.

"What does he want with you?" he asked.

"Whatever it is," I said, "he'll get it over my dead body."

Turns out, I wasn't the one who ended up dead.